GLITCH KINGDOM

GLITCH KINGDOM

SHEENA BOEKWEG

FEIWEL AND FRIENDS

NEW YORK

A Feiwel and Friends Book

An imprint of Macmillan Publishing Group, LLC
120 Broadway, New York, NY 10271 • fiercereads.com

Glitch Kingdom. Copyright © 2020 by Sheena Boekweg. All rights reserved. Printed in
the United States of America.

Our books may be purchased in bulk for promotional, educational, or business use. Please
contact your local bookseller or the Macmillan Corporate and Premium Sales Department at
(800) 221-7945 ext. 5442 or by email at MacmillanSpecialMarkets@macmillan.com.

Library of Congress Cataloging-in-Publication Data is available.

ISBN 978-1-250-20979-5 (hardcover) / ISBN 978-1-250-20980-1 (ebook)

BOOK DESIGN BY KATIE KLIMOWICZ

Feiwel and Friends logo designed by Filomena Tuosto

First edition, 2020

10 9 8 7 6 5 4 3 2 1

*This book is dedicated to my husband and my kids,
and to all the video games they played while I wrote it.*

1
RYO

The rules of the game were simple.

The goal was four shovels and a song. I fanned my hand of cards. Three boats and two birds. Blast. I inhaled and fought to keep my breathing shallow; hold my shoulders still, and keep my face free of the thousands of tells I'd learned to hide.

There would be no winning this round.

At least not if I played the cards.

I peered over my hand and studied my opponents around the table instead. A haze of smoke coming from Lady Maramour's pipe blocked her expression, but the tapestries I'd crisscrossed over the arched windows of my rooms sent a sliver of sunlight that cut through the smoke and highlighted the creases at the edge of her eyes. She was sharp as the knife at her waist. She held her cards close to her chest, a hint of a smile hiding inside the folds in her cheek. Lady M had the mind of a general when it came to stealing my coins, and with that smile I'd best fold now, count my losses as education.

Unfortunately, a pretty girl was watching. The chair usually occupied by my best friend, Grigfen, had been filled by Lady M's eldest granddaughter, here from the country. The girl seemed more interested in making eyes at me over the top of her cards than paying any semblance of attention to the game. No clue what her cards held, although what she wanted was clear, and it wasn't a kiss—it was my crown.

I slid a pile of coins to the center of the table.

My guards, Davi and Fio, folded immediately, although Davi

seemed reluctant to let go. I wished he would have stayed in—he could use the money; his girl was in the family way, and the married barracks were barely comfortable for two. But my guards always allowed me the win when we gambled real coin. Probably on my mother's orders.

Where was Sir Grigfen? He should be here by now. I glanced about my chambers. Three tables full of players in pale silk dresses or sharp suits seemed content enough with their cards. When my gaze settled on Lady M's granddaughter she flushed pink and then folded her hand, her smile a thrown game I didn't have to do anything to win.

Lady M matched my pile of coins and picked up a card. I grinned at her, but inwardly I fought a panic. Last time we played she took my coat.

"Guess it's just you and me now, my lady."

Someone entered my rooms. I turned, hoping it was Grigfen. He'd been known to get caught in tables less savory than mine.

Close, but no dice. A boulder of a man blocked my doorway. Tall and thick, with corded arms and a bushy blond beard, Sir Tomlinson seemed completely devoid of his son Grigfen's good humor. As the head of agriculture, the man was more farmer than noble, despite his fine coat, and from the dark angle of his eyebrows, he wasn't pleased to find my rooms set up as a gambling den on a Thirdday afternoon.

I pulled at my vest. "Sir Tomlinson," I said. The room's chatter quieted at the presence of a member of my father's council. "What brings you to my den of iniquity?"

Sir Tomlinson was not amused. "News. A Savak Wingship landed not twenty minutes ago."

A chill ran up my neck. This was news for my parents, not idle gossip to throw at my friends. Every man in the room, except me, stood. Several people spoke at once, but I ignored them. If a member of my father's council believed the news urgent enough to speak freely, then another game had started.

"Military?" I asked from my chair.

"Religious," Sir Tomlinson answered.

Lady M twisted her fingers. "Not much better. How many?"

"One. A lone cleric in her red robes. She surrendered her wings without a fight."

Fio lowered his voice and leaned near me. "I didn't know they had female heathens."

I hid a smile, but Sir Tomlinson caught it. "Watch your tone, sir. They may believe in a different god, but we don't want to war with their bloodthirsty queen. It's best we avoid the notice of the seers, and calling them such a word—"

"And why does this involve me?" I asked, leaning forward.

"She's requested to meet with the council of six, and your father wishes you to observe."

My cheeks flooded with warmth. "When?"

Tomlinson didn't answer. He simply turned his heel and left my rooms.

Now, I gathered.

I followed him out with my guards at each flank.

My father wanted me to observe a council meeting.

Do not skip, Ryo. My father's council was meeting with a Savak cleric. Now was not the time to skip.

A slight bounce to my step, however, was acceptable.

Tomlinson scowled when I caught up with him. "I do *apologize* for taking you away from such noble pursuits," he said with a sneer.

I rolled my eyes. "I'll have you know that card game was well within my mother's code of conduct."

He clearly had more opinions, but he ducked his head in a bow. "How Your Highness behaves is none of my concern."

We turned a corner from my hallway. My collar felt hot all of a sudden. "It isn't. Especially since Sir Grigfen didn't show, and Lady Dagney wasn't invited—"

"That is Lady Tomlinson to you. If you speak to my daughter at all. Which you should not, unless you are in a crowd of witnesses and I am observing with my grip on my sword."

I chuckled. "Honestly, Sir Tomlinson, you have no reason to fear. It's very unlikely that Lady Dagney would break my heart. Though I am touched for your concern for me."

Davi broke in, "You see, Sir Tomlinson. Girls, for the prince, are like coins. Easy to win, easy to lose."

"Better in piles," Fio supplied.

I snorted. In truth the only similarity between girls and coins was that I had to make a full accounting of each to my mother. "Unless, of course, you weren't worried for your own crown prince's heart?"

Davi gave a false gasp. "The disloyalty to the Crown!"

I placed my hand on my heart and mock fainted.

Sir Tomlinson stopped his quick assault down my halls and raised a finger. "My daughter would rip you to pieces."

I bowed. "I thank you heartily for your warning. I shall endeavor to leave your daughter far from my attention."

"Good."

I grinned and made my way through the polished stone hallways, through arches of sunlight that warmed the floors. Now he was following me. "Though now that I've thought on it, Lady Dagney is interesting, in her own way. I believe she bested me in an archery tournament once, and there was something so fascinating about the crease between her eyebrows. Most other noble young women of my acquaintance view me as a path to becoming queen, so they store their patience in large vials. She, however, seems to not understand that I am *constantly joking*. A serious girl, your Dagney."

"Some things are not jokes, Your Highness," Sir Tomlinson said.

I'd worked my way under his collar. My cheek lifted, despite my attempt to keep a smile off my face. "Of course that does make her more fun to tease. I wonder if she plays cards."

Sir Tomlinson turned a shade of pink I'd not yet seen, so I decided to lay off him about his daughter. Truth was I sometimes forgot Grigfen even had a little sister. She was always so content to stay home with her books. Besides, I wouldn't risk Grig's friendship over a pretty set of shoulders. There were plenty of other options out there. I loved women—their intelligence, their kindness, their stubborn bravery, not to mention the softness of their skin—but once I met the right girl there would be room in my heart for only one. I wanted a love like my parents had. A love of equals, that could last forever, long past legends.

But I'd yet to meet a girl who could see past my crown.

Sir Tomlinson fumed down two flights of granite stairs and across the wood-paneled entrance hall, each slammed heel a punch line that tickled me no end.

We crossed into my father's council room and I lost my grin.

Perhaps it was the length of the ancient table, the carved map that covered the length of a wall, or the shadows on the council members' faces, but the mood seemed sober and ominous. Sucked dry, as it were. A chorus of Historians in raven-feather robes and silver masks surrounded the edge of the room. At the center, my father's council and the Savak cleric sat around a long table.

Sir Tomlinson took his seat at my father's left, and my father dismissed my guards.

The lone empty seat was reserved for my uncle, so I stood among the Historians.

"Seen anything naughty lately?" I asked the closest Historian.

They did not respond. Not even a chuckle.

I could never read the Historians, not with their expressions hidden behind their carved masks. They were tasked to record everything of note for posterity, refusing to influence history, only to observe it. Truth was I barely noticed them anymore. They were simply always there—watching me eat breakfast, studying me sword fighting with Grigfen in the armory; one always observed me as I slept, in case I were to die while dreaming and my last gasping sounds were worth recording.

Prince Ryo ne Vinton's last words: gurgle gurgle.

Who would want to lose that?

The cleric wasn't speaking.

Her red hood rested at the crown of her pale hair. Silver wings—the emblem of the Savak—painted across her brow, her dark red robe puddling around her chair, and a silver and glass sphere necklace tucked between her collarbones. Her face was flat, devoid of emotion, but I could not say that of the rest of the council. Sir Tomlinson crossed his arms, the general's jaw pulsed tight, and Lord Reginal's tongue peeked from the side of his false smile. A sign of his greed as well as his suspicion.

My mother watched me, not the cleric. And my father? My father sat like a spring wound tight, pinching the bridge of his nose, his foot tapping against the marble floor, his twisting mouth rebelling at the silence.

"What is your business here?" my father expelled, his voice rough and serious, like he only was to our enemies.

She stayed silent.

My father, the most powerful king in the world, asked her a direct question, and she sat in silence and the king did nothing but huff in impatience.

Mother waved her hand. "Perhaps you'd like something to drink?"

The cleric pressed her lips together. "Not until every chair is filled."

Well, at least we knew she had the ability to make sounds.

The last chair stayed empty. By rights of the council it belonged to my uncle Edvarg, but as emissary for the Abbey of the Undergod, he wasn't likely to show his face in order to appease the Savak. No matter how many times the king sent a messenger to the Abbey, he would not come to hear a heathen's words.

It would be a council of five.

"Son." The king gestured toward Uncle's seat.

"Me?" I touched my chest. Tomlinson sighed, but the rest of the council seemed to soften with affection, looking at me much the way they did Mother's pet cat, Chompsens. I cleared my throat. "Yes, Father?"

"Take your uncle's seat, please."

I bowed to the council, and I fought back a grin as I touched my forehead in a salute to the Historians. This I wanted them to record. I looked back at the king and in that moment, I saw my father. The man who always welcomed me to sit by him no matter how busy he was, who cheered at my tournaments even when I was bested, the man who told me that there was nothing I could do that would make him not love me.

And then in an instant something behind his eyes went blank, and he shifted from the man who was my father to the man who was my king. But I could handle this opportunity. All that I wanted, more than any win or tournament, was to see my father look at me with pride, the way I remembered.

I slid into the chair at Mother's right.

"You must give me your kingdom," the cleric said.

The council shared looks. Ridiculous. I laughed, and General Franciv gave a snort. Sir Tomlinson's giant hands batted at poor Lord Reginal, but the scrawny little man was giggling so hard he didn't notice. Mother pressed her fingers over her lips, trying to remain polite in case it wasn't a joke.

It had to be, although the Savak were not known for their humor. Their cunning, their betrayal, their strange religion? Yes, of course. Humor? Not famously reported.

The cleric tipped her head to one side as if she did not understand our reaction. Her golden eyes seemed sharp in the light coming from the arched windows.

Father did not smile. "Is there a threat in your words?"

I narrowed my eyes.

"Not in my words." She pressed her lips in a tight grimace and reached into her long sleeves.

My father's guards drew their weapons.

There, hidden behind swaths of red silk, was a bag, brown leather, tucked tight next to her body.

"In the future."

My breath caught.

Out came a clay vase, sealed with wax. It thudded as she placed it on the table in front of her. She withdrew five small clay cups.

The guards did not put away their weapons.

We all eyed the vase . . . or pitcher, most likely. Filled with the only thing the Savak possessed that made this cleric welcome to the court.

The clear water of the Seer Spring. One sip and the future no longer remained a mystery.

I cocked my head to the side as the cleric filled the cups.

It would be considered blasphemy to drink of the spring water, but anyone who did could see the future. Imagine knowing what enemy might attack, or what the clouds would bring—drought or famine, richness or surplus. We could prepare for war or for illness. Blasphemy seemed a small price to pay for such a vision, yet there were rumors the seer water was also a judgment. If their goddess didn't consider the partaker worthy, the water would kill.

I leaned forward.

Oh light. I seemed eager. My reputation would never live that down.

"Generations ago," the cleric said as she placed a cup in front of my mother, "we were allies. I ask you to remember the time before the Seer Spring was discovered. Back before the first seer drowned in his vision of the future."

"Before the walls," Mother said, her voice measured.

Sir Tomlinson's voice was not. "Before the hibisi." Sir Tomlinson's anger was well placed. He'd lost his wife due to the lack of those flowers.

When they discovered the Seer Spring, the Savak built walls around their island, and they stopped sending aid or emissaries to any other kingdom. The Savak closed their gates by the edge of the sword, only allowing certain traders to come, and only if they brought the seeds of the hibisi flower. A century later, they owned every hibisi flower on this side of our world, and they dotted their island like little white specks of light.

The cleric placed the small cups in front of my father, Sir Tomlinson, General Franciv, and Lord Reginal. She did not place one in front of me, which was wise, because I might've thrown it in her face. She lowered her gaze. "We, like you, regret the lives lost to the gray illness."

Lord Reginal clasped his heart. "The Undergod was well fed."

"By our greed," the cleric said.

I agreed with the cleric, which felt fundamentally wrong. Six years ago, an illness spread throughout my kingdom. Thousands of lives were lost. Harsh ugly deaths. Nothing we tried could stop it, not until the Savak revealed the cure.

Brewed from the bloom of the hibisi.

They knew the hibisi held healing properties, unlike anything we'd ever found. They'd seen it in their visions. Centuries before the disease first spread, the Savak knew the lives it would take, and yet they hoarded the truth. The clerics came to our shores with the cure, which they offered for a price, and only if the recipients would praise the Savak goddess for her goodness. The Savak watched, holding the cure, as people—our people—who could not afford to pay, or who were too pious to blaspheme, died gasping in front of them. And the Savak never shed a tear for us.

And now she wanted us to trust her? There was not enough fortune in the world.

Father leaned away and clasped his hands under his chin. "You wish to ally yourself with us?"

The cleric's expression was still as a bluff. "Not as such. We need to be united to save as many lives as we can from what is coming."

I glanced at their seer water, despite myself.

Mother tapped her fingers on the table. With her black hair cascading over her shoulders, and a thin golden band tracing the line of her brow, she was the picture of a queen. "You come alone. Do you have your queen's blessing?"

"Our queen does not know," she whispered. Her shoulders hunched. "She must never know."

"What is coming?" Father asked.

"War," the cleric said. "Our young queen has assembled an army. She will make herself empress. We have seen it. We have seen the loss of life, the destruction she will reap in her rise to power. She will not govern well. She will not take prisoners. But there is a path to survival. You must drink to see it."

"How do we know this isn't poison?" Tomlinson asked. "How do we know she's not sent you here to kill us all?"

"I will drink with you," the cleric answered.

Not enough. Still, curiosity drove me forward. I lifted Lord Reginal's cup to my nose and sniffed. It smelled clean and fresh, almost sweet. I gave it back.

The cleric lifted her eyebrow. "It is an honor to drink seer water. No one outside our island has ever been offered of our spring, and this we freely give to you. There will be no price."

I clenched my jaw. "The Savak always have a price."

She acknowledged my anger with a softened look. "At least not for you. If the queen finds me, my life will be forfeit for smuggling this water and for giving it to you. But I shall give my life gladly. For there is a future you must see. A future we must avoid. And we can, but only with your help."

The Historians stepped closer.

Father had been still. Considering. "What do you say, General?"

General Franciv considered her cup. Her dark hair framed one side of her face, but the other was shaven close to her scalp. Her crisp white uniform was similar to a common Everstrider uniform, except for the rows of jeweled awards on her lapel, and the line of black kohl from her forehead to her neck.

"If her life is forfeit anyway, there is no guarantee of our safety. It could be poison, or a trap. If it's poison, they would take out the spine of our kingdom in one act. We can't let our greed destroy us—"

"It's not greed," Lord Reginal interjected, his voice polished from all the time he spent in the university. He tugged at his fine collar, and his gray mustache twitched beneath his wide nose. "The pursuit of knowledge is never greed. If we can learn our future, we can change it for the better. I vote we drink."

"Well, I will not," I replied. "Father, I would not trust a Savak to post a letter, let alone drink their piss—"

Tomlinson coughed.

No heathen war. Right. I bowed my head and said nothing.

"We must face the future. Together," the cleric said. "Or we will not survive."

"If she's lying, it's a risk," Sir Tomlinson said. "But if there is a chance danger is coming, it may be worth it."

I tapped the table. "Then we let a servant drink. Someone we trust."

The cleric looked about. "Only a chosen few are worthy of our goddess's tears. It must be this council."

"A king never asks a servant to take a risk he would not take." Father's gaze was sharp.

I tensed, my tongue slid over my teeth, and I refused to look at anything except the shining wooden surface of the table.

Father was wrong. A king's life was worth more than a servant's. My father never listened to me when it came to the greater good. He only summoned the King's Executioner when the taking of one life would save hundreds. He couldn't see that if we smashed a threat when it was small, the kingdom would be at peace.

Mother folded her hands. "I'd rather trust and be prepared."

"Trusting an enemy is a good way to get killed," I warned.

"If we only take knowledge from those who agree with us, we will be led into a trap of our own making," Mother said. "We can't let our biases leave us blind."

"I've reached my decision," Father announced. "Kings must have longer memories than generals or sons. I know the source of their spring's magic and I do not fear it. I will drink."

I dropped my hands. "Father, no."

Our people would not approve of this. After the hibisi, my people saw the Savak as murderers, as monsters more foul than any Lurcher.

To side with one and share seer water with a cleric? It wasn't just blasphemy. To many of our people, this would be treason.

"As king, I must know what threatens my people." He sighed. "Be brave, my son."

The general reached for her cup. "My king. Wait."

She dipped her kohl-darkened fingertips into the cup and drew them to her pale mouth. She paused as she tasted, then she licked her lips and gave a brief sniff. "I am nothing if not brave. I will drink with you."

They all ignored my warnings. I might as well not have even been there, if they weren't going to take my counsel over a Savak cleric's.

The cleric smiled and lifted her glass. "To a new future," she toasted.

She pressed the cup to her lips, and the rest of the council, including Father, followed her example.

I watched, in horror, as my parents fell victim to the seer water's pull. Their eyes rolled upward, flashing white, their skin paling to a soft gray. The council slumped in their chairs. Lord Reginal nearly fell off his.

And they didn't wake.

I sped to my father's side and struck his back. Once. Twice. Again.

"Father. I beg of you. Wake up!" My pulse raced with a panic so sharp it seemed almost a memory. "Father!"

I knew they shouldn't have drunk. I knew they should have listened to me.

My father's guards rushed to the cleric's side and held her bound. Those at the door lowered their weapons and searched about for something to do. The fools.

"Get a doctor. Quickly!"

The cleric never fell to her vision. Her eyes were clear as a mirror as the guards shoved her into the table. "He will awaken in twelve heart-beats," she said, her voice strained.

I didn't trust her words. I couldn't. She drank it too; why wasn't she swept up in this vision? "What have you done to him? To all of them?"

"Do not fear, Princeling. All will be well."

I wasn't afraid, I was angry. Anger could sometimes make my heart pound, and my jaw quiver, and my throat tighten as if I was about to cry, but I was not scared. A future king was not allowed to be scared.

Mother woke with a great cry. Oh, thank the light. She reached forward and drew me into a hug. Her arms trembled, and she held me too tight, her tears wetting my collar.

I pulled back when Sir Tomlinson screamed himself awake, reaching for his sword and lifting it high above him, as if he were facing a monster. "You're all right, Tomlinson," I shouted. "It was just a vision. It wasn't real." His arm lowered slowly, and the sword clattered on the table. The sound awoke General Franciv. Her hands twitched to the dagger belted to her waist, before she fell to her knees and clutched her grip together as she prayed. Reginal's eyes flashed open, and he held his fist over his mouth, fleeing from the table to be sick in a vase.

Father woke, his face filled with grim resolution.

I closed my mouth. I'd seen that look on my father's face before. Once. When the sickness tore through my people. It was the look of a king at war.

"What can be done?" he asked.

The cleric extracted a large contract from the folds of her cape.

"You must sign your kingdom to the queen of the Savak, and you must come with me. We will protect your people, and keep the oaths our creator gave us."

No one laughed now. Father only hesitated for a moment before laying his palm out in request for a quill.

I stood. "Stop! That's my kingdom you're giving away."

"Not yet, my son."

"Not *ever* if you do this. You can't just hand over our kingdom to the *Savak*?"

"I feel the sting of this too, my son. But the cost of leaving is nothing if it stops what's coming."

Mother stepped toward me. "If we bow to the Savak queen now, she will save our kingdom for last, and we can give assistance to our allies while she thinks us cowed. It is the only way we all will survive. It is our only path to peace."

"By giving her our armies?" They would not see sense. "We cannot leave." My voice betrayed my emotion, so I cleared my throat and began again. "What will become of our people if you take our armies to other shores?"

What would become of me?

Father's eyes softened. "You will keep them safe until I return."

Me? "Against the Savak queen?" It was too much. "I can't. I can't do this. Not on my own."

"That is not all, my son. The only way to win this war is if you gather the Armor of Irizald before the queen of the Savak tracks it down."

I stilled at the mention.

The Armor of Irizald was a secret we never spoke of beyond our family walls. The witch-made armor created a power immeasurable when all the pieces were combined. We should have destroyed it—it was too dangerous to continue to exist—but we could not. Instead, long ago, my grandmother separated the armor and hid each piece in far-flung locations, which only my father and I knew. It set my spine to ice to think of our armor in the Savak queen's hands.

My father gave me a nod. "Once you find the armor, the true heir will return to the Throne of Honor. Our kingdom will be restored."

Mother wiped her cheeks and stood. "Your uncle will help you until then. Get him to drink the seer water. He will manage the kingdom as you quest for the armor."

I crossed to my father's side. "Father, no. Please. Whatever is coming, we can destroy it on our own. We can gather the armor together. You'd be invincible, no matter what weapon she aims our direction. We'll face her as a united kingdom, not as servants to these heathens."

I waited for someone to correct me, but the room was silent.

"It won't be enough," General Franciv said. "There is only one solution now. I've seen it. We must lead the charge from different shores."

"What?" The world shifted. If the general agreed, there was no one on my side. "Are you certain?"

"It won't be enough," General Franciv repeated. "There is only one solution now. I've seen it. We must lead the charge from different shores."

Why would she repeat herself? The council stood still, as if they were waiting on me to make a choice. But what choice? Why would they be silent now?

Was it possible the cleric was right? My people hated the Savak; they would not understand this. How was I supposed to change their opinion when it matched my own? How could I protect my people and gather the armor at the same time? Could this really be the only way?

I leaned over my father's shoulder and read the contract.

WE, THE UNDERSIGNED, DO HUMBLY SWEAR OUR FIDELITY AND SUBMISSION TO THE HONORABLE MCKENNA SHARPWING CARRINGTON, QUEEN OF THE SAVAK. WE PLEDGE ALL BORDERS, RESOURCES, AND LEADERSHIP IN HER ESTIMABLE NAME, IN EXCHANGE FOR THE SAFE STEWARDSHIP OF OUR PEOPLE.

WE DO SO PLEDGE UNTIL THE DAY OF BATTLE ENDS, AND THE RIGHTFUL HEIR SITS UPON THE THRONE OF HONOR.

Treason.

Cowardice.

But in truth it was a distraction. The council would undermine the queen from within her circle, and buy me time to collect the armor.

"All right," I whispered. "I'll do it."

A flare of light struck through the glass windows. I stood taller, like something had given me strength.

A servant gave Father a quill and he signed. Father passed the paper to Mother, and she to the rest. My hands trembled and I shook my head.

As they signed away my home, my title, and my future.

As they left me with nothing but a family legend to protect my people from a war that was coming.

And my uncle. He would love a chance to manage the kingdom while I searched for the armor.

The trick would be to remove him once Father returned.

"Can I trust Uncle to help me?"

My parents shared a glance, but the cleric stepped forward. She placed the near-empty pitcher on the table.

"Goddess bless us all if he does not drink."

My tutors never taught me the proper etiquette of abandoning one's kingdom. Turns out it involves a grand helping of silence, and servants mooring the ship to the royal docks, while the harbor men work and whisper and watch.

Mother pressed back a curl and kissed my hair. "Keep yourself safe."

She cocked her head to look at me, as if memorizing my face. My mother had fought a thousand battles, but never with a sword. She came from a far-off kingdom and she had to fight tooth and bone to gain the respect she'd earned at court. She could protect my father from this. She could protect herself.

"I'll try my best," I whispered. This task had set my voice to hiding.

"Thank you for doing this," my mother said.

The cleric unstrung the necklace from around her neck, lowering her hood over her shoulders to do so.

"For when the time comes, Princeling." She gave me a small blue glass sphere wrapped tight in metal filigree, strung between two threads. "It was drawn from our holy spring after our plans were made. If our plans succeed, you'll see what you must do to find your victory."

"And if they don't?"

Mother broke the silence. "Then this is goodbye."

The sphere full of seer water hung heavy in my palm. A part of me wanted to drink it now, to know why my parents were doing this, and another part of me wanted to throw this sphere into the moons-lit waves.

My father closed my fingers over the sphere. "Promise me, son," he said. "Promise you won't drink until you are sure nothing will stop you from finishing."

I met his eyes and nodded.

He pulled me tight, his scruff scratching my neck, his hand clasped around the back of my head. When he leaned away, his cheeks were wet.

Then they climbed into the boat, my parents touching their noses in prayer. The general gave me a salute, which Tomlinson copied, and I stood tall, trying to look like one who could accomplish this impossible task, not letting my doubt curl my shoulders or my spine. I slipped the necklace around my neck before I tucked it beneath my collar.

And I turned my back on the people who were turning their backs on me. Alone, I made my way through the courtyard toward the stables. Whispering servants ducked away from me while watchful eyes peered from windows. A Whirligig, a pumpkin-sized mechanical with fluttering wings, rose from the mechanical shop, carrying gossip in its spinning gears. The news had begun to spread, soft and slow like kindling catching. I needed to enlist my uncle to our cause, before the city turned ablaze with words of a king's treason.

Uncle could help me douse this fire.

Or he could fan the flames.

I raced into the stables, after my mount. Sir Grigfen guffawed from a stall near mine. His foot was caught in the stirrup, and he was spilling coins and laughter as a servant tried to pull his boot from the metal.

The tension in my neck loosened for a second. Grig's grinning eyes met mine. "Ryo! Sorry I'm late, pal. I had the Undergod's own luck at the Fisherman's Haul. I got twenty coppers before some chap decided I was cheating and tried to . . ." He trailed off as he took in my expression. "Wait. What's gone wrong?"

I could give him no answer. "Nothing. I need to see my uncle."

"I'll go with you. I've just got to figure out how to get back on this horse. Were they always this tall?" The servants pushed him back up onto his saddle.

I didn't answer him. I checked that the cleric's leather bag tucked at my side still held the seer water and the contract, then I climbed astride my horse and kicked my heels.

"What's the rush, Ryo?" Grigfen asked as he struggled to keep pace. He'd always hated riding with me; he said I either needed to push my horse to a full gallop, or walk. Still, he smiled—I could not recall if I'd ever seen his face not in the midst of a toothy grin. His shaggy blond curls hung over his eyes, and his vest was unbuttoned, stains on his cravat. "You look like you've got a prank on countdown. Should I fetch the feathers?"

"Har, har," I muttered over the sound of our horses running at full gallop. "You don't need to follow me."

He held the reins tight as we rode down the cobbled streets toward the Abbey. He squinted at me, his face shadowed in the torchlight. "The fact you keep saying that makes me think I need to. You look all squirrelly so I know you're either heading toward trouble, or you're heading toward a lot of trouble. Either way I'm not going to miss it."

He grinned and I almost smiled back. I'd like the company . . . no, I'd love the company, and I'd love to not be the only one who knew this secret; I also knew that word was going to spread, and once news broke . . . Mine was not the only father who had left.

"You need to be with your family when the news breaks."

News was already spreading. Peasants stood at the edges of the road, calling out to us, but I did my best to ignore them. They'd find out soon enough.

We reached the Abbey gates, and I dismounted. The Abbey chapel was walled with bones, fused together with iron smelted from swords donated with the bodies of soldiers. A circle of painted glass reflected the moons-light in the grand chapel, but I wouldn't find my uncle in the chapel. I ran past the glowing building and around the back to the catacomb tunnels where the high priests and my uncle kept their offices. Grigfen followed close behind. As a child, we used to play in the hallowed hallways of the catacombs. Now I rushed forward through the catacomb doors, a sealed cup in one hand, and the bound parchment with my father's signature in the other, trying not to vomit on the holy bone walls.

My uncle would help me carry the load of this. Right now, we were the only ones leading this kingdom, and if we wanted to restore the rightful heir to the throne and protect our kingdom from the Savak, then my uncle and I needed to be united.

I turned the candlelit corner to a maze of skull-topped hallways. How could I find my uncle in this catacomb? I usually preferred to wait in the main chambers, or in the chapel, let Uncle come to me when he could. But my uncle's office was back here somewhere.

Grig scratched the scruff on his chin and stopped me. "Oh. It's serious, is it?"

"It is."

"Then I'm not leaving."

I sighed. "Grig."

He folded his arms over his stomach. "You know, your pride is going to get you killed one day, and it's my job as your best mate to protect you from your own self."

"Are you certain?" The task in front of me was dangerous, but it would feel almost achievable if Grigfen was at my side.

He stepped closer. "You're my friend, and this might be because I'm floating over my winnings at the Fisherman's Haul, but I'm not ashamed to say you're my hero, Ryo. Whatever it is, I won't let you do it alone."

The weight on my shoulders lightened. "It's too dangerous. You should—"

"It doesn't matter. You're my future king, and I can't leave you to your adventures without a squire."

I offered my palm and he shook it. Torchlight brightened against the bones, and I must have squeezed too hard, because he winced.

"Light's bosom, you are strong." He shook out his hand and I laughed.

"You won big, then?"

He shook the coin purse at his belt. "Forty coppers in all. You?"

"Lady M took me for twenty-five golds."

He whistled.

I lifted a shoulder. "She brought her granddaughter."

Grig chuckled. "Poor fool Ryo. She found your weakness."

I picked up my pace, and he matched my footing. "Where are we going?" he asked.

"To see my uncle."

"Grrreeaat." Grigfen had a way of saying things so I always knew exactly what he was thinking. "And what's with the cup and the scroll?"

"I wouldn't touch that." I lowered my voice to a whisper. "It's Seer Spring water."

"You're bringing your uncle . . ." Grigfen let out a rumbling giggle I tried to hush. "Oh, this is a mighty prank. I'm glad to see it."

I desperately wished it were as simple as a prank.

A Devout stepped forward. Her hair was shaved, her nose was dotted with red paint, and she wore gray and shapeless robes. I tugged at my coat and then chided myself for showing my nerves. The Devout could use a portion of the Undergod's power to see the dead and perform miracles the unbelievers called magic. The truly dedicated, the priests of the Undergod, could command bones to move or control the monstrous beasts that crept from the underworld. "Hush, Grig." I bowed to the Devout and Grigfen followed suit. "Peace and honor to you for your devotion."

The Devout answered our bows with one of her own. "And to you for your reception."

I held the cup behind my back. "I'm looking for my uncle."

"His holiness is in his chambers. May I be permitted to lead you toward him?"

"I thank you for your service."

The Devout turned. Grigfen barely held back a laugh. The shadows of his almost laugh echoed against the walls like a flickering candle.

A bead of sweat traced down my back. Well, I'd found him.

Now what was I going to say?

As the second son, Uncle Edvarg was encouraged to go into the priesthood of the Undergod. He took to it well—too well, some said. It showed too much ambition the way he ascended to the rank of high priest. People whispered about deaths they could not explain, in which Edvarg profited. My parents ignored such rumblings, and so did I.

Uncle Edvarg would help me. He had to.

The catacombs air tasted of silt, torch oil, and candle wax. The bone walls seemed almost made of bricks, each bone slightly different, but united in their anonymity. The office of the Holiest was open, the wrought iron door held ajar by a loose stone. Inside a room of bones,

Uncle pored over a map at his gilded desk. The ceiling was formed of rib cages, with a striping of sunlight cascading on my uncle, unleashing the creator's wisdom on anyone the light fell upon.

Uncle Edvarg's lips pressed lightly before bending into a smile. "Nephew! So good to see you. So tell me, what did the Savak cleric want?"

"What cleric?" Grigfen asked. "I may have missed something when I was down to the tables."

"Ah, Sir Grigfen. I thought I smelled cheap cologne."

Edvarg waved away the Devout. She gave a low bow, touching her forehead to her wrist before exiting.

The door stayed open.

I let out a breath. It was a relief to no longer be alone with this.

"The cleric brought a gift."

"Ah?" Edvarg squinted.

I lifted the cup.

Edvarg gestured it away, but I held it firm. "You have to see the future. Our kingdom depends on it."

He turned back to his papers. "Says the heathen."

"Father drank."

Edvarg stilled.

I pushed the drink forward across his desk. "So did the other four members of the council. And their vision—"

"Wait." Grigfen's face flushed red. "My father drank from the Seer Spring?"

I gripped Grig's shoulder. "What they saw . . . It's terrible, Uncle. The Savak queen will try to destroy us all, but we have a plan to stop her. You need to drink, so you can see the plan and help us survive."

"The council drank seer water?" Edvarg murmured. He pressed his index finger over his lips, considering. He pointed to the scroll. "And what is that?"

I unrolled the parchment and laid it out over the papers on the desk. I knocked over a small idol, but I didn't right it. "After they drank, they all agreed this was necessary to save our people."

Uncle's neck pulsed. "They disavowed our *god* in favor of the heathen spring?"

Father said Uncle would help. He had to. He was the only family I had now. I'd give him one last chance—one last opportunity to be who my parents thought he was. "Trust me, Uncle. They are trying to save us." I moved around the desk. "Please, Uncle Edvarg. You need to drink to see the future and help protect us from what is coming."

Grigfen stepped to the desk, his fingers tracing the scroll as he read the words. "They left us for the Savak? Why would he leave without saying goodbye?" Grig ran both hands through his curls and stepped away. His face crumpled.

"They wouldn't have, if the danger wasn't real," I insisted. "Please, Uncle, you need to believe me. Drink the seer water, and I'll let you rule as adviser until Father comes back."

Uncle Edvarg's cheek creased, and his eyebrows lifted as he read the words. My muscles tightened, but I had to trust that his ambition would be stronger than his piety. I was offering him the throne.

"I could believe you, but never the Savak. My foolish brother has been tricked by them and he's turned a traitor," my uncle announced.

"No. He's trying to save us. If you drink the seer water, you will see why."

"My brother has renounced his god-given duty to our people, and in the Undergod's name, I must assert my claim for the throne he's left behind."

I shuddered. "I'm giving you the throne."

"No. You, my traitorous nephew and your disheveled friend, are the only things standing in my way."

Edvarg raised both hands, his thumbs touching in a summoning pose. A green mist spread from my uncle's fingers, lighting the curve of his cheekbones, leaving shadows under his eyes.

I rocked back. The glowing light filled the room.

"Stop," I commanded. I darted a glance to Grig, my body flushing hot. I should have never allowed him to accompany me.

"What're you doing?" Grig's eyes widened.

My uncle pulled his arms down and the bone walls shuddered. A crack and a whiff of bone dust and floating bones flew toward him and congealed together into half-formed, animated skeletons.

I flinched back. The Undergod's own power.

Grig swore and joined my side. His hands lifted into fists.

"Uncle," I whispered. I couldn't stop staring at the half-formed creatures. Bones formed where bones should not be, deer antlers for hips, a skull from a beast I could not name serving as a set of ribs. The Undergod's power to move the dead was a sacred gift bestowed only on the most righteous. Such holiness should only be used for protection from the lich and against our enemies.

Never against me.

"Will you disavow your father," Uncle asked me, "and kneel before me as your king?"

We huddled in shocked silence. "Not bloody likely," Grig said.

I shook my head. No matter what power my uncle wielded, I would never betray my father. Uncle knew that. Uncle leaned forward, his eyes firm on mine, the side of his mouth hooked up like a jagged lure.

He wanted me to stand against him. He didn't want me to cower. He wanted me dead.

My body tensed and I found a store of rage I'd never cracked into before. I bared my teeth, drunk with my anger, off-my-head tipsy with a need to right this wrong. How dare he threaten me? He didn't just betray me, he betrayed my father. I drew my sword.

Uncle pulled more bones from the wall. The ceiling above us cracked.

My heart thundered in my chest, and my throat tightened. "I won't."

"Shame." Edvarg sat at his desk. The side of his mouth twitched like he was hiding a smile. The bone-formed creatures crept toward us at his command. "If you won't stand with me, then you must be removed."

My heart thundered. The whispers had been right. My uncle was more ambitious than my father or I had ever realized. He would kill me to get me out of the way.

But I could not let him ruin my father's plan.

Grig and I shared a look.

The skeletons lunged for my throat. On instinct, I swung my sword, slicing through bone. The skull flew backward, but the creature kept marching forward.

Grig chucked his sack of coins at the skeleton coming for him then raised his fists. I swung my sword again, and again, but bones pressed against my arms and held me back. My arms stopped in midair and nothing I could do would move them. Uncle raised one hand and spread his fingers. The bones threw me backward. I slammed into the wall. Clay and shards rained around me. Grig lunged to help me, but the bones holding the door frame twisted forward and wrapped around his neck, slamming him back against the frame.

I scrambled to my feet and ran to his side, prying at the bones that pressed against his throat. I had to pull them off him. He couldn't breathe.

Grig's face turned red, then purple, his arms thrashing against the bones. Grig.

"Uncle, stop!" I slammed my sword against the bones. They shattered, and tightened closer. Harder. Sharper, shards cutting his skin. The other skeleton grabbed me with strength beyond muscle. It pressed me against the wall. Too rough. I could feel my ribs cracking.

"Uncle!" I gasped.

"Will you join me? Renounce your claim to my throne?"

My head ached. I could never do that. But I couldn't let him kill Grig.

"I will. I swear it," I lied. I licked my lips.

"You *lie*, Nephew. I've seen you play cards. I know your tells. And why would I allow any uprising to threaten my claim to the Throne of Honor? It should always have been mine."

The bone at my throat snapped in two.

Then a shard of bone slammed into the base of my throat and speared my body into the wall, like a dart through a board.

"No!" Grig shrieked through too little air.

My hands formed fists. I couldn't breathe. It was so quick. So cold. I didn't feel the pain until blood spurted into my lungs. The copper taste coated my tongue, and speckled the pale calcium. Blue sparks crackled in my vision, and a spot of ache between my shoulder blades seemed like a heavy rock collapsing through my back.

The pain came. Harsh. Stinging like a scream that wouldn't release. Every nerve sharpened; even my hair follicles stung.

The bone spear held me standing as night slipped over my vision.

Blood filled my mouth and I could not find air.

— — —

I awoke in the doorway of my uncle's office, a scream still caught in my throat. I grabbed my neck, but there was no wound; the only proof of my death was a puddle of my blood, a pile of shattered bones, and one foot to my left, a bloody femur stabbed into the wall.

My mind raced as I fumbled backward. I searched my uncle's blood-splattered office, trying to find answers, but there were none. I was alone. Still breathing. Somehow still breathing. Free from the spear that had stolen my life. I held my head in my hands. I'd died. I knew it.

In the hall behind me, my uncle shouted lies. "Guards! Guards! This assailant killed the prince."

I tilted my head to the side and peered into the hall. The walking bone creatures held Grig's hands above his head, their unnatural backs to me. My uncle marched ahead of them, not one drop of my blood on his robes.

I leaned against the door frame and fought for air. Every inch of my skin hurt. An ache in my skull hummed, as if a spark of lightning had left me scalded. The room stank of blood, bones, and rancid incense.

I clutched my throat.

"It wasn't me," Grigfen said through sobs. There wasn't any weight behind his words. He spoke as though he knew he'd seen me die and now no one would believe his word over the Holiest himself.

But I would. I planted my bloody hands and pushed myself through the doorway.

I was alive and it was a miracle I could not explain. "Stop!"

My uncle shuffled around, his eyes wide, his color pallid.

"Holy . . ." Grigfen flushed. "Ryo. What . . ."

Uncle averted his eyes, his jaw trembling at the sight of me.

"Edvarg ne Mark." I spat out blood that clouded my throat. "You've committed treason in front of a witness."

"How is this possible?" Uncle shook his head rapidly.

The nerve of him. "I didn't know your heart was this dark, so full of sick ambition."

"I killed you," he snarled. "You were erased."

He froze. His expression lagged as he processed.

I lifted my head. "You are forthwith removed of all title, rank, and by my father's authority I swear—"

"Your father gave away his authority." He shook the scroll in his hand. "You are the one who has aligned with the Savak. Some blasphemy saved you."

"It was our god—"

"You don't speak for the Undergod. Not in my catacombs." He spoke through his teeth. "You ask me to commit treason, to deny the Undergod. I will not. You've been corrupted by the Savak. I will kill you a thousand times to get the heathen out of you. It is my duty as your uncle."

I rushed forward. If I knocked him out, he couldn't control the bones. Edvarg's spindly hand twisted and a wave of ghostlight tossed me back easily like I was a child still learning how to fight. His nails dug into my freshly healed wrists, stronger than his frail form led me to believe.

I raised my fist.

Grig sputtered behind me as the sharp shards of bones aimed at my best friend, cutting into his neck.

Edvarg massaged his temples as if he'd grown weary of this conversation. "Stop or I will kill him."

I couldn't bluff my way out of this. Not with stakes this high.

But I could try. "Let him go."

"Yeah, seriously, let me go. I'm nothing to you. I won't say anything, I promise." It shook my core to hear the fear in Grig's voice.

"He only lives if you surrender."

My fist trembled, but I didn't swing. If I moved, my uncle could kill Grigfen as quickly as he had killed me. The bones at his throat drew blood. Grig leaned his head back, his eyes glistening with tears, but his hands rolled and his arm muscles tensed. He was about to fight back. Any movement would spell the end of him.

"Do you promise you will let him live?" I tried to signal Grig not to attack, but his eyes were wild, past listening to reason.

Edvarg's jaw pulsed. "Yes."

"That's not enough." I stepped closer. "Swear it to your god."

A muscle twitched on his neck. "Will you trade your life for his?"

Grig's head shook back and forth as though he thought he wasn't worth it, but how could he say that? I couldn't allow him to die. Not when he was willing to die in my place.

I lowered my knife. "I will."

Edvarg's anger melted from his eyes. "And you, Sir Grigfen. I can't have you blabbing what you've seen, so the only way I will allow you to live is if you devote yourself to the Undergod himself. Will you accept the Devout class and vow to keep my secrets? It is the only way you will leave this catacomb with your head attached."

Grig glanced at me and then nodded. A green mist swirled around him, before it tunneled into his mouth, brightening the whites of his eyes.

I closed mine. The life of the Devout wasn't death, but it might as well have been. He couldn't marry, he couldn't own his title. I'd stolen my best friend's future.

Edvarg turned his sharp smile on me.

———   ———   ———

Later, in my cell, I berated myself for not fighting back. Later, I thought of a hundred things I could have done differently to save Grigfen, a hundred things my father would have done against his traitorous brother. What someone worthy would have done.

But I'd raised my hands and dropped the fight.

The moment I needed it, all my bravado had disappeared.

And it had taken my hope with it.

I could not eat the silence in my cell. I could not drink the absence of light. I had nothing to gnaw on except my nightmares.

I woke from one, the memory of a sharp bone paring through my flesh, to the sound of a subtle movement in the dark. I crawled forward, ignoring the dust and filth that littered the ground. The bars of the cell were cold on my cheek. My dry mouth opened, pleading to the noise for light, for water . . . For kindness.

Uncle had stolen everything from me, except the clothes on my back, and the necklace he had not found.

A window somewhere opened slightly, sending a lost saint's whisper of light.

It was a Historian, her legs folded, her carved mask tucked on her brow, like a low-hung hat. I knew this Historian well. She was the one who always came and watched me sleep. It was almost a comfort to have her there, because the expression on her face wasn't predatory.

It was motherly.

Faded black paint spread across her nose and forehead in perfect streaks only marred by the line of tears dripping from eyes I almost recognized.

"Help me," I pleaded. I crawled up onto my hands and knees and held the bar. "Help me," I raged again, my voice shaking with anger and need, like an open wound.

Her tear-streaked eyes recorded my agony, but she didn't move. I pulled at her cloak, trying to bring her closer, to force her to action, but she stayed planted.

Her cloak slipped off.

Underneath the cloak was a structure of rusting gears and green misty ghostlight, a skeleton of pipes, sparks, and machinations. Historians were nothing but walking Whirligigs, with a face of someone I almost remembered.

I dropped the cloak and found a corner on my own.

She recorded my deaths.

Again and again.

I died of thirst, a slow death that rattled my lungs and set a sharp pain in my abdomen.

I reawakened a foot away from where I'd lain, only to die from poisoned food. Each time I awoke, my body was battered, but my heart was still beating. I didn't know how long I could live, clutching on to life with only one heart left to beat. Three times she watched me die. She stood sentinel as I shuddered awake, vomited on the cold stones, and screamed into the darkness to let me go. I didn't want to live, only to stay dead.

She watched, but she never said a word.

— — —

Hours, or days, or years later, a door opened, and a lantern's sharp light burned my retinas.

"Still alive?" Edvarg said nonchalantly, like he wasn't surprised, or as if he simply didn't care.

The Historian was gone.

"How many days?" I croaked. My throat was rough as used sandpaper—dry and full of muck.

Edvarg's cape flicked in the breeze. He cocked his head to the side. "Perhaps if we remove your head entirely."

"How. *Many.*" I stopped to fill my lungs.

"Eleven." Edvarg scratched his beard. "Perhaps if there were enough witnesses . . ."

I ignored my uncle's casual inquiry in how to kill me and clenched my eyes closed. My parents were eleven days gone. I'd lost eleven days of my quest. My palm brushed the bauble around my neck. I died from a lack of drink, yet I had crystal-clear water strung around my neck that I would never consider drinking.

Not until I knew I'd be strong enough to do this.

3
DAGNEY

I was in the market when the Executioner gongs rang out. Loud. Mechanical. I clutched the book against my chest and glanced up at the moons above me.

There was time. There was still time.

The bookseller pulled his embroidered books from their stands and packed them in a large trunk. I stepped quickly to his table.

"How much will you give me for this?" I asked. I showed him the bindings, but did not let go. You never let a trader hold your wares. Father taught me that.

"Lady Tomlinson." He eyed the title on the spine, and then shook his head. "I don't deal with traitors."

And I didn't deal well with people calling me names. I grabbed a handful of his lace cravat and pulled him until our noses were almost touching. "Jecky Varnes, I've bought enough books from you to furnish your entire house, so you will deal with me. How much?"

His eyes bulged at my violence. "One silver."

I let go. "I bought it for five not twelve days ago."

"Prices go up, prices go down." He fiddled with his collar and went back to stacking.

I folded my arms. "You are cheating me? I'm your best customer."

"You were a council member's daughter," he muttered. "I could call the guards on you. I'm sure King Edvarg would love payment for your father's betrayal."

I lowered my hands. "My father left me too." My throat tightened, but I refused to let it weaken me. "He loved me more than anything in this world, and he and my brother left me with nothing. Please. I have a household to feed."

He met my gaze, a spark of light back in his eyes. "Five silvers."

"Thank you." I handed him the book and it slipped into his trunk before I could count my silvers. "I'm looking for information about my brother."

"Be glad you got the silvers." He slid his last three books off the shelf and collapsed the thing in one winding twist of a gear. I'd always admired his mechanical bookshelf. "The King's Executioner's been summoned. Market's closing."

I stared up at the twin moons. It was getting late indeed if I could see their faces.

"I heard the gongs." I slid my coins into the pockets of my market dress. "I'm sorry about your cravat. It's been a difficult few days."

He slammed his trunk closed and locked it. Jecky Varnes used to be friendly, almost a friend. I shared sweet rolls with him, and he always saved me the best books.

But now I was just grateful he didn't spit on me.

The market emptied. No one here would trade with me, not even for information. I needed to know where my brother was. I had to find him.

But there was no one here, except one woman, huddled in the shadows, counting coins with trembling fingers.

I didn't know this trader. She sat with her legs folded on a woven rug. Small carved stones lined her table. I crept closer and she looked up. Her eyes were lined with kohl, her pale hair reddened with dye, her face creased with wrinkles. She wore a dress made of scarves and feathers, with tiny shells sewn as embroidery, and nestled in her skirts was a small black-and-white dog.

"You aren't heading to the execution?" I asked.

"I've seen enough death." Her husky voice barely reached me. Her pale gold eyes found mine. "Why aren't you running off to join the crowd? You aren't afraid you will miss it?"

I *wish* I could miss the execution. I glanced toward the castle, and I wrapped my shawl tighter. "I've heard tale Sir Grigfen Tomlinson was with the prince the night of the treason. But no one has seen him since. You haven't heard any rumors—"

"About your brother?" She scratched her dog's ears. I lowered my eyes. "Aye, I know who you are, miss. I also know you'd do anything for information, so how's about a trade?"

I knelt before her table. "I have few coins."

"No, coins aren't enough. I'm looking for land. Far away from the city."

I scoffed. "You expect me to trade my family's land for information?" This was not my first market day.

"No, miss." She bit her lip. "There's no information to be had. Not one soul knows where your brother is. I tell you true. I'm offering you more than information." She glanced over her shoulder before she pulled an unassuming silver bottle from a shell-lined pocket. "I'm offering you answers, and a path to a good future, for you and your family."

I leaned away from the table. King Edvarg published every word of that contract my father had signed, and the Devout proclaimed to everyone who would stop at the Abbey gates about the council's decision to drink the Savak seer water. With her words and the twisting in my stomach, I recognized the contents of the bottle without a taste. Seer water. Treason and answers in one gulp. But why reveal it to me now? Seer water was worth a thousand gold pieces at the least.

I stared at the woman. This kingdom was such a melting pot; there were merchants from every kingdom, each one a different height, weight, nationality, and gender, but somehow, they seemed stamped from the same design.

Except her.

Her dyed silver hair. Her pale eyes. Of course. She was a Savak in hiding, and if she wanted to flee . . . The Savak hated deserters more than any enemy. If she was found here when they came to claim our throne, she'd be among the first to die.

"One year's lease," I offered. But where would she be safest? "The orchard at Avenlo. It's been closed for decades, but there should be wild apples, plenty of squirrels and rabbits. The house isn't much, but it should be warm enough when frost comes. Three days west, follow the river until Forest Hill when you turn south."

"My wife and I thank you heartily." Her eyes shone. "Goddess blessings on you," she whispered.

The moons-light brightened and I felt a swelling of hope in my chest. I would find my brother. I had to. No one else was looking.

I took the seer water and sniffed it. Not well water or wine. I'd never smelled something so crisp before. There was no trick. She'd sold me seer water for a year lease. I'd never won such a bargain before. I closed the stopper and tucked it away before anyone could see me.

"Best hurry, my lady," she said. "Don't want to miss your summons."

I swallowed. "I don't know what you mean."

Her leathered face creased in a grin. "I'll keep your secrets if you keep mine."

I offered my hand and she shook it. "That's a deal if I've ever made one."

The gong sounded again. Third time. I drew a breath. I couldn't delay any longer. I had to be about my father's business.

— — —

God below, guide my axe.

My thoughts were more prayer than plan. I stood alone in front of the tall stone doors, as nervous as the first time I attended a ball, but this time my older brother wasn't here to push them open for me. This time I was heading toward death, and it was not my own. My knees shook, and I couldn't move. I wasn't ready to step out of the dark tunnel and into the gallows.

Not yet.

Heavy drums pounded in the distance, each boom echoing in my rib cage. The black robes of the King's Executioner covered my corset and bloomers, and the weight of the gilded axe pressed into my shoulder, heavy as a bag of laundry.

Would the blood stain my robes?

Don't think about it.

I drew a breath, but didn't open the door.

The tunnel smelled like my father—of ink and blood, sweat and polish. It smelled of his tears. He'd warned me taking a life would not be easy. He said it destroyed a piece of his soul to do it.

But he still did it. And with Father gone, I had to take his place.

If only my brother were here to answer the summons. If Grigfen had worn the robes, he wouldn't have stood out. His height was closer to my father's, his shoulders larger.

Perhaps it was good he wasn't here for this. It would kill him to kill another. He'd received the muscles, but I was the one who'd inherited my grandmother's strength.

I tugged the sword belt lower on my hips and widened my stance. I was a large woman, thick as my father. Perhaps they would not think me a woman below the robes.

I could do this.

My fingers twitched inside the witch-made gloves. I lowered the black hood over my mask and tried not to think of the person I would kill on the king's orders. It could be anyone. A dissenter who spoke out against our new king. A traitor, like the servants who helped King Vinton leave.

The new king demanded a show of strength. With war looming on the horizon, our people needed it. And there was no stronger hero than the King's Executioner—he who came from below the streets to kill in the king's name. He mingled with the Undergod. He was holy and secret and sacred.

His title was the mask my family wore, and that was worth protecting.

I pressed the door with the palms of my golden witch-made gloves. The solid wall slid open in front of me, and I stepped through into the night.

At the base of the castle, where some kingdoms would keep a moat, my kingdom held an arena. A half circle of steps made risers to aid the crowd's view.

The awaiting crowd scattered away as the wall behind me closed. Half-melted candles arched around the wall, where names were etched.

The onlookers cheered for my arrival as if I were the star of a theatrical. It'd been too long since I'd heard a kind word, so now this mob celebrating my presence felt like a feast to the starving. Almost comforting. But the lie in their love made the warmth curdle at the base of my throat.

I'd been spat on for my father's actions. They were cheering for a title, and not the girl behind the hood.

I focused on the raised platform, covered in straw at the center of the arena, and the blackened block that awaited me. I walked the way my father would have, shoulders wide, hips straight, keeping silent as the lowborn moved out of my way. No one could see the tears scratching my cheeks. No one could hear my pulse racing.

No one except me.

I could face this. My father had. My grandmother had. My family had carried the secret title and responsibility for four generations, hiding our heavy duty behind our noble name and lands. I'd always been proud of it, of my grandmother's kills, which had stopped the Devani revolt, of my father's high standing with our old king. But I never thought twice about those who died.

And now all I could think about was a name I didn't know.

The drums stopped as I reached the block and lowered the axe to the straw. King Edvarg joined me at the block. Tall as a mountain and thin as a river on a map. He'd been king for a few days, yet he still wore the gray robes of the Holy Order of the Undergod—now edged in royal silver and king's bronze. A tight silver crown traced his brow, pressing down the sacred cowl of the high priesthood. He always seemed sickly to me, with his face lined in shadows. He raised his spindly fingers to the crowd circled about the platform. They silenced.

"It grieves me to meet on this dark night." His soft voice rumbled like a distant thunder. "My brother's treason has led to this, and here this sad business will end. Our god will be appeased, and his justice will rain on those *heathen* Savak who stole the best of us with their vile lies."

The crowd cheered. He spat on the dark cobblestones and I drew backward. To King Edvarg, heathen meant anyone who didn't worship the Undergod. To anyone else it was only an insult, but from King Edvarg it was a holy judgment of damnation.

"We will not betray our god," King Edvarg's voice echoed. "We will not give in to my brother's blasphemy and cowardice. When the Savak try to claim our lands, we will show them our swords are mightier than any traitorous contract. Our fight against the Savak begins tonight, with one death. A death I mourn already."

The torches flickered. I caught a whiff of burnt oil.

A crowd of men dressed in long black robes lined with raven feathers moved to the edge of the platform, holding back the crowd with their silent presence and sharp gaze. Historians. I couldn't look them in the eye. Even behind their carved silver masks, the Historians' vision was too sharp. My brother had told me it was best to stay away from their notice.

They were watching me now.

I slouched and tried to hide beneath the thick black robes. I was only doing this at the king's command. It was the king's kill, not mine. He didn't even know who the Executioner was. No one did. They should be focused on him.

A bell tolled, and the lanterns sputtered. I heard the footsteps first, the first hint of the life I would take. The crowd roared as the prisoner walked forward, chains linked around his wrists, his eyes and mouth tied with filthy coverings.

I closed my eyes and clenched my jaw. My hands would not settle.

Not Prince Ryo.

Any name but his. My brother would never forgive me for this.

The crowd circling the platform spread down the long roads. They only avoided the Executioner's wall. With the bewitched gloves, I could press the wall open and reach my father's tunnel. That would be my escape. If it came to that.

But there was no way out for Ryo.

I stared at Prince Ryo like I had the night of my first ball, like he was the only person in a crowded room. Except this time, Ryo marched toward his death in bare feet, dressed in a poor shirt, made dusty red from dirt, sweat, and blood. He'd hate that. He was always so meticulous with his clothing, so concerned with the way his people saw him. The crowd quieted, for this, even in rags, was the prince whose birth sparked a three-week festival, the prince we waved to when he was a small boy, sitting high on his father's shoulders as he grinned from the castle balcony. He'd grown handsome as he aged, with his strong jaw and intelligent eyes. It seemed like god spent more time designing him than others. I knew the details of his face, the scar above his eyebrow, the curve of his lips, the halo of black hair, which seemed a crown. We all did.

He was ours.

And he'd betrayed us.

I should have seen it coming.

No one hated him more than I did. That first ball I'd thought him handsome, and when Grigfen introduced us, he looked me up and down, his lips curved in an appraising dismissal as though he thought me plain. No one danced with me the whole evening. The other girls mocked my ribbons and the boys shoved me to the back of the ballroom. I cried myself to sleep that night, and every other time I'd stepped into his company, Ryo had made another joke at my expense, which would echo and repeat through meaner tongues.

Long before my father signed that contract, I was the lowest girl in court, and I knew exactly who had given me that role.

The king's guards dumped him at my feet, next to the blood-darkened block.

The crowd rumbled, none louder than a row of Everstriders lined among them. Their matching bleached leather coats hung to the top edge of their boots, belted tight at the waist with three buckles and strings of holy bells. They eyed the king's guards and the Devout with distrust. One Everstrider kept his eyes on Ryo, his hand touching the sword handle at his belt as if he would protect him. The rest formed a line at the back of the platform.

I pulled my thin knife from my boot and slipped the blade between the fabric and Ryo's cheek.

King Edvarg protested, "His mouth must be bound." He loomed closer.

But I would not be intimidated. "He has a right to a last word, sire," I answered, my voice deep as my father's.

"His words are lies. Blasphemy."

"And he has a right to it, Your Highness."

The king's glare burned, but he didn't silence me. The crowd was too close, and with the Everstriders watching so sharply, this moment was a scale too precariously balanced. King Edvarg couldn't push me, not if he risked tipping.

Prince Ryo licked his dry lips, but he didn't speak right away. I'd nicked his cheek with my knife, but with the blindfold on, he'd never see it. One of the king's guards shoved him onto his hands and knees, and pressed his throat onto the blackened stone. Ryo's jaw trembled, but he made no plea for forgiveness. No demand of innocence.

"My father has a plan," he said instead. The crowd silenced, hanging on every quiet word, as I was. "The council of five did not betray us. They've saved us."

I leaned in, wanting desperately to believe him.

The vein on King Edvarg's forehead throbbed. He gestured to the crowd and raised his voice. "So we should allow the queen of the Savak to reach into our hard-earned borders? Should we give away who we are because of some contract?"

Prince Ryo broke through the crowd's roar. "I didn't sign it. I'm only suggesting we trust our king—"

"I am the king now."

"Not my king. My father lives, and I do not relinquish my claim to the throne."

The Everstriders stepped closer to the platform.

Edvarg's hand rose, then he gestured at the king's guards. "Hold him down."

They pulled the prince's arms back so high, my own shoulders ached in sympathy. And for what? The rumors were rampant, but he hadn't signed the contract the way our fathers had. For all I knew, Ryo could have done nothing wrong except stay loyal to his own father.

The crowd roared now, some moving to stand behind the Everstriders, their eyes uncomfortable at this scene, some shouting about blasphemy and treason, whipping up to a frenzy, led by the Devout.

But I was the one holding the axe.

Father had struggled to bear the weight of it, but it was too much responsibility for me to carry. I should be reading my books, or drawing my bow at a Whirligig target, not killing someone.

But I gripped the axe with both hands and inched forward. I could do this. I had to. Only it wasn't just killing my brother's best friend. As the King's Executioner I was choosing which king to follow.

King Vinton left. My father had abandoned me at his royal command. As foul as he was, at least King Edvarg had stayed.

There was no choice here. I had to do it. Our people needed to be united under our new king if we were going to survive the onslaught of the Savak. And I'd tested the new king by allowing Ryo to speak. If I did not do this, I'd make a powerful enemy. If I didn't do this, there was no way I could stay here and find my brother.

The weight of the axe would do the work for me. All I'd have to do was lift the axe and let the blade fall. It wouldn't be murder. I was following orders. That was all.

But it was Prince Ryo. He deserved a slap across the mouth, not death.

My guilt and his ghost would haunt me forever.

The crowd roared out for blood, but I couldn't hear them over the sound of my pulse drumming in my ears. The prince muttered feverishly, "This is wrong. This is wrong. Please don't let me die."

Father wouldn't want me to do this. So many nights Father would stay awake speaking with Grigfen about the influence he could have on Ryo. The prince had the potential to be a great king and a great man, if we guided him. But Father had left me with nothing. Not a word of goodbye, not a coin for food. What he wanted me to do didn't matter when he'd left us to starve.

I lifted the axe high. The prince gasped for air, his frenzied pleas clear as starlight as the mob silenced. Strange the stars still shone, even on such a night as this.

King Edvarg was the only one not grieving. His slimy tongue slipped over his lips, curved in celebration so sharp it could only be lust. For all his pious words, he was glad to see his rival killed, even though it was his own nephew.

The idea of Edvarg as my king made my stomach roll. My heartbeat stilled. There was only one opinion I could trust now.

My own.

The weight of the axe made my arms quake, but I could do this. I arched my wrists and swung the axe.

Deep into King Edvarg's stomach. His blood sputtered out around the axe blade, dripping down the handle and staining his fine robes.

"You are not my king," I roared into the shocked silence. "And I'll have no hand in this execution."

Then the night caught fire.

4
DAGNEY

Torchlight blinded the stars, and the heavy gloves lightened as if I'd gained strength by that act of violence. Ryo's shallow panicked breathing was the only noise audible, until King Edvarg's body collapsed to the straw and the crowd erupted in screams. I stepped back, my hands held close to my chest. *The axe. I need the axe.*

The Devout priests rushed to the king's side, whispering incantations, their hands quickly becoming blood-covered as they tapped prayer dots down his nose. The axe was surrounded. Not worth it.

The lowborn scattered with voices ragged with coarse laughter and bitter terror. The Everstriders split ranks, half the guards rushing to the king while the rest turned their swords to me.

I may have broken out in hives.

An inner compass behind my eyes pointed like an arrow toward safety. I jerked the prince by the rope stringing his arms together, trying desperately to breathe through the thick black hood covering my face and mudding my vision. We had to get out of here.

I shoved through the line of Historians. The crowd scattered away from me like I was diseased. What was I thinking? I saved *Ryo. RYO.* I axed the Undergod's appointed king, and my father was missing, and I couldn't find my brother, and WHAT WAS I EVEN DOING?

Running toward the Executioner's wall. That's what I was doing.

I pushed through the crowd, pulling the bound and blindfolded prince behind me.

We were surrounded.

Breathe, Dagney. Breathe.

"King Edvarg is dead!" a priest cried out.

Ryo let out a breath. "Long live King Vinton!"

The crowd pushed forward. "That traitor."

"Blasphemy!"

Sharp hands ripped at us, pulling at Ryo's tattered clothes, as if trying to find something to sell. Everstriders fought to keep the crowd under control, pushing back, while the king's guards advanced on us.

"Go!" an Everstrider hollered. "We'll hold them back!"

I cut the ropes keeping Ryo bound. He ripped his blinder off and shoved a lowborn back.

"This way!" I grabbed the prince's arm and led him toward the tunnel.

I'd never fought anyone except my father or my brother, but I held tight to Ryo's arm and shoved the crowd out of our way. I was no weak lamb. I was thick and strong.

We ran like a hole in a stocking.

A king's guard blocked our path. He raised a crossbow at us.

"For King Edvarg," he shouted. The guard pulled the trigger and the shaft ripped through the air. I yanked Prince Ryo toward me as the arrow's sharp edge sliced my hood.

And lodged into Prince Ryo's shoulder.

He fumbled into my arms and grunted in pain. Royal blood stained through his shirt.

I swore.

The arrow breached any semblance of order in my mind. I fought a wave of panic and shoved Ryo toward the Executioner's wall. The guard lowered his crossbow and reloaded with a new shaft.

The crowd surged closer.

Forward. Move forward. The rough wall pressed solid against my arms, no handle on this side of the massive stone doors, the witch-made gloves the only key. I shoved my palm against the door, and it slid backward.

Ryo fell inside the dark tunnel, and I yanked the glove from the wall, and the bricks slammed back into place behind us.

Muffled shouts echoed inside the tunnel. The crowd and the guards struck the other side of the Executioner's wall, cheering for the end of the royal line, vowing death when they caught us.

But no one could enter without the golden gloves.

I slipped the black mask off my face and gasped like I'd surfaced for air. I pried off the heavy gloves and they clattered against the ground.

Holy night, holy excrement, holy lamb's stomach ground to stew.

I knelt by the prince's side. The ground was damp with what I assumed was his blood. Ryo cursed and moaned in the dark. I leaned over his body, my arms outstretched toward the wall where I'd left the lantern. My fingers scraped the wall and the ground, until finally they brushed the cold glass.

I struck the sparker and lit the wick.

Blood had turned my father's tunnel red.

I couldn't force myself to check the wound on Ryo's shoulder. I should. I should make a list, make a plan, but instead the searing island of light burned my eyes and I focused on the storage in my father's tunnel—broken cupboards and wardrobes, some with doors half-hung or missing shelves. A rug we no longer used was rolled across glazed chests full of my mother's things. A dusty bed frame with rotting hay sticking through the padding rested under a tattered map nailed into the carved dirt wall.

We'd be safe here. There were tunnels like this one all under this city, either made to commune with the Undergod or to escape the notice of his Devout.

Could we use these tunnels?

Edvarg was dead, I knew it, but without a king the factions would turn on one another. Devani magic against the Devout. The Savak would find us easy pickings divided as we were.

The chaos in the street above sent a rainfall of dirt on us. Ryo moaned.

I turned away. At the end of the long tunnel, a rickety door led out into the streets. No one but my family had that key. No one knew that cobbled door led to the Executioner's wall.

I twisted my mother's ring around my smallest finger. I had to find Grig.

But I couldn't leave Ryo to die.

A splatter of blood lined Ryo's profile in the flickering lantern light. He sprawled against the wall, his face pressed against the stones. Tears painted missing lines on his blood-covered cheeks. The arrow sprouted from his shoulder.

His glossy eyes widened as I leaned over him. "Do your worst," he said, his voice quiet. "I won't tell you anything."

I pulled back the hood that had shadowed my face. "Try not to speak." I removed the hood and pressed the fabric over the wound to stop the bleeding.

His Adam's apple bobbed. "You're a girl?"

I rolled my eyes. I'd literally just saved his life, and now he was complaining that I did it as a female. "Why not? Anyone could be anything in this city. Hold this tight against your shoulder." I stood. I raked through a cupboard. "Father has to have something for—"

I opened a drawer hiding a slew of knives, took one, and moved on.

The next drawer held maps, and the one after that clothing. I opened a cabinet door. Bandages. *Yes.* Maybe I could bind his mouth closed.

There wasn't time for my anger. I carried the bandages back and moved the soaked fabric to inspect his shoulder. The blood seeped around the shaft. When I took out the arrow, more blood would burst through his wound. I needed to move quickly.

He held his neck tight. "So the Tomlinson family is a line of Executioners. I'm surprised Grig didn't let that secret slip." He drew a deep breath. "I always thought your father had too much influence for a farmer."

I pressed his wound with my thumb and he winced. It wasn't the insult to my father's position that chafed my nerves, it was the word *had*. I knew my father would never leave me unless he was trying to protect me from something.

But who was going to protect him?

"I'm going to have to remove the arrow," I said quickly. "I don't know if you'll be able to use your shoulder or your arm ever again."

I didn't know what I was doing. I fell against my heels, the moment he was struck echoing in my mind. "Perhaps I should go get help . . ."

Grigfen would be the best at this. He was more healer than executioner. I'd only started Father's lessons. "I don't know what I'm doing." *Do not cry, Dagney.* He already thought me weak.

I stood and rummaged through my father's things. I opened a cabinet and found my father's alcohol.

His voice softened as I knelt by him. "It's all right, Lady Tomlinson. I've faced worse."

Ryo's open expression hid no lies. But how could he have faced worse than this?

His bloody hand was warm on my arm.

"Sit up for me." I leaned in and inspected the injury again. The filthy shirt was in the way, so I ripped the tattered fabric, careful not to move his shoulder as I removed deteriorating cloth.

The arrow was lodged just below the shoulder joint. I set my jaw. "The arrow has torn through the muscle, but it may have missed your ribs. If we're lucky. Here, hold still."

I poured the liquor over his shoulder. He flinched and wrenched the bottle from my grasp, throwing back a drink.

"Who taught you healing, a torturer?" He shook his head, his hair falling over his clenched eyes. He folded a rag and placed it between his teeth.

"Yes," I growled.

His eyes widened.

I bit my lip and stared at the shaft of the arrow protruding from his back. I could handle this. I could. I axed a king and fought a crowd. This was almost simple in comparison. I reached and snapped the head of the arrow off in one quick motion. He tensed and his jaw trembled in pain.

I clenched my teeth. "That was the easy part."

Ryo swallowed hard.

I twisted my palm around the shaft. "Keep the arrow straight. Quick as lightning," I muttered to myself. *You can do this.* I ripped the shaft out of his flesh.

He let out a gasping groan. I applied pressure to his shoulder and wrapped the bandage around tight to his skin. Father had me take care of Grigfen when he broke his arm in training. I'd have to treat this wound the same way.

Only there wasn't as much blood when I'd helped my brother. I needed more fabric to hold the bandage in place. Blood was already seeping through.

"Press this against your shoulder." I placed his hand over the bandage. His grip seemed weak, like he could barely hold his hand up.

I touched his forehead with the back of my fingers, and his skin burned. He had a fever. Could be an infection. It was too soon for it to have come from the arrow, so the infection must have come with him from King Edvarg's dungeons.

One problem at a time. I needed more bandages. I could do that. I would have to take the bedding off the bed and pull strips of the sheets into thin slits. No saying how clean it was, but there weren't many options.

"Can you stand?" I asked.

"I don't know if that's a good idea. My head is swimming."

"Oh." I rubbed my forehead. "Lean on me. Let's get you to the bed."

He raised his eyebrows twice before he started giggling.

Was he drunk? "Imbecile," I muttered under my breath.

His good arm wrapped around my shoulder, clutching tight. His sharp chin leaned into my neck, and I tried to carry as much of his weight as I could. He radiated heat and let out a string of curses at each step, his muscles tight like they were made of iron.

When we reached the bed, he more fell than sat. He kept his grip on my shoulder to hold himself steady.

I tore the sheet into makeshift bandages, wrapped them around his shoulder, and tied them tight. "There we go."

He leaned forward, his breath hot against my damp skin. I'd never had any man this close to me before. I bit my lip but didn't move.

His pulse was too slow. He fell forward against my shoulder, his body heavy against me.

"Ryo," I breathed, my voice affected by his proximity. "I've done everything I can; now it's up to you. Don't die."

I pushed him backward, and he collapsed back onto the bed, his eyes dim and unblinking.

I wrung my fingers. "It would be just like you to die, when I've gone through all the trouble of not killing you."

His dry lips opened. Water. He needed water.

He reached in my direction as I moved toward the pump.

"Thank you," he said. "For not killing me."

I cocked a shoulder. "It's still an option."

I put the jug to his lips. The slow stream wasn't enough, judging from the eagerness of his swallows, so I tipped the rest of the jug into his mouth and he drank the whole of it.

Then he slowed his swallows so I lowered the jug. His eyes drifted closed, his eyelashes fluttered, but he'd lost too much blood to stay awake. Which was fine. His body needed the rest. My stomach twisted into tangles.

I refilled the jug with the iron pump, returned to his bedside, and left it where he could reach it when he woke. I balled my father's robes in my hands. He'd wake. He had to.

His breathing was slow and ragged. I watched the rise and fall of his chest and studied the filth from his neck and his hair. Here was the most recognizable face in the kingdom, wanted for treason.

The most handsome too. Not that that mattered.

No one had known where he'd been. Rumors speculated he'd left with the council, or even married the Savak queen. From the crusted dirt and blood along his hairline, it was clear neither of those rumors were true.

"What happened to you?" I asked. "How were you captured?"

He didn't answer. His eyes didn't even flutter. He was completely asleep.

Blood covered the floor. Undergod knows it covered me as well. The Executioner robes were soaked through. How much could he lose and still live?

In the flickering light, Prince Ryo lay too still, too silent, his skin almost gray. I tiptoed out of the light and pulled the soaked robes from my shoulders. They slid to the ground. I'd stand out on the street covered in blood. If I was going to find my brother, I had to do it as a lady.

And that meant I should probably change my clothes.

I glanced his way, but Ryo still slept.

Part of me had not healed from the time last Summernight picnic when the changing tent I was in *accidentally* attached itself to a rogue horse's leash, and *accidentally* left me standing in mid-change. When my fury brought me to my brother's side, his best friend, Ryo, asked, "What's wrong, pink cheeks?" That name followed me for a whole season, and I think if he woke and saw me changing I would die or I would kill him.

Ryo's head turned away.

It didn't matter. I couldn't stay in these clothes. My bloomers and corset were clean, but blood and dirt stained my arms and I'd left bloody footprints to and from the basin. I pumped water and scrubbed my arms until my skin ripped raw. Blistered.

The pump slowed to a dripping.

My hands were clean and Ryo's wound was tended, so I could move to the next item on my to-do list.

Panic.

OH, MY LOST SAINTS, *what had I done?*

I axed the king. I slammed an axe into the king's stomach. I murdered a king. No matter how many times I said it, it still didn't make sense. I was not the kind of girl who committed treason. I had a life. I read, I baked, and I was saving money to buy a dog. And yes, I mostly stayed in my room, but I liked my life behind walls I'd decorated with my own coins.

And now it was over. If the wrong faction won control of the city,

I'd be executed for this. I'd betrayed my family's title and my kingdom for a boy I loathed.

But I couldn't stop the feeling my father would have wanted me to save Ryo. My father must have had a good reason for signing. No matter what rumors whispered, I had to believe my father would never betray me.

I placed my head in my hands. There. I'd panicked. Now, perhaps, I could move on.

I gathered my thoughts with my breaths and pulled my market dress from the chair where I'd left it and covered myself with the cool silk. I slid my arm into one sleeve, and the other, tying the ribbons closed. The dress was covered in pockets, the ones over my thighs heavy with coins and the weight of a jar of seer water.

I'd almost forgotten my earlier trade. If anyone needed answers, it was me.

I licked my lips then cocked my head.

The tunnel was too quiet. It took me a moment to recognize the missing sound.

Ryo wasn't breathing.

I knocked over the jug as I rushed to his side. Ryo's skin had gone cold, his eyes glassy. I pressed my fingers to his neck and his blood was still. No pulse. No life.

I punched his arm. "No!"

I axed the king for him and he *still* died?

That jerk.

I had an itemized list of rude things Ryo had done, but this. This was uncultured.

I fell back on my heels and let out a breath. A tug of grief and loss tightened my throat, but my eyes refused to water.

No. No.

I was still panicking; I did not have time to grieve.

It was just a goodbye. I'd said those before. I didn't even like him, so what did it matter?

But it mattered. I didn't want to face this on my own. I wanted to face this with him.

I reattached my belt and dagger before I stepped into my lace slippers. Everything about me had gone cold, and a part of me wanted to sit on the ground and give up. Let Edvarg come back from the dead and rule our kingdom. Let the Savak wage their war.

The King's Executioner might be able to do something, but I was only one girl.

I stood. Nothing had changed. I still needed to find my brother. I pulled a dusty leather bag from the top of a cupboard and opened a drawer. I needed supplies.

"Wait," Ryo called.

I slammed backward into the cupboard.

The lantern light warmed the curve of his cheek. He sat up in the bed. "Are you leaving?"

I screamed. I pointed at him and screamed again.

Ryo chuckled.

"What was that?" I yelled when I found my voice.

He blinked. The man blinked. He blinked and he looked at me like I was the crazy one when he was dead.

"You were dead. You died." He did die, right? I wasn't losing all sense?

Ryo closed his eyes and pulled his legs over the side.

I brought the lantern closer. "I saw it." He was dead. I'd touched his cold skin, his chest not breathing, and his lack of pulse. I knew it. I reached for his throat to check his heartbeat.

Ryo raised his chin and met my eyes.

I curled my fists and stepped away. "What are you? How is this even possible?"

He stood, the color returning to his face. He pulled the wrappings off his shoulder, wiping away the fresh blood. His skin wasn't raised. There wasn't even a scar on his cheek from when I'd nicked him. He smiled, but his eyes were a storm of emotion.

"Would you believe me if I said I didn't know?"

"No!"

"Really? Girls usually believe whatever I say." He glanced down at his chest. "Perhaps it's all the blood. This is not my best look."

As he crossed to the pump, I remembered my legs could move, so I moved. Away. From whatever that was that was scrubbing his blood off his skin as if he'd never been injured.

I shook out my hands. "Good luck to you, Prince Ryo. Undergod's demon. Whatever you are. This is where our paths end. I need to find my brother."

"Stop," he commanded. I turned, and he offered me a forced smile. "I'm afraid my blood has dirtied your cheek."

I scratched my nails down my cheek, and then I remembered I didn't care. I didn't care if Ryo never answered my questions. I didn't care if he was the Undergod reborn. I tugged the bag up my shoulder and loaded whatever I could find that might be of use to find my brother, or to lie low until my father returned, or to stage a rebellion against the factions I'd made my enemies. Knives I'd need. Spyglass? Possibly. Bandages and oats. I shoved them in my bag.

Ryo stepped closer and I abandoned the cupboards, my hands flailing for the walls.

"Stop this ridiculous reaction. I need to find your brother too. I need him. You too."

I shook my head and kept packing. "I don't know where he is."

I didn't even know where to look. I'd already searched everywhere for my brother, and all I'd found was a pile of unpaid debt from the tables.

I glanced at my hands. "I haven't seen him in twelve days."

"He couldn't go home."

"What do you mean he couldn't go home?" I drew my dagger. Prince Ryo had seen my brother last. And if Ryo ended up in the dungeon, then where would my foolish brother have ended up? I fought the image in my head of my sweet dumb brother's body bobbing under the docks. If Ryo's foolishness had hurt my brother, I would hate him until I died, and then I'd come back and haunt him until his healing finally stopped. I held the knife to his throat. "Home from where? Where was the last place you saw him?"

He yawned, big and wide as a cat. "You do know how pointless threatening me is, right?"

"This knife has a point."

He pushed the dagger away, and he ducked his head under the pump. "I'll tell you everything, once I know I have your loyalty." He washed the blood from his hair, and then flipped his head back, splashing my family's things like they meant nothing.

I sheathed my dagger in my belt. "I've no need for your assistance. I'll find him on my own."

"Don't leave; I know his haunts better than you do."

I let out a laugh. "Haunts. Well-chosen word, you spawn from hells."

"That line of insult is both blasphemous and tedious. I heal. I don't know why. It is a new development, but I'm still human. I'll lead you to him when I'm good and ready."

I clenched my fist. "You're the Devout's biggest enemy. It's best to stay here where you are hidden. I'll save my brother and we can regroup."

He scoffed. "I'm not going to be left here like some damsel in a tower."

That's it. I threw a clay pot at his face. He dodged and the thing shattered. But not loudly enough. "If he truly was your best friend, then perhaps you should have thought of him before you betrayed us all."

He winced. "But you . . . You saved me. I thought—"

"You thought you'd flirt your way into my heart, and you'd walk all over me like you do all the others?"

"Well . . . Yes."

His eyes widened as I stepped forward. "I didn't save you because I had some twitterpated foolish feelings for you, you smug fool. I saved you because Edvarg needed to be stopped. I did it for your father, who is a good man and a great king." I pointed my finger into his chest. "You are not what you were supposed to be. Not by miles."

I let out a breath. That was good to get off my chest.

The glass bauble around Ryo's neck glistened in the light. I brought it closer. It was Savak. I was sure of it; the thing was covered in tiny white birds. Perhaps the Savak had found a way to heal him. I wrinkled my nose in disgust and turned away.

"I will not trade one dark dungeon for another," he said. "I will not be left alone to die again. And I have a task set by my father, the rightful king. I will face what's coming on my feet."

"It's not your choice, Ryo."

His eyes flashed. "Your Highness."

"What?"

"You should call me Your Highness."

"I should have dropped the axe on your skinny neck." I curtsied deeply. "Your Highness." I met his glare with one of my own. "Now tell me where my brother is."

"I won't. But I will lead you there."

He was impossible. I forced out a puff of air. "*Fine.* Get dressed."

Father's old clothing should fit him. I crossed to the cupboards and threw a white cotton shirt at him.

"Why?" He plastered on a grin. "Do you find me distracting, Lady Tomlinson?" He gestured to his naked chest, now clean and very distracting.

My cheeks flushed. "Let's keep one thing clear. There will be no flirting. I am not interested in a spawn from hells, nor a prince who is more card shark and womanizer than royalty. I wouldn't dance with you if you asked, wouldn't help you if you were on fire, and I wouldn't flirt with you if you turned into a whipped pie."

He pulled the shirt over his head. "Do you often flirt with whipped pies?"

"More often than I'd flirt with you."

His lips twitched into the shadow of a grin, which I did not find amusing. He sat on the edge of the bed he died in and tugged his boots back on. "We'll need supplies first. Stay close to me on the way. I know how to navigate these streets, and if we happen upon an Everstrider, let me do the talking. We're going to need them in order to survive what's coming."

I opened a trunk. It was mostly empty except for two identical training swords. I grabbed the plain wooden hilt and offered the other sword to Ryo. "Why? What's coming?"

He tested out the sword by slicing the air twice, and then he grinned. "Don't worry your pretty head about it. You'll be safe at my side. I will protect you."

I narrowed my eyes and stood my ground.

He didn't know me at all if he thought I'd be led by someone who wouldn't treat me as a partner. I was done being left in the dark. I could find my own answers without him.

I pulled the seer water from my pocket and glared at Ryo as I drank every drop. The spring water tasted crisp, like sunshine, but the aftertaste was sour, almost metallic.

Ryo's jaw dropped. Take that, you pretty boy.

The world shifted green.

Oh no, what did I just do?

5
DAGNEY

I was dreaming. I knew it.

Symbols and letters swam past like a school of fish, before the images multiplied into a swarm with sharp teeth that nipped at me as they rushed past. My nerves ached and my toes trembled.

The flow silenced and the world brightened.

The ground beneath me disappeared and I soared over a castle. My stomach sunk at the heights. A Whirligig zoomed past me, all gears and ghostlight and flapping wings. Then an image of a gigantic girl filled the whole sky. She was about my age, lounging in a throne, holding a bloody sword thicker than her waist. The Savak queen, I guessed.

A man's voice filled the sky, "Welcome, adventurers, to the land of traitor kings and vicious queens!" The image shifted to a battle on the ground between ghosts and machines, and then shifted again to a Whirligig's view of an island filled with jagged mountains. "Who will win the throne in this epic RPG by the makers of *Ashcraft*?"

There was a flash, like static from a Whirligig. The briefest of glimpses into a dim world filled with people wearing the strangest clothes.

A man walked past dressed in plain blue linen, a shirt with a V at the neck, and simple cotton trousers. A silver necklace lounged like a snake around his neck. He removed it quickly, placed two ends in his ears, and a third he held to the chest of a woman in a bed. He placed the end on her chest and turned his ear to one side like he was listening, perhaps to her heartbeat.

My bright vision came back and the voice with it: ". . . is great, but so is your victory. You've selected the Trader class. You will aid your party by—"

Sparks and static cut through the bright picture.

I was in the dim world again. Strange machines lined the walls, each with lit mirrors, or windows open to strange worlds. A disembodied voice shook the walls.

"Dr. Garcia to the players' hall. Dr. Garcia to the players' hall."

I retreated three steps back. Something cold and metal pressed against my skirts.

I turned. It was the curve of a bent bed. A young woman lay beneath blankets, silver jewels attached to the end of her eyebrows, a silver band twisting across her forehead like a wire crown. She appeared to be sleeping, but I stared at her like she was a monster reflected.

I knew my own face.

My memory was reversed, though, the freckle above my eyebrow on the other side. This odd world was a lie, or a dream, but I knew the scar on my eyebrow, and the faint bruising on my temple.

I'd lived through that bruise, and I could remember it now, flashing white when Seth had shoved me into a locker.

No.

I covered my face with my palms and this strange world silenced under a flood of symbols.

Ones and zeroes, I recognized now.

That didn't mean anything.

"I know you were expecting a cut scene right here," a woman spoke from a chair near the metal bed, "but I needed to send you a warning. Don't get hurt."

I held on to my knees. I knew that face. Nao Takagi. She had smiled at me as I sat in a chair and they'd strapped the wire crown edged with sparks to the sides of my temples. I'd watched her turn away and flip a switch.

Her face was the last memory of a different dream.

And now her expression was tormented.

I palmed my skirts.

It was a trick of the Savak, that's all. A lie called a vision, meant only to confuse me.

"Don't get hurt," she repeated. "It wasn't supposed to be very painful. But there's a glitch in the safeties on the pain receptors."

"What do you mean 'a glitch'?" I asked "What's going—"

"It's okay. You're okay." Her voice cut me off. She wasn't listening, or maybe she couldn't hear me. "But you need to know this is the real world. These are your real bodies." She gestured to the beds next to mine, where other teens about my age lay strapped to medical devices. "The world you know isn't real. You're inside a game."

Nonsense.

It was nonsense.

What sort of game? I swallowed and reached forward. My fingers broke through the numbers that formed her face, but didn't interrupt her train of thought. Like her words, they didn't stick; they were only mist.

"We coded pulses to the medulla to make your experience inside the game truly immersive. We put safeties on the pulses, of course, so they would never go anywhere near high enough to really hurt any of you. But they would let you know when you've been struck, allow you to feel the sunlight, speed up your heart during action scenes."

My stomach knotted. I shook my head, but the mist was getting into me now, blurring my thoughts.

"The safeties regulating those pulses were part of the initial programming, buried deep inside the code. But when we launched the game we found a stowaway program. Someone added something to the neural net and it's corrupted the source code. The safeties on the pain receptors were the first to go."

I didn't understand what she was saying, but my pulse sped up like my heart understood before the rest of me caught on. My feet itched to run away, but how could I run from a vision?

My hands balled up. I didn't understand any of these words. They didn't mean anything to me. They couldn't.

Wake up.

The voice didn't stop for me; she spoke on like a rock falling downhill, growing speed until a crash.

"And we can't pull you out. Now instead of sending an electrical pulse into your brains, your brains are sending information and neurons back through the neural network. It's locked us out, and now we can't break you free."

I crumpled to the ground.

Her voice cracked. "What we know is that your brains and my game are linked. And those initial electrochemical pulses tightened the walls of the system. You're stuck there. Your brains are convinced it's real so you've forgotten you're in a video game."

My heartbeat thrashed behind my ears.

Video game.

Those words didn't exist, but I still knew them. How could I know them?

Those two words rocked through my whole world like a hurricane, every inch of my brain stimulated, a rush of memories blowing back into the empty spaces, and only wreckage was left behind.

I'd wanted Lady Tomlinson to be real—her life, her family, the whole world. I'd wanted it to be mine.

But it wasn't.

No. It couldn't be true. If it was true . . . I didn't want to let this go. This world was kinder, this world made more sense. Wake up. Wake up. I covered my eyes with my hands but I could still hear the voice echoing with static and scratching feedback.

"We never meant for this to happen. We had safeties in place. Dagney, tell Ryo I would never have put him in this position if I'd known it was dangerous."

I dropped my hands. *Ryo?*

"I'd never put any of you in danger."

Ryo was in on it. His face was slightly different, but I could remember him now. From before.

I froze. There was a before.

Was it possible? I opened my eyes, and I remembered more than sitting in the game pod, more than the impact into a locker. Every moment of my life seeped in, trickling in flashes of memories. The taste of ice cream. The whispers of my classmates before PE as I got dressed. My third grade teacher's name. Cruel names and fists. I remembered my life until I remembered how much I wanted to forget.

The game wasn't supposed to be dangerous. It was supposed to be something else. A vacation from my real life.

The voice, this vision, was real.

That meant my memories of my life as Lady Dagney Tomlinson were planted in my brain for a video game.

"We're doing everything we can to help you from our side, but you're going to have to break yourself out. The only way out is to win the game. Place an heir on the throne, dressed in the armor, and then the neural net should release the door. Please. I need you to help my son. Get as many players as you can and work together to crown him. I programmed his path through the world first, so as the source code damages further, his path should be the last to corrupt.

"I hope." She pressed her fist into her stomach. "If you can't get out before the source code breaks down more . . . the neurologist says you all could die. I've spent the last seven years envisioning every detail of this project, and now it's swallowed my son, and it's hurting him, and I have no idea how to get him out."

She clutched her chest, her face flickering in the light. "I'm sorry. If this is the last message I can get into the game, please know I'm so sorry. And we're doing everything we can to get you out."

The image shut off, leaving only darkness and my memories.

The light flashed, then the too-loud man's voice rang out over an image of a throne and my own face in a crown, light brightening. "And you, too, can win the crown!"

The light flickered again, and my world shuddered back into being. Ryo held me close to his chest, his dark eyes searching mine. His eyebrows shot up and he let out a relieved breath that sent my hair spinning back.

Then the side of his lips turned up. "Oof, you're heavier than you look."

Jerk. I shoved him with all my might and it felt great. I swung my fist into his stomach then fled back until I fell, my knees slamming against the ground where I'd dropped my sword.

I could kick him, stab him, kill him, but I couldn't fight back against the truth.

The cold ground gave no comfort as I pulled my legs into my chest and let out a groan.

It shouldn't hurt. Not if it's not real.

Why do the things that aren't real hurt the most to lose?

I caught my breath like it was a living thing and tucked it back into the dark tunnel of my heart. But I couldn't stand. I could pretend to be Lady Tomlinson for the rest of my life, but I couldn't put weight on my feet, and leave the safety of the floor.

Ryo knelt by my side, a circle of candlelight lighting his cheek. He hesitated then touched my arm.

I shouldn't hate him as much as I did. But if Lady Tomlinson was still the girl who'd been bullied, then he must still be the jerk who'd joked at other people's expense. I didn't care that he was a player too.

I turned away. Last thing I needed right now was one of Ryo's insults, or for him to try to sneak beneath my defenses.

He didn't say anything about the dust on my sleeves, or the blood staining the hem of my dress. He listened to the sound of my lungs exhaling, his hand hesitant as he cupped the back of my neck, his fingers twisting through my hair.

"Whatever it is," he said, "you won't face it alone."

In the dim light, I couldn't tell if that was a line. It didn't seem like one, not from his steady gaze.

It seemed real.

I pushed myself up to sitting and winced at my raw knees. Ms. Takagi wasn't lying. I needed to be more careful. This game hurt.

He leaned closer and flicked my skirt up to reveal my gashed knee.

I protested.

"Hush now, Lady Tomlinson. We need to check for infection. Can't have you slowing us down, now, can we? Besides, you already ripped my shirt off; it's only fair I return the favor."

I scowled and his lips lifted in a smile that didn't touch his eyes.

His fingers whispered over my calf as he checked out my injury. They weren't my real legs; my real legs would have had a soft bristle of hair and a pair of moles on my knee. The shadow of his touch sunk heavy in my stomach and sparked along my nerve endings.

I knew better than to let him affect me.

This wasn't him. I'd met Ryo twice before this game started. Ms.

Takagi's spoiled son got to play as the main character, even though he never placed in the competition. He was so dismissive of us players, as though *we* were the ones who didn't deserve to be here. His face was altered now—only hints of the real him left over. His deep brown eyes were the same, but now his eyebrows were thicker, his brow ridge pressed out like a mountain range. His jawline cut sharp, a false dip at the center of his chin. He looked like a photoshopped version of the Ryo I'd seen. There were similarities, sure, they were both tall, and strong, their arms like rolling hills of defined muscles, but the real Ryo had a delicate nose and pissed-off eyes. The real Ryo was quietly handsome. The real Ryo made me look twice, but I was not interested in this man who wore a different face like it was a Snapchat filter.

His face was a lie, and I'd had my share.

"I'm fine." I tucked my legs away from his reach and pressed my dress down.

I couldn't tell you how many times I'd said that lie.

Before the game, I'd said it after I was locked in a dark janitor's closet. I'd said I was fine after I found dog poop at the bottom of my bag. Every day for five years, I'd lied and said I was fine, and that those names they called me didn't bother me. I'd said I was fine after a jerk named Seth made me his pet victim, and every teacher I'd told let him get away with it.

He tortured me, and everyone looked the other way. He was smiles, good grades, and trophies for the case by the office, and I was the girl who yelled about the patriarchy and argued with my teachers about incorrect history in the textbooks. I was the girl who wore the wrong clothes and showed cleavage in a tee shirt. Maybe I distracted the class with my body, so wasn't it my fault when boys picked on me?

But I was fine. I was a fat girl who liked herself. I was a girl who took up space, and would not shrink to make others more comfortable.

I was the girl who took first place in an eSports competition and won a chance to be among the first to play an incredibly immersive game by my favorite developer. I was the one who walked alone out an empty hallway while a school full of people cheered on our third-ranked 2A football team after another preseason loss. I closed that door, and I didn't think once about those people who would never like me.

That was fine. They couldn't hurt me.

I was fine.

Outside the doors of my high school was an entire world full of people who wanted this chance I'd won. I could play in a shared world, learn magic or how to be a warrior, or play the game of politics and strategy as we tried to put the true heir on the golden throne. When we chose our characters, I chose the body that looked the most like mine.

Because I was fine with who I was, and if I said it enough, maybe that lie would become the truth.

A faint purple diamond floated above Ryo's head. I squinted and the diamond light brightened.

"Would you share your thoughts aloud?" Ryo asked. "I'm having a devil of a time reading your expressions."

I reached my hand into the diamond of misty purple light above his head. He leaned away and the diamond moved with him. It wasn't a diamond, it was a player indicator.

I stood.

"What?" His eyebrows dipped and he leaned away. I took three steps back and squinted at him. Above the diamond of light were small light squiggles, like the spaces between the shadows of leaves. Only . . . No, they were numbers, not squiggles. *1,240. Lv.4.* One heart shape and a long rectangular bar edged with numbers. *97%.*

A stats bar! He was at 97 percent health.

That was why he came back to life. He must have had extra lives.

But there was no indication that he had any more. Or that I had any extra, for that matter. Most RPGs only give you one life, and death means a restart.

A chill ran up my neck. If the pain receptors were damaged, what happened at game over?

I looked above me, and there was a diamond over my head.

I grunted. "Pink. 'Cause I'm a girl, right? Might as well tie me up with bows and call me Ms. Pac-Man."

Ryo pointed at my dress, which happened to be tied with several small bows.

"So I like ribbons!"

He chuckled. "I happen to think pink is a fine color."

I grumbled under my breath and looked up. Could I adjust my view so I could see behind me? As I stared at the diamond hovering over my head, I made out stats at the corner of my vision. My health was at 89 percent and my points were more than double Ryo's. I was listed as a Trader class, with high levels of Intelligence and Constitution. The word *abilities* appeared, and as I stared, the image shifted to a short list.

Pathfinding

Trading

Would you like a tutorial?

Why yes I would.

"Are you having a fit?" Ryo asked. "I've never seen anyone make that particular expression before. Are you about to make sick?"

Ryo's confusion, hilarious though it was, would have to wait.

"No. Shut up for a second." *Pathfinding*, I thought. A circle appeared directly in front of me, with dots in different places. Player locators, I bet. A compass appeared above the circle, and an arrow spun.

I punched the air and grinned.

"Was that a smile? I did not think it possible." Ryo's eyes warmed, like my reaction had given him a glimpse of hope, and he hungered for more.

Speaking of which, we needed to get more food. "I smile, on occasion."

"Fascinating. Are you ready for my questions, or will you punch me again?"

"Yes."

"To which? Punching or questions."

The side of my mouth tugged up. "Both are always options."

I searched the tunnel again, this time not for supplies, but for things to trade. My father had a few hibisi petals on a top shelf. I tucked them into my top pockets. I needed to trade for as many health potions as possible.

Only Sir Tomlinson wasn't my father. So why'd he feel so real? My real family seemed so far away, but I could remember every kind word, each time Sir Tomlinson held my wrist and trained me to throw a punch or a knife. And Grigfen was my brother, though we weren't related. He was my responsibility.

I knew one thing—I didn't want to die like Ryo had. Even if I had extra lives too, I didn't want to risk it. Was I the only one who got this message from his mother? I stared at Ryo. How much of this should I tell him?

"Is that seer water around your neck?" I asked.

He swallowed and tucked his necklace below my father's shirt. "It is. And I'm not drinking it."

"Why? It'd be so much easier if you'd drink now, while we're safe."

"I made a promise to my father. That promise might be the only reason I'm alive."

"The only reason you're alive is because you're in a video game and you had extra lives."

He squinted at me, that hope I'd handed him gone completely from his expression. "What?"

"Just drink your seer water. Everything will make sense once you get your game vision."

He turned away. "I'm sure you believe so. But I didn't drink despite being tortured, so I will not drink despite your nonsense. I keep my promises. It's all I have of my father now."

That stubborn idiot. "Fine." If he wouldn't listen to me, then I would let him fumble without answers. Let him be confused. I didn't need his help.

We needed to add to our team if we were going to win. I needed to find my brother. My almost brother. Grigfen314 had to be okay. He was one of the only other players I knew before the game. Decent guy. Great sense of humor.

Someone needed to tell him not to die.

Yellow letters scrolled across my vision. *Recruit Sir Grigfen to Your Party*.

The compass behind my eyes spun, and this time the arrow pointed up and north.

Awesome. "Come along, Your Highness." I pulled the strap of my bag over my head and then picked up my sword. "It's time to play."

6

MCKENNA, QUEEN OF THE SAVAK

ONE WEEK EARLIER

My queen," a cleric said, "are you all right?"

I clasped the bridge of my nose between my fingers. A migraine sparked behind my eyes, brief but sharp, as the vision left me.

The pain left in an instant, and only a distant numbness remained.

Clerics of the Seer Spring lined either side of me, their red cloaks backed to the sparkling mosaic walls, their worried faces in profile as I preferred. Servants fanned me with massive white feathers as I placed the seer water on a tray next to a zomok steak. My first glass of seer water, though they didn't know it.

But they weren't real people, so they didn't know much of anything.

Welcome, adventurers, to the land of traitor kings and vicious queens!

The voice from the video still echoed in my mind, but I didn't break character as I processed. I sat taller in my throne, mindful of the cameras. Any camera angle could be used in the promotional materials.

So let's give them something to watch.

I lunged for the cleric who had remarked on my moment of weakness, grabbed the chain around his neck, and yanked down until his fear-widened eyes were level with mine. One thing I knew about this character, the queen of the Savak could not appear weak in front of the clerics. "Are you questioning my mental fitness, cleric?"

He shook his head rapidly, but I spied other clerics sharing a look. The Savak queen could not show mercy. My fingers, clad in filigreed bronze rings molded to claw shapes, would teach them a lesson. I traced his jaw with the ring on my index finger. If I killed him, it would look cinematic, but if you take the stakes to a ten, you have to keep them at a ten, and I prefer a slower build.

A messenger entered with small fanfare. "My queen, your armies are ready for your inspection. They come bearing the spoils of war."

I shoved the cleric off my dais and sucked in my stomach.

"Good," I said. I crossed toward a large arched window, each step purposeful, my shoulders wide, hips twisting, borrowing from the walk I used when I played the Witch in the Walnut Creek's community theater's production of *Into the Woods*.

Confidence. You are a queen. Think of Bernadette Peters. You can do this.

Improv had never been my strong suit. I performed best with solid choreography, blocking, and the phenomenal lyricism of one Stephen Sondheim. But I missed the fall musical to do this, not to mention serious PSAT studying time, so I was going to crush this role like I'd crushed every audition I'd gone to since I was eleven years old.

This was my big break.

I pressed my hand against the pebbled glass window. My clawed rings scratched the glass. Below me, hundreds of Wingships landed on the battlefield. One Wingship to a soldier. Shining armor reflecting daggers of sunlight, though the uniforms seemed battered, covered in blood. Some were injured, while others tied trophies in ribbons, the spoils of the raid against the Biallo wrapped across their necks.

Across the sea, a column of fog shot up from the mainland. Two more brilliant columns appeared next to the first pale green one, a bold purple and a musky pink. As I looked, names and stats appeared like dots in my vision, too far away to read.

We were told we'd receive game vision to guide our tasks. This must be it.

"Did King Vinton sign the cleric's treaty? Or will the Kingdom de Mark be the next stop on our world tour?" I asked the messenger.

"He did sign; however, his brother, Edvarg, has made himself king and is rustling up a small resistance. We await your orders, my queen."

I didn't move. A map appeared in the corner of my vision. Names and dots showing their locations so I could always find them.

How many players were there again? I turned slightly, leaning my head to the left. Across the ocean toward the Kneult harbor, two more columns of color were visible. Yellow and gray. Specks of light fractured in the distance far behind them, like particles of light shooting from a prism.

Eleven columns in all.

So many players to defeat.

I should have known with the backstory they'd provided, but assassinating all the other players was the only way I could win the game. Once I knocked them all out of the game, I'd be crowned empress. Great, right? Except I somehow had to defeat nationally ranked gamers to do it, when I hadn't had time to pick up a controller in seven years, what with all the dance classes, play rehearsals, and piles of homework. But I was not panicking. The more players I killed, the more screen time I could get, and even if the very first player took me out, I could still make the kind of impression that could lead to something cool, like maybe national commercials, or a TV pilot, or, at the very least, this would look good on my college applications.

The rings scratched the glass, and I realized I'd cupped my fists. It would be fine. There were no small roles, only small actresses. This was not my only break.

Oh, who was I kidding? I was a theater person. Competition came as naturally to me as a perfect box step. I wanted to be the lead, so dang it I would do whatever it took to do it.

"Excellent." I pursed my lips. A scene where I welcomed my troops would be very cinematic, and Past Me was not thinking of the cameras when she chose this dress, so I needed a quick change, stat. "I'll meet them when I'm good and ready. Sabi, to me."

My maid servant squeaked, and then followed after me, her eyes downcast and flinching. Servants opened the doors with their heads bowed as I exited the throne room.

But there was no exit stage left. I wished I could just be offstage for like a second to shake out my hands and do some vocal exercises.

Letters scrolled across the top of my field of vision. *Stealth mode on?*

Stealth mode? *Sure.* Something hummed like a light switching on.

I glanced back and Sabi's eyes darted back and forth like she couldn't see me. I read the stats quickly. As a Rogue class I could go invisible for up to ten seconds. Oh, thank Lin-Manuel Miranda. No one could see me, so I shook out my arms and jumped up and down, stretching out my mouth so my jaw wasn't so tight.

Although going invisible was the opposite of what I was aiming for. I wanted more camera time, not less. Still, at least I'd be able to get some off time. Villains made meatier parts, especially for women, but keeping in character kept clashing against my need to be liked. I sighed and my neck muscles loosened. It was really hard to be in character twenty-four seven. I mean, I was a method actor, but even Daniel Day-Lewis sleeps.

Now that I thought of it, stealth mode could be useful in a stage fight. Like how completely dramatic would it be to just pop into existence with like a dagger raised or something? I'd totally have to use that. I just needed practice to master it.

Turn off stealth mode, I thought. The humming stopped like a switching off of a light. Poor Sabi almost ran right into my shoulders. I gave her my meanest glare, and she wilted like a scared little flower. I bit my lip, but reminded myself she was not even a person so there was no reason to feel guilty. I cleared my throat. Don't break character, McKenna.

We managed to cross into my rooms and toward my closet without making the girl cry and I waited until she opened it for me. The closet was three times the size of the one I had at home. Marble floor and glittering crystal lanterns. And the clothes . . . Silks, sheers, lace, straps, and ribbons. Miles of shoes, delicate boots and spiked heels.

I squealed in joy. My dad totally hooked me up with the best costume closet this side of Broadway.

I pulled a blue lace gown to my chest and cocked my head at my gilded mirror. No. Too basic for the cameras, and a bit too soft. I needed to look threatening. Regal, but villain-like. I put it back and grabbed a military coat with ribbons on the sleeves. The neon light of game vision showed lines where I could alter to shorten the coat, fabric I could add, places to connect mechanical accessories. If I lengthened the sleeves, I could add a blade-throwing tool under my wrist. And if I paired it with these jagged black goggles, my aim percentage would be nearly perfect.

The stats changed like someone swapped cue cards. I had two abilities, stealth and crafting, which meant not only was I going to be lead actress, I was also props, costumes, and director.

I couldn't breathe for a second. I loosened the stays and closed my eyes.

It's okay. Think about how this will look on a college résumé. You just have to be a triple threat.

In more ways than one.

I pulled pieces from the wardrobe, a mix and match of color and fabric, until I designed something incredible and way more badass than I'd have dared to try at home. When I wasn't in costume, I tried not to stand out too much. My talent had always made me weird. Different. People might use me to borrow the spotlight, or include me because we were all part of the same cast, but it always felt like I was separate from everyone else. No matter what I did, there was this wall between me and my friends, because I got what they wanted. And plain, sometimes baggy clothes made me look like other people, like I wasn't bragging about who I was. I had clothes for Normal Me to help me fit in, and clothes for Audition Me to help me stand out, and clothes for Character Me where I get to be someone else. I always knew exactly which role I was playing based on what clothes I'd chosen.

And this outfit needed to say I was a killer queen.

I hummed Freddie Mercury as I designed exactly the right look. Something strong. Someone who never got scared. Someone who made others fear instead.

Black silk gown and a red sheer lace overcoat with velvet-lined bell sleeves. I picked up knives and placed them in the shooter thingy at my wrist. Actual weapons, not the flimsy plastic ones I usually found at the props table. Then I hooked the sharp goggles to my tiara with a click, like they were always supposed to go there. Of course they were. I was the wicked queen of the Savak. People cowered when they heard my name.

I practiced turning stealth mode on and off as I stood before my mirror and made sure I looked enough like me for the facial recognition and enough not like me that I could lose myself in a different character.

Goose bumps arched up my neck and I held my head high. Perfect.

Let's go make the camera love me.

— — —

The sun kissed the Wingship armor and my cloak flowed behind me like wings as I inspected my army. Glowing neon lettering pointed to the Wingships, too faint to make out. But as I narrowed my eyes to squint at the connections where screws attached to the feather blades, images of weapons appeared where I could attach them. Each weapon was made with sleek design and rumbling gears. If I changed those blades to something sharper, filed the edges, their attack value would strengthen. And if I painted lines where the carvings of feathers were, they'd stand out more, amp up style points. I grinned. It was all design now, like the largest fashion game ever, now with a deadly expansion pack.

"Your spoils, my queen." A captain gestured. Chests of gold coins, barrels of hibisi blossoms, and piles of salted meat sat like set dressing. "The Biallo would not sign the treaty, so we burned their capital and staked their nobility to our coast."

I leaned away. "What do you mean 'staked'?"

"We placed their bodies on stakes, as is our tradition, and as their bodies rot, the birds carry their remains to the goddess of—"

"Oh, that's creepy. And gross. Mostly creepy. I *can* see how that could be effective as a warning, but I don't want you to do that on Savak shores anymore."

"My queen, it is our way. Your rivals will not be removed until staked."

It must be a game condition. "Well, then just leave them where you killed them. I want this island to have a very different aesthetic. No dead bodies, nothing rotting, or oozing. We are crisp, shining, and gorgeous. I'm thinking art deco with a bit more gold trim. Velvets and silks. No wool. No spiderwebs. Like danger is hiding behind that velvet curtain, not skeletons, okay? We want to impress, not look like a cheap Halloween display."

The captain blinked at me.

Anachronisms. Knowing my real life did make this more complicated. I raised my chin and narrowed my eyes. I couldn't be expected to keep character while directing. I'm sure they could just edit that part out.

"Anything else?" I asked.

"One noble escaped. A farm boy, the youngest son of a lower house. He meddles in Devani magic."

I glanced toward the Biallo coast. An orange column of light shone up to the clouds. A player. I needed to snuff that column out.

I swallowed.

Once I was ready.

"I want my own Wingship," I announced. "And we need to do some tailoring before I send my army out again. And I want to redo the servant wardrobe. This place has the makings of a great aesthetic, but we can do better than monochromatic wool."

A pair of servants shared glances.

I cupped my fingers together. "I know things were different before, but I'm your direct"—nope—"queen, and I demand perfect obedience as we fulfill my vision here. Do you understand, or do you need a demonstration of what will happen if you don't listen?"

I stared heavy, letting the reputation of this character do the work for me.

The general of my army knelt before me, his shoulders covered with a red vapor that matched the color of the diamond shape hovering over my head. The rest of my army dipped to their knees, the brilliant red spreading like a wave, until every member of my cast and crew showed their loyalty to my colors.

"Wonderful!" I smiled. I had never had such perfect obedience. It was so nice to be working with professionals. "It's going to be such a good show. Hands in!"

7

RYO

The cheap sword matched this poor excuse of a jacket, but it was a comfort in my grip. I wasn't prey now. I wouldn't let this sword go. I lowered the hood and grimaced at the fabric. This homespun thing itched like a demon's teeth against my newly healed skin.

Lady Tomlinson shoved past me. Her bag hit my shoulder. "Slouch if you can. Wouldn't want you to stand out while sneaking."

She blew out the lantern light.

I trembled in the sudden dark.

Get yourself together, I told myself. You're the hunter now. It's not going to happen again.

I followed Lady Tomlinson down a long tunnel, through a wooden door, and into the light. I poked my head out and peered both ways.

The narrow alley was empty. Above the torchlit street, the night sky reached out to forever. I could see the night sky. How perfectly novel.

I sharpened my focus. If the wrong person saw my face I'd be back in a cell.

She took off without me.

I grumbled. Someone should inform Sir Tomlinson he had an unfaithful wife, because clearly his daughter had been sired by rabid wolves. My ribs ached from where she had punched me, and she kept switching from anger to fear to who even knew what, her eyebrows and twitching expressions impossible to translate.

But I did not want to lose her.

Members of the Merchant class rushed through the street, a royal guard shoving them away from the high ground, yelling out commands about curfew.

I slunk into the shadows. She crossed to a pile of boxes against a wall, struck the crates with her sword, and the poorly constructed thing broke with a loud crashing noise. I flinched but no one on the street reacted.

Her sneaking left much to be desired.

A gold coin hid inside one box, a salted salmon in the other. She pocketed both and moved forward.

The thief. I grabbed her arm. She couldn't take things without permission. "Are those yours?"

"They are now." She pressed her flat pocket where she'd stuck the salmon against her waist. "Oh, sweet. This is like the TARDIS of dresses."

"The what?"

"Bigger on the inside." She grinned as if teasing but I had no response. She should not smile at me like that if I could not tease back. In addition, her smile was no guarantee she wouldn't punch me. I couldn't trust her expressions, or her nonsense.

But she should not be stealing. "You should not take something which does not belong to you."

"I'm sure this is all very confusing to you. If *only* there was something you could drink to make this all clearer."

Her green eyes flashed with what was clearly a dare. Unfair. A pretty girl daring me to do something reckless was a particular weakness of mine, and it was rude of her to use that weakness against me after I was so recently dead. But I wouldn't drink the seer water until I saw my father, and that was final.

She sighed. "If you can pick up an item, you can collect it."

"I believe that's called stealing."

"No, it's . . . I don't even know what to say to you. This world is an arpeegee, and we're stuck here until either we win the game, or the source code corrupts—"

"What sort of code? A code of honor? Then we shouldn't steal, no matter the stakes . . ."

She clenched her fists. "I don't have time for your morality right now. Trust me, or drink. Those are your options."

Lady Tomlinson slipped into the crowd and I followed her, my head low and my pulse racing. Trust her? A rabid wolf who stole and spoke nonsense? An elbow hit my back, and the person in front of me stepped down on my foot. I reached for a loose ribbon on her dress, to keep track of her.

She was the only ally I had. And if anyone in this crowd was loyal to the Devout, I'd make a fine trophy.

Lady Tomlinson met my eyes and gestured. We slipped away from the crowd through an open alley, ducking under lines of stale laundry and broken wine bottles until we reached a street that had already been cleared.

"Where are we going?"

"North, it feels like. Toward the Abbey." She looked my way. "What is Grig doing in the Abbey?"

I swallowed. How did she know this?

The seer water, of course. "He was forced to become Devout."

She smiled. "Sweet, we need a Mage class in our party."

Why wasn't she upset? Her brother had vowed to lose himself to the Undergod's will. It was my fault. And she smiled.

She was either incredibly brave, or the seer water she'd drunk had been laced with poison, which was slowly rotting her brain. One of the two.

"I'm going to pick up some supplies on the way. This sword keeps taking damage."

She led our way up the hill, slipping into shadows at any noise until we reached the top. The dual moons danced a promenade across the sky, lighting the shadowed homes of the city, which towered like a judge in fine robes. This hill overlooked the bay, where the docked noble ships were packed and ready to flee. The dark horizon seemed clear of the Savak Wingships that would come to claim my kingdom.

Above us, a Whirligig flew through the sky—all forged metal and flapping wings as it shot a misty green ghostlight through the city streets. Made of rusted pipes and copper trinkets, the inner gears spun with a flow of ghostlight. A beam of light traced the doorways and the cobbled streets.

Searching for me.

I ducked beneath an overhang until it passed. The Mechani were loyal to the Devout and my traitorous uncle because the high priests sold ghostlight to the Mechani to make Whirligigs fly. If their mechanicals found us, we'd be dead.

A wire door creaked open and a Historian stepped out from a tavern into the street.

I'd wondered when they would show up.

Dagney struck another box and drew the Whirligig's attention.

I pulled her behind the Historian's long cloak. He would make good cover. She crouched down next to me, hiding behind the feathered cape. The ghostlight traced over the Historian's cloak and registered no alarm.

The Whirligig moved on with a rumble and a cough of exhaust.

The Historian turned to face us, but I didn't trust him much further. I grabbed Lady Tomlinson's arm and took off, caring more for speed than secrecy, keeping to the shadows between buildings, staying out of the Whirligig's sights.

"Don't worry so much," she said. "We're still in the lower levels. We should be able to hide from enemies until we gather enough weapons and level up so we can fight."

Her nonsense was unnerving. "I've already died several times, so I will worry as much as I care to."

"You're only level four, and you've already died a bunch? No offense, Ryo, but you suck."

The impropriety. "Offense taken."

She turned. "I'm sorry."

"Offense not removed. I'll have you know I am a very good kisser. I do not suck, unless the occasion calls for it."

She laughed so hard she had to lean against a wall to hold her up.

I couldn't believe she laughed. I tugged my lips down and refused to smile. I was not the butt of a joke. Though now that I knew she could laugh, maybe next time I could get her to laugh on purpose. The way her eyes sparkled was quite bewitching.

She stopped and looked me head-on. "Did it hurt?" she asked. "To die, I mean." She spun a small jeweled ring around her little finger. A nervous tick, I gathered.

I tugged my hood lower. "Every time."

"I'm sorry. Sincerely. But buck up, dude. You aren't alone anymore. I'm the highest ranked *Ashcraft* and *Swordmaker's Chronicles* player in over three states. And Grigfen314 is even better, though don't tell him I admitted it."

Why did that nonsense make me feel better?

The narrow streets were empty except for the whirling sound of the Abbey's spies flying above the two-story buildings.

A Historian stepped out from a rooftop, and Lady Tomlinson stopped me. "We can use them as a warning."

"How?" I ducked low. We were near the market, a few streets from the Abbey. The fishmongers' side of the market, from the smell.

She lowered her voice. "If the Historians only show up when there is something to record, then we hide whenever we see one."

She peered around a barrel of fish and pressed her hand into my chest to stop me.

I stole a careful look. A group of royal guards turned down the street. They were sloppier than the Everstriders, both in movement and also in their wrinkled uniforms. No way would that pass my father's inspection. They turned down another street.

Should I try to enlist the Everstriders to my cause? They had been very helpful.

But I couldn't tell if they'd be loyal to my uncle. "Let's go," I said softly. "They've gone and Garbage Row reeks."

"Not yet." Her eyes were on the Historian. The thing was still studying the streets. I ducked back.

A Devout priest turned the corner, black cloak billowing, bright red dots along his nose, and his arms painted to show the bones beneath his skin. His hands fogged with a pale green mist of ghostlight. He stilled as if listening, then turned his gaze to Garbage Row.

I yanked Lady Tomlinson's arm and pulled her into a pile of stale garbage and rotting refuse from the fishmongers. We fell behind a wooden bin. I took Lady Tomlinson down with me, pulling her tight against my chest so she didn't fall into the rancid puddle. No one who knew me would look for me behind a pile of dead fish and empty boxes.

She squirmed away, but I held her tight in my lap. "Stop. He'll kill us," I hissed.

A wave of ghostlight pulsed down the street, pulling a crate from the pile and smashing it against the wall in front of us.

She drew her legs into mine.

Each step the Devout priest took thudded in my ears like my pulse. I peered over the bin edge and saw his wide shoulders.

I tucked Lady Tomlinson in my arms, folding in as small as possible. She stiffened against me, but kept quiet. I didn't dare whisper a warning.

I didn't think I could heal without my head. I did not know the limits of these strange recurrences. I'd died five times in the last twelve days. Each time, surprised as ever, to breathe once more.

The hilt of her sword pressed into my ribs, and our breaths echoed in my ears. Too loudly. Even our heartbeats might give us away. The back of her warm neck pressed against my nose, her hair brushing against my eyes. She smelled of fresh soap. I inhaled. How could anything smell clean right now? She moved and I could feel her pulse against my cheek, thudding slower than my own. Steady. I matched my breathing with hers. Inhale. Exhale. My rising chest pressed against her back.

We were in danger, so I should not be enjoying this.

The priest took his time patrolling the street. He seemed unsettled, his pace unfocused and wandering, his eyes sharp, but not looking to the side where we hid. He didn't seem to be looking for us in the garbage. A pulse of ghostwind shot forward again, swinging a few clay pots toward us.

Dagney startled in my arms, shaking like a leaf as those footsteps crept past us.

Her shoulder brushed against my nose as she peeked over the bins.

"The priest and the Historian have gone," she whispered.

I let out a large breath and dropped my head back in relief.

"He might come back." I moved my grip from her arms to her waist. "We could stay here for a few minutes, if you'd like? To be safe."

The point of her lips tipped up but she shoved my shoulder. "You smell like fish guts."

She climbed out of our hiding spot and my side went cold.

I picked at my borrowed shirt and sniffed. *Oh.* I recoiled from the smell. "You're not wrong."

I wiped off my hands as she searched the streets. All clear.

"You should have tried to charm him to our side," she said as I picked out a path.

Dead fish. Dead fish. I stepped around filth until I reached the clean cobblestones.

"So you think I'm charming?"

The sky flickered with an odd blue light, like lightning, but all along the edges. I stared at the sky and tried to find a logical reason. The sky was not ripping apart at the horizon, it was simply lightning striking. Again and again. At the same spot.

That was all.

She tapped my neck as if she were annoyed I wasn't paying her attention. "I'm not flirting. Your ability is charisma. You're so ridiculously pretty everyone just wants to help you, protect you. Haven't you noticed that people give you more time to make decisions? You can add members to our party. I can't be the only one to do everything."

I tapped a finger right back into her collarbone, see how she liked it. "You were squirming so much you'd likely have gotten us both caught if I hadn't held you still."

"I know how to be quiet."

"I was only trying to protect you."

She clenched her jaw. "That's benevolent sexism."

I narrowed my eyes and waited for the perfect retort to come, but the well of witty retorts had run dry. "I try."

Her dimple dipped.

I ran my fingers through my hair. "Fine. I'll recruit the next guard we see."

"Make it an Everstrider. We need a warrior to balance out our party and their start weapons should be better. Ooh. Bluebird of death is playing as a Warrior class, she'd be excellent." She spun on one foot and made her way into the market.

Bluebird of death? Who was that?

Dagney moved quickly, but I didn't follow right away. Instead I watched the sky as lightning struck again. Three quick times. Same location, right over the mountain's edge by the Biallo border. There was a pause, and then three slow strikes. Each one timed with a drummer's precision. A pause, before the sky sent three bright flashes again.

"Did you see that?" Dagney asked.

"The lightning that brightened the entire night sky? No, I missed it."

"SOS." She squinted. "It's Morse code. I wonder if that's another player."

I caught up. "Morse code? Is that the corrupting code?"

"No, that was the source code. Morse code is something completely different."

"Of course. How silly of me to be confused."

She raised her hands. "Let's just not talk."

"Fine by me."

I kept behind her. I'd have preferred to be in the lead, in order to stop any attack before it came. But I wasn't going to complain about the view of her plump backside.

I lowered my hood over my face as we entered the market square. A few traders were still packing up their wares. They glanced up when we entered the Fools Walk, the path in front of the stalls where buyers traded.

"I need every healing blossom you've got," Dagney announced. "Who has hibisi brew or blossoms to trade?" A few traders raised their hands, and she reached into her pockets.

I scanned for swords or threats and stepped in her shadow as she traded most of our food.

My stomach rumbled. "Won't we need food for our journey?"

"We can hunt, and I'll craft some things." She glanced above my head. "Your health is fading. When was the last time you ate?"

I couldn't remember. "Days," I admitted.

She handed me a salmon.

A raw, pocket-warmed, whole fish she'd found inside a wooden box. The thing still had a head. She mimed taking a bite.

Disgusting. "Am I a bear?"

She snorted. "I'm sure you've eaten raw salmon before, you're Japanese."

Her words tugged at a memory I could not see. I shot her a look. "I highly doubt this was the preparation."

"Fine." She turned to a trader, a man with a jerkin and a careful gaze standing behind a pile of cheeses and baked bread. Oh lost saints, the smell of fresh bread.

I grabbed a loaf. Still warm.

She made a face. "You can't take things from a trader, what's your problem?"

"So now we can't steal, because someone is looking? Fascinating how your morality is based on observation."

She tossed the baker a few coins and gave him the salmon from my hand. "Sorry. My friend is from far away. He doesn't understand how trading works."

The gall. "Explain the rules, then," I said with my mouth full.

"Drink your seer water, then." She smiled at the baker. "Just the one he grabbed. I'm looking for weapons and armor, and no, I'm not going to hunt down a goat for you to make leather. No side quests or barters, I'm trading with food or coin only."

Dagney traded quickly, sometimes smiling to get her way, sometimes coldly calculating. She was clever. And useful, I could admit, albeit grudgingly.

A trader near the entrance watched me. My mouth went dry. I crossed to Dagney's side and lowered my voice. "We need to go."

A Historian stepped into the market.

Dagney swore and then led us out through a back route. Carefully we stayed in the shadows of the buildings as she led us in a strange path through the city. She'd duck low whenever a Whirligig sped past, and then break open more boxes, which drew more to us. I said nothing of her thievery, though I noted each occurrence, in case there was ever a chance to repay.

She stopped suddenly, eyeing a corner of a roof, moving back and forth to try to get a better angle.

"Is it a threat?" I ducked low.

Her eyes lit up. "There's definitely something glowing up there."

I peered up, but could see nothing that warranted a positive reaction.

Her footsteps creaked against a table as she pulled herself up to the top of a wall and then toward the corner of the roof. She reached up, but unable to reach, she turned to me. "A little help."

Honestly. I made my way toward her, searched the streets for any spies, Whirligig or Devout, then bridged my fingers for a footstool. She held my shoulders and stepped up, her soft stomach pressing against my cheek as she retrieved a box hidden at the roof's edge.

Her skin was so warm, her curves so close. She was trying to torture me by pressing herself against me, I just knew it.

She found something shiny. A pair of silver boots, of all things. On a wall.

I very much doubted they belonged to her.

She stepped back down, and I moved away quickly, not staring at the large curves I liked so much, especially now that I knew how they felt, not staring at the way her cheeks had turned pink with exertion, or the way her joy at discovering these new shoes took every trace of scowl from those plump lips, and the way the crease between her expressive eyebrows had disappeared.

When she laced them up, moons-light flared upon her face, and afterward each step she took was quicker and muffled. "Boots of sneaking." She grinned at me with so much light, I could not help but smile back. I'd never seen a wolf smile like hers. You'd think it would be a cold thing, a baring of teeth, a warning accompanied with a low growl.

But when Dagney smiled, her whole face changed. Perhaps it was the dimple near her lip, or the spark of light in her green eyes, but she no longer seemed like a wolf cornered, she seemed like a wild wolf running free.

It was disarming.

And I was not staring.

Every step she took from then on seemed quieter. Softer. My own steps still echoed as I followed the rest of the way to the Abbey of the Undergod. I crossed into the gates and looked up at the glowing bones of the chapel.

I touched a spot on my neck.

Edvarg was dead. I knew it. He couldn't hurt me again.

But every person in this Abbey was loyal to Edvarg, and might take my life. Our lives. I held the gate but didn't step any farther. Dagney slipped under my arm and hit me again, but softer this time, with her bag.

I followed her in and the gates closed with a heavy clink.

I started down the manicured path toward the chapel's large arched entrance, but she snapped once to get my attention and cocked her head toward the back. I'd hoped Grigfen would be in the chapel, with the newly Devout. But of course Grigfen would be in the catacombs, the tunnels dug into the hillside leading to the great pits, the very mouth of the Undergod himself. I'd lost all my good luck when I lost my family.

We took the Death Walk, the paved path my people used to carry their dead to burial, moving toward the catacomb doors behind the grand chapel. I licked my lips. We'd been lucky, so far, not to run into anyone, but our luck was ending. I could feel it like the pulse in my new heart. As high priest of the Undergod, Edvarg had ruled the dark tunnels and the holy chapel. There was no telling how many of the Devout were loyal to him.

"I wish we could press save," Dagney whispered.

But I was no longer sure salvation waited within. I crossed to the catacomb entrance and pried opened a door made of bones leading into my uncle's territory.

I put on a smile she couldn't see. I didn't do it for her. It was my own fear I couldn't show.

Then we walked into the place of my nightmares.

8
DAGNEY

I hated exactly two things: entitled boys and haunted houses.

So guess how happy I was to be stuck in a dungeon level with Ryo.

The catacombs of the Undergod were a classic labyrinth level, so I knew to look out for traps or ghouls hiding in the dark tunnels. Didn't mean I liked it.

I looked for a flicker of a candle or some kind of sign ghosts were near, but the two torches lighting the bone walls near the entrance kept a steady wave. I grabbed one from the wall, and Ryo stood behind me, his sword twitching at each dark echo.

He'd gone suspiciously quiet, but maybe that was because the soundtrack had increased in volume. When I drank the seer water, it gave me game vision, which included a music score. The undercurrent traveling music had been light and bouncing, but now the soundtrack had turned ominous, like the thudding of a heartbeat mixed with the bass of thunder.

It was as annoying as Ryo himself, although the compass behind my eyes was worth the cost of the accompaniment. Each time we reached a fork the arrow would spin and settle on a tunnel. Most often the darkest tunnel.

Just flicker for me, torch. Give me some kind of warning.

Three left turns and one right later, I stopped.

A body in shapeless robes lay on the ground. An aura of green mist surrounded him. My heart lurched. Was it Grig? The arrow in my mind pushed past him. No, it was an NPC. With his throat cut. I looted through his coat, the few coins I found not worth the look of disgust that crossed Ryo's face. We crept around him, only to discover another body, this one covered in a black mist. From the bloody knife in his hand, and the spear in his gut, it looked like they'd taken each other out and died in the process.

The Devout were fighting each other?

A skitter of bones fell.

Footsteps.

The flame from my torch spluttered, and a damp wind shoved through my hair.

"I hate this," I muttered. "I hate this." I drew my sword, so now I held the sword and the torch ready to smack the spooky out of this level.

I take it back. Warnings made it worse.

"You hear that?" Ryo asked. Drums thudded in the distance.

I'd thought it part of the soundtrack. But if Ryo heard it, it must be part of the regular game play since he didn't have his game vision yet.

A tunnel opened to the right, but the arrow in my mind said to keep going straight, toward the sound. This game was the literal worst. We tiptoed forward. I saw a flash of ghostlight in a dark tunnel to the left of us.

Where a bone-dry horse's skeleton shot out at us.

We screamed. I sliced the thing with my sword. Again. And again. The skeleton was in splinters, but I hit it once more for good measure.

Ryo wiped a shard of bone from his shoulder. "Feel better?"

"A little." I checked the damage level. Crap. This sword was one hit from shattering. I tossed it to the ground. The tunnel where the Devout who'd tossed the dead horse bones at us was empty.

If I was playing this level at home I'd be a pint deep into mint chocolate chip ice cream by now.

Ryo shuddered. "Why would he use the Undergod's power to scare us not kill us?"

"Who cares, at least it wasn't a trap."

Ryo took my hand.

I narrowed my eyes. I was scared, but that didn't mean I needed comforting.

"So we don't get separated," he said. His jaw pulsed as he looked away. The torchlight found shadows beneath his cheekbones and lined the curve of his nose.

I dropped my glare. I wasn't the only one who'd screamed. He was scared too. Maybe he wasn't trying to give me something I didn't need, maybe he was asking for something I could give.

I was a strong confident person so I didn't need a man to hold my hand because this place was all kinds of creepy, but . . .

I liked his hand in mine. It made me braver to hold his racing pulse against mine. I squeezed his hand and held on.

Together we crept through the tunnels, following the drums and the arrow in the top left corner of my game vision. We found more bodies, covered in green or black auras, casualties of a battle already fought.

The tunnel led to an open cavern lit by torches and a soft green ghostlight. About fifteen men and women with shaved heads and faces marked with red paint were in the midst of a fight, but not with swords. The Devout and the high priests dueled against one another with ghosts I couldn't see. I could only see the evidence, a Devout shoved several feet back by an invisible wind, bones drawn from the tunnels to create barriers, and hear hymns sung as battle cries. They fought against one another, my game vision marking a glowing aura on every Devout, green marking one side, black the other.

We ducked against a rocky outcropping. I snuffed the torch's flame into the dirt.

The arrow in my mind disappeared as the catacomb surrendered to the darkness. We'd reached our destination. Grigfen314 was in there somewhere.

A cascade of bones slammed into the boulder I'd hidden behind.

"Poor Grig," Ryo whispered as he let go of my hand. "I did this to him."

"We'll get him out." A green diamond floated above a crowd of Devout surrounded in green. A player indicator. Finally. "There! He's with the green group."

"The what?"

"You don't see the auras?"

"What's an aura?"

"It's like a cloak on their back. The group around him is mostly all green." I gasped. Of course. "They're marked by their loyalties. Grig's in the green, and the other half is in black."

"Like a tournament," Ryo said, a strange look on his face.

"Exactly." I drew my dagger. "The green must mean they are loyal to Grig, and the black . . . I don't know, maybe loyal to Edvarg."

Ryo peered over the edge. He ducked back behind the rock. "Erm. It seems I have forgotten how good-looking I am, because someone just made a remark about my face when they saw me just now."

"They spotted you?" Honestly.

Well, then, I hoped they'd see the knife in my hands. I stood. A Devout cloaked in black widened his eyes as Ryo stood at my back. "It was the prince," he hissed. He raised his hands. "For the Holiest!"

A slimy wind pushed us forward, away from the shelter of the rocks and out into the open. I crouched and braced against the wind, but Ryo was taken unprepared and fell backward. A wave of dusty bones whipped around us, circling like a tornado, trapping us in the eye of this storm.

Ryo scrambled to his feet and attacked the bones, smashing and slicing with his sword, but the only damage he inflicted was to the sword's stats. The cyclone kept spinning around us, pulling at my dress and thrashing my hair against my face. I flipped my dagger in my palm and waited for an opening. It'd be a waste of time to go after the attack. If I killed the magic wielder, the spinning bones would drop.

I threw the dagger through the swirling bones, but a femur knocked the hilt and it lost its trajectory and slid past the Devout.

Well that was embarrassing. I pressed my pockets. There was another knife somewhere. I knew I grabbed more. I dug into my bag.

"We're trapped," Ryo said, his sword at the ready but his eyes darting back and forth, like he didn't know what to attack.

I pushed up my sleeves. "Nah, it's just a bit windy."

The twister of bones drew more Devout and high priests, their black-lined robes marked in red paint, their auras showing black loyalties as they tightened around the bone tornado.

I found another dagger. "Slice the bones right in front of me!"

Ryo complied. As soon as his sword cut a hole in the wall, I threw my dagger through the bones.

It struck right between the Devout's eyes. Yes!

The bone-circling wind fell with a clatter, and we were free.

To face two Devout and a high priest.

Round two. I wished I'd had time to trade for more weapons. Where was a battle-axe when you needed one?

I scanned the room. There had to be a cache around with more weapons. Something cool. Something we could use to end this battle.

"Stop! Vengeance isn't the answer now!" someone shouted from a wall of green. I recognized the lilting sound of his Scottish accent. Grigfen. "We need unity!" The green auras brightened around him.

I grabbed Ryo's arm. "Come on!"

We ran past the Devout into the center of the open cavern. Stalagmites cut through the ground, and stalactites dripping from the ceilings made floating candles of stone above us.

In a crowd of Devout marked loyal to him, Grig's purple aura showed his loyalty to Ryo. He looked so different from the last time I'd seen him, his blond curls shaved close to his scalp. Red dots ran down his nose, and his Devout robes folded over his shoulders like a cape to reveal a sleeveless black tunic tucked into dark green pants. His lean arms were lined with painted bones and his copper eyes shadowed with lack of sleep or guyliner. Health at 32 percent, but skill set maxed.

Grigfen314.

Badass.

"The Undergod gives protection, and comfort," he preached. "It is our job to emulate him and protect and comfort his followers. Including Prince Ryo. With Edvarg dead, our people need us firm at the Crown's side."

I tugged Ryo behind a rock. But if Grigfen was loyal to Ryo, and all those marked in green were loyal to Grig, then they only needed a small push to shift their loyalties to Ryo. He could handle that. As a Royal class, he'd have the Charisma he needed to shift the loyalties, even the black cloaks of those loyal to Edvarg. If he could pacify them, we could have every Devout on our side.

But how could he convince them?

"Give a gift, Ryo," I said. In *Ashcraft* the Royal class could offer a gift and change the tide of a war.

"Is now the time for gifts?" He pressed his pockets. "Besides, they could take this cloak, or my damaged sword, but I have nothing else."

"I'll find something." I reached into my bag. What did you give the Devout who had everything?

"I've just got to roll the dice." Ryo lowered his hood and walked into the center. "I'll stall, and you find me something I can give as a gift."

I glared at his back, and then rummaged through my bag.

The fighting stopped, the NPCs pausing to allow Ryo's action. His Charisma manifesting. The NPCs wouldn't wait like this for me.

He pressed his palm against his chest. "Peace and honor to you for your devotion. I come bearing a gift!"

What gift? I held up the bag as I stepped out after him, riffling through everything I'd traded for while he tried to stall.

Grigfen gasped when he saw us, his shadowed eyes grinning. He bowed and pressed his wrist to his forehead. "And to you for your reception, you pile of rat dung."

Ryo and Grig clasped each other around the neck.

I lowered the bag, the gift less important. Grig wasn't dead and bobbing. He wasn't imprisoned or sick.

"Grigfen," I said.

"Dags?" He stepped forward and lifted me off my tired feet in a tight hug. He was still strong. My brother was still alive.

Task completed.

The shine of my leveling up brightened the cavern. I felt stronger, less tired, like I'd awoken from a full night's sleep.

"So what do I give them?" Ryo asked.

I handed him my bag. "Something that shows you understand what they value."

"Is there a naked woman in—"

I punched his arm.

Grig watched our exchange with his eyebrows furrowed. "What are you doing with Ryo?"

Ryo dug through my bag. "One moment," he said to the crowd, holding up a finger. "Where is that gift?"

I lowered my voice. "Edvarg summoned the King's Executioner to kill him."

His shoulders drooped. "Sorry I wasn't there. How'd you find me?"

"I drank seer water, and it showed me the way," I answered. I reached into a pocket and handed him a hibisi bloom. "Mind your health."

Grig palmed the blossom and glanced over his shoulder. I blocked the crowd from him as he ate. His health raised 25 percent. I gave him another.

"You are a traitor, Ryo ne Vinton," a high priest marked in black said. "A blasphemer who spoke against the Holiest. Why shouldn't we kill you right now?"

Ryo stilled and then dropped my bag. He took a deep breath, and I hoped for one second that he could use his Charisma and charm them to our side.

But I'd met him, so I made a plan B.

"You need to drink seer water as soon as you can," I whispered at Grig. "Have you seen any?"

He grabbed my arm. "The cup Ryo brought," he whispered eagerly. "It's still in the Holiest's office."

"Where?"

Grig pointed behind us, and the arrow at the top of my vision spun deeper into the dark cavern behind us. *Find the seer water.*

Great.

"I know what to do," Ryo said softly. He raised his voice. "The

Undergod has marked me worthy. Edvarg is dead. He did not come back from death, but I have."

Oh no.

"Prove it!" a Devout said.

"I've seen it happen," Grig shouted. "A bone spear struck through his neck, and an instant later, he was free, with no injury." A few Devout loyalties shifted green at his words.

Ryo reached for a dagger. "You value miracles," he said. "I will show you one."

No. I ran forward. "Don't!" I hissed.

"It's all right, Dagney." Ryo held his knife to his wrist. "The Undergod will bring me back again."

"You don't know that."

The Devout behind us chattered at the delay. One by one the green auras dimmed and darkened.

Ryo studied their faces. "I have to do it."

He sliced his wrist, the skin flayed almost an inch deep, deep enough I could see his bone.

No!

I threw my hand over the cut, as if covering it would erase it. The idiot. The idiot. I shoved a handful of hibisi into his protesting mouth. He fought me off.

"He has no faith," a high priest said. She stepped forward and pointed. "He relies on the Savak healing flowers!"

Around us the Devout's loyalties shifted black.

Every single one.

I shoved Ryo. "RUN!" I took off after him into the cavern's darkness, following the arrow only I could see.

As the very shadow of death chased after us.

9
DAGNEY

The moron. The absolute idiot.

Hi, I'm in the middle of a battle, let me kill my own self, I mocked him to myself as I ran.

At least now we had Grigfen in our party.

Grig spread his fingers and the blood on my palm shot forward, twisting in front of him, before he threw his hand in front of him, sending the blood and a wave of bones from behind us flying forward. He formed a barrier.

Solid. Well made.

It took nearly five seconds for them to break through it.

We ran forward into the dark. I had the arrow before me, and Grigfen knew these catacombs, but Ryo ran with only his trust in our footsteps.

He clutched his wrist to his chest. The healing should help him.

It had to.

A strange mist rose from a line at the horizon. I glanced over my shoulder at the priests and the Devout and their skeleton army chasing after us.

Four out of ten. Would not play again.

Ryo thrust his hand across my stomach and stopped my run.

We'd reached an end of a canyon.

No, not a canyon. The edge of the Undergod's pit. Looking down, I could see ghostlight rising from the rotting bodies of the dead below.

Our people brought their dead to this pit, and as their bodies rotted, ghostlight formed.

The Devout drew closer, and the arrow in my mind pointed straight across the pit.

"We can't go around," I said.

Grig swallowed. He gave a nod. "Well this is a fine kettle." He thrust his hand forward and raised bones from the pit until a thin bridge formed across the whole of it. "Quick, I'll hold up a bridge."

Oh crap. I hated this trope.

But there wasn't time to argue. I took a breath and stepped forward. The bones bobbled under my weight, but Grig's power held them up.

"Go quick now," he said, his face straining with pressure.

I leapt forward. *Don't look down*, I told myself, and then I shook my head and looked down all I wanted. That was a cliché. This whole thing was a cliché, and I hated Nao Takagi so much for coming up with it. A femur slid beneath my boots and I growled under my breath and rushed forward, propelled by the power of sheer annoyance. My hands lifted at my side to keep my balance like this was a tightrope, and I was a cliché. She could do better. *Ashcraft* was a visual masterpiece, and so much more creative than this ridiculous game. Sure, the graphics were immersive, and whatever, but this whole story left a lot to be desired, and relying on heights? Yes, some people were afraid of heights, like me, possibly, but do better. Some people were afraid of peanut butter. Couldn't this be a soft leisurely wade through a river of peanut butter? That would be way more creative.

Behind me, Ryo stepped on the bones. The whole bridge under me shook with his steps. My knees were made of goo and my thighs ached and I hated this.

The pit was too deep to show the bodies, just green mist and gray shadows that seemed vaguely human. *Don't look at the dead things. Keep going.*

The Devout reached the edge and started a hymn I'd never been taught. Grig ran after us.

The bone bridge dropped a foot lower.

Pieces of bones disappeared under my feet. My stomach sunk and I fell forward to my knees, and used my utter hatred of this cliché to propel me forward and all the way across.

When I reached solid ground on the other side, I hit the dirt on all fours and sent an apology to Ms. Takagi for all the yelling. Not that she could hear me. Could she hear my thoughts? It didn't matter.

Ugh.

The Devout sent a wave of ghostwinds, making the bridge oscillate like a snake slithering its neck. More sections of the bone bridge fell.

Ryo's face was green as he clutched the swerving bridge, though maybe that was all the ghostlight keeping it up.

I reached forward. "You're so close! Jump!"

He leapt for me. Our fingers slid against one another, but I grabbed him hard and yanked backward. My heels dug into the dirt, his weight sliding me forward. My arms strained from the effort, but his feet found the cliff's edge and he climbed. Loose dirt slipped under his steps. I pulled back with all my strength. I wasn't going to let him fall.

He landed on top of me, his weight heavy on our entangled legs, his breath sweet and warm on my cheeks. His jaw grazed my lips.

And suddenly I didn't seem to hate this trope quite so much.

No. Come on. Growing feelings for someone while you were in mortal danger was like the biggest cliché of them all, so no. No to his damaged heart, perfect swooping hair, and false jawline, and no. Just no.

The pressure lightened as he hauled himself off me.

We both climbed to the edge. Grigfen was only halfway across.

His health percentage was fading fast with all the magic he was using. Only a few floating bones still hovered for him to make his way across on.

I couldn't hold them up for him.

"Grig!" I shouted, my voice raw. He had to make it. He had to be okay.

"I know you can do this!" Ryo shouted by my side. "I need your help, and as your prince, I command you to jump!"

Grig looked at us and nodded, the purple aura marking his loyalty growing brighter. His healing slowed its drain, and he leapt onto the last bone—a skull that didn't seem quite human, some seven feet away from the edge where we waited.

I was not going to let my brother die. "Grab my waist," I said. Ryo locked his arms around my stomach. "Jump, Grig!"

I threw myself forward as Grig took a mighty leap, his hands extended behind him, shooting a green mist of ghostlight back, propelling him to me. Ryo's arms restrained me as I grabbed on to any part of Grig's clothes I could hold. My tired arms rebelled, and his robes slipped out of my grasp. He flung his arm around my neck. Ryo roared and rocked us all backward, dragging us into a tangled pile of limbs and cloaks and heaving breaths on the safety of the other side.

I threw both hands in the air. "We did it."

Ryo exhaled. "And may we never have to do it again."

"Amen, brother," Grig whimpered.

I gripped Grig's shoulder and sighed. He was okay. We were all okay.

What would those punks at school say if they saw me now? Huddled with two of the most handsome boys I'd ever seen, though my memories as Lady Dagney wanted me to stab my eyes with her knitting needles for thinking our brother was attractive.

I pressed myself up and shook off the dust.

Across the pit, the Devout argued about what to do with us, half already walking around the pit. I offered my hand to Ryo to help him up.

I checked their health. Leveling up had raised them both to almost full bars.

"Come on," I said. "We need to get Grig his seer water."

We walked inside a bone-walled tunnel. Grig summoned a ball of green ghostlight, which kept the mood remarkably spooky, especially as the labyrinth soundtrack started again.

"Have you both had the seer water?" Grig asked.

Ryo sighed. "Don't get her started."

"*I* have," I said. Ryo gave a half smile.

The arrow behind my eyes spun left so I gestured, and Ryo followed after me.

Grig hesitated then followed my lead. "What did you see in the—Ah!"

My heart clenched. A Historian stood at the end of the tunnel, where the pathways forked. A woman Historian, judging by the way her raven-feather cloak curved around the small set of her shoulders. The green light lit her silver mask and sent shadows where the eyes should have been. She raised a spindly finger to the left.

My arrow pointed right.

"The placement of the bones indicates we should turn right," Grigfen said. "If you get lost, pay attention to the stacking of the bones; there's always an arrow point showing which way to turn."

The Historian shook her head and pointed left again. There was nothing down the hall. Was she warning us against something?

Ryo's forehead creased as he met my eye, and then he shrugged.

"What are Historians?" I studied the Historian as we crept closer. Her aura betrayed no sign of her loyalties, and no player indicator hovered over her head. "Can we trust her?"

"I don't know if we can," Ryo answered. His arm was warm next to mine. "They've always stayed out of the Crown's business. I've never seen one help anyone before."

Grig's back bumped against mine. He guarded our backs, ready to pull at the bones if the priests or the Devout caught us.

"I think we should go right," I said.

The Historian shook her head, the silver mask waving back and forth. She pointed again to the left.

"They're Whirligigs." Ryo's lower lip disappeared behind his teeth.

"What?" Grig screwed up his face. "But they look so human."

Ryo brushed his chin with his index finger. "I believe they are a combination of Devani magic and Mechani skill. They were made to watch and record our history in the great book."

Interesting. "They watch, but don't interact." This was a video game. Why would there be characters written in simply to observe? I tiptoed closer. Unless . . . "Are you behind a screen?"

She nodded.

She was from outside the game. "We go left," I announced.

The Devout drums pounded closer, and we turned left.

Grig's ghostlight dimmed, leaving us in pitch black.

"It was a bloody trick," Grig's voice shouted.

"No. It wasn't. Grab hold." I grabbed a hand and what was probably Grig's robe and stepped forward into the dark. We walked forward until a warm yellow light highlighted an open door and a bone wall passage hidden behind shadows.

We turned and saw a different door, this one made of iron and edged with skulls and candlelight.

"The office of the Holiest?" Grigfen said. "But that was still several turns away."

"She found us a shortcut," I said. The Devout drumming was

muffled by the distance. They were still coming for us, but we had a major head start now.

Ryo opened the iron door and Grig rushed inside. "This room has been sealed since Edvarg's flame snuffed out."

He lit a candle and I entered.

The room smelled of dried blood. A bone stuck through the door frame. Ryo flushed pale. He closed the door behind us and then grabbed a rolled parchment from the desk.

And on top of a crowded desk was a full cup.

The arrow in my mind disappeared.

I grinned. "Bottoms up, bro." I handed him the glass.

Task completed.

"Are you certain this is a good idea?" Ryo asked.

Seriously? "Would you trust me already?"

Grig cracked his neck and puffed his cheeks. He sat in a gilded chair, popped his heels onto the desk, and lifted the glass. "Cheers."

He drank it all down.

10
GRIGFEN

Three notes sounded, as familiar to me as a lullaby, and then a low voice shouted:

"Welcome, adventurers, to the land of traitor kings and vicious queens!" I waved my hands as ghosts and machines fought one another right in front of me, but I made no contact. So I closed my eyes and thought back on my Devout training as the voice continued. "Who will win the throne in this epic RPG by the makers of *Ashcraft*?"

My eyes cracked open. *Ashcraft*?

I'd heard and said that word so many times that in one instant everything clicked. Right. This thing was a video game.

Static flashed, skewing the image for a moment and then the cut scene continued. Pretty standard, all in all, so I didn't watch. Instead I tried to find my stats. There we were: Mage class, Magic high. Intelligence low (that seemed faulty) and Constitution—super squishy. Grand. That's the problem with Mage class. Phenomenal cosmic powers, itty-bitty healing space.

It was all right though.

There were three things in life I was better at than any other living person. Number one: remembering ska band names from southern Edinburgh in the late nineties. Number two: making the best seven-layer bean dip in the galaxy (the secret was nine layers). And number three: winning top score at *Ashcraft*.

"There are two ways for you to win the crown," the voice continued.

"The first is as a member of a team. You will aid your party with your Devout magic, and they will protect you with their might."

An image flashed with a girl I knew well, in full Everstrider uniform, looking so different from the first time I'd met her.

Bluebird.

I grinned. Six months ago, I took high score in *Ashcraft* by five thousand points and qualified for the eSports competition to be one of the first to play *The Heir's Ascension*. I was in my room (where else would a seventeen-year-old be on a Friday night?), and I lifted my arms above my head and the crowd cheered, or actually the radio played from my dusty speakers while my granddad snored down the hall.

"Griffin!" my mum yelled at me from the kitchen. "Take out the bins!"

"Hold yer horses, woman," I muttered.

"What?!"

I cleared my throat and pressed pause. "Yes, Mum."

And by the time I got back, someone else had taken the top spot. Some chap named bluebird_ofdeath had done the impossible. It cost three Vimto sodas and a burnt stovie, but about three the next morning I finally won the top spot again.

Seven seconds later, bluebird_ofdeath had stolen it again. I hadn't even finished my victory dance.

"Wut?" I wiped some grease from the corner of my mouth and pulled up the chat to call the lad a cheater.

But then, of course Bluebird had to reply,

It's skill, not cheating.

I was going to say something mean and get in a real row, but then I kinda noticed Bluebird was a girl.

A real live, breathing, about-my-age female.

And this girl . . . Mother of Dragons, she was adorable. A black girl with light pink hair and blue-framed glasses, wearing a *Firefly* tee shirt, her fingers parted in "live long and prosper" like she was manga drawn straight out of my nerd-boy fantasy. I sat up so quickly I knocked over a half-full can of Vimto and had to mop it before it stained my wood floor, and by the time I figured out what to say back, she'd logged off.

Which was, you know, fine and all. It was late and I had to get my granddad breakfast in a few hours.

She'd left a message though. She'd spied on my high scoring game and thought I needed to look out for the smoke demons near the falls, which I knew, *obviously*. Later, while my granddad napped, I loaded the game and followed the smoke demons, and behind the waterfall was a whole secret room full of jade, and in the next moment my score soared higher than ever.

And my subtle attraction morphed into a beast of epic proportions.

I thanked her without saying anything too awkward, and she messaged me back, and I replied again, and so on, and so forth, and typing was the best. I could really obsess about how big of a knob I was being before I pressed send and dial back the nerdometer. It got better over the next few weeks as we swapped tips, jabs, high scores, and a string of swears when she beat me at head-to-head, and I realized a high nerd rating was one of the many things we had in common.

That and we both qualified for the eSports competition.

Bluebird had to be in this game somewhere.

"And the second way to win," the voice went on, "is to gain your team's trust, until the very last moment when you betray your friends and steal the armor for yourself."

That took a turn. The image shifted to one of me with glowing green eyes, stabbing Ryo through the heart before I stole some strange crown and sat on a gilded chair.

"Then you, too, can win the throne."

Not bloody likely, to be honest. I wanted top score for myself, sure, but I owed Bluebird. We trained together.

We'd video chat before we played, which was a bit awkward, like I had to shower and comb my hair flat before I played a game, but I got used to it, and to cleaning the bits of my room where the camera might see. It was worth the effort, because video Bluebird was like profile pic Bluebird to the nth degree. My crush/obsession with this girl had evolved from a regular Eevee into like Vaporeon by this point.

So we'd play the game, but by this point, the best part was the talking. We'd talk for hours about everything except the bits that regular people seemed to go on and on about, you know? I knew what fandoms she obsessed with, what OTPs I could tease her about, and what ones were sacred. I told her the secret ingredients in my bean dip, and showed her my dad's vinyl record cover where he played a trumpet with his mates in matching shiny purple vests.

I knew she was from the States because of the time difference, but I didn't ask where she lived. Luckily we both stayed awake late into the night so we caught each other waking up and going to bed.

Once she left her game logged on while she slept. She just said "Alexa, turn off the lights," and then she didn't shut her laptop. I didn't like stalk her sleep or anything—I had things to do, like take Granddad to the park and get his hearing aid adjusted—but I checked in on her from time to time. It was so peaceful, watching the dim light of her laptop glowing against the freckles on her brown shoulder.

I left my laptop on that night while I slept. And the next night, hers was on again.

We didn't talk about it. But it couldn't have been an accident, so we smiled and talked around it.

She knew more about me than anyone else did, but she didn't know my real name, and I didn't know hers. She called me Grig, because the name I wanted, Gryffindork, was already taken, so I went by Grigfen314, which meant nothing, but at least no one else was using it.

Somehow that made it better. Like I couldn't mess it up, if we were still strangers.

I fell hard for the way her mind worked, and for the way she understood how those things that mattered to no one else mattered so much to me. When my granddad's health took a turn, there wasn't much room for anything resembling a social life, so talking to Bluebird while we trained became a kind of holiday from caretaking. She had a disability, so she understood when I talked about doctor visits and my fears for the worst. She knew how to joke our way through it.

Then my granddad died.

And it left me in this funk. I couldn't talk to her. I couldn't talk to anyone, let alone play in the tournament. I shut off my games, my computer, my phone. Everything that had distracted me from the time I had with him.

I didn't know how much I loved him until I lost him.

It took me weeks to even be able to open my phone. I didn't intend to look for Bluebird. I didn't know how to talk to the girl I'd used to escape my granddad, but I couldn't ignore the heap of messages from her, some swearing at me for quitting, some in caps lock—all date stamped about two weeks earlier.

The second I connected to our chat, she was there.

You all right?

It took me a minute to answer. I always said I was fine when any-one else asked. But I didn't have to lie to her.

No. I'm really not.
Is it your granddad?

I didn't answer.

Oh Grig. I'm so sorry.

It was later, on video chat, when she convinced me to try to get back in. I'd forfeited a few matches, but there was still time. If I won the final match with a high enough score, I could still get into the game. The best part of *The Heir's Ascension* competition wasn't the experimental immersive technology; it was that the winner would also get an internship at the company, on-the-job training, and the promise of a future that didn't require a degree.

I didn't want to leave my home. But as I glanced around my half-cleaned room, I realized I didn't really belong here anymore anyway. My granddad would want me to live my own life.

All I needed was the ability to get a high score.

One of my top three skills.

Just behind the bean dip.

Bluebird was already in. She told me all she could about the other players, their strengths and weaknesses, and tips about that final round.

When I won that match, I was giddy like a fool, because it meant I could meet her. Once we met, whatever it was we had would become real.

I couldn't betray her.

Not for all the money in the world.

The cut scene ended, and Dagney knelt by my side, Ryo next to her. They seemed to be in the middle of an argument of sorts. I closed my eyes. "Oh, would you just kiss already and get it over with?"

"Grig," Ryo said, though I noticed his cheeks reddened, the poor boy.

I let out a laugh, and I couldn't stop. Suddenly my whole fake life was just the funniest thing in the world.

"Are you all right?" Dagney asked. "Does your head hurt? You overwhelmed? What are you thinking?"

Oy. There comes the headache.

I pressed the side of my head tight until the pain receded, cursing my squishy Mage class.

Dagney clung to my arm.

"I'm all right," I told her. "I've just got to find my Bluebird."

Then it wouldn't matter what world I was in.

So who is this Bluebird person?" I asked. I had several questions, of course, but that seemed the most pressing.

"Bluebird of Death," Dagney said. "She's incredible. If we get her, we'll win the game for sure."

This was the second time I'd heard the world called a game.

"Of course she'll join us," Grig said. "She's my, erm . . . partner."

"What sort of game?" I asked again. Perhaps now Grigfen would explain, since Dagney did not have the patience.

"I told you," Dagney said. "It's an arpeegee."

I tapped my foot. "As though that were clarification."

"If you really wanted to know you could *drink your seer water*!"

"Ah, get a room, you lovebirds," Grigfen said.

Dagney scoffed and then took a step away from me. "What? No . . ."

I would have scoffed as well, except I was busy looking everywhere other than at Grigfen, or at Dagney, or at the bone spear that had once impaled me.

The desk, basically. I was looking at my uncle's desk.

"So what do we do next?" I asked.

"Did Ms. Takagi say anything to you?" Dagney asked Grigfen.

I scratched my jaw. My mother's given name was Takagi. I'd have asked more questions if I'd known my mother had spoken to her through the vision.

"Wait, she spoke to you?" Grig said. "I just watched a cut scene giving an overview of the game, and then went into a detailed win condition."

"How do you win this game?" Dagney asked.

"Me personally? Either as a member of Team Ryo, or as a Devout—I'd need to win the loyalty of the high priests, retrieve the Armor of Irizald, and take the throne to rule as a theocracy, after betraying the prince, of course." He shrugged. "Pretty standard secretly evil sidekick storyline."

My stomach twisted into a betrayed knot. "Grig!"

"Relax yourself, Ryo. I wouldn't tell you I'd betray you if I were planning on it." He squinted at me. "Is that an icon over your head?"

"You're getting your game vision!" Dagney's eyes shone. "It seeps in slowly."

I stepped away and glanced around the Holiest's office. How exactly did I come to be here with this madness?

"What'd Ms. Takagi say to you?" Grigfen asked.

Dagney pulled her hair over her shoulder. "She said there is a glitch in the pain receptors, so we should do our best not to get hurt. She said we are trapped in the game until someone wins and we break out, and that the glitch is affecting the source code."

I understood about one word in five she said, but Grigfen paled and sat back down. "I'm pure done in."

"I know."

She sat on the edge of the desk.

"What happens if we die?" Grig asked.

"I don't know." Dagney gestured to me. "Ryo here comes back from the dead. Best-case scenario we feel every inch of death, so I can't advise it. And that's if we have extra lives. I don't think we all do. I think Ms. Takagi gave Ryo extra."

She twisted her ring around her finger.

I stepped forward. "I have a few questions."

"I'm sure you do, mate," Grigfen said. "Just let us plan for a wee bit and we'll explain things on the road." He turned his back on me. The impudence.

Dagney's lip was a thin line. "So we go after the Armor of Irizald. Did your vision say where to find it? My vision was interrupted by *Don't get hurt, please save my son.* I don't even know my win condition."

Grig cupped his jaw. "Mine didn't say where the armor was either."

I lifted a finger. "I know where the armor is."

They turned to me. Finally.

"Seriously?" Dagney asked. "Why didn't you say anything earlier?"

"I don't know, perhaps because you seemed *so* receptive to everything I had to say."

She huffed. "You could have told me." She glanced down and then met my eyes. "I love game lore."

I swallowed hard.

"I think the Historian's shortcut bought us a moment of peace," Grigfen said as he slid open a drawer and riffled through. "We're listening now." He pulled out a sharp knife with a polished bone hilt and claimed it as his own.

Thieving ran in their family, apparently.

If Grig was distracted by looting Edvarg's desk, at least Dagney seemed interested. Well, if she insisted. "Irizald was the last queen of the Devani. They made the armor for her."

"I love that the armor was made for a woman." Dagney leaned forward. "Sorry. Continue."

I closed my mouth. I was only going to tell the pertinent information, but with Dagney's rapt attention, I had the strangest desire to tell the full story, the way my father told it to me.

"Before my family claimed this land, it was ruled by the Devani witches. They weren't one nation or race, but many, drawn together from every continent to pursue magic. They gained their power by making deals with powerful spirits, friendly bogeys, and the Lurchers— monsters two stories tall with sharp teeth and an unending hunger." Dagney's eyes widened so I curled my fingers like claws.

"But every deal they made strengthened those monsters, and they couldn't turn against them. The monsters crept out of their forests and hunted our people. The Devani changed, learning to imbue magic inside objects, or weapons, so they could reuse the same spell without strengthening the monsters. But it was too late. The Devani couldn't stop those monsters they'd freed alone."

"That was when the Everstriders formed, right?" Dagney asked.

"Indeed. Together they fought those monsters with honor, but a few Devani would not stop making their deals. Until one day, my grandmother Verelise discovered a way to steal the ghosts' energy."

"The first high priestess," Grigfen said. He opened one of Edvarg's trunks and glanced up at us. "They taught us about her back at the chapel. She drew ghostlight from the lining of the magical barrier between the living and the dead, and the more ghostlight we drew, the weaker those monsters became."

I folded my hands. "She worked with the Mechani to create the first Whirligigs to aid the Everstriders. With an army of mechanicals and the Devout on her side, she had more power than the queen of the Devani. When the Devani struck back, our people revolted. They were tired of being hunted. Tired of their witch queens. It was the Devani's turn to be hunted. Those who survived imbued their power into a set of armor, sacrificing their lives in order to create talismans anyone could wield. They left this armor to Queen Irizald. If she survived, she'd sit on her throne and bring back the day of witches."

Grig and Dagney grinned, as though they didn't hear the pain in my voice. This was a story I did not care to tell.

"The day of battle came. My grandmother Verelise survived. Irizald did not. Afterward, we scattered the armor, for using the armor could bring those monsters back. We sent each item to one of our allies, and they hid them. No one, except my father and I, know where every item is hidden."

I crossed to Uncle's desk. "The Crown of Visions went to the Savak clerics. They were our allies then. From my father's reaction to the seer water, I'd wager it's at the bottom of the Seer Spring. Then there's the Traveling Boots. The wearer can travel leagues per step, reach our farthest ally in only moments. We buried that one on the feet of my grandfather." I put on a grin. "Hopefully he's still in the King's Crypt. The Axes of Creation and Destruction were given to our most trusted allies, the Kneult. No clue where they've kept it, although judging by the power of their trading ships, I doubt it gathers dust. It can tear down a forest in an afternoon and build a house before morning."

"That's bloody awesome," Grig said as he replaced his cloak with one he'd found in a trunk.

I smiled without showing my teeth. "I also know where the Breastplate of Healing is, but I swore never to reveal its location, for the wearer could live forever. If I had the boots, I could get it. Probably. But in order to get the boots, we'd need the Gloves of Freedom, which we gave to the King's Executioner for safekeeping. They can open any door. Or crypt."

Dagney touched the pockets at her hips and opened her bag. "And what will you trade me for them?" She flashed the gloves like they were a trophy.

"Come on, I just revealed a royal secret. That has to be worth something."

She shrugged a pretty shoulder. "But is it worth my King's Executioner's gloves, kept secret in my family for a generation?"

"I'd throw in this cloak as well. Many women would value seeing me with my shirt off."

She rolled her eyes. "How about I give the gloves to you if you promise to stay clothed."

"Deal." I took the gloves in my hand, and my skin lit. It wasn't a brightening of torchlight; something had made my own skin turn lantern.

Grig put his feet down. "You don't want the armor for yourself?" he asked his sister.

She bit her lip. "I guess I'm Team Ryo," she mumbled.

"That'd explain all the purple."

She looked down at her bare arms and groaned.

I raised an eyebrow. "What now?"

She glared hard. "Nothing."

Didn't seem like nothing to me. I fought a smile and looked at the golden gloves. They'd seemed large on Dagney's hands earlier, but when I put them on, my skin tingled, and they fit as though tailored for me. Solid metal on the outside, but the inside seemed lined with calf skin. Carved with Devani symbols, and imbued with history.

I wore a piece of the Armor of Irizald. Perhaps my father's faith in me had been well placed after all.

"Oh no, I've seen that look," Grig said.

"What look?" Dagney asked.

"Ryo at full power. It usually means a prank is in order."

I grinned. "Don't be foolish, Grig. A prank's always in order."

"That's not funny." Dagney glared at me. "We still have to exit a labyrinth level with an army of pissed enemies searching for us, and once we get out, we still have to get through a world full of traps to find the armor before the source code corrupts or before the queen of the Savak finds it. This is not the time for a prank."

"How about a question instead?" I asked. They looked at me with tested patience. "Does anyone else hear drumming?"

12
MCKENNA

The large ship shifted beneath my feet, the dark waves crashing against the hull, hiding my sneaking footsteps. I stepped in time with the soundtrack. It was so dark, I didn't need to turn my invisibility on, but I still did because it was dramatic as all heck to step out of the shadows and reappear, look side to side, and then disappear again.

For sure they'd use that shot in the promotional materials.

The tips of my Wingship scraped against the wooden deck as I sneaked into the cabin of the boat. Sailors slept on hanging hammocks, or lounged out on the floor, while one girl slept in a large rolled mattress. She seemed young for a player, maybe fourteen. And small. A slip of a girl dressed in a plain muslin dress, freckled across the nose, her hair braided at both sides and loose curls at the top. Nothing very special, except for the player indicator hanging above her.

I flicked my wrist and a dagger shot into my palm.

Stealth mode, I thought. The soft hum sounded. I stepped around the snoring sailors, lifting my black cape so it wouldn't trail over their slobbering faces. I crept to the sleeping girl and stood over her, with my dagger raised.

Stealth mode ended, as though someone pulled a cloak of invisibility off my face. "You made it too easy, Catherine," I said.

The girl woke. I lunged for her, but a hand shot out of nowhere and shoved my stomach hard. I tripped over a sleeping body and fled back. The player indicator rose, and it wasn't over the girl. Instead, it hovered over a young woman who'd slept behind the mattress—her skirt covered in fringe, her shaggy hair mussed from sleeping, and her mouth twisted into a dangerous snarl.

That made more sense. I wish I'd been able to find her photo before. I flicked my wrist, but by the time the dagger snapped to my palm, the player was on me. She punched my jaw. Clawed at my hair. I shoved backward. My wings carried me toward the ceiling. The NPC sailors awoke with angry startled grunts.

Stealth on.

I flew back, toward the exit. The men on the boat surrounded the young girl, blocking her and the player with their bodies. My chance to knock Catherine out of the game while she slept was gone.

"You can't have her," she shouted, searching the room for me, but not finding me. "My young queen will take back the Devani throne, and not one soul can stop our rebellion."

She must not have drunk the seer water yet. Once she had game vision she'd be harder to tag out, especially since I almost caught her. She'd watch for me closer than I watched the standby line last time I went to New York.

This was bad. The Savak queen's reputation would be damaged by this failed attempt. I couldn't let anyone know how off this had gone, or else my stats would drop. I had to be scary. Who would buy a game with a weak queen? They'd shift the marketing focus toward the heroes, and I'd be edited out of the commercials. I couldn't let news get out, no matter what I had to do to keep it silent.

I closed my eyes.

You practice what you perform. Every time I'd get caught with a dose of stage fright, Ms. Fields told me those words. I'd practiced enough. Catherine was one of the lower-ranked players. I'd run all the tutorials, researched the players, tailored my wings to the highest stats I could. So all that planning should work out now that it counted.

The humming stopped.

Sailors shouted when they spotted me.

I opened my eyes.

Stealth mode on. I landed on soft feet while the sailors fired their weapons where I'd just been. Daggers in both hands, I spun low, slicing stomachs. Then I jumped before they registered an attack. Blood dripped from my daggers as I spun in a flip. My wings caught me. I flicked the stealth mode off so I flashed visible, then on again as I kicked off against walls toward another round of sailors. Slice. Slice. Slice.

Three more NPCs dead.

Catherine threw a glass of something liquid at me. If she ruined my hair, we would have words when I woke up from this game. She lifted a metal-clad hand, palm up, and struck me with some sort of magical fire. It hit my shoulder, burning my dress, melting the Wingship bronze into my skin. I could smell my hair burning, hear the flames roaring.

But it didn't hurt.

It should have. I remembered falls back in training that stole my breath, cut palms from when I learned how to catch my daggers. But no sting of pain had struck me since I drank my seer water and gained my game vision.

It made for an excellent acting exercise.

Stealth on.

There wasn't time for fake wincing. I flew forward, but that water she'd thrown on me must have shown even through stealth mode, because her Devani firebolt followed wherever I flew. A large man with a face tattoo swung a sword at me and struck my Wingship.

I shot a dagger into his neck. "Do you have any idea how long I spent designing that?"

I disappeared and took out three more sailors. Twist, stab—*five, six, seven, eight*. Repeat. Until it was just me, the player, and the small girl.

"You won't harm her," Catherine said, standing in front of the girl.

Smoke rose from my scalded shoulders like fog from a fog machine. My legs barely kept me standing. I flicked my wrist. Palmed the blade. Aimed between the player's eyes. "I won't need to," I said.

The dagger launcher fired. The look of pain that crossed Catherine's eyes before the dagger dimmed them once and for all was a work of genius. Seriously. I was so glad to be working with professionals.

Her head shot backward. She fell in a crumpled hunch.

She was a true talent, not over-the-top at all. Subtle almost. She'll be good for television.

After Catherine fell, the young NPC queen's eyes lit white. She raged at me, her fist slamming into my chest, but I couldn't feel it. I held her by her throat, and then lifted her until her feet dangled.

"Save your rage for the sequel, little queen."

I tossed her to the ground. Her head slammed against a pole and she was still.

I gathered myself for three breaths and then turned stealth mode on so I could have a freak-out moment in the privacy of invisibility. I could not believe I'd just beaten Catherine. She'd won the national competition three years back, and while the new crop of players had overtaken her when she went to college, she was still serious competition.

I clicked a button and a warning whistle sounded above me. Two of my soldiers dropped from the clouds where they'd been circling. I pulled Catherine out of the room and onto the dock.

Wordlessly, the soldiers planted a stake into the boards at the front of the boat. It didn't count as a victory until the players' bodies were staked. And I was the one who had to do it.

They helped me lift Catherine's body and slide the stake through her.

Her inventory fell out of her pockets into a perfect circle with her staked body at the center. The servant pulled out the plaque I'd made and hung it around her shoulders. I didn't give it a second look.

Instead, I picked up a silver bracelet that linked to a ring, with a small jewel chained to hang in the center of the palm. This was what she must have used to make the fire. Devani magic wouldn't work for me, but it was pretty, so I pocketed it anyway. I bent to retrieve her unused healing potions and drank. Just because her magic didn't hurt me didn't mean it didn't damage my health. I was at 5 percent before the hibisi tea restored me.

She'd almost gotten me.

While I was looking at my stats, the skill set crafting highlighted. What? Why would there be unlocked crafting abilities?

The Devani bracelet. I couldn't use the fire magic hidden inside it, but I could use each magic-infused link of chain to amp up my crafting and create a mechanical fire launcher. Not as powerful as Devani magic, but the possibilities it unlocked were phenomenal.

But each chain could make only one mechanical.

I glanced at the unconscious queen. I bet I could convince her to make some more, provided she was sufficiently motivated.

I bent next to her body and tested her heartbeat. Good, she was still alive. Then I sat in the middle of a ship full of bodies as I crafted enhancements into my costume wings.

One player down.

And I'd need every power-up I could find to take out the rest.

13
DAGNEY

What did it mean that my loyalty was purple? Nothing. Except that I wanted Ryo to win. Well, sure. Ms. Takagi asked me to help him, and we needed to get out of this rotten game, so who cared who won it? I didn't even know my win condition, and if Grigfen could win as a member of a team, then helping Team Ryo to victory seemed like my best shot.

That was all it was.

That was the only reason.

The drumming grew closer.

Exit catacombs. The arrow spun, pointing out the door. Grig had grabbed everything of value in the office, so we should amscray.

We raced through the catacombs, turning ourselves in twisting circles. The bones glistened beautifully, stacked carefully to show the way out. I'd caught the pattern, but still trusted my arrow for directions more.

Grig slowed to a stop. "Last turn until the exit," he whispered.

"Let's go," Ryo said, moving forward.

I grabbed his arm. The soundtrack had just changed to battle music. "We've got a boss to fight first."

I peeked around the corner. Three priests blocked the exit, swaying softly, their hands alit with ghostlight.

I gestured three fingers and Grig nodded.

"Can you turn their loyalties?" I asked.

"No time," Grig said, his eyes sparkling. "Besides, I've got a few new spells I want to test out."

"I'll tank," I said, unsheathing Ryo's sword before he could protest. "Ryo, protect Grigfen as he does magic."

Grig gave a brief nod, and we moved forward. Ryo trailed one second behind.

The bone walls of the catacombs around us shook, and then a monster of bones formed, blocking our way. I checked, but it wasn't Grigfen's doing.

Now we had to fight three priests and a bone monster? I was so done with this level.

I lifted my sword and sliced at the bones. Shoved the thing backward.

Grig lifted his hands and chanted a single word over and over, "Vixhe, vixhe, *vixhe*."

I ducked as his magic shot from his hands. The bone monster imploded, sucking tight into itself, and then, as Grig closed his fingers into a cupping shape and then spread his hands out, the glistening bones exploded. Grig pulled his hands in front of him and gestured vertically, whispering a word I couldn't catch over the boom.

A shield blocked the shattered bones from hitting us. But they destroyed those swaying priests, just completely eviscerated them.

Grig swayed on his feet, his color pale, but still he grinned. His knees buckled, and Ryo caught him.

I put a hibisi in his mouth, and he chewed the blossom like a cow.

"When did you learn that?" I asked.

"I may have found Edvarg's book of spells in his desk." His head dropped to the side. "Can I bother anyone for a horse, or a cart, or maybe you could wrap me in a blanket and carry me like a wee baby?"

"I've got you," Ryo said, wrapping his arm under Grig's shoulder. He lifted him easily. "I left my horse at the stables. Do you think they're still there?"

Oh, he was asking me. I ripped my gaze away from his rippling arm muscles. "Probably."

I turned away quickly and almost ran into a dead priest.

"Watch where you are going, dude," I said, not embarrassed at all. Stables. Stables.

Find stables. Thank you, Pathfinding arrow, for working when my brain just wasn't. I didn't even think to loot the dead priests.

We made our way to the horses, and then out of the city to a hill overlooking the castle. Grigfen drooped forward on his horse, but he was sitting steady enough that I didn't worry about the galloping. We made it out. The twin moons lit the city with my hope. The sky had brightened, morning on its way. Whirligigs scanned the streets for us. The docks were full of ships ready to flee the kingdom before the Savak came to claim what we'd given them. And the empty castle glowed like a candle left in a window.

Ryo's throat bobbed.

"We'll come back," I said. "This isn't a forever goodbye."

Ryo met my eyes. A lie was not a lie if it was kind.

Truth was, there was no guarantee we'd make it back here. But we would get Ryo home.

Nao Takagi asked me to.

I searched the tree-covered hilltop. We had the gloves, so we should get the Traveling Boots next. From my understanding, they were like Seven League Boots and would help us collect the items faster.

The words *Retrieve the Traveling Boots* scrolled across my game vision in glowing yellow light.

The arrow at the top of my vision shifted and pointed east, away from the city.

"This way," I said.

Their horses followed my lead. I didn't look back, but Ryo did. He kept checking for the spires of the castle until we were too far away and the mountains had swallowed the city.

A fox darted across our path. The moons-light kissed wildflowers, and branches swayed in a gentle, dawn-breaking breeze. We traveled until we found a clearing with a rock circle, the perfect place to make camp. We needed to rest and heal up a bit if we wanted to make it to the boots. I was starving, and tired, and my butt hurt from sitting on the horse, and it was a game, so I shouldn't be feeling any of that.

WHO THOUGHT IT WAS A GOOD IDEA TO GIVE US PAIN RECEPTORS?

"I'll hunt," Grig said as he dismounted. He still seemed tired, but not like he couldn't carry his own weight anymore. "I can hear some vultures chewing on some bones not ten paces from here."

"Creepy." I dropped my bag and threw him a spare hunting knife. He caught it.

"We'll need to gather some supplies tomorrow," I said. The arrow spun west.

Side quest—find peddler wagon ran past my vision.

"I'll start a fire," Ryo said.

I knelt next to my bag. I needed to take inventory if we were going to trade in the morning.

I pulled out the blanket that had been on that wire frame bed in my father's tunnel. We had fifteen gold coins, a jar of peaches, the signed contract, strikers, my old boots, seven knives, and a pouch of hibisi blossoms. I needed to be on the hunt for more treasure chests. Maybe we could look in the morning, after we'd rested enough to sleep off our aches.

Or afternoon. Dawn had painted the sky a warm yellow. A line of white ran straight up the sunrise, like a crack on a phone screen.

One error in a perfect world. I didn't know when it appeared, but it was there now. Proof that this world wasn't real. The source code was beginning to corrupt. A chill ran up my neck. I wrapped the blanket around my shoulders and turned my back to the cracked sky.

Ryo searched the underbrush, a handful of small branches in one hand.

He seemed so focused, his eyebrows furrowed.

I leaned back. "How does a prince know how to start a fire?"

"I'm capable of far more than you give me credit," he said. He snapped a branch in his bare hands and wouldn't look at me.

I folded my legs under me. "I'm sorry." I sighed. I'd called him all sorts of names. I'd become exactly the kind of bully I hated. "I've been really scared and angry and I guess I took it out on you."

"It's all right. In truth, I wouldn't have gotten through this without you. Whatever *this* is." He glanced at the sky and then back at the branches in his grip.

"You're handling all this better than I expected." There was so much he couldn't understand.

He broke the branches and placed them in the firepit. "Despite not drinking the seer water?"

I grinned. His eyes softened. But I turned back to my inventory as if this jar of peaches I'd found in my father's tunnel were fascinating.

If he drank the seer water, then he'd remember who I really was.

Before the game started I'd caught him arguing with his mother in the hallways of Stonebright Studios. At the time, Nao Takagi was my hero, and he seemed so ungrateful for this chance I'd fought so hard for, so when he stalked past me, I shoved my shoulder into his. He'd looked me up and down and sneered so dismissively.

Once he drank seer water, he'd stop flirting with me.

Which was clearly what I wanted.

I stood and hunted around the campsite for anything promising.

Some kind of environmental decor that also held items inside, like a treasure chest, or a barrel, or . . . A glint of light sparked within a large hollow log. Great. I really wanted to smash something. I kicked the thing harder than necessary, and it shattered into chunks of wood pieces.

Inside, I found a frying pan. Score.

I loaded the shattered wooden pieces in the pan and carried it back to the fire.

"Here," I said.

He leaned back. "Perfect." He assembled the wood pieces into a tepee, with kindling and underbrush underneath.

I grabbed a striker from my bag, or match, I guess, and gave it to him.

He slid the striker against the stone circle. The fire lit his cheekbones with a warm yellow glow. Then he lit the kindling with no trace of hesitation.

This wasn't his first time making a fire. "You go camping a lot?"

He bent on all fours and watched the flame take hold. He blew softly on the fire, and the wood caught.

"Often as a child." He sat up. "Not as often as of late. My father and I would scout locations in case of a Savak attack."

"Of course." I sighed. These memories weren't true, just a past planted to make the game more immersive.

Ryo sat next to me on a log, his focus on the flames. "I loved it. We'd catch fish in a stream, and at night we'd sleep under blankets like peasants. And as the stars woke, my father would tell me stories under the light of the moon."

He cleared his throat and stared into the rippling flames.

Moon. Singular. How much of that memory was real?

He waggled his eyebrows. "Though it wasn't this romantic."

I shoved his shoulder with my own. "Two whole minutes as a human being. That's a new record."

"All hail the triumphant victor!" Grigfen shouted from the wood. He lifted a dead bird by its claws.

"Well done." I left the blanket at Ryo's side and took the bird from him.

Ick. I placed the bird, feathers and all, on the pan, poured some of the peach juice, sprinkled a few sprigs of pine into the pan, and shoved the thing in the fire.

The flames overtook the bird and the space filled with smoke. When the choking gray cleared, the bird looked like something Martha Stewart would serve for Thanksgiving. If only cooking was this easy in real life. My dad and I tried to make Thanksgiving dinner last year and we nearly burned the whole house down.

I used the blanket as a potholder around the handle and placed the cooked bird on a rock. The pan was barely warm. You'd think it would be burning hot, but crafting never made much logical sense. I pulled off a leg and took a bite.

That bird was the most delicious thing I'd ever had.

"Anyone care for a ghost story?" Grig asked.

I rolled my eyes. "You are so on brand it's ridiculous."

Ryo licked his fingers. "Yes, I've had quite my fill of ghosts for the time being."

Grig laughed and then grabbed the other vulture leg and made his way to the other side of the fire. "So what I'm hearing is that you are looking for a ghost story."

I sat back on the grass and offered the blanket to Ryo. He'd had the worst time of the game so far, and he needed comfort more than any of us.

His expression seemed guarded. "It's all right, Dagney. This cloak is not only the most hideous thing I've ever seen, it also doubles as a wool blanket."

Oh. I took the last bit of meat from the bone. Why would I be disappointed? I threw the bones in the fire.

Grig lit a sphere of ghostlight below his face like it was a flashlight. Dork.

"It is pitch-dark," he said, "and you are likely to be eaten by a grue."

I stood. "I'm going to sleep." I scouted for a spot with the fewest number of stones and plucked the empty bag to use as a pillow.

"I think I'll join you," Ryo said as he crossed to the other side of the fire from me.

I punched the bag to make it softer and covered myself with the blanket.

"No stories this time, then," Grig said. "That's fine. My feelings aren't hurt at all."

"Grig," Ryo said.

"No, no. You rest up. I'll take first watch."

"Are you sure?" I asked.

"I napped on the horse. I'll wake you if I get too puggled."

Okay, if he was sure.

I lay my head back on the bag but didn't close my eyes. The encroaching dawn had brightened the sky. The sunlight sent an unearthly red glow over everything it touched. A river of soft green grass waved in a gentle breeze. Each blade slightly different, each blade drawn with precision. How much time went into designing each blade of grass? How much time had Ms. Takagi spent on this game that was trying to kill us?

Grigfen hummed and Ryo . . .

Across the flickering fire, Ryo lay with his back to me. He didn't make eyes I could ignore. He didn't try to make a pass I would shut down. He slept as though I were just another teammate on this adventure.

I grumbled under my breath. That was exactly what I wanted. He treated me as an equal. I'm glad he'd listened when I told him I didn't want any flirting.

Stupid boys making me feel weird ways about them.

Ryo rustled a little. Then he stilled and his breaths grew even.

I glanced over. My heartbeat roared behind my ears. Louder than it had when we were in danger, louder than when I'd crossed that bridge.

But he never looked back my way.

It took a long time for my heartbeat to slow enough so I could fall asleep.

And when I woke a Whirligig hovered over my head.

I changed my mind. I hated everything.

14
GRIGFEN

The crick in my neck almost woke me.

It stirred my dreaming, breaking the darkness behind my closed eyes. Dark like an unlit laptop screen, startup memory humming, ready to start up a new game, or load a new world, or best of all, seconds away from seeing my Bluebird again.

She'd smile, tuck a strand of tightly curled hair behind her ear, and say, "Hi, Grig."

And I'd melt into a lumpy puddle all over my keyboard.

Sunlight burned my cheek, but I didn't wake. Gears squeaked and wings hummed, but I kept my eyes closed.

"Help me!" Dagney shouted. And that did it. My head bonked against something hard and splintery, like wood.

I opened my eyes.

Spoiler alert, it was wood.

I'd apparently not kept as good a watch as I'd hoped, because I'd fallen asleep next to a tree, and now something metal and round floated right over my sister's head.

I sat up. The mist that covered the forest around me should not have been green. It should not have glowed like ghostlight, or have sung an undead song. While I'd slept, I'd drawn ghosts to me. Soft spirits of deer, birds, and bears nestled around my legs and slept by my side.

And those ghosts had drawn a Whirligig to suck them up. And the Whirligig had brought two Whirligig friends, floating behind it in the fog.

I leapt to my feet and touched the red prayer dots down the line of my nose.

Let's show these things what a Devout could do. I cracked my knuckles and threw my open hands in front of me like I was trying to catch a ball. The ghostly beasties at my side woke. Their bones, ripped from the forest behind, came to a hover in the air in front of me.

Meanwhile, Dagney had flung her massive bag up over the Whirligig above her head and tackled it to the ground, holding it down with the handles. The bag squeaked and beeped, rustling against the leather as she cursed the thing out.

One of the other two Whirligigs' ghostlight flashed red as it scanned the mist with a sharp beam. Only the beam wasn't coming *from* it, it was sucking the light into it. A ghostly bunny looking at me with its endless eyes twitched its little bunny nose, then its ghost was gone, sucked inside the Whirligig.

Not my ghostly bunnies! I hummed the words of a hymn and shot bones at the machine. They thudded and cracked the metal.

Boom, you garbage machine.

Something creaked, and then small metallic arms and swirling knives folded out, spinning like an oscillating fan with sharpened blades.

Aw bollocks. "Ryo!" I shouted. Why hadn't all our noise woken him?

He jolted awake. He plucked his sword from the ground next to him and raised the thing.

"Don't hurt them," Dagney said. "We can sell them!"

I sighed. Exactly the kind of thing a Merchant class *would* think about a spinning death machine.

The Whirligig I'd struck came straight for me, blades spinning and slicing at me like I was a loaf of bread. I jumped backward, the blades barely missing my robes and cutting my arm. Och.

I slid my robes over my shoulder so my hands were free and shot a burst of bones into the gears. They spluttered until the gyroscope inside it stalled. It crashed to the ground.

I stomped it with my boot. "You're going to have to sell this one for parts."

Across the firepit, Ryo's sword clanged against the metal of the other Whirligig, its whirling blades slicing sparks against his sword.

A ghostly bear nudged its head against my arm. "Go on, bear."

I gestured forward, and the bear leapt over Ryo, swatting the machine to the ground in a burst of ghostwind. The Whirligig crashed and the ghostly bear played with the thing within its translucent paws and ripped pieces of metal with its teeth, spitting and clawing, until the ghostlight at the center broke free and back into the mist. The gears stopped spinning.

Good beastie.

Dagney wrestled with her bag. "I'm going to need your Charisma now, Ryo."

He lowered his sword and crossed to her side. "What can I do?"

"The Mechani serve the royal family, so this thing is programmed to follow your instructions. If you can reset it, it'll be worth a lot more with the peddler; maybe we could even get a better sword or two for it."

"A battle-axe would be grand," I said.

"I call dibs," Dagney said. She gave us both a look. "Don't destroy it."

Once satisfied, she opened her bag. The Whirligig emerged, slightly frazzled, red tinted light dim inside its gears, gyroscope spinning slowly as it searched about for an attack.

I held my ghosties back, but ready.

Ryo placed his hand against the metal. "It's all right," he murmured. "Nothing's going to hurt you. I'm Prince Ryo. My mother is very proud of her Whirligigs. I know you're simply doing your job."

"Your mother is the head of the Mechani?" Dagney said.

Ryo shrugged. "All my secrets find their way out around you."

The red light inside the Whirligig shifted ghostlight green, and then Ryo's purple. His XP raised.

He tickled under the Whirligig's base. "It's kind of adorable. In a stabbing kind of way."

I cocked a grin. "Your favorite kind of adorable, innit?"

Ryo cleared his throat and I snorted. Teasing these two was a particular joy.

"Well, I'm sufficiently rested." Ryo retrieved his horse's reins. "You want to come with us, Pumpkin?"

Dagney adjusted her dress. "No, we can't keep it. That thing is a battle-axe with my name on it, and if you get attached, then I won't get it."

It fluttered its wings over to Dagney and spun its gyros prettily.

Ryo followed. "She doesn't mean that, Pumpkin. You're more than your value."

I gestured the ghosties back into their forest. "Did you name it?"

"No. It is not a pet!" Dagney curled her fists. Ryo grinned at her and her hands uncurled. "Oh, you're teasing me again."

"Never." He usually smiled at me after a teasing or a prank, but I might as well not have been there.

"You are just teasing, right?" she asked.

"Nothing I do is ever serious, Lady Dagney." He climbed on his saddle. "This way, wasn't it?"

"West!" Dagney collected her items back in her bag.

The Whirligig hovered over Ryo's shoulder as he turned his horse into the afternoon woods.

I picked up a pair of boots and handed them to Dagney to repack in her bag. "I'd have named the thing Artoo."

"It's not a pet." She shoved the rest of our items in her bag and huffed away. "Do not get attached!"

"Too late for that, innit?" I said with a pointed look at Ryo's back.

"No." She shook her head. "I don't know what you're talking about."

"I'm talking about you having the hots for—Ow!" I rubbed my arm. "I'm telling Da you punched me." I grinned.

She shook her fist and stepped up into the stirrups and then kicked her leg over the plain brown horse. "Nothing is happening. You don't have to worry about me."

I pet the neck of the gentle horse I'd napped on earlier. She was black with a speckling of white spots on her hindquarters.

I mounted my horse and nudged her with my heels, following after Ryo. "I'm not worried about you; I'm worried about him. I don't know how many of these memories are true, but I'm the same person I was before the game, and I think he is too. And I've never seen him like this before. You can't see the way he looks at you, but his heart is not something you can sell, or stab—"

"You know nothing about me."

"No?" I had so many memories of her. Memories I'd never lived. But somehow I remembered standing outside her door and knocking after some bastard from the court had made fun of her. I remembered her tears as she opened the door, her stubborn refusal to tell me who it was. I remembered the day she stopped crying, the day she stopped coming with me no matter how I'd asked. "So I don't know that you've been bullied enough to grow spikes, but inside you have a gooey center?"

She scowled. "Nothing is happening, because he doesn't even know me. This"—she pointed at her body—"isn't the real me."

I didn't know what to say to help her here. "I've seen the real you, and you're quite fetching."

"I know! I like who I am. I'm fine. Don't talk to me about this stuff."

I sighed and dropped the subject. This was a bigger issue than I could help her with in one conversation.

"All I want is for us all to get out." I lifted a branch for her to guide her horse under. "But there's no guarantee here. Look at the sky. The source code has corrupted. They should have woken us instead of sending messages through the seer water. We shouldn't still be here."

She paled. "So since we might all die, we should all make out while we still can?"

"Ew. Dagney. Gross. I'm your brother; you can't say things like that around me."

She snorted.

The sun lit the trees and glowed against Ryo's loyal Whirligig. It felt like he stood at the edge of a cliff, and I didn't like being this far away from him.

But Dagney needed a push.

I stopped walking and she turned. "I just lost my granddad." I let out a heavy breath. "And the thing about losing people, what hurts the most, isn't that I loved him. It's all the times I chose not to."

She stared at the trees.

I nudged her arm. "Take the risk, love." She stared after Ryo and bit her lip.

I grinned, tapped my heels so the horse moved to a gallop, and caught up with Ryo. Dagney's horse trailed after us.

In the woods, beneath a pine tree, a Historian stood. I believed she was the same one from the catacombs. She raised her hands like she was telling us to stop.

I tugged Ryo's arm.

Dagney joined us, taking Ryo's other flank.

The Historian pulled a branch from a tree and wrote in the dirt with the stick. I dismounted and stepped forward.

Lurcher twenty steps west. Go around.

It was nice of her to give us a warning. And that shortcut in the Abbey gave us loads of breathing time. Whoever she was, she was trying to help us. So heartbeat of mine, calm yourself.

"Hello," I said softly.

She lifted her hand to below her chest and wiggled her fingers in a small wave.

I inhaled sharply.

Ryo and Dagney moved closer.

But I almost sprinted. It was her. It had to be. I pulled off her mask. Behind the mask was a blank silver sphere. No eyes. No mouth.

But I recognized the way she moved her hands.

"Bluebird?" I asked.

Static interrupted her feed, sending sparks across her raven feathers. She disappeared in a rip of lightning and I was left holding the carved mask.

15

BLUEBIRD_OFDEATH

The sudden exit shook my processors.

"No, no, no, no, no, no, no," I muttered. I rolled my wheelchair to my third computer and typed as quickly as I could.

My VR glasses blurred like I'd stepped back through a window. I adjusted my visor, flexed my hands in the sensor gloves, and turned up the volume, but the game had shut me out again. The best I could do was smudge my nose against the barrier.

I should have been using real equipment, controls that tingled in my hands. If I had the real stuff, I'd be able to help him, but I'd had the bright idea to tell my parents.

It was one thing to sneak off to the studios for testing, because I lived local, so I could take the bus home every night. But once the game started, I'd have been away full-time for nearly a month. I didn't want my family to worry, or drag me back home.

But that's exactly what they did. Right in the middle of the selection party. I'd rolled out to gather my awkward self because I knew I was about to actually meet Grigfen for the first time and the idea made my insides go all *woohawoohawoohah*, and there were my parents, mad as I'd ever seen them.

I didn't even get the chance to meet Grig.

I pulled off the duct tape and the homemade diodes stuck to my temples. I blinked a couple of times in order to see my bedroom. This was real life, where my subscriptions to *Wired* and *Teen Vogue* were delivered, and where I hid a twelve-pack of Mountain Dew under my desk. The world of the game was such vivid multicolor that real life was stick-figure scribbles in comparison.

Maybe that was because Grig was still in there.

Or, you know, maybe it was the drab, gray paint color I'd chosen for my bedroom. Mom had punched it up with a teal comforter and designer accessories, but the only thing I liked about my room were the decoupage birds hanging from the ceiling that I'd hot glued plastic vampire teeth on.

Those were pretty rad.

What had kicked me out of the game?

The scrambler should have hidden my whereabouts, but the securities team at Stonebright wasn't like my online school's private server, and I really wasn't trained for this.

But I'd set up a warning system to guard for the team at Stonebright, and none of my sirens had gone off. Not sure if that was a good thing or a bad thing. If it was a good thing, I was a hacking genius and no one knew what I was doing. Bad thing, they'd already found me and I'd have no warning.

It was the Schrödinger's cat of good/bad things.

Someone knocked on my door.

"Not now, Mom! I'm in the middle of something." I was pretty sure I could check for—

"Zoe?!" It was my sister.

She rapped on the door again and I lost all my civility. "I swear on a stack of comics, if you bang on the door one more time I'm . . ." I rolled my wheelchair to unlock my fortress of solitude and slushies with the clear intent to break my big sister's pretty white teeth.

Except.

Oh no.

It wasn't just Abigail at the door.

Nao Freaking Takagi stood next to her.

I blinked.

There was a good chance my parents might find out about the overages on my data plan.

I gripped my power chair controller and rolled my chair backward. Nao Freaking Takagi folded her arms. Strands of hair slipped from her loose braid and her elegant blouse wrinkled at the waist, but compared to my stained pajama pants and tank top, she seemed way too fancy for my suburban bedroom.

"Bluebird of Death, I presume."

OH MY GALAGA, NAO FREAKING TAKAGI KNOWS MY NAME.

Breathe, Bluebird. Now was not the time to ask for a selfie.

"May I come in?" Nao F. Takagi asked.

A tiny part of me realized I'd yet to move or speak, and that was what the cool kids call social ineptitude, so I twitched a nod and rolled out of her way. "Hello, Ms. Takagi. May I ask what this visit is . . . okay, no there's no way you're going to buy that. If you're here in my house then you know who I am, and what I've done, so I'm going to stop talking now, or now adjacent, and aw dang, is that the head of security?"

Yup. Totally that was the massive muscle-having suit-wearing head of Stonebright's security. In my hallway.

Silver lining: not the feds.

Nao F. Takagi entered the fortress of solitude and slushies and plucked the diode I'd made with my soldering iron from my sloppy desk. I wiped my nose with my thumb as she opened my laptop. It popped to life right on the feed of Grig's face.

And that was not embarrassing at all.

Nao F. Takagi smiled. "I'd thought it was a shame when your parents refused to sign the release form and pulled you from the game, but now I'm grateful."

"You're not mad? I broke into your game."

"Why would I be mad? You've only done what I've been trying to do. The source code glitch blocked all my back doors. Except one. Because your character was coded into the game, you're the only one who has been able to break in. And now I need your help."

I pulled my pajama pants to the side in a curtsy. Not too shabby for a self-taught sixteen-year-old.

"Zoe?" Mom interrupted from the doorway. She wore her work clothes, freshly glossed lips, and an expression that could melt a hard drive. "Why is there a bearded white man in my front room?" She paused when she saw I wasn't alone. She offered Ms. Takagi a hand and a warm fake smile. "Hello. I'm Zoe's mother, and who might you be?"

Mom didn't seem to notice the cover of *Wired* magazine stapled to the wall with Ms. Takagi's mirror image on it.

"I'm Nao Takagi." Ms. Takagi met warm smile for warm smile. "We spoke quite forcefully on the phone a week ago."

Mom lost the game of Fake Smile Chicken. "Oh. You're from that game?"

"Yes, the one your daughter is still so very interested in." Ms. Takagi turned the laptop until the screen faced my mother. Oh no. "I'm here to offer your daughter an internship at my company, as clemency for a series of crimes she's committed against us, including—"

An internship? "There's no need to give a laundry list of—"

"Theft, breaking digital copyright protections, securities fraud, and lying on an entrance form."

I clenched my eyes closed. "Technically that's not illegal."

Ms. Takagi raised a polished eyebrow. "It's an opportunity of a lifetime. Our internship programs feeds right into the company and into top colleges. We have thousands of applicants, and Zoe was among the final selection. And the fact she's been able to hack around our security system makes it clear we either recruit her now, or we'll all work for her later."

My mom stared at me. "But she's sixteen. And—"

Ms. Takagi's eyes tightened. "Exactly. It's quite an accomplishment. I've personally read her transcripts. She's not being challenged by her online school. This is an opportunity for her to reach her full potential. Of course if you prefer, she can face the charges against her."

Funny, the articles didn't mention Ms. Takagi dabbled in blackmail.

My mother folded her arms. It would take more than this to threaten a black mom with a disabled child. "Is this dangerous?"

I wanted to know the answer to that one too.

Ms. Takagi laughed. "Of course it isn't dangerous. It's training to become a video game designer. She's a smart girl." *She's right here.* I didn't say anything, though, because I was penciling these compliments into my dream journal. "I believe we've caught her at a crossroads between a possible life of cybercrime and a chance at an extraordinary career. But as she's a minor, she will need your permission."

Good luck, Ms. Takagi.

Mom pinched her lips. "How long would she be gone?"

Halle-fricken-lujah. "Just twelve days, Mom."

Ms. Takagi shook her head. "Three days at most. It's a weekend immersion program, where she'll shadow some of the best in her field. She'll stay in our on-campus housing with world-class medical facilities. And of course she'll be permitted as much contact with you as you would like."

I shot her a look. There should be twelve days until the game shut down.

Ms. Takagi wouldn't meet my eyes.

This was worse than I expected . . .

I propped up my elbow on my desk and pushed up my glasses. "I want to go, Mom. This game. I can't even explain how much I love it, how hard I've worked to try to be a part of it, and to be right there watching how they do it will teach me more than years at college. Please. It's three days, and it could change my whole life. You always tell me that there's nothing I can't do. Please let me do this."

My mom closed her eyes and tapped her fingers against her legs. Behind her Ms. Takagi clenched her hands tight.

Mom opened her eyes and moved toward me. "I don't like that you broke the law, Zoe. This is not a reward, and we will be talking about the consequences when you get back." I nodded and she smiled. "Then, if you want to, I give my permission."

Just kidding. She didn't say that. It took about twenty minutes of pure flattery on Ms. Takagi's part, and about twenty minutes of me reminding my mom that opportunities like this one were limited before she finally relented.

I swallowed. But I couldn't take it back. I wanted to be the one to save Grig. And I could see the pride in my mom's eyes. Usually she saw me as something fragile. My mom told me I could be anything I wanted to be, but she always seemed so surprised whenever I tried.

I turned to Ms. Takagi. "I would love to help with this very serious project. Thank you for your kind offer."

"Good. Welcome to the team."

She left to speak with the head of security, and my mom bent and kissed my forehead.

"Mom," I said.

"Oh, sorry." Mom rubbed the lip gloss off my forehead because I couldn't take it off without a mirror and somewhere to prop my elbow.

"Zoe?" Ms. Takagi called.

Apparently they wanted me to start right now.

That wasn't worry making at all.

———

Nao Freaking Takagi opened the rear door to her luxury SUV and tossed my bag into the back. I grasped the powerchair controller and drove from the front door down the ramp toward the vehicle. My mom and sister waved at me from the door, while the head of security watched me like he'd like to lock me up for breaking through their technical defenses. I thought, briefly, of abandoning my duffel bag and rolling back into my mommy's arms. How much did I like those clothes?

"Do you need help?" Ms. Takagi asked me when my chair stopped a few feet away from the door. My parents usually parked in the driveway, and when my friends picked me up, usually someone offered an arm to lean on. But getting help from Ms. Takagi meant admitting to my idol Ms. Takagi that I needed help. I thought about Grig and sighed. Every time I think I've spent the last of my pride, it reanimates in time to pay up again.

"Yeah." The step from the curb to the SUV was a little too far for me to climb in by myself. I planted my feet on the ground and struggled to bear my body weight through my unsteady legs. Ms. Takagi pressed her hand at my back as I walked. I gripped the door to hold me steady, but my knees buckled beneath me and I half fell into the seat from the force.

I wouldn't get top scores for the landing, but I'd made it into the car. Mostly.

"Can I help you in anyway? Perhaps lift your legs into the car?" she offered, because clearly she'd noticed how tired the transfer had made me.

I could have done it. I still have that ability, but the exertion necessary would mean I wouldn't have the energy I'd need later.

"Yes," I said, resigned. "Thank you."

She lifted my feet into the car. I settled into the passenger seat as she pulled the seat belt down. I grabbed it once it was low enough and fastened it myself. I watched as Ms. Takagi pushed my wheelchair to the back of the SUV. My mom couldn't help herself and all but ran down the driveway to take over. A slight tension in my neck relaxed. My wheelchair, which I called Voyager, both for the NASA implications, and also for Star Trek reasons, was more expensive than my dad's car and the idea that it could be damaged set my already nervous system into hyperdrive. Voyager was my ticket to freedom; it was like another part of me. My mom made sure it was loaded correctly and that the extra battery was charged, and then she had to come kiss my cheek one more time and to ask about the level of care at the facility and if they'd have any mobility devices ready and then about the accessibility of Stonebright's campus and seriously she would never let us leave.

"Mom," I said. If she kept talking, she would talk herself out of letting me go. "I'm fine."

She stood and waved as Ms. Takagi shut her door.

We nodded at each other, both of us trying to hide our nerves.

The car hummed and pulled forward, blasting pop music from the radio. Ms. Takagi always seemed so posh and elegant. Weird she'd be so interested in a former member of a boy band. The head of security followed behind us in a shiny car.

"What's really happening?" I asked.

Her knuckles tightened around the steering wheel. "There's something wrong with the game. The source code has corrupted and now the players are trapped. At first I could get in. As soon as I realized the source code was deteriorating, I found a back door and tried to get Ryo out. Instead, I had to watch him die in the game. I watched my game hurt him, as the code corrupted even more. Eventually I couldn't get back in, so I found another back door and sent a message through seer water to the next player to drink. But now even that back door has closed."

"It's okay, Ms. Takagi. I can still get in. And with your equipment, your *gloriously not duct-taped equipment*, I can do whatever you need."

"There's a chance you'll get stuck in the game as well." Her eyes clouded. "There's a chance this could kill you."

"What?"

She turned away. "There are so many lives to protect. I'm doing everything possible to get everyone out. But if you keep breaking in without our assistance, you will damage the source code further."

I stared at the passing streets, hoping it was the speed that blurred the buildings and not tears.

"You're so young. If there was any other choice, I'd keep you out of this. The last thing I want is to put another life at risk. I've tried to take over your avatar, but it's biocoded to you. You are the only one who can get in there and help. I need you to go in there and give them a message. Ryo needs to drink the seer water and get game vision. I'll help you. You won't have to go through my security system. The team thinks we'll be able to give your avatar the ability to speak. I'll pull you out right after. If you get stuck in the game, you could be affected by the same glitch. There's a chance you could feel pain. And if you do, there's a chance that you could die."

I swallowed. I'd faced worse odds every day of my life. "I want to help. I'll be safe."

She looked down at her hands. "But . . ."

I filled in those dots. "I have muscular dystrophy."

"That only means I want to protect you more."

I leaned back. They thought when I was younger I was only a carrier of the gene, but once I became symptomatic, everyone started treating me with kid gloves. When I was twelve, the muscles in my shoulders weakened until I could no longer raise my hands over my head. I used leg braces for a while, but then when my muscles wasted to the point where I couldn't walk for more than ten minutes, I found my freedom in a wheelchair my mom had painted bright yellow.

I swear to Galaga, sometimes that's the only thing people ever see of me.

"I want to help," I said more softly.

Neither of us had much to say for the rest of the drive.

— — —

I'd been to Stonebright Studios before.

It was different coming here with the owner of the company and the head of security. At the entrance the focus was on Ms. Takagi, so I could check out the tech on desks, but as we moved deeper into the belly of the building, the lab coat people stopped watching Ms. Takagi, and their attention switched to the black girl in a wheelchair following behind her.

Meaning me.

Meaning everyone needed to turn their attention back to their own papers, thankyouverymuch.

I'd stepped inside the firewall now. And everyone I saw was doing everything possible to keep the players safe.

But they were also doing everything they could to keep this secret. The front desk had private security manning the doors, phone check-in, and full body scanners in front of the entrance.

The mood was somber. Urgent. Screens showed the game play of the world, places I'd stepped a virtual foot in and so many societies and side quests I hadn't taken. I'd located Grig and read the code around him, but I hadn't searched any of the other players. There were two with the Kneult, two with the Savak, and . . .

Where were the rest of the players?

Ms. Takagi cleared her throat.

I lowered my gaze to the ground and slipped behind her into her office. The ceiling of her office was impossibly high, with one wall made of glass and the city beyond it. At the center, a steel-framed chair glowed—her own personal gaming pod. There were massive monitors on the other three walls, two showing views of the game, the other four split to show different camera angles of her building.

And I thought I was paranoid.

"Here is where you'll plug in. This is where I plugged in to play a Historian," she said. "The restroom is through here, and there's plenty of food in the mini-fridge."

She touched the screen and the camera on her own office enlarged to full screen.

I touched the diodes and the visors. The tech in this room was a thing of beauty.

A white man knocked on the open door. I remembered him. Preston something. It'd be hard to forget someone so meticulous, from the sharp part in his hair, to his tailored suit and his trimmed nails. He was the CFO of Stonebright and he intimidated the crap out of me.

He cleared his throat. "Now, before you panic—"

A woman in scrubs broke into the conversation, and into the room. "We lost another one."

Wait.

Everyone in Ms. Takagi's office quieted.

"Who?" Ms. Takagi asked.

"Not Ryo. Sylvania."

Ms. Takagi pressed a fist into her stomach and her shoulders curved in. "*No.* Have you notified her parents?"

A chill ran up my neck. Her parents?

"No," the CFO said. "Of course we haven't."

What was happening? Warmth burned my eyes, but my thoughts were frozen. I turned machine, recording everything without processing it.

"They need to know. We can't be the only parents—"

The CFO touched her arm. "As soon as we alert the parents, they will call the police. Any investigation will be a distraction from getting our kids out. Our stock eval—"

My insides turned to ice.

"I don't care about stocks," Ms. Takagi said. "Any success in slowing the damage?"

He shook his head.

I rolled back against the machine and something crashed.

I fought my own mouth for words. "How many?"

Ms. Takagi lowered her chin. "Sylvania makes five."

"FIVE?!"

"Of the twelve players selected, only seven are still alive." Ms. Takagi's voice held the weight of the world.

But it wasn't her world. It was mine. I knew their faces. I'd smiled at them. I'd beaten them at video games. We were the final twelve, and five of us were gone.

Sylvania had taken my place. She was unlucky number thirteen, the one just close enough to miss it.

Maybe there was something wrong with me, because when I heard the news, I didn't cry. Those tears that stung my eyelids didn't fall. I was numb. It couldn't . . . Video games didn't kill people. Games were a safe place where I could be myself, and be excellent. They were killing people? That was as wrong as someone saying sunscreen causes skin cancer. Video games were there to protect me.

They were my friend. Sometimes my only friend.

And they betrayed me.

Now the tears fell. "How did they die?"

"You don't need to worry about that," the CFO answered.

"TELL ME. I want every bit of information you have. Don't sugarcoat it, or dumb it down. I want the declassified truth or I'll find it myself."

Ms. Takagi stared at the screen. "They die of pain."

The doctor stepped forward. "The coded pain becomes lethal due to the effects on the heart, blood pressure, and release of stress hormones." She had to pause to breathe again. I still couldn't. "We officially list the death as cardiopulmonary arrest, or medullary hyperstimulation."

"So when they die in the game, they really . . ."

If I hadn't called my parents, Sylvania never would have gotten in.

"None of this is your fault," the doctor said.

She was wrong. Grig wouldn't be here if it wasn't for me.

He could die. They all could.

"Why three days?"

Ms. Takagi blinked slowly. "That's when we estimate the source code will fail completely."

I shook my head. "Can you give them extra lives, like you did Ryo?"

She shook her head. "That was before the game launched. I've tried. We're all trying. But I only gave extra lives to Ryo, and now the code is too fragile to change."

I pressed my shaking hand against my stomach. "Can I see them?"

Ms. Takagi clicked on the keyboard and the screen switched to the launch rooms.

I'd thought the slick metal sphere in the center of the room had looked so cool before, but now the flickering lights seemed menacing, like lightning sparking through a cloud. Seven doctors in lab coats surrounded a few of the pods, but they ignored the five empty ones.

That was all I saw at first. The players who weren't here. Then my focus shifted to those who could still survive.

Four boys and three girls.

"Pull them out," I said.

"We can't."

My voice broke. "Why not?"

"They didn't all die inside the game. After the first death, we pulled Jefferson out. And he . . ." Ms. Takagi turned slightly green.

My lungs tightened until they wouldn't expand. "I don't want to know."

I'd never said those words before. Not once. But now it was the only thing running circles in my mind.

Grig's blond hair curled against his scalp, wet with sweat. He looked pale and too thin, his eyelids sunken and his skin tinted yellow. I tried to match the faces in all the other beds with the people I'd met in the game: Dagney's sharp eyebrows, dark hair, and large curves; Marcus's pale freckled skin. It was hard to see anything of Ryo except for a shock of black hair; he was so covered in wires and tubes. His face was slick with sweat. His body shook like an addict in withdrawal.

If there was a sixth death, it would be his.

"What can I do?"

Ms. Takagi pried her gaze away from her son. "I know my stubborn son. I had a character tell him not to drink the seer water until he was further along, because I was worried he'd quit, but he needs it now. They all do. You will not be hooked into the pain signals. I will not allow another young person to risk their life for this game. Tell him to drink, and then log out immediately."

Grig's lips twitched.

She tapped my arm. "We need you to come back." She leveled her gaze. "I need you to save my son. But do not risk your own life to do it."

I bit my lip and then I nodded. "Strap me in."

16
RYO

The peddler carts circled the middle of an open field. They were a lively bunch, children playing with a mechanical spinner, fiddles humming, food and drink at the ready. Supper was some sort of rabbit. My stomach rumbled. It'd been a long time since the vulture.

Perhaps that was what gave me this headache.

We emerged from the trees. "We are here to trade," Dagney announced.

The peddlers stood and the camp came alive at her words. Children were tucked away and a fiddler began to play soft looping music as a few cart fronts opened.

Fresh clothing. Was there anything more beautiful?

Dagney followed me. "Grig, can you walk around the carts? I'm looking for healing, armor, weapons, and any gossip."

"Right."

I touched a silk shirt, and Dagney led me away toward a few weapons while Grigfen took the other way around. Pumpkin floated after us.

The peddler woman smiled warmly as we approached. She sold weapons: swords, daggers, arrows. Dagney went straight for a battle-axe.

"This looks . . . fine," she said, her jaw held tight, as though she were trying to hide how bright her eyes lit when she saw it.

I snorted.

Dagney grabbed a bronze sword. "Be nice, or I won't get you any-thing." She tested the balance, her eyebrows furrowed.

"I like that sword." I opened my palm so she'd hand it to me.

"Thanks." The point of her lip turned up. "Find one for yourself."

But I'd thought . . . it didn't matter. Hmm. Which sword?

Ooh, jeweled handle. Beautiful.

"No," Dagney said, taking the jeweled handle out of my hand. She grabbed a warrior's sword instead. It was finely made, but . . . plain.

Dagney studied the wagons. "Let's get you some armor."

"I support this mission completely. I will not abide the itching of this foul cloak any longer."

"Don't mock my father's cloak." The crease between her eyebrows deepened. "Your charisma could really help us get a good deal here. So try to be charming."

I scoffed. "You think I have to try."

"Hello!" Dagney said in her prettiest voice. A group of children flocked around us, tugging at my cloak, reaching for my coins.

I touched the Whirligig. "Play mode." I grinned at the children. "If you hide, Pumpkin here will try to find you. And by Pumpkin, of course, I mean this floating thing and not my adorable companion."

Dagney scowled, but the color on her cheeks reddened slightly. I loved her blush. Most of her other expressions read as if she hated me, but her flushed cheeks were a tell she didn't mind my teasing.

I spread my hands. "I am Prince Ryo, lord of three mountains, heir to the Throne of Honor. I come to you, in this my most desperate hour, asking for your assistance."

The peddlers bowed in subservience. "Your Majesty, you honor us."

"I hate you so much right now." The upturned corner of Dagney's lips told a different story.

"Show us your finest armor," I said. "For I battle our enemy, the Savak queen. And I need protection from our kingdom's finest crafters."

The peddler pulled the edge of his wagon front. This wagon seemed different from the others in the circle. Wider somehow, and on springs closed tight for traveling. The thing wasn't stuck as much as it was wedged unopened. Perhaps I could help with that.

"Allow me," I said.

The golden gloves would not come off my fingers. Grig had suggested this was because I was a Royal class, and my duty to our party was to open doors others could not.

The good news, gold went with everything.

I gripped the stuck edge of the wagon with my witch-made gloves and pulled.

The wagon spread open, wide as a ballroom, full of silks and armor and boots.

Dagney held up a purple silk tunic with gold embroidery. "Take this one."

Good choice. I complied, but not before she threw a worn red belt at me.

I sniffed. This seemed . . . dare I say it, used. "Is there something in gold?"

"This is cheaper and it's plus ten accuracy."

How would a belt affect accuracy? She handed me a yellow-and-black-diamond crisscrossed cape, a black leather breastplate, and a helmet that looked like the skull of a bison.

Honestly. "Have you seen clothes before?"

She sighed. "I know it doesn't match, but this is the highest stats assembly."

Grig came from around the other end and burst out laughing. He held a glass jar of hibisi blossoms. "Were you dressed by the rock troll from *Witcher 3*?"

Whatever that was.

"Style counts," I said. I returned everything except the purple tunic and scanned the wagon. An ermine fur-lined gold silk cape. A pristine jerkin, fresh violet pants, gold greaves, and a white helmet with a purple peacock feather.

Hello.

Dagney touched the material. "Royal purple. You might be right. The outfit upped your charisma stats."

I turned to the peddler. "Before I dress, I'd like to bathe. Would that be possible?"

The peddler clapped his hands. "We have a Mechani cleaning system!"

"That would be wonderful." I followed the peddler around the back of the wagon and listened patiently to his instructions. When he left me alone, I hung my new clothes over the fold-out screen they wheeled flat. A bucket of rainwater attached to a hose and a spring of whirling gears. I undressed and wound the handle five times as instructed, until the water ran up the tube and through a spout, falling over my shoulders in a continuous downpour. A small store of ghostlight warmed the water. They were nearly out; perhaps Grigfen could sell them more.

Sell. I was becoming as pragmatic as Lady Dagney. These were my people, and they had a need. It was my duty to fulfill it.

The water was colder than I preferred, and I may have dumped in nearly all the contents of the little soap bottles so the bath was more slime than water, but it was a strongly pleasant scented slime, and for a moment the entire world was safe, and not intent on killing me.

What a novel experience.

"What news?" I could hear Dagney talking to the peddler on the other side of the screen.

"What will you trade me for it?"

She paused. I peered through the crease in the screen. But I couldn't see her, so she couldn't see me, which was good considering what I wore.

"Will this ring do?"

"Heartily. I've heard rumors of war, my lady. Falidin has been razed by fire, the royal family killed in the night; no survivors remained to tell the tale. Rumors speak of a Savak weapon. Some call it a beast. Some say mechanical. In the night you hear a whir of wings, and then when you wake, whole households have been killed. I saw a ship razed in the harbor with mine own eyes, but never saw the creature that slipped in and killed it. The Savak army has taken the Lacice harbor, *and* the throne of Talmour. There is hope, though. I hear the Kneult have offered great resistance. A brilliant general has arisen from their ranks, and they face the Savak queen now. We're heading inland, toward the mountains. May the Undergod keep us safe."

But the general who faced the Savak wasn't from the Kneult, as this man believed. It was General Franciv and my parents, I'd bet my life on it.

The council was with the Kneult.

The water slowed to a dripping. Someone had hung a thick white cloth over the wood separator. It gathered shadows as I wiped away any dirt or blood the water did not cleanse.

Still I took my time getting dressed, running my fingers across the embroidery of my tunic, the shining jeweled buttons of the jerkin, and the supple leather boots. I reattached my sword to the new belt, and the gold handle matched perfectly. I'd missed the trappings of the court. I'd missed the civilization of a pressed collar.

The impact was immediate. I stepped outside, and the peddler families saw me differently. Even the children bowed.

But they were bowing to their own clothes. I was the same man in that itchy wool cloak.

"Oh, get up," Dagney said. "He's not a god."

I gave her a silly grin. "You've not seen me play cards."

"You're ridiculous." But she smiled. I'd learned to read her smile by now. Her words and her expression didn't always match, but she saw me the same way, no matter what clothes I wore.

She didn't see the crown. She saw me.

She raised an expressive eyebrow and her green eyes sparkled in the afternoon sun, and I wanted to giggle and be sick all at the same time.

Oh light. I was in trouble. I liked her. But how did you talk to a girl who you actually liked? And where did you put your hands? Like in general I had forgotten how a normal person held their hands. On your hip? No, that looked ridiculous. I'd fold my arms. That was fine. That was very natural.

Her nose crinkled. "What's wrong with you?"

"Nothing. Excuse me. I'm going to see a man about a horse."

"Good idea."

She was following me. Why was she following me?

"Grigfen!" Dagney shouted.

I glanced back. The afternoon sun lit the ghostlight Grig had made for the Whirligig to pick up, much to the children's delight. His eyes widened when he saw my expression. He joined us.

Dagney had procured a notebook from the traders and scribbled a list. "The peddlers could use more ghostlight for their mechanicals. Conjure them some, would you? And help Ryo inspect the horses."

She placed the end of her pencil against her bottom lip. It was like she was trying to wound me with her adorableness.

Grig tapped my shoulder. "Are you going to be sick?"

"No, I'm fine. Why does everyone think there is something wrong with me? I'm completely normal." Why was my heart beating so quickly? "I'm going to go look at some shields for a moment, excuse me."

Why was I overreacting?

I'd been told this world was an arpeegee, whatever that was. I'd seen a split in the sky, I'd died five times, and not one thing had made me flat-out panic like this.

She was only a girl. Not a monster. *Breathe, Ryo, breathe.*

So I liked a girl. That was not the end of the world. I was fine.

"Your Majesty," a peddler with moon-rimmed glasses said. "There is of course the matter of payment."

"Of course." I inspected the swords and drew a few breaths. "Lady Tomlinson will handle our trading. Including that jeweled sword, if you please."

The peddler's eyes lit with greed. But if he thought a girl quarter-master would mean a higher profit, then I'd looked forward to seeing Dagney trade him silly.

I tilted my head to the side. "May I ask about the ring the lady traded for information?"

"Heard that, did you?"

"I'd rather she not lose her property as she is in my aid."

"That's right gentlemanly." The peddler held out the ring.

I inspected it. It wasn't anything fancy, a simple band of silver with a small black stone. "Never mind about the jeweled sword. I'll take the plain one and this ring instead."

The peddler gave a nod.

Static shook the sky, and the Historian stepped out of charged air. She was the only Historian I'd seen since before we'd entered the catacombs. She wore a mask again, even though I knew Dagney had already added the one she'd lost to her bottomless bag.

"Bluebird!" Grigfen dropped the reins in his hands and ran toward her.

I pocketed the ring.

The Historian removed her mask. This time she had a face. Big brown eyes, warm dark skin, and hair the color of a spring rose.

"Hi, Grig," she said.

I reached for my hilt. I'd never heard a Historian speak.

"Are you all right?" Grig asked. "Where is your player indicator?"

"I'm outside the game. My parents wouldn't sign the permission slip."

"You're outside the game?" Dagney asked.

This Bluebird person rubbed at her arms. Her neck corded. Something was wrong. I could read the pain on this stranger's face from ten feet away. I stepped forward.

Dagney's concerned eyes met mine. *Stop looking at me, woman.*

"How'd you get in?" Dagney asked. "I thought the game was locked."

"Ms. Takagi helped me."

"Can you send her a message?" Dagney asked, but she didn't wait for a response. "What on earth were you thinking? Why weren't there more fail safes?! HOW DID YOU LET THIS HAPPEN?" Her cheeks flushed red and her fists clenched. "That's it, end message, press send."

I brushed her shoulder with my own. "Do you feel better now?"

"A little. I may think of a postscript."

I faced Bluebird. "What's gone wrong?"

Dagney sighed. "I've told you, the—"

I held up a hand. "No. There's something new. Out with it."

Bluebird drew a shaky breath. "Five of the twelve players are dead."

Grig pressed his fist into his mouth and swore.

Dagney narrowed her eyes. "Five? Which five?"

Bluebird rattled off a list of names I didn't know, but which seemed somehow familiar. "And Ryo is next."

I swallowed. I definitely recognized that name.

"What can we do?" Dagney asked.

"He needs to drink the seer water. Players who have the game vision seem to be doing the best. The doctors think the game vision helps your brains realize the pain isn't real. Psychosomatic or something. The competition is over. It doesn't matter who wins. Once someone claims the victory, everyone is freed, no matter where they are on the game map or what side they are on. So long as they survive."

They glanced at me with faces lined with worry. But it didn't matter one fig. "We've discussed this. I'm not going to drink."

"Shut up." Dagney clenched her fists and faced me like I was her opponent.

I held out my hands. "Now, don't—"

She lunged for me and tackled me to the ground. Both her knees pressed against my shoulders.

This was unfair. "Not that I don't enjoy—"

She grabbed at my necklace.

I reached for her wrists. "Dagney, stop. People can see us."

Her loose hair brushed my face as she pulled our hands toward her neck. "You are going to drink this seer water if I have to pour it into your mouth."

I let go of her hands and lifted her under her legs and rolled her onto her back. See how she liked that.

She pinched my arms.

Ow. "Grigfen, help me."

I grabbed Dagney's wrists, but it was like she was made of snakes. She would not stop squirming.

Grig stayed at Bluebird's side. "You need to go before you get sucked in."

Bluebird watched us with mild curiosity. "I'm safe. Just win the game and come find me."

The disloyalty. He barely glanced my way, and meanwhile Dagney elbowed me in the stomach and she rolled me onto my back again.

I really should not be enjoying this. "Grigfen, honestly. Tell your sister—" She punched my jaw and I swore.

"YOU NEED TO DRINK." She ripped my necklace and broke the chain.

I shoved her off me. But now she had the seer water, and I swear she'd turned into a rabid animal.

And I still liked her. Oh lost saints, was I in trouble.

Bluebird turned to me. "Your mother says to drink the seer water, Ryo."

I rubbed my jaw. "You've spoken to my mother?"

"She has a message from your father." Bluebird's face turned silver for a moment, like she'd leaned back out of her own face. "The sultan of the three moons says it's time." She scrunched her nose and turned toward empty air. "Are you sure? That doesn't make any sense."

But it did to me. My father used to tell me stories before I fell asleep as a child, and the sultan of the three moons was one of his favorite characters. No one else knew that name except my parents.

The message was true.

I sat up and held out my hand. "All right, I'll drink."

Dagney cocked her head to the side, her eyes narrowed like she didn't trust me.

"What, like it was so hard to change my mind? Give me the seer water."

She held it to her chest. "Don't dump it."

I offered my hand once more and she placed it in my palm. My instincts still rebelled at drinking. My father had told me not to drink until I was ready, and what if abiding by his instructions was the only thing that had kept me alive? However, I'd seen too many miracles, and I'd followed Dagney and Grig's lead long enough that I had to conclude they were telling the truth. And I knew my father's message was from him, so none of my doubts or confusion mattered.

I had to be ready. I had to be enough.

I popped the top of the glass sphere and downed the contents.

Dagney's stubborn eyes were the last thing I saw as the darkness swallowed me whole.

— — —

I woke from the cut scene and brushed the dirt from my new armor. I couldn't look at them. I couldn't look at the false sky or my mother's idiotic game.

I marched into the forest and sliced a digitally rendered tree into as many chunks as I could cut. Then I dropped my sword and fell to the ground. My hands pressed over my eyes, my breathing heavy.

Every memory I'd had before I drank the seer water was true. To a point.

I'd gone camping with my dad like I'd remembered. I'd trained, not for tournaments, but for football games. I'd been surrounded by adoring fans who viewed my worth through my mother's accomplishments. I was still a spoiled rich kid who desperately wanted to make my father proud. There was just one massive detail my mom forgot to mention.

My father was dead.

My dad had died from a stroke three days after my twelfth birthday. But in this world, he was still alive. King Vinton had my dad's face, my dad's voice. We ate his favorite foods. The sky was his favorite color; this whole world was a place my father had invented and shared with me one bedtime story at a time. He invented the Savak and their magic spring that told the future. He told me stories of the Kneult, who traded their way to power, and a story of a good king and his pious but twisted brother, who plotted to kill him and take over his kingdom.

I thought my mother wasn't listening. Her whole life was her ridiculous job, and after my dad died, she threw herself into her work and this game, like she'd forgotten she'd even had a son.

My mother had recreated the world my dad had invented. And now it was killing me.

In the last . . . I didn't remember how many days, I'd been tortured and jailed, and lost my life over and over again. But the worst moment in the game was this one. When I no longer had a dad to make proud.

I wiped my wet cheeks. A branch snapped behind me. I grabbed my sword and turned to face it.

Dagney held a branch. "R . . . Ryo? Are you okay?"

I lowered my sword. It took me a moment, but I could remember her. From before. Same angry green eyes, thick dark hair, her real curves made of all things soft. But this beautiful girl was small consolation for losing my dad all over again, or this torture my mom had put us through.

This wasn't real. I wasn't this handsome prince from my dad's stories. Lives were at stake, people were watching our every move, and we didn't need any kind of distraction if we were going to win.

And I was the next to go. If I pushed this further, it would only hurt her if I reached my game over.

I lifted my jaw. "Why do you care? I don't even know you."

Her jaw trembled as she looked way. She clenched her fists. "Seriously?"

I lowered my voice. "It's a game. It isn't real. So any feelings or connection between us was a lie anyway."

"Because you remember who I really am now? Not going to flirt with a fat girl?" There was a challenge in her glare.

It nearly broke me. She had no idea how beautiful I thought she was. "You're ridiculous."

She glared. "You're such an—"

"I'm dying. Maybe give me a second to process before you make this all about you."

That shut her up.

Part of me wanted to apologize. Put on the flirtatious mask I wore around school, and used as the prince. I could play the part and make her smile again. Make her want me again. But then a fresh wave of grief curdled in my stomach and made my arms hang heavy. My dad was dead, and this world made of his stories wasn't going to bring him back.

She took a step closer. "What's going on with you?"

I pinched my lips so they wouldn't tremble. "I'm not sure I want to go home."

I closed my eyes. I hadn't meant to say something so honest. I wanted to rage, to insult her, to do something cruel in order to make her walk away. It was better for both of us. She didn't need my damage.

Before this game I was so good at putting up walls. Why did they always crumble around her? Why did the expressions on her face make me want to tell her all my secrets?

Dagney marched forward, her face pink. "You might not want out—but the rest of us do. Grig needs to get back to Bluebird, and there are six other players stuck in this hellscape who don't deserve to die." She brushed her hair behind an ear. "Stop being such a baby and pull your weight. And if you want, once we're out of this game, we never have to talk to each other again. That's fine by me."

She stalked out of the woods and I growled after her.

That did not go the way I wanted.

I punched the air, shook my fingers through my hair, and tucked away my grief. Then I picked up the sword I'd dropped. I had to play the dutiful son.

I knew how this story ended.

17

DAGNEY

My eyes burned with tears and that pissed me off. I stomped out of those woods and away from that jerk. I did not look back at him. Not once. I didn't replay him slashing trees and damaging his sword, or the way he held his head in his hands like he couldn't hold his head up for one more second, and I did *not* worry about the anguish in his eyes. That would be foolish, and I was not a fool.

When we emerged from the trees, Grig stood with his arms folded and his shadowed eyes careful. Pumpkin floated over his shoulder.

The mechanical squeaked its gyroscope and floated to Ryo's side.

Screw him. "Whirligig half price. I'll sell it for parts if it means a higher profit."

The peddler squeaked in excitement, and I ripped the drawers open, searching for anything, everything. I'd outtrade this peddler; I'd prove I was . . . I wouldn't let anyone make me feel small.

I was not nothing.

I glared at the peddlers so they would leave me alone and then took stock of the items I'd trade for that Whirligig: five rolls of cheese, plenty of bandages, Ryo's ridiculous clothes, twelve weapons, and twenty-seven hibisi blossoms. With Ryo now a full player, I'd stay back and play as a healer. Then I wouldn't have to talk to him except for emergencies.

Grig touched a cheese, and I ripped it from his hands and tucked it into my bag. "I'm gonna miss the thing," Grig admitted.

"Don't get attached," I said through barred teeth. "It's only pixels."

"You all right, sis?" Grig nudged my arm. "You two've been bickering since I knew you, but that didn't sound like banter."

"I'm fine."

"Funny, that's what Ryo said."

"Well, Ryo says a lot of things and most of them are lies."

Grig sighed and crossed back toward Ryo. Grigfen took him aside and they talked in quiet whispers. He put his arm on Ryo's shoulder, and when he let him be, Grig's loyalty still shone vibrant purple.

My hands unclenched.

What was wrong with me? I'd yelled at him, called him names, tackled him, and tried to force him to drink something he said he didn't want to drink, and now I was pissed because he wanted to walk away from me?

I was like a barbed wire fence. It made no sense for me to be mad that he would let go.

I folded a bandage and watched him. He pressed his hand to his chest. "Sun's greeting, travelers! I thank you for your fair trading, and I ask in our lost saints' name for more. It is not for me that I do ask, but for our people, our roads, and for our king. The Savak queen has threatened, but we do not cower. Here, in this clearing, beneath this warm sky, is where we turn the fight to her. This is where the rebellion starts." Their loyalty shifted purple. "This is where the tides turn. Who is with me?"

The peddlers shouted in unison.

He was actually good at this now. He called those peddlers to arm and left them smiling and proud to follow behind us.

"How'd you know what to say?" Grig asked.

"My game vision has an etiquette manual. There is very little I don't know," Ryo said, pushing his hair out of his eyes. I sighed. Great.

Ryo's special ability was to know everything and then mansplain it back to us.

That wouldn't get annoying at all.

"Clearly the NPCs have pixels for brains," I muttered.

After I packed what I could carry, the peddlers got ready to leave with us.

"Which way, Dagney?" Ryo called. He rode a white horse, because of course he did.

I found my horse. "Don't bite me, horse." A peddler put a stool out and I climbed onto a leather saddle. I closed my eyes. *Find Traveling Boots.*

The arrow spun. "Northeast. Here." I handed Grig and Ryo hibisi blossoms. "In case we come across anything."

"And we're likely to," Grig said.

Ryo nudged his horse and took off, stopping at every sign of life to recruit people to our cause. He kept collecting loyal people, but not one of us shone as bright a purple as Ryo himself. Before he was kind of this cute little obnoxious puppy I had to protect.

Now he was assembling an army.

By the time we settled in a camp for the night, he'd acquired servants, a militia of untrained farmers, and a massive violet silk tent I would not enter if someone paid me. It was rolled up at the back of a servant's horse.

We had almost reached the King's Crypt when a shadow raced across the moons.

"What was that?" I pulled on my reins. The horse stopped beneath me.

"Not dead. That's all I know," Grig said.

Ryo squinted at the sky. "A zomok. A flying creature that prefers fresh oranges mixed with salmon, and is loyal to its masters if trained from a hatchling."

Another shadow flashed past. How many of these things were there?

"So like a pet dragon," Grigfen said.

"No, dragons are not trainable."

The smell of oranges and the flapping of wings almost masked the whiff of copper and rust, and the whirl of a Savak Wingship.

But nothing could mask the soundtrack changing into heavy drumming. I stopped my horse. I hated when the battle music came on, but I didn't see any enemies.

"To cover!" I shouted.

The caravan behind us pulled toward the trees, and parents shoved their children under wagons. I searched the night's sky. There, near the smaller of the two moons, three Savak Wingships flew in formation. A Wingship carried a single person. Armor, weapon, and transportation in one. Sleek silver wings twice the length of a human were strapped to warriors dressed in Savak red, and the ends of the wings were razor sharp, like they flew with swords for hands. The detail to their costume was awesome, but much cooler at, like, a distance.

Grigfen summoned a mist around us, hopefully blocking us from their view.

The Wingship at the front hovered overhead for a full second—no player indicator over her head, only a collection of pixels flying through a damaged sky. She whistled at the zomok then dived straight for us. The zomok dived with her, but its wings were faster.

Before the Wingship reached us, talons ripped at a servant's shoulders. Right behind Ryo. This silver dragon-like thing lifted him from his horse with a roar, his legs kicking at the air. I clenched the hilt of my sword. The zomok took half the servant, and dropped the rest.

Grigfen shot ghostlight at the beast and Ryo lifted his sword high and let out a battle cry.

The Savak knew where we were now, and Ryo just drew their attention.

He needed more than a healer.

A Savak dropped an anchor. I ran forward.

Ryo shouted, "For my father!" Every farmer he'd acquired charged at my side. They ran with pitchforks and tin swords, huffing like they weren't trained to run full-out like this. I wasn't either, but these silver boots had plus twenty stamina.

I yanked the rope anchor as hard as I could.

You want to come down? Here, I'll help.

I jumped and used my body weight to pull. The Wingship lost air and crashed to the ground about fifteen feet away from me.

Yes! *I did that.* The NPC farmers rushed the downed Savak, striking her wings with their low-level weapons. She stood, her wings folded over her like a shield. Then she twisted in a sharp spin, the wings cutting through those farmers' bodies.

I slowed. My breath caught in my throat. They were NPCs. That's all. A child cried from under the wagon, her voice raw with grief as she called out to her lost father.

The zomok circling above us sniffed the air.

There wasn't time to grieve for fallen fictions.

Grig conjured a mishmash of animal bones into a vaguely human shape. He shoved forward, and the bone creatures rushed over the Savak Wingship. Hitting her again. Again. A cry of pain coming from within the wings.

Two more anchors dropped around Grig. The Savak flattened their wings and they tried to stop his assault on their ally. Feather-shaped blades shot from their wings, cutting through him, dropping his health like nobody's business.

"Heal! Heal!" I shouted, rushing toward him. "Grig, heal now!"

"I'm a little busy at the moment." He shot a wave of ghostwind that sent a Savak ship flying.

"Check your stats!"

The other Savak lifted his arm and aimed the tip of his wings at Grig.

But he aimed at the wrong girl's brother.

I pulled out my battle-axe and took off running. I jumped on a wagon, ran across a horse's back, and thrust myself up, up to the Savak Wingship who aimed at my brother. I wrapped my fingers around his harness and stabbed right into his neck. Then I threw my weight backward.

We crashed to the ground with a thud I'm sure I felt in my real body on a different world.

Ow.

Grigfen shoved the Wingship off me and helped me stand. I swallowed a hibisi blossom. Ick. The thing tasted like kale, my least favorite of all vegetables.

I stepped on the body and retrieved my axe.

"Get to the bushes," I told Grig. "And don't use too much magic at once."

"I know what I'm doing. Watch out for Ryo. Any damage could kill him in real life."

The last Savak shook off the ghostwind. She flapped higher and lifted her anchor so we couldn't reach her. She whistled twice, and that beast of hers followed her command.

Ryo stood on the top of a peddler's wagon, above folded springs. He raised an orange above his head and shouted at the beast. "Come here, girl!"

No. Now was not the time to play a hero.

The beast lunged for him. Ryo held steady as the zomok tucked its wings. It wasn't slowing. It opened its mouth, flashing sharp teeth. That idiot, that idiot.

Ryo threw the orange straight up in the air and leapt off the side of the wagon. The beast caught the orange and flew back to the Savak, its spiked tail wagging. The Savak warrior pointed at us twice and whistled, but the zomok wouldn't dive.

"You tried to train it?" I said as I reached him.

Ryo brushed off dirt from his fancy clothes. "There was no try about what I just did."

He ate a blossom, but his life only went up a little. Grig was still lined with scars from the Savak Wingship, and we'd only taken out two.

In the distance, from the direction my arrow pointed, a fleet of Wingships took off. About a dozen. Flying right toward us.

I glanced back at the untrained farmers who'd been too scared to attack and the peddler children huddled under the wagons. Ryo had recruited them to fight, but they assembled now to die.

And there was a good chance that I would join them. The choices I made mattered here, because they might be the only choices I got.

"We go for the boots," I decided. "Now. The farther we get from these children, the more likely they will survive."

"They aren't players," Grig said. "We could use the farmers to distract—"

"I'm not going to let a kid die. Not even an NPC."

Ryo's eyes warmed. He'd spent the whole day assembling this army, and he looked at me like he was proud to let them go. "Let's go."

He didn't even hesitate.

We ran for our horses. I climbed onto the saddle and kicked its flanks, urging my horse to gallop as fast as it could go. The white horse kept the pace I'd set. Behind us Grig galloped with his eyes toward the sky. Ryo's cloak billowed out, like a bull's-eye to our location, and for the first time, I was so glad for the fancy clothes he wore. Look at us. Follow us. We're the ones you want.

We galloped over the hillside and down to the valley of the King's Crypt. My lungs galloped with our horses. We made our way through the houses and buildings that surrounded it. More ruins than houses. Burned by a fire that still smoldered and sizzled inside the wreckage.

The crypt itself remained untouched. Three stories high and covered in sparkling carved marble, etched black with smoke. Solid iron doors had been fused together, keeping the building locked. The Savak Wingships circled above. Voices carried in the night wind. But I couldn't hear their plans.

Though the goose bumps on the back of my neck recognized their anger.

"They can't get in without the gloves," Ryo said. "They haven't retrieved the boots yet. We still have time."

Above the crypt, a pair of Wingships cut off from the group. They each unfurled a weapon from their wrists, a silver carved bracelet, which shot flames that lit the night.

I glared at the sky. "Why would you give them flamethrowers?" I hissed.

When this was all over I would be having words with Ms. Takagi.

Their weapons scalded the metal roof. It was only a matter of time before they broke in.

"There are so many bones here," Grigfen said. "I'll find a hiding place and summon a few skeletons and zombies for the Savak to fight. I'll set up a distraction."

"And then we'll break into the crypt," Ryo said.

I gripped Grig's hand tight. "Watch your healing. Summoning ghosts drains your health, so eat a blossom every few minutes."

"I will. Awa' an bile yer heid, Dags. I'm higher ranked than you are. I'll find a nice safe place and take a nap if I need."

"We'll be right back to get you."

Grig tapped my nose. "You don't die on me either."

Ryo dropped his cape next to where we left the horses and then he pressed his hand against my back, like we were on good enough terms for him to touch me. We slipped through the shadows and waited under a branch, until Grig gave some sort of sign.

The ground in front of the crypt rumbled, and decomposing arms sprouted from the ground. Creatures climbed from the earth and leapt up. The Savak Wingships fell for Grig's trick. They dropped anchors and focused their attack on the dead warriors he'd conjured.

"Now," I whispered.

We shot from the trees and pressed against the marble building. Ryo pried at the iron doors with the gloves and I slipped inside. My heart thudded when the doors slammed closed. The soundtrack cut off abruptly with the light. I could only sense the warmth of Ryo's arm next to mine and the sound of our breaths. The crypt was dark as a cave; only a circle of heated metal lit the ceiling three stories high above us.

A sharp blaze cut through the metal. They were almost in.

Claws tore at the ground. The screech made me flush cold. I turned, but couldn't see a thing. Something shuffled in the dark. Something clawed against the stone floor.

We weren't alone in the crypt.

18
MCKENNA

The tall waving grass sounded like soft wind chimes and dampened the sound when I landed on the Biallo coast.

I strutted forward as though I was making my way to the front of the stage to accept an Academy Award. And why not? I'd killed four players now. Nationally ranked, egotistical players who were back home sulking that a no-name nobody came and showed them how it was done.

My Wingship armor even shone like an Oscar, maxed out to its most lethal. I did a quick check to make sure I was camera ready, and then I turned off stealth mode.

The orange column of light I sneaked toward brushed the horizon. *Andrew Sanderson. Ranked fifth. Mage class, talent unspecified.*

I hated when I couldn't research my scene partners, and in this environment, it could get me ejected from the game. I needed to tame my ego and be careful. Sylvania almost caught me last time, because I was too busy celebrating a particularly dramatic strike. I should get this over with quickly; keep that pace quick and rising toward my showstopping finale.

Stealth mode.

The humming noise sounded shrill against the numb echo in my head. If I could feel pain, I'd be feeling it now. I glanced at my stats, and my health had dropped. I froze. No, *was* dropping. Something was wounding me, but no one was around. No one but the cameras. The light between the grasses pulsed. A bright swirling vapor lingered beneath the pads of my feet.

The threat came from below. I leapt and my wings caught me, but somehow that orange vapor rose with me, twisting around my ankle like a stinging trail of invisible liquid. The liquid grew taut, and I couldn't fly higher.

I checked my healing. I'd crafted a helmet and hidden a hibisi drip line on either side of my cheeks, like a wireless headset mic.

It was poison magic. I'd stepped inside a large orange circle, the circumference thin and shuddering. I'd walked into a trap.

My healing dropped.

I searched the ground, the sky, anything for that column of light, or something I could do to fight off poison. The map showed him just beyond the reach of my weapons. Just offstage.

I flicked my wrists, and my Devani bracelet sparked. I ignited the flames and shot straight down. The vapor caught in the flames. It exploded with a force of sound and air that shoved me straight into the sky.

That shackle of poison burned and released me. I flew high as I dared, swallowed hibisi tea, and then rushed for that column.

Stealth on.

Andrew hid in the bushes, his health weakened from his magical trap. He seemed disheveled, his clothes sloppy, his cheeks as hollow as his eyes.

Stealth off.

I reappeared. He lowered his chin, his shoulders curved in defeat. He didn't even attempt to fight. He knelt to the ground and put his hands on either side of his head, elbows up.

I lifted my palm and aimed a dagger.

"Please," he said. "Before you kill me, can you just tell me how to get out of this valley?"

I did not lower my weapon, but I didn't fire either. He seemed so . . . pathetic. His health was at 14 percent, and his bare feet were bloody. He didn't seem awake enough to be a real threat. "When was the last time you've eaten?"

"You mean something other than grass? I don't know. How many days has the game been playing?"

The game. He has his game vision? "You've drunk seer water?"

"First day in the game. You sent a treaty to the king of Biallo. I stole my father's glass of seer water and told them not to sign, and then the Savak killed all my people anyway. I barely made it out. I can't go back, because there's flying morons circling the walls, and the cliff that way is too short to kill me; guess how I found that one out." He closed his eyes. "Aim between the eyes or in my heart. I mean it. I have a hard time dying."

"You have extra lives?" How was that fair?

"No. I wish. I'm a Devani healer, and all I have to do is rest for a bit and my health goes up."

I checked his stats. Health at 21 percent. "You're a healer?"

"Yeah. It sucks. I'm only really good on a team, and the player I was supposed to team up with, Jefferson, died in his sleep."

"I could use a healer."

He scoffed. "Right. And I'm supposed to trust you?"

"Oh, of course not. I will kill you. I have to in order to win the game. But I could save you for last, if you're nice. In the meantime, I've got plenty of real food. A castle with all kinds of luxuries. And I can fly you out of this valley right now."

He opened his eyes. Looked me up and down.

"You'd do that?"

I opened my mouth but couldn't speak, like I'd forgotten my line. He played at my sympathies, but the queen of the Savak shouldn't have any. He was useful. She'd use people. But did I want to help him because he looked pathetic, or because I could use him?

Or was it because I was lonely?

While I debated with myself, his health slowly reloaded. A speck of orange vapor seeped from his fingers.

He was stalling, I realized. I lifted my palm, but he shot that vapor out like a rope that slid around my neck and pulled me to my knees in front of him.

No. The Savak queen couldn't kneel for anyone.

A numb tingle ran up my neck, but I didn't feel any pain. I milked it, though, grasping the magic rope with my fingers, coughing. His grip started shaking. We both waited down my health. 9 percent. 7 percent. He pulled me close, until our noses touched.

"I'll just take your wings for myself," he said, his voice strained. Weak. Mine was not the only health that was dropping.

I waited until his grip went slack. I fell to the ground, my head turned so my health stat was hidden behind me. He collapsed to the ground, heavy breathing rumbling over me.

Health at 2 percent. The numbness echoed behind my ringing ears. I licked my hibisi-dusted lips and the numbness quieted. I waited until he stood to collect my loot, and then I sat up and shot him with feathered blades. One in the side. One in the neck. One in his gut.

I stood as he fell. "You wouldn't know how to use them."

I whistled. A zomok stopped circling the clouds above me. It dived; sharp claws paddled to the ground. I cocked my head to one side as the zomok joined me. Her head turned to the side in copy. Having a healer on my team could be useful, but I'd crafted a hibisi-delivering system, and honestly, I didn't need the baggage.

"What do you think, Sunshine?" I asked the zomok. "Does he look like lunch, or should I use him?"

"Please," he whimpered.

"Please what?" I asked. "Please kill me quick? Please forgive me?

Which please are you pleasing now? Sunshine here is hungry. Aren't you, you beautiful girl?"

"I don't know," he said. I didn't trust him for anything. Trying to use my sympathy as a second trap. He was supposed to be harder to beat. He was supposed to be a challenge.

"You are a disappointment," I said.

I flicked my wrist and palmed a feather-shaped dagger.

He covered his face. "Wait! Wait!" The haze of loyalty around his shoulders turned from gray to a dark red. Not my color, not really, but closer.

Scrolled writing tagged to a bracelet around his wrist. My crafting file unlocked. Something new I could build. I opened the crafting file, and twenty, no thirty, new upgrades unlocked. Poisoned blades, traps, and he'd hidden a Devani necklace that captured lightning.

I could use that.

I pulled that bracelet off his wrist, connected it to a chain already made magic by that Devani queen, and connected it to his wrists again. His own poison had turned against him now.

"You'd better hope your healing wasn't a lie," I whispered. I whistled twice, and Sunshine grabbed him by his ankles. I took off after them, flying back toward my castle. My armies were returning, and there was still so much to do before the finale.

I'd need something stronger to keep him in line, and I knew just the thing.

As my Wingship carried me over the Biallo coast, I reloaded my hibisi distiller, dusted my lips with powder I'd dyed bright red, and tried to settle my nerves.

This was the first player I hadn't killed.

I really hoped that wasn't a mistake.

Sweat drenched my skin.

Scratch. Thump.

I searched the darkness, my eyes throbbing.

Scratch. Thump. Closer to me.

Dagney struck a match and lit the torch she'd pulled from her inventory. The light illuminated the arched ceiling of the crypt.

Dad's image was etched into every sparkling wall. Carved moments of his life; one of him receiving his diploma, one of him marrying my mother, and right beside these large double doors, a carved moment of the first time he held me, his grin completely taking over his face. My father's entire life was recorded in the walls of this monument of fallen kings.

I softened my jaw. My mom made an Easter egg for my dad.

She hid an Easter egg in every world she'd created. In *Ashcraft* there was a secret room with my father's initials. In *Swordmaker's Chronicles* there was an underground tunnel with a painting of me taking my first steps.

The carved walls arched over skeletons in fine clothes on slabs, arranged in a circle in the center of the room.

Nothing else.

Nothing that could have made those sounds.

Something scratched. We both flinched at the sound.

Dagney handed me the torch and grabbed the battle-axe from her back. "Keep to the walls," she whispered.

"Is your arrow pointing to any particular body?"

"No." The torchlight made dancing shapes in her irises. "It disappeared as soon as the doors closed. The boots are in this room, but that's all I know. We're going to have to search for them."

We moved across the crypt, each of our steps echoing against the crypt walls.

A thump. A scratch.

"They're footsteps," Dagney whispered.

Great.

The torch blew out.

Dagney swore.

"Give me a match! I'll light it." She turned.

Her axe was too close to my cheek. "Careful." I stepped away and relit the torch. At the edge of the light, a foggy shadow loomed. I lifted the torch.

Nothing behind us.

Then, in an instant, the shadow returned, too tall to be human. A line of light cut through my game vision. As fast as it appeared, the shadow winked out, leaving only a suggestion of what might have been horns or fangs. The crypt was ripe with the aroma of fresh blood.

An indicator pointed to where the shadow had just been. "Lurcher," I warned.

We waited, watching for movement or shadows deepening. The torch warmed the side of my face and flicked against the walls.

Darkness gathered against the wall, the center tinted green as ghostlight.

We stepped backward. Something brushed against my legs. I flinched around.

But it was just a dead body.

How screwed up was this, that *that* was comforting?

A footstep scratched behind us. I turned, but Dagney still faced the doors. "Do you think there are two of them?" she asked.

"I don't know. Only the Devout can see most ghosts. Not unless they want to be seen."

"And Lurchers?"

I read the info scrolling across my game vision. My stomach twisted. "Lurchers like their prey to see them before they eat them."

"Great. Super great. How can we kill something we can't see?"

"I don't think we can kill it; it's already dead." I lifted my chin. "But it has to be possible. My mom would make the game playable."

The ghostlight solidified at the center of the looming shadow. It did have horns. Something crackled like a skeleton coming to life.

The torch dimmed but the flame held steady. Come on, torch. Don't fail me now.

At least not until I find those boots.

I didn't know which of the finely dressed skeletons had once been my game grandfather's body, but their feet faced the walls, their heads close together, like a demented star shape. A half-melted candle rose from a candlestick near the wrapped head of a woman dressed in a soft, purple, moth-eaten gown. I lit the candle and moved on to the next.

Each lit candle made the disappearing shadow more substantial. I lit another. The crypt brightened and the shadows lost the dark they hid inside. There were three shadows. The horned one in the center seemed twice the height of a man, the other two, maybe ten feet tall.

Candles lit, I thrust the torch into a crevasse and started searching for the boots. I lifted the shroud covering one of my musky ancestors. Nothing. I moved to the next slab and pulled off the shroud. A skeleton with wiry silver hair and a vivid green silk dress. No league boots. I puffed out my cheeks. The next had a bronze crown and deep red, moth-eaten robes.

The sharp dragging footsteps quickened, the sound rising as it moved toward Dagney. She lifted her axe, a smile curving her lips as she raised it and waited for the shadow to reveal itself.

My pulse raced. I needed to find those boots.

At the center of the circle, the horned shadow solidified, colors shining through the darkness. It looked almost human, except its pale gray skin sunk into deep eye sockets and its mottled cheekbones looked almost mummified. My stomach churned as it lurched forward. Those weren't horns.

They were a crown.

"Hello, Nephew." The voice sent a chill up my neck. The shadow receded as King Edvarg stepped into the light, taller in his second form than when he was alive. His bony features seemed to drip ghostlight.

"Uncle Edvarg," I said. "You're looking unwell. I must say death does not suit you."

Edvarg laughed. The sound was as shrill as a ref's whistle. His head rolled off his shoulders and down to his hand, and then back up to his neck. I couldn't speak. My throat tightened. I couldn't look away from my uncle's glowing eyes.

My hands trembled.

What would it feel like to be eaten?

Beside me, Dagney smiled. "Didn't I kill you already?" She moved forward, her battle-axe lifted like a baseball bat. Two Lurchers appeared at Edvarg v.2's side. Smaller, their heads spinning in time, their ghastly bodies sunken into spiny skeletons.

Edvarg v.2 disappeared.

Dagney swung an axe and knocked off a Lurcher's head. That didn't even slow it down.

It grabbed at Dagney. She twisted out of its grip. She swung her axe again, this time into where its stomach should be.

I thrust my hands onto a bone ankle. Nothing. I needed those boots so I could actually help! Charisma couldn't do much against ghosts.

Think. What could I say to keep Edvarg distracted and substantial enough that Dagney could kill him?

"UNCLE!" I shouted. "You're no king! You don't belong here!"

A roar shook the royal corpses. Uncle flashed visible. Gotcha. I threw a femur at his too-long neck. He vaporized, and the bone went right through him. He watched the bone shatter against the wall. "You always were a disappointment."

"Oh yeah, well, your character development is shallow." From this angle, I could see a circle of ghostlight at the back of his shoulder. "Aim for his back!" I shouted.

Dagney nodded and ran forward. A Lurcher reached for her, but she ducked under the swinging arms, jumped on top of the slab, and threw her axe. It landed right between Edvarg's shoulders.

He let out a primal scream. The candles flickered and then Edvarg disappeared. Dagney landed. She looked at me, her face lit in a grin as the bar marking Edvarg v.2.'s health cut down by a third. The axe fell to the ground with a thud.

Dagney raced to rearm herself.

The other Lurcher appeared behind her. My breath caught. "Behind you!"

She picked up her axe and swung it behind her, then backkicked that Lurcher in the stomach. Impressive.

While she fought, I ripped off the next shroud. A metal plate covered a body—solid iron and covered in Devani symbols. Finally. I wrapped my fingers under the plate and lifted.

Edvarg reappeared. Dagney didn't see him reaching for her.

"You never deserved to be king!" I shouted.

Edvarg's beady corpse eyes met mine. They flashed a furious green. Ghostlight swarmed around his spindly fingers as he called the bones in the crypt and threw them toward me.

I shoved the plate up, like a shield, and climbed onto the slab on top of a royal corpse. Yuck. I didn't even have time to be disgusted before bones slammed against the metal, the ghostlight tugging at my clothes as it rushed around me.

I couldn't see it, but I heard the thrash of an axe, and Edvarg's yell. The rush of bones stopped, so I peeked from behind the iron shield. Dagney's axe was glowing with a soft green mist, and Edvarg's health had dropped by another third. We almost got him.

So maybe I should get off the dead guy. Beneath me, the golden boots were pristine against my grandfather's dusty bones. I picked up the boots and stood. The metal was etched with Devani markings similar to the ones on the gloves. The boots formed with no ties, just a latch around the ankle.

The plate slid off the slab and landed with a crash.

The monsters reappeared. And their attention was focused on the dumb guy holding golden boots in the center of the room.

Edvarg's eyes lit with greed. All three ghastly monsters zoomed toward me. Gah!

"Dags! Catch!" I chucked those boots like they were footballs, perfectly spiraling into Dagney's waiting hands. But the Lurchers and Edvarg didn't stop coming for me.

I had to defend myself. I drew my sword.

Problem was, any injury might hurt my body back in the real world. I yanked the iron plate up as a shield. The Lurcher slammed into it, forcing me down to one knee. The iron sizzled against its mottled skin, where it touched suddenly turning back to shadow. The pressure let up. I sliced into the dark where the iron had touched. The thing screeched.

The other Lurcher loomed behind me, its talons sharp as knives. I twisted and swung my sword into its chest, then I knocked its head off with my shield. It spun off the thing's shoulders, crashing into the wall, and dissolving like a ball of smoke.

The iron could hurt them.

Edvarg and the Lurchers disappeared.

Dagney stood in the boots. "The boots don't work!" She stomped her feet. "They aren't even showing up in my inventory."

I checked out my inventory. *Traveling Boots.* I wasn't wearing the item, but I was the one who found them. "They're in mine."

A Lurcher and Edvarg reappeared. The headless one was too injured. Edvarg lifted his hands, and green mist began to form.

"Hurry," Dagney said as she tried to pull the boots off her feet.

There was no time. "Trade me for them."

She dropped her foot and then looked at the axe in her hand. "Catch!" She threw the axe, and I caught it. I turned with a grin and I ran for Edvarg. I swung the iron shield into the Lurcher that blocked my path and knocked its head clear off, then, while Edvarg raised his mist-clouded hands above his crown, I slammed that gorgeous axe into the glowing circle on his shoulder.

He dropped his hands, his bar of health dimmed to a speck. I shoved the shield into his chest, and Edvarg fell back to the ground. I stood over him.

"I'll kill you for this," he said, trying to push up to sitting. I stepped on his chest and held him down.

"Not this time." I slammed the iron plate into his neck and trapped him down to the floor. His body shuddered, arms flailing, fingers outstretched and then curling upward. The damage bar drained to empty. His body disappeared in a flash of green gas, sharp and acidic. My axe clattered to the ground.

My skin lit as I leveled up. Yes! I defeated a boss! My hand lifted, but I dropped it. My dad wasn't here to give me a high five.

This was why I never played video games anymore.

My lungs tightened as I breathed in the rotting green gas. My skin flashed cold, and I coughed. Once. Twice. I couldn't breathe. The gas was poison. "Stay away!"

Dagney's face paled. She rushed into the gas. I flinched. She should stay back; I could find a way out on my own. If I could only breathe. She didn't listen to my pleading thoughts. Instead she grabbed my jerkin and pulled us backward.

The witch-made boots teleported us out, like a tunnel of multicolored lights. Warm electricity surged, binding us tighter together. But Dagney didn't stop. Her golden boots stepped backward again.

Her skin glowed as she leveled up. The spark of energy heightened my senses—the sweet smell of sweat at the base of her neck, the taste of sunshine on my tongue, the purple-and-red nova of lights behind my closed eyelids. My foot hit solid ground, and a flash of stinging heat burned my shoulders as we stilled.

We'd moved about five miles away from the King's Crypt, to a long open stretch of sand and desert heat. I coughed again and green vapor released from my lungs, like a dragon snorting. I gasped a long deep breath of air. My shoulders wound tight.

I stared at her, at the round curve of her cheek, the light in her eyes, her dark hair wild. I wanted to take a picture of her, remember the way she looked for the rest of my life. "I can't believe you ran into poison to save me."

Her lips were tinted with a soft green powder. "Of course I did, you d—"

I rubbed her bottom lip with my thumb, wiping off poison like I was wiping off her lipstick. She broke off before she could land whatever devastating insult she had planned.

"Are you certain you are all right?" I wiped the poison on the shoulder of her dress.

"I'm okay," she said, her eyes wide. "We're okay."

Now perhaps I could breathe. No monster was about to kill us. We had the boots and we weren't locked inside my mother's crypt. Dagney was standing on her own feet.

Very close to me.

I let out a relieved laugh. One hand still brushed her cheek, and the other held her waist close.

I couldn't stop looking at her mouth. The corner of her lip pointed up, and her dimple tucked inside her cheek.

A question awakened between us, a question I didn't say out loud. I traced her neck with my fingers and she closed her eyes, her body arching up. Her fists clenched around my shirt, coaxing me toward her.

Well, if she insisted.

My lips brushed against hers. She growled softly and kissed me the way she argued, with every bit of her. Her body pressed against my chest and I cinched her waist tight, my fingers entwined in her stays, but not close enough.

She stepped toward me. The tingle from traveling electrified every sense, the taste of her sweet as whipped pie, sparks crackling between my fingers and trailing every inch of her, my lips burning embers against her mouth, her neck, her jaw.

In a tunnel of speckling light, I lost all sense of direction, but she didn't stop moving, rocketing us through step after step. One step wading through rivers, while her fingers gripped my hair and lights shot past us. The next step thrust us through a circling wind. It rattled my clothes and froze the sweat up my back. She tugged my shirt up and touched the bare skin. I flooded with heat. Those enchanted boots transported us farther through a snowbank, a crunch of snow pressing to my knees as I lifted her higher by the slope behind her thighs and we stopped shooting forward. I walked us instead, until her back hit a stone wall, and finally, finally, we were close enough.

And right when I was about to surrender all sense, her lips parted into a smile.

I pulled back and we breathed together. Her cheeks flushed pink, and she wouldn't look at me.

I cocked my chin. "'Sup, girl."

She threw her head back and laughed.

I chuckled with her, everything else in the world forgotten except the way her lips curled into a smile.

20
GRIGFEN

There were seven Savak Wingships, all aiming bursts of fire at the King's Crypt. They flew above the ruins of the burnt town while Dagney and Ryo ran into their flames.

I'd have to set a distraction. A right good one too—fierce, strong, and quite a ways from where I hid. I climbed up a shadowed tree and made my way out onto the largest branch, arms held at both sides for balance. Through the cover of the leafy branches, I called for the spirits, bones, and ghost beasties hidden in the forest surrounding me. Indicators lit over the bones. I glanced through my list of spells until I knew just the song to sing and words to say to enchant them.

I settled down on the branch, legs dangling, and gathered my balance on the swaying branch. I twisted my fingers. The flame-parched earth cracked. Dusky skeletons emerged from the billowing ghostlight. First a human arm, an antler, and then a skull. The bones congealed into one creature. But it wasn't distraction enough. I hummed an ancient made-up word, and a cyclone surrounded the bone monster, spinning ghostwind swirling in a dance around the distraction.

It worked. The Savak turned away from Ryo and Dagney's goal and attacked the creature.

I grinned and popped a hibisi in my mouth, watching the battle like it was a movie. The battle could last for as long as my health held on, so I kept chewing on hibisi blossoms as my magic usage dimmed my health, creating new skeletons whenever my magic and health were strong enough.

I kept going until my head ached and my fingers stiffened in a chill that didn't seem to be caused by the weather. Even healing couldn't repair the exhaustion that settled into me.

I couldn't hold the bones any longer. The skeleton collapsed in a scattered heap. Oh. A nap would be so fine right about now. I settled back against a branch. Well done, Griffin.

Hopefully that was distraction enough.

I felt the branch give before I heard the crack. I threw my hands back to catch myself.

But it was too late.

I more slipped than fell. I tumbled down. Thick branches slammed into my stomach. My head. My vision flashed black.

When I came to, the world was drawn at an odd angle. The King's Crypt had gone all scallywampus in the background.

Two Savak Wingships marched toward me, just meters away. A pilot cocked her head to the side. They crept forward, their flame-throwers scorching the underbrush. I murmured curse words under my breath, and a weak fog rose from the ground. It only brought them faster. My fingers twitched, dark spells darkened my tongue, but I was too drained to raise more resistance. I couldn't even pull a femur toward me.

The flames burned through the mist and a Savak kicked through the splotchy fog. She stood over me, her arched metal wings pointing to the sky. She grabbed my arm and yanked me so close I could smell blood on her breath, sharp as a mouth full of coppers.

"You are now the property of the Savak queen. Your life is hers to take or tailor. Congratulations on being used for her glorious vision."

Aw bollocks.

21
DAGNEY

When our laughter faded, every unspoken thing echoed in the silence between us. I didn't look at him. I couldn't.

So I just looked at my hands clasped in his cravat and waited for the world to stop spinning.

That kiss. I drew a deep breath. Maybe it was the connection to the game or the thrill from traveling, or maybe it was Ryo himself, but this felt different from all the times I'd kissed people before. Kissing Ryo was better than a brownie Blizzard sundae, and screw everything I wanted another bite.

But. Like. Priorities.

What were my priorities again?

Finally I met his eyes. His perfect hair was ruffled, his lips swollen, and his eyes, oh no, his eyes were as hungry as mine. He looked well kissed.

And like he wouldn't mind if it happened again.

Infuriatingly kissable boy.

I'd read thousands of books, written essays on interesting topics, and said swear words when I really meant it, but my favorite words I'd ever thought were those—*infuriatingly kissable boy*.

Get a hold of yourself, Dagney.

"We should probably . . . ," I said.

"Right." He released my waist and I let go of him.

He ran his fingers through his hair, throwing glances back at me, like he was checking to make sure I was still there. It'd be embarrassing if it wasn't so ridiculously adorable. I pressed my warm cheeks with my hot palms. There was nothing to be embarrassed about.

Except that . . . um, his mom was probably watching. Oh gosh, I forgot we were on camera.

"So . . . where exactly did we end up?" Ryo asked.

I glanced around. We'd traveled someplace damp, someplace that smelled like dirt and blood, and somehow familiar, lit by a still-burning lantern. Somehow I'd walked us to the King's Executioner's tunnel under our own city. The walls empty of the maps in my inventory, his blood-soaked bandages still on the bed.

I had no idea how these Traveling Boots worked. After the battle and during the kiss, I'd just moved out of desperation, by instinct and desire, but now I had these metal things strapped to my legs that could rocket me hundreds of miles away, through walls and distance, and I didn't dare move my feet.

Okay, game vision. Give me your magic.

When I gained the Traveling Boots, a vertical column appeared on the left side view. Percentages were marked in lines up the column, like a ruler but marked in tens. 10 percent, 20 percent, and so on. I lifted my foot, and a pink line filled the column, and then lowered, up and down, up and down again. I'd have to time my distance like I was timing a swing. I gathered that at 100 percent it would send me the farthest distance away, and lower would send me a shorter distance.

There had to be some sort of calculation I could use to make my steps less chaotic.

I glanced at Ryo. I needed all the control I could get.

His shoulder bobbed. "Hey, um, so . . . should we talk about—"

"Nope."

He rubbed the back of his neck. "Oh."

Shoot I didn't mean . . . "Maybe. But let's go find Grig first. I don't like that we left him on his own."

"Right. Okay." He took a loping step toward me. "How do we do that?"

"Um, well, you moved with me before. I'm guessing it was because we were touching so . . ." He grinned. I made a face. "Do not look so eager."

He put his hand in mine. "You don't tell me what to do."

I fought a grin, but then stopped myself. Why was I fighting this so hard?

"How far should we jump, do you think?" Maybe my maps could help. I checked in my bag and pulled out a map. "Okay, the King's Crypt is here, and we are here, so . . ."

Find the King's Crypt. The arrow behind my eyes spun. I knew the direction; now I just had to figure out the distance.

Ryo leaned over my shoulder. "Can't we just leap?"

"No." I bit my lip as I measured the distance between the tunnel and the King's Crypt, and then compared it to the widest distance on the map. "It's not magic, it's math."

"Okay, but don't bite your lip, it's distracting."

I grinned at him. "Oh, do you find me distracting, Prince Ryo?"

His eyes warmed, no trace of humor masking them. "You know I do."

My breath caught. Math. Think math. "So . . ." What was I saying? "Let's try ten percent." I tucked my map back into my bag. "Brace yourself, and don't let go of me."

"I won't."

10 percent. This time I ripped us from the tunnel with my eyes open. The setting blurred as we raced through it, through city and forest and dry desert. Then through mountains and a grassy coast that smelled of salt water.

My fists clenched. I'd overshot. The world was way bigger than I'd estimated. I tried to dig in my heels but nothing could slow my step. We plunged into the ocean and deep under water. That's when finally the traveling stopped. I clung to Ryo's drenched fingers as waves pulled him away from me. His hands shot forward, clutching me against him.

I turned under the water as we reached the bottom and aimed my steps again. A shadow swam past, large and not worth waiting to see. Bubbles burst out my mouth as I held tight to Ryo and waited for the pulsing column to reach the bottom. 5 percent.

We shot forward. Out of the ocean and into a coast covered in hip-high grasses as far as I could see. We were soaked, my clothes plastered to my body. I let go of him and shook out my messy hair. Ryo's hair lay flat against his face. I laughed. Seaweed covered his nose so I plucked it off.

"Maybe smaller steps?" Ryo suggested as he pulled a piece of seaweed off my shoulder.

It took three more steps, but as we traveled closer to the crypt I got the feel for how far each percentage would take us.

The Savak had stopped attacking the crypt. Scattered bones lay still on the ground. A chill ran up my neck as I took that last step toward where we'd left Grig. The horses still grazed, all three of them, but I couldn't find Grig. Where was he?

Deactivate Traveling Boots? my game vision said. I nodded.

My damp clothes chilled as I searched the woods. *Find Grig*, I told my vision. The arrow in my eyes didn't spin. My damp clothes chilled against my back.

I let go of Ryo's hand.

"What's wrong?" he asked.

"My arrow isn't pointing to anything." My jaw trembled. "Grig's not here."

"What?"

Find Grigfen, I thought again, sterner this time. The arrow behind my eyes spun and then tipped upward.

I followed where the arrow pointed to where the Savak Wingships flew in a V.

"They got him," I said. "The Savak grabbed him."

22
GRIGFEN

The last time I flew across an ocean, I had an aisle seat, so I did not enjoy the view this much.

The claws digging into my shoulder, however, were less of an improvement. I'd write a sternly worded letter to the airline, if it wasn't actually a scaled beast lifting me a hundred meters over an ocean filled with sea creatures and a fathomless bottom.

A chill wind whistled through the quiet air. My powers were stripped by the height, too high for the ghosts' song to reach me, let alone their bones. My pocket, once full of healing blossoms, now felt suspiciously flat. It was silent and cold, but Mother of Dragons, that view. Horizon to horizon, clouds painted the blue sky, marred only by the line of error.

Savak Wingships filled the sky, carrying Devout and Devani prisoners, some awake, some injured but not past the power of a hibisi blossom. What were they going to do with us all?

I scanned to my left. A pair of Wingships carried a large chest hanging from chains. Another Wingship held a Devani woman, her legs kicking, like she was fighting her capture. Devani symbols drawn in kohl covered her eyes. She swore and the symbols began to glow. Blue as cobalt. No player indicator hung over her head so she must be an NPC. She drew ice from her fingers and shot blades of glistening blue upward and into that soldier's stomach. The Savak screeched as a blow caught him, and then he dropped her. I gasped, my gaze falling with her until a massive horned creature with the teeth of a shark leapt from the glittering water and snatched that Devani as if she were a piece of kibble.

I held on tighter to those claws cutting into my shoulders. Not fighting, not fighting.

Not yet anyway.

In the distance, far as the horizon, a noble ship burned, a pair of Savak Wingships pilfering its contents. I was grateful to be carried by a zomok, or whatever Ryo called them. The thing seemed almost friendly in comparison, except for the claws and the serpentine face and the armor across its scaled wings.

Fog seeped over the rocky shore, like the clouds had fallen from the sky. Rocky peaks broke through, tiny islands with jagged green cliffs. A jagged spire of stone reached toward the clouds. Nestled inside the mountains, a pristine castle cut through the sky.

The Island of the Savak.

As we sailed into the fog, a chill sent shivers up my back. No one who landed on the Savak shore ever returned. The sea-salted air changed as we bobbled toward shore, the rich scent of the hibisi in bloom, fragrant as a cheap perfume, mixed with the smell of something strange.

Off.

Rotten meat.

When we crossed over land, the Savak Wingships split into two groups: one heading toward the castle, the other toward caves and the nests of zomoks. I didn't care for either destination. Below me trees ripped past. Solid ground. No sea creatures.

I think I could survive a fall.

Och, I was going to regret this.

I tugged at the whispers of ghosts in the trees below me, drawing their light and their bones. A spirit of a zomok soared up, up with the shards of its bones. I thrust my hands up, and the bones stabbed the creature in the neck. It released its grip on my shoulders.

And down I fell. My stomach tightened as air ripped past me, ruffling my robes. The ground grew closer. I pulled at ghostlight to soften my landing, and bones came from the ground, hitting the pads of my feet, slowing me down. I kept tugging, whispering an ancient word. The bones formed a frail stilt beneath my feet, long as my fall. It snagged against some underbrush, and the thin stilt bent, then cracked. I free-fell about three meters, and the impact stung like a thousand pinpricks up my back.

Oy. Ouch. Ow.

I rolled my landing, scrambled to my feet, and hid behind a tree.

The zomok screeched and drew attention.

But I was well rested now, thanks to the bump on the head. I summoned a fog, and scanning the new spells I'd unlocked from grabbing Edvarg's book, I found a spell that could shift me transparent.

I gripped the tree trunk and held tight until the world stopped spinning from the fall. I couldn't take a straight step for a good minute. I kept turning left, like my controller had jammed sideward.

Above me, the zomok searched the ground, snorting and slobbering, a bone still stuck into its side. I crept into the woods, ducking under tree branches above me, each step light and careful to not alert the zomok. That wouldn't be enough. I pulled ghostly beasties to use as cover. A translucent bear joined me, followed by an ice-blue fox, a deer with a missing leg. I wasn't alone. A ghost was as good as a friend to a boy who'd about died.

Now if only I knew where I should be going . . .

I wandered through the forest, collecting items where I could, hunting meat or information. Anything. I had to stay alive until Dagney and Ryo won the game. I could hide in these woods, grind some points, and keep out of danger. I could survive out here.

But I'd prefer to do more than survive. I mean, I was a top-ranked player. Just because my character was a tad squishy, that didn't mean I couldn't help.

And an item from the Armor of Irizald was hidden somewhere on this island. Ryo said the Crown of Visions was in the Seer Spring.

And this boy of Scotland was ready to do some light thievery.

My robes snagged a thorny plant and it ripped the hem. I walked westward until I heard some zomoks chomping on something not dead enough to sing to me.

Not that way, then.

I crept backward. Away. East, perhaps. I wandered until I found a path. I glanced one way toward a dark forest and the other toward a castle. All right. Which way? This was a lot harder without Dagney. Hopefully they were doing okay without me.

I puffed out my cheeks then held up my palm and summoned a ghost. Something small. Something whistled a mourning tune within the dead tree branch. I twitched my fingers and coaxed it out.

The ghost of a black-and-white bird followed its bones to my hand. I pet its head. "Where to, bird?" I tossed the spirit up. It flapped its wings then flew away from the castle.

So not that way.

"The Seer Spring," someone whispered.

I closed my eyes and grinned.

I turned. "You shouldn't be here."

"Glad to see you too," she answered.

I opened my eyes. This version of my Bluebird wasn't quite right. Her face was plumper, her arms thick with muscles, even under a raven cloak. But by Galaga did she make my heart flutter.

I crossed to her side. "That's not what I meant. It's not safe."

"Okay, bye." Bluebird waved, static flickered, and she disappeared.

I let out a laugh. "Wait! Come back."

Leaves crunched. Where'd she go to now?

I dropped my hands and called to the sky. "If you're insisting on helping, I guess I wouldn't mind knowing which way to the spring?"

Bluebird reappeared in the bushes. She staggered back, her hand on her head. Her gaze met mine.

"You all right, pal?"

"I'm fine. I just." She sighed. "That seemed easier in my head than actually doing it."

"Ain't that the way."

"I'll take you to the spring. Ms. Takagi says that's where the Crown of Visions is hidden. Apparently it's supposed to help you see the future. But how is that going to work in a video game, especially with all your brains all tied together? If all your brains are adding input into the neural net, then maybe it makes predictions based on the inputted history and thought patterns. You could see what people are likely to do, make real-time predictions. Like the application possibilities of that technology is absolutely staggering when you think about it."

Her raven robe billowed behind her as she made her way up a hill. Her bare feet didn't make prints on the ground.

I jogged to catch her.

"I'm sorry. I'm babbling."

"I like your babbling. And truth to truth, I'm kind of used to it. How long did you go on about Stormpilot—"

"How dare you, you know I'm still hurting about that."

I grinned.

Her return smile was small, and full of light.

Jings was she beautiful. "Let's go," I said. "Me and you. Let's go nab us a crown."

"I want to, but . . ."

"But what? It'll just take an hour or so, I figure. We go in through the clerics' halls, maybe do a couple of side quests, earn some buff resources, and then we go get the Crown of Visions and do a victory dance."

"I can't."

"It doesn't have to be a good dance."

"It's not—"

I didn't know why it was so important she stay with me. I just didn't want to say goodbye just yet. I didn't want it to be our last one. This was the way the game was supposed to be. Me and her.

"I know it's a risk, but we've been training for this for months. We can't do one mission?"

"Grig."

I knew the way she said my name, and this time she said it like it was a no.

"Oh." I scratched my ear and searched the woods for, well, for a reason to look away, to be honest.

"It's . . ." She inhaled sharp and deep. "I want to live."

"All right, that's fine. You can point the way, and I'll do it on my own, that'll be fine."

She reached for my arm, but her fingers slid through my freckled skin. "Grig, there's something I need to tell you."

I drummed my fingers against my chest. "I appreciate what you're risking to help me. I really do. But it's not worth risking your life, so it's probably best—"

"I have muscular dystrophy."

My eyes found hers. "Wut?"

"I know you know I have a disability, and that I can't reach above my head, but it's more than I've told you. I can't . . ." She trailed off, her eyes closed tightly. "I hate admitting when I can't do things, because I can do anything, you know? I can drive a car, I can go to college, I can sneak out of my house and qualify for an international contest, and find an amazing guy from across the globe, but I can't stay here. My life matters, and I have to fight extra hard to say that."

"Why didn't you tell me?"

She wouldn't look at me. "I liked when you didn't know. I liked who you thought I was."

Apparently I wasn't as bright as I thought I was. How much work did she go into to hide this from me? That time when she fell asleep with the laptop by her . . . Was that because she couldn't move it?

How serious was muscular dystrophy? I didn't know enough about it. I wanted to run a search for it, to know everything about what we were going to face. But my heart settled quickly. No matter what would come, it didn't change anything, not for me.

"You could have told me." I said. My voice was calmer than my mind.

"I know. I know."

But I could have asked more questions. I looked at her, really looked. She always seemed so tough, but she seemed so breakable now, like she was made of porcelain.

She closed her eyes. "And *that's* why I didn't tell you. I'm not . . . argh." Her eyes flashed open wide. "I can't log out."

I remembered, suddenly, my granddad, the way he hated when

people didn't know what to say, when people talked around his illness. I knew how to handle this. "Why would you log out? We're having a conversation."

"When it comes to fight or flight, I have wings and I run."

"Not very fast."

Her face froze. "That's not funny."

"It's a little funny." I touched her arm, and I could feel her skin. I swallowed back my worry. "I don't run. It's not in my nature. So you can flit around all you like, little bird, but once your heartbeat settles, you can come find me. If you need to go, I'll be okay. But I'm not quitting on you."

"You sure?" she asked, her eyes glistening.

I had to be enough for her. "You can trust me with who you are. I promise you, love. I can handle it."

"I'm Zoe. By the way."

"Zoe." I savored the way her real name felt in my mouth.

She bit her lip. "I like how you say my name."

I smiled. "I'm Griffin, by the by."

"I know," she said. "I looked up all your information before we ever talked."

"I figured. You're a curious girl."

She drew a breath like she drew a sword and she faced me like she faced certain death. "I'm not going to get better, Grig."

I drew a shallow breath. "That doesn't matter."

"In fact, I'm just going to keep getting worse."

"I'm not going anywhere." My voice trembled, and I fought it. I wanted to be strong for her, but the idea of losing her like I lost my granddad broke my resolve. I stepped close. So close the feathers from her robe tickled my skin. So close I could see the fear in her eyes, see the moment she almost gave up on me. "I'm not running." I touched her cheek and she leaned into my hand. It was a promise. An oath. And I'd break all my bones before I broke it.

What did it mean that I could touch her? "You can't log out?"

She stepped back, her eyes wide with panic. "Oh yeah, no, that's bad. I'm trying. Just give me a minute."

Her skin raked with static. I reached for her and couldn't feel her. The sky flashed red. I heard thunder and lightning flashing at the horizon. "I'm going to have to damage the source code to break free."

My throat clenched. We both turned away from the sky.

"Go," I whispered.

She pointed up the path. "That way," she mouthed.

I nodded and she disappeared. And when she left she took a pixilated line of sky with her.

——— ——— ———

I felt more alone after she left. But I'd get back to her. I made a promise I wouldn't run, and I was going to keep it.

I followed the path until I found a cleric holding a lantern at the side of the path, like he was just waiting to give me a side quest. Silver hair, pale skin, his long red robe stained on the edges. And when he bowed, the light glinted off the gold markings on his forehead. "The Seer Spring said you were coming to aid us in our fight against the queen."

"You are an enemy to the queen?"

He bowed. "I am but a simple servant of the goddess. I am no warrior like you. We could use your help."

I nodded and he turned. I flexed my fingers and followed him, ready at any moment to draw bones to me. One thing I knew about video games was that the enemy of my enemy could very possibly be another enemy.

There wasn't anything suspicious about his bare feet walking the path, or the flash of his pink heels, though that was the most color about him. He seemed sapped of color, his skin almost gray. The roots of his hair were a deeper brown than the pale tips.

As we walked through the forest the trees seemed to dim. The colors shifting paler, leaves turning almost gray. Dwellings strung between branches, like treehouses high above the ground connected by rope bridges.

As we climbed closer to the spring, clerics began to emerge from their treehouses, and every one of them was unnaturally colorless, their clothing and skin shades of gray like a black-and-white photo.

I stared at a cleric praying from the top of a tree. "When did we step into Kansas?"

It wasn't just the clerics, even the trees had barely a trace of color. I clicked my heels. *There's no place like home, there's no place like home.*

The cleric gestured. "The Seer Spring steals our color."

I stepped lightly. I was pale enough already.

At a certain point along the trail, the houses stopped. A river babbled in the distance. A stark white insect crawled across the pale ground.

I didn't like this. The cleric stopped me at a line of pebbles across the path. The line of rocks continued into the forest, black and white on one side, soft brown and green on the other. Beyond the line of rocks, the slender trees were in grayscale, each leaf glistening and white.

"You must remove your shoes," he instructed. "This place is hallowed."

I nodded. The path to the Devout took many a hallowed detour.

I pried off my shoes and stepped over the rock line into the black-and-white woods. The ground on the other side of the marking was several degrees hotter. It burned my bare feet. I yelped and startled a bright red bird perched on a pale branch.

"Sorry. I didn't expect the ground . . ." They didn't need an explanation. "Never mind."

By the time we reached the spring, or at least the cliff across from it, my calves burned from the climb. Only the cleric's breaths were even. The ground broke free around us, sharp drops that hid their edges behind stark bushes and thin trees.

We clumped tight along the path, mindful of a misstep.

Beyond the canyon, a massive stone statue cried waterfalls from each carved eye. I stopped as my jaw dropped. The spring was a she. And she was breathtaking, a massive statue etched into the cliff face. Like Mount Rushmore, but female.

Bluebird would have loved this.

I moved toward the edge. Rickety wood and rope bridges crossed from cliff side to cliff side, the ropes bleached pale and frayed by time. Eight different bridges stretched higher and closer to her eyes, and if I had the time I could have climbed them. Clerics crossed the bridges, holding cups that drained of color as they filled.

At the end of the path I followed, a massive stone hand jutted off from the edge of the cliff. Seer water filled the base of the palm, maybe three meters across. A hawk circled directly above it.

Goose bumps shot up my skin. "Incredible."

Seer water seeped between my toes as I walked onto the upturned hand, leaned over the edge, and peered down. The carved hand was like a perfect diving board. Across from me the waterfall cascaded dozens of meters down to a clear sparkling pool where bone-white fish swam in perfect circles.

"Careful," the cleric warned. I stepped back.

He pointed to a cleric on the lowest bridge. "That cleric needs a key to unlock the gate that protects the only beach. One of the clerics on the bridges will have it, though I do not know which one. Perhaps if you assist them with their duties, they will give you a prize for your efforts. But beware, the farther down we collect the seer water, the clearer the sight. The clerics may speak prophecies, or they may speak riddles that will aid you on your journey."

The air smelled of fog, deep and murky.

There wasn't time for riddles. I glanced up to the damaged sky. Squares of light blurred, like they'd dissolved. One disappeared as I watched.

A Savak Wingship took off from the tallest spire of their castle. The soundtrack drummed heavy and menacing.

Word must have spread to the Savak queen that a player was here. They were coming for me.

The cleric lost his smile. They were coming for him too, I didn't doubt it.

"No time. I want to jump."

"Without wings?"

I trusted the cliff more than I trusted the Savak wings. My stomach tightened as I tiptoed back to the edge. I couldn't just hide. Not when the crown was so close. And this was so obviously an Indiana Jones leap of faith moment. I might die from it, but I doubted it. It was only about a skyscraper high. People had jumped from higher cliffs before. And I needed the velocity to reach the bottom of the spring.

I knew this was a risk, probably a daft risk.

But Bluebird was waiting for me, and if I hid or waited until they could catch me, the window of opportunity to grab the crown might draw its blinds. If we didn't get the armor, I'd never get back to her.

I let out a breath and stepped off the cliff.

My body arched like I was an Olympic diver. Not on my own skill, mind you. *I* was more like an Olympic belly flopper. My robes shook from the wind, and I knew this moment was making the most amazing cut scene. My heart thundered as I fell. My stomach flipped. I breathed until the fear faded, leaving only exhilaration behind. Falling was like running, like a rush of joy and freedom and victory.

The cleric shouted as I fell, the others creeping out to watch.

I felt alive in every centimeter. The wind rippled my robes and pulled at my cheeks, but I would not give in to fear. I was a bird, breaking the rules of flight. I pointed my fingertips above me in a perfect V.

The pool rushed closer.

I let out a steady breath and counted for the moment of collision with the water.

Three. The fish scattered, and my shadow shrunk on the surface of the water.

Two. Deep inhalation of breath. The air was sweet and the visions already blinding.

One.

I broke the surface. The impact sent tingles through my whole body, but they weren't painful. Underneath the water, the spring was even more beautiful than the falls that crashed into it, the water crisp and cold, the light scattered through it glittering. Stark white fish swam away through the pure water, like they were flying in a rippling nothing.

Gorgeous.

Another carved hand reached from the polished sand, and at the center of the palm was a crown. Silver and sparkling in the water, more a diadem than a crown. The orange stones were vivid color against this pool of white.

A circle appeared at the corner of my vision, like a timer slowly draining as my air ran out. I just had to grab the crown before the circle emptied.

A shadow ran over the crown—long, thick, and slithering through the water.

Bloody underwater levels.

23
DAGNEY

There were woods everywhere, a rocky mountainside, and a ceiling full of sky, but we stood like the trees had crowded us tightly together. The branches left eerie shadows and stripes of darkness through the muddy ground. My shoulder pressed against his chest, my skirts brushed against his legs, my bag dug into his hip.

He was my personal space.

I'd gotten so caught up in Ryo I'd lost track of my brother.

"We'll see Grigfen again," Ryo said softly. But that wasn't something he could promise. We couldn't know how much time we'd have left.

I pressed my palms against my stomach. But no matter what words he said or pressure I put on my stomach I couldn't smooth the tangle of worry inside me. He wrapped me in his arms and held me tight.

He was strong and steady. I could almost believe him that we'd make it out of this, or that Grig would be fine out there on his own.

Almost.

"Where to next?" I stepped away and he let me go.

"The Axes of Creation and Destruction." He glanced above me. "Are you hungry? Your stats are dropping."

"I'm fine." That was a blatant lie. "We should go."

"Are you sure? I can make you something. Might be good to press pause and regroup before we travel to the Kneult."

I ran a hand up my arm. "Do you even know how to cook? You are a prince."

"True. Prince Ryo has never cooked a meal in his life, but I can."

"That's confusing."

"Tell me about it."

"Who is real? What are you really like?"

He shrugged. "I don't know. I'm still me. Except, well . . . I play football." Great. "I'm lousy at math, but my mom sent me to a school with a STEM focus, so that sucks. I lost my dad, and my mom creates worlds." His smile seemed false, like something he put on to cover how he really felt. He met my eyes and the mask slipped. "Prince Ryo never lost his dad. And that kind of grief, it changes you. I have a bigger temper than Prince Ryo does, but I'm more likely to take risks. Something in me broke when I lost him, and it's broken again every time I've died in this game. I'm not really sure who I am anymore, having gone through that."

I reached for his hand.

He squeezed my hand and kissed my fingers. "How about you? Who is the real Dagney Tomlinson?"

He said it with a smile, but I couldn't respond with one. "Hungry," I said after a second. "I'm hungry."

"Let me take care of that." He opened the bag and gave it a dirty look. "Why would you pack an entire bag full of cheese?"

"It travels well."

"Always so practical." He made a face and dug deeper.

"But not quite to your taste?"

He gave a crooked smile. He could smile when he said he didn't like something; was that what his face would look like when he decided he didn't like me?

Activate Traveling Boots.

"One second." My heart raced so fast, I barely timed my step before I ran away. 3 percent. Far enough away I wouldn't see him, but not so far I'd plunge into an ocean. Again. I took a traveling step with my boots and he disappeared. One second he was there, grinning, and the next I was alone in the woods, dressed in the flickering light. I combed my fingers through my tangled hair and braided it back with nimble fingers.

WHAT WAS I DOING? He was a football-playing, egotistical, and yet secretly broken boy. This was not a good idea. Maybe you don't even like him. Maybe he's just tall, have you thought about that?

Side quest, find peddlers, I thought.

The arrow in my mind spun, and I measured the distance between where they were and where I'd stepped. I'd stepped 3 percent away from Ryo, and they were that 3 percent plus some. *5 percent.*

I took a step and landed just outside the peddlers' camp.

Deactivate Traveling Boots.

I walked through the camp. There was a flurry of activity throughout the carts: grieving people burying their dead, tending to wounds, and a woman assembling our supplies into a pile they were clearly about to abandon. The children leaned on their parents' shoulders. At least they were alive.

She faced me. "Ah, Lady Tomlinson. You've survived the onslaught. How fares the prince?"

Her face was blank of emotion, but something in her eyes seemed tired.

Maybe it was all the deaths in this game, but something in me had shifted. "I won't ask you to do more."

Her shoulders slumped with relief.

"I'm just looking for food."

"Take what you'd like," she said, gesturing her hand toward the pile.

I loaded my bag with dry crackers, drink in sealed bottles, and dried meat. I glanced around. I didn't know if I could come back for more supplies. The league boots made traveling easier, but we'd have to carry what we needed on our backs.

I licked my lips. "I'd like to trade back for my ring."

Why did I want it? It wasn't attached to plus accuracy, or style. But it was my mother's ring. On my eighth birthnight my fictional mother had knelt with me up in our attic and asked if I was old enough to be trusted with her greatest treasure, a ring she'd gotten from her mother, and her mother before that. And then she died, and it was all I had left to remember her.

And at the same time, the ring was only a token from a story, an implanted memory with a side attachment of grief and guilt, so I'd traded it like it was nothing.

"I'm sorry, my lady." The peddler I'd traded the ring to pressed his hand to his chest. "I sold that ring."

I closed my eyes. My real mother was still very much alive outside the game. We used to be so close when I was younger, then the bullying started, and my mom didn't stop it. I knew she tried, and I knew she loved me, but she wanted me to be more like them. She wanted me to diet and wear darker colors, told me if I wasn't so angry all the time and if I kept my opinions to myself maybe they'd leave me alone. She treated me like I was a problem she could solve, and I gave her nothing but my anger for it.

But when I touched Lady Tomlinson's ring, it was like remembering that someone missed me. Someone wanted me to come home.

"That's fine," I lied.

I packed anything that seemed useful and stepped back to where Ryo waited. My full bag pressed against my leg, and I held two roasted turkey legs.

Ryo's hair was carefully parted, his cape back on. I wasn't the only one who took my time away as a chance to gather myself.

"Tell me you paid for this." His eyes twinkled as he took the turkey leg.

I smiled at the memory. "I traded so well, they paid me."

I took a bite. Oh gosh, this was heaven. Whatever hack they did that made us feel pain also made us able to eat, and I thanked them for that. I loved food. I loved the char on this meat, the crunch of the crackers. If we were in real life, we'd need to drink a lot more water, but then again if we were in real life we'd have to pee a lot more often.

I couldn't think about that anymore. I was giving myself a headache. "Can I ask you a question?"

He wiped turkey grease off his lip.

"Your mother is Ms. Takagi. But your face was different so . . ." I trailed off, not quite sure how to continue.

"Are you asking why my mother photoshopped her own son's face?"

"I'm trying not to."

"It was a bad call, right? The real me is super hot." He grinned, but I didn't think he was joking. "But only my brow ridge and this massive chin have changed. The rest of me is exactly the same. I mean these abs are photorealistic."

I rolled my eyes and wouldn't look at him. "Would you put your shirt down?"

He laughed and tucked in his shirt, but not before I caught a glimpse of the skin beneath. My cheeks burned. I was in so much trouble.

He stared up at the damaged sky, his hair flopping to the side as he moved. "The marketing department thought the game would sell better if the main character was more traditionally handsome. Appeal to the broadest range of consumers."

"That's horrible. And your mom just let them?"

Ryo took the last bite and tossed the bones into the bushes. "I guess so. And it's stupid. Everyone has their own type, so the idea that I have to look like someone else in order to appeal to the greatest amount of people is, well, insulting and dismissive, and man. I didn't realize I felt this much about this. It's messed up. Isn't it?"

It really was. "It's like being a girl."

His eyes flashed and he scooted closer. "I bet. The girls at my school, I swear, just keep trying to morph into the same person. Bleaching their hair, nose jobs, color contacts. All of that. It's like they think a girl has to look a certain way for a boy to woo her."

I hit his arm. There was an insult in his words, either to me, or to other girls.

Or maybe the truth just pissed me off. I looked away. "Did you just say 'woo'?"

"It's a word we handsome princes say."

I laughed, despite myself.

He pressed his hand to his heart. "Warn me before you do that. your entire face lights up and you're completely adorable."

"You're completely adorable," I grumbled.

I expected a look of triumph when I flirted back, but he didn't even pause. "I know. That's what I've been saying." His gaze slid to mine and that was when he grinned, and I had to smile back.

I was so dead.

He rubbed his knuckle under his nose. "That's why it doesn't bother me that it's not my jawline on the game. It's marketing lies"—he licked his fingers—"but I'm still me. Besides, I don't want to see an exact replica of my face on billboards, or banner ads, or TV commercials, when the game launches."

"Do you think it will still launch?"

"I don't know. I hope it does."

I scooted closer. "What's it like being the child of Nao Takagi?"

He winced. And then that polished mask came back on.

"Sorry," I said. "I didn't mean to sound like an interviewer or something."

"No, it's okay." He leaned back like he was suddenly mindful that we were being watched. "It's good." His shoulder bobbed and he lowered his voice. "It was good. My mother smiled in all the family pictures, came home at night and ate the food my dad made for us all, and we'd play Mario Kart as a family. We were all so proud of everything she made, but sometimes it felt like she never really wanted to have kids." He stared at the ruins around us. "Like I was the compromise she would not make twice. I think I only exist because of my dad. He always wanted to have kids, and she fell in love with the wrong person."

"That's hard."

He shook his head. "It wasn't. I had a good education, everything I'd ever wanted. My dad made my childhood a joy. But . . . when he died when I was twelve"—he swallowed—"my mom and I were both stuck with a life she didn't want."

"How'd he die?"

"He had a stroke." Ryo bit his lip. "We were playing *Ashcraft*. Level three by the waterfalls. It took me a couple minutes to realize why his character wouldn't stop running into a rock."

I put my head on his shoulder. "Oh my gosh."

"I haven't really played much since then."

"I don't blame you. I wouldn't either."

"And then after, it seemed safer to keep separate from her world. She had this game and I had a security guard named Thomas who looked quite a bit like Sir Tomlinson."

"Let me guess: he didn't approve of your friends, but he thought you had potential."

"It's like you've met him." He smiled. "So I don't mind the anonymity of wearing a different face. Honestly I'm not used to being a part of my mom's world."

I touched his arm. "That sucks." He shook his head, but I stopped him. "Look, you have the right to whatever you are feeling. You don't always have to be agreeable."

He swallowed. "It's my job to make my mom happy."

"No," I said. "It's her job to keep you safe."

He wrapped his gloved fingers around mine. We were both quiet.

"I really like you, Dagney," he said softly.

His heart thundered so hard, I could feel his pulse racing, even through the gloves.

I took a breath. "I really like you too, Ryo."

"Dagney." He sounded so surprised, and so happy. He couldn't fake that kind of happy. His hands cupped my cheek. "If I kiss you, will you hit me?"

"I have no idea. I might."

He bent closer. "Thank you for the warning."

I was smiling when our lips met and smiling when he pulled his lips away. He breathed me in, both of us silent and feeling the aftershock, not of our sparks, but of our honesty. He moved first, bending his neck until his lips reached my hand, and he stole the last bite of my food.

I shoved his shoulder with my arm. His nose crinkled as he chewed with his mouth open, blatantly trying to make me smile.

I didn't like mirrors, but I liked the way I reflected in his eyes. "This is my favorite level." I cleared my throat. "But we should go."

"All right. To the Kneult!" He made a soft accent on the *k*, then offered his palm.

I wished we could stay here longer.

I took his hand and aimed the boots. The step power meter raised and lowered. The words *Obtain the Axes of Creation and Destruction* ran across my vision, and the arrow in my mind pointed south.

I reached into my bag and pulled out my map. "Okay. Let's do some math."

"Here." He handed me a pencil. His expression seemed eager. I scowled at him. Why did his expression seem eager? "You can hold it against your lip, if you'd like."

I whacked his arm with the pencil, my cheeks warming. "This was a mistake, I can already tell." I turned back to my map.

Okay. If I stepped about 15 percent we should be able to see the mountain peaks, and then I could course correct after pinpointing our location on the map.

I glanced at him and he grinned. Dang it. I'd placed the pencil on my lip.

I grabbed his arm and we took a step.

Traveling dried out my eyes, with the wind rushing forward. I could almost see our surroundings, like we'd fast-forwarded through them, but not clearly enough to pick out images. We stopped. There was that peak. Saint Gial's Tooth. There was a story there, but I didn't have time to ask.

I found our exact location and then measured the distance again. I'd say 20 percent. Or should I go 25? *Hmm. Best to not overshoot, I think. Give us some time to make a plan as we approach the Kneult.*

I stepped forward, but halfway there, we snagged to a stop. The momentum shoved me to my knees and knocked Ryo clear to the ground. The ground shook beneath us, like we got kicked out of traveling. Even the boots deactivated themselves, and my arrow just spun in place, like a loading screen restarting.

What on earth?

We were on a hill, overlooking the ocean. What had stopped us? Far to the west, near the Island of the Savak, the red sky tore at the horizon. And then another scar through the sky, three times as thick as the last one, ripped up and over, like a rainbow of broken pixels.

"That's not good," Ryo said. Way to make an understatement. I met Ryo's eyes, and somewhere, behind that damaged expression, hid a boy who was dying. He could joke all he wanted, but I couldn't forget that. He was programmed to be the main character in a game that was breaking down.

Of course it was breaking him too.

I wrapped my arm around his waist. "To the Kneult?"

"You meant K-neult."

I pulled out the map again and tried to gather my bearings. "Why do you pronounce it 'the K-neult'? I thought the *k* was silent."

"Oh. It probably is for the game. My mom might have forgotten that my dad liked to pronounce the silent *k*. He'd say, "I k-now," and then we'd laugh, or when he'd knock on my door, he'd always say, 'k-nock, k-nock.'"

"That's k-adorable."

He smiled at me like what I said was actually funny, or maybe like he was just glad to have someone to talk to about his dad. Ryo smiling in his full armor was a sight, like some drawn perfection glowing in digital sunlight. But all I could see was the boy behind the screen. Lost and broken and the next to die.

I clenched my fists. He wasn't just tall. I couldn't let him die for real.

Engage Traveling Boots.

The bar reappeared at the side of my vision, but it didn't go up or down. *Resume step?*

I clutched my fingers in his cloak and nodded. My spine tingled with the step, and the ground began to change from brown to deep red sand as we moved south toward the coast.

The staggered lights forced my eyes to blink, the movement sending drag on my back, pushing me closer against Ryo's chest. Each blink brought a new vision as we rushed from horizon to horizon, following the packed dirt road toward Freedom Square, the capital city of the Kneult.

The step stopped us outside the city.

Disengage boots.

"So, we're going after the Axes of Creation and Destruction," I said.

"And hopefully a few more players with the Kneult," Ryo said. His eyes narrowed as he read something in his vision that I couldn't see. "Isabel and Marcus are the players in the Kneult sector."

"What do you know about the Kneult?" I asked as I started walking up the road.

Ryo matched my stride. "My dad invented them, back when he would tell me bedtime stories, or when we'd go camping. They were short angry people with mold growing from their knees. Both the men and the women wore long tangled beards, and they traded their way to power, the person with the most money ruling the kingdom."

"A plutocracy. Or is it capitalism?"

He chuckled. "That's not the message of the stories."

"So what is?"

He smiled a little. "There were a few stories my father told about the Kneult. One was about a boy and a girl, children of rival trading houses, who always competed for the best trade. They would haggle for a pair of shoes, and the girl would win, haggle for a sword of iron, and the girl would win, haggle again for a harp that played an angelic song, and the girl would win. But when she asked the boy why he never traded in his crops or his carvings, even when he had more and could have won the trade, he kissed her and asked her to marry him. And though the families despised the match, though he was a penniless fool, he'd won the one trade that mattered. He'd won her heart."

I leaned into his shoulder. "I like that story."

"I like it too. Because that's how he got all the girl's stuff."

I elbowed him in the side, and he laughed again, free and easy. Lighter somehow.

My smile faded as I stepped into empty streets broken with streams and bridges—not one mold-specked person in sight. Freedom Square's harbor was crisscrossed with empty piers, faded docks, and not a single ship. Empty streets fled through brightly painted buildings and a street market with no bustle except the clothing hanging from wires across alleys. The entire city seemed deserted.

Ryo scanned the street. "No welcoming committee?"

"It is only us."

"We are incredibly impressive. There should be banners, ribbons, parades."

I picked up a handful of the strange red dirt and threw it in the air. "Better, Your Highness?"

He didn't smile. His eyes scrutinized the street. "No." He took my hand and held me close to his side. "We should have allies here. The king, his council, General Franciv. This was supposed to be the last stand against the Savak."

No shadows moved in the city. No footsteps sounded except our own. There was no movement except the water that seeped between the cracks on the cobbled streets. Constellations of mold speckled the base of all the buildings. The road led forward to an open area. At the center was a large dry marble fountain. Instead of a stream of water, a pair of axes balanced at the top.

I let go. "Well, that works for me," I said as I crossed to the fountain edge in one step.

"Careful. It could be a trap."

The streets were empty, and the soundtrack was incredibly generic. "There's no one here."

"Exactly. Where is everyone? Don't touch it."

"Why not?" I climbed over the stone lip into the dry basin. "We should grab them and go before the Savak catch up to us. This is why we came, Ryo. Have a little trust." I stretched my arm and plucked the axes from the fountain's base.

I froze as light struck my arms.

There was a soft rumble.

Items 3/6.

I took quick steps back and jumped over the lip. The fountain released a stream of water, and with the motion came the rumble of the city around us. The empty streets filled with Kneultians wearing bright colors and mucked boots that covered their knees. The women did not have the long beards that framed the faces of nearly every man, but they did wear gray aprons tucked right under their chins. They bartered in the markets and scolded children, and they barely gave Ryo and me a second look.

Why would retrieving the axes wake the city?

I held the axes in each hand. Their weight perfectly balanced and the workmanship seemed even finer than the axe I'd yielded as the King's Executioner, and way better than the one I'd traded for the

Traveling Boots. They felt natural in my grip. Solid. Better than any sword. Any dagger.

This was my character the way she was supposed to be, daughter of an Executioner, axe in both hands.

"Look at their expressions," Ryo said. "Everyone seems so sad."

I lowered my axes. He was right. Black mourning ribbons were tied around the necks of the villagers. At the end of every street, a man or woman carried a tin bucket to a door and slapped black paint on the door casings.

"What's happening?" I asked a Kneult woman.

She covered her mouth with a lace handkerchief. "Down to the docks. It's horrible. The Savak." She blubbered on more words I couldn't understand.

The arrow in my mind pointed to the docks.

Ryo took off at a full run. I struggled to match his pace. As I ran I could hear the names of those they mourned. Isabel, the daughter of the trading House Takkan, and Marcus, son of the trading House Biento.

Two of the names on the player guide.

We found their bodies struck through on spikes. A silver plaque hung heavy around both of their necks. The words *Killed Personally by the Queen of the Savak* were etched in fine calligraphy.

"We're too late," I whispered into Ryo's chest.

While we'd kissed and talked and eaten lunch, the players we'd come here to save had died. That was why this area of the game was so quiet. It'd shut off.

There was no one here to play.

24
BLUEBIRD_OFDEATH

I threw myself back against the chair and ripped the VR screen from my eyes, like they were dollar store sunglasses and not the most advanced thing to come out of E3 since . . . well, anything.

I clutched my knees. *I'm alive. I'm alive.*

The neural net didn't just catch me. I didn't have to damage the source code in order to break out. I didn't just make things so much more dangerous for Grig.

"You're okay, Zoe. You're okay." A nurse checked my pupils. There were so many nurses on this floor it was hard to keep track of them. But I tried. I checked her name tag: April.

"Where's Ms. T?" I asked.

April checked my pulse. "How are you feeling? Your heart rate is racing."

"I'm alive, and I'm out. What's happened since I plugged in?"

Behind the nurse's shoulder, a massive flat-screen held camera feeds showing an overview of the players' hall. A doctor sat with his head in his hands, and two more beds were empty.

My heart stopped, and April heard it through her stethoscope.

We lost two more? I sat up to look at the screens. I just saw empty beds. Who was missing?

April attached a blood pressure cuff on my arm. I tried to look beyond her.

Isabel and Marcus.

No. My vision blurred and I slumped back onto my pillow. They were doing fine before I hopped into the game and now they were gone.

It was too quick. I couldn't fight the idea that I could have gone in there and done something to stop it.

Something to stop her.

After April tested my nerves for further damage and took my blood pressure, she helped me transfer from the game chair to my wheelchair.

She backed away as I rolled my chair to the screens.

I closed my eyes and started praying. There wasn't anything else I could do. This room was too small, and there weren't enough people in it. I zoomed in the image until all I could see was Grig's sleeping face. His breathing slow and his heartbeat marching on, steady and calm.

I couldn't say the same thing about mine.

My thumb traced the screen.

"Hi, Grig," I whispered. "Wake for me. Please. Shake yourself free and come say hi to me."

His heart beat on but he didn't speak.

I ran my fingers across his hair. "That's okay too." A nurse pulled his blanket so it covered his shoulder.

I wanted him to grin at me again, to flash me those dimples and kind eyes. I wanted to go back in time to see him through my laptop screen, his hair rumpled, wearing a hoodie from a band I'd never heard of, three days' stubble on his chin, drinking tea in a fancy cup. Or when he stayed up late talking to me with a fluffy blanket wrapped over his head, or the time I logged in wearing Princess Leia buns in my hair, and he wore a Batman mask, and neither of us planned it, and it was nowhere close to Halloween.

I touched the glass like the thousand times I'd touched my laptop screen.

He couldn't feel it now either.

I zoomed out to check on the others. Ryo lay in one corner. Dagney's and Grig's beds were next to each other. Andrew had a thick tube coming out his mouth. And next to him was the girl who played the queen of the Savak. She smiled as she slept, beautiful even in a coma. Her skin shone like a night-light, her hair draped over her shoulders like it was styled, and her eyes . . . Eyes should not be that big, not if they weren't animated by Disney.

McKenna Carrington. Only daughter of Preston Carrington, CFO. Player killer.

25
MCKENNA

I had not spent enough time at the Seer Spring. The waterfall and carvings were so theatrical and glistening. I really should have done more training here. The camera angles would have been gorgeous with the waterfall as a backdrop. I landed at the cliff's base, and the clerics scattered away.

I ignored them.

There was a player here. The indicator column rose from under the water.

Green.

That was Sir Grigfen Tomlinson's color. Or, by his real name, Griffin McNaughton. In my prep work before the game I'd almost counted him out, but that last qualifying match was impressive. Almost like seeing Liza perform at the Palace. Just a genius in his art, working at the top of his craft. I didn't know enough about game play to know how he did it, but I knew enough to be impressed.

This would not be an easy kill.

I leapt from the cliff top and let my wings carry me down slowly, gliding to the lowest bridge.

The water of the spring frothed at the base of the waterfall, but I could see through the cresting water. Below the surface, Grigfen fought a massive snake, which seemed to disappear in the light.

Stop stealing my act, snake.

He drew bones from the ground, the water churning as they struck forward. Devout magic. Interesting.

It took three magic spells, and each approach to the surface for air seemed slower. The use of magic made him tired. Weak.

Hmm, last thing I wanted was to fight someone who felt cornered.

I flexed my wrist, palmed a blade, and aimed where he'd next surface.

It would be best to kill him before he could hurt me.

But he didn't surface as I expected. He dropped to the bottom and then twisted, shooting daggers of bone into that water snake, and as he did the snake grew visible, silver and sparkling like it was scaled with mirrors, seeping blood into the water from its wounds.

He claimed the Crown of Visions. It didn't slip through his fingers like it did mine.

A tunnel opened out of the spring.

Shoot. If he exited into the clerics' tunnels he wouldn't get out for days. The first time I came here, they conned me into side quest after side quest, and all I got for the trouble were a few thousand pearls.

But Griffin didn't take the tunnels. Instead, he surfaced, the snake wrapped around his neck, the crown in his hands. His giant grin covered his face, and then he started convulsing . . . no, I think it was some sort of dance. My jaw loosened. He was charming in his dorkiness. He wasn't my type of attractive, more cute than handsome, like a puppy dog right after a bath. Slightly pathetic, but arresting all the same.

But Andrew had taught me not to fall for any tricks. Grigfen hadn't noticed me yet, but he was deadly enough to kill that giant water snake.

I fired the dagger.

His eyes met mine, and he stopped dancing. He moved his hand

and my dagger changed its trajectory as if an invisible wind had knocked it off course. It splashed in the water.

Oh no. I palmed a new dagger and prepared for battle.

He raised both his hands. "I give up!"

What kind of trick was this? I fired again. Two blades this time. He gestured again. This time the blade barely budged, and it nearly got him. His eyes were shadowed; though maybe it was just that the kohl on his eyes had smeared. I couldn't tell if he was angry or scared. Either way he was about to attack.

He dipped below the surface, and I followed his swimming toward the shore, firing blades one after another and spreading ripples in the blood-tinted water.

He surfaced again, his pale hands shaking. "Wait, wait, *wait*!"

"For your health to refill?" I pressed the button on my wrist to switch from blades to flame. "I don't think so."

"Don't kill me okay?" He swallowed hard, his Adam's apple bobbing. "I can help you."

I aimed my flame shooter. "I don't believe you."

"That's not even the hard-to-believe part."

I sparked the oils.

He yelped and ducked under the surface. My flames created steam as they evaporated the surface of the water. I'd boil him out.

But it'd also make my hair frizz.

I turned off the flames and went back to my blades.

"Please, please, *please*," he said as he breached the water, treading low. "Okay, *okay*. I give up. Don't kill me."

His acting was a little over the top, but there was something that felt sincere. But Andrew had seemed sincere too. I pointed my wrist.

He closed his eyes and sunk below the surface. He spat out water. "Please. I can't believe I'm going to die because I can't talk to a girl."

"It's not . . ." I inhaled. I didn't want to break character, but he seemed so honestly scared. I didn't want him to think he was actually dying. "You'll be okay," I whispered. "You'll just wake up at Stonebright."

He didn't open his eyes, he just muttered under his breath.

They could edit that part out.

I rearmed, but he didn't move to fight back. I fired.

The dagger hit him between the ribs.

He dipped below the water. His health was already low, but the blade dropped the health lower.

He didn't fight back, but miserable red eyes met mine. "Please. It's part of my game condition to turn on my friends." He spat out blood. "Let me help you. I'll do anything. Just please don't kill me."

I raised my palm again. He didn't fight back.

How was I supposed to work with someone who wouldn't participate?

The crafting ability in my stats lit up. More tailoring skills must have unlocked.

I guess having a Devout wouldn't be so bad.

I mimed firing, and he winced. But I didn't shoot. Instead, I reached for his arm. His health was too low. I might kill him just from the flight back to my castle. I pulled him up until our noses touched and then turned my head slightly so the hibisi tea would drip down onto his bloody mouth.

"You are now the property of the Savak queen," I hissed, trying to cover this breach in character action with very on-character words. "You try anything, and I will kill you. No lies, no tricks, and in fact, no words. I don't trust you, and I will kill you to win this game."

I clipped him to my Wingship. Before we left, his loyalty colors had turned red.

Though maybe that was all the blood.

I had a final battle scene to prepare for, and a nearly dead new ally to get costumed.

It was almost time for places.

The docks were in ruins. Flames had scorched the shore; the docks themselves barely kept floating. And all along the dark pebbled shore, bodies wrapped in stark-white clothes lay like keys on a piano. Even with how fast we could travel, we'd missed the last stand against the Savak queen.

"We should go," I said. I didn't move.

And Dagney didn't either. "How can we leave their bodies staked through like this?" She ran her fingers through her tangled hair. "I know it's not real, but . . ."

"It's real enough."

We helped lift their bodies off the stakes, and Dagney helped wrap them. The Kneult offered us hibisi for the effort, a jar of brewed blossom tea, with stronger healing properties than chewing the leaves on their own.

Then they led us to the bodies from our own kingdom.

General Franciv, Lord Reginal, Sir Tomlinson. The queen.

And my father.

All lay wrapped in white fabric, on the edge of the ocean they believed was a god called Mother. Funny, I called the god of this world Mother too.

We didn't tell them our names, so they couldn't know we knew them. They couldn't know that this side quest meant more to me than the vague promise of treasure at the end of it.

And now they'd arranged a way for the ocean they called Mother to welcome our dead back home. They carried their bodies over our shoulders to boats made of paper. Some boats were thick and finely crafted, some barely covered the water.

The council's boats were gifts from the Kneult. My father's boat seemed almost holy, marked with dripping candles. Dagney and I carried the council members' bodies, one by one by one. We pushed them into the waves, watching the paper disintegrate slowly. The paper boats lasted a small distance into the ocean, until the bodies sunk under the glistening water.

It was heavy, hard work, until there was only one body left. He was already wrapped, and he wasn't my father, not really. I'd already buried my father.

So thank you, Mom, for making me live through this twice.

The lapping waves pushed against my legs, my father's weight heavy over my shoulder. Dagney carried him too, strong and steady. I felt as flimsy as a fishing line with no lure, no anchor. The waves could knock me over, and they tried, they tried. We lowered him onto the boat made of money and then we pushed him out.

The lapping waves carried me forward without my permission. My memories wanted to follow him out there, to watch him sink until the darkness sealed him away forever.

Dagney held my arm. The sunset sent streaks of orange and red across the brutal sea. Their families mourned them with wails and songs and tears of grief, quiet echoes of my feelings, like my grief was outside me, dressed in white, singing a mourning song. The Kneult lowered Marcus's and Isabel's bodies into their boats. Marcus's name was too close to my father's, and when his family wailed out his name and sang hymns of grief, it echoed a reminder of the moment I'd watched my father's casket lowered into the earth.

I couldn't face those memories.

But I missed them too. They'd started to fade into the years since I'd lived them. In a small way, it was a gift to get them back, to remember the smell of leaves and upturned earth, and the moment when my father disappeared. One moment I said goodbye to his casket, and the next it was covered by dirt.

When my father died, there'd been a short paragraph listed in the news. He was called Nao Takagi's husband. There'd been no grand list of achievements, nothing to share how proud I'd always been of him. It didn't list the way he always pulled over when he saw someone stranded with a stalled car. It didn't show the way he paid the bills on time, or cut his sandwiches into triangles, or ate mayonnaise with a spoon, or his Mickey Mouse impressions. No obituary listed the way he listened without judgment, or the way his attention made me feel like I was royalty.

And then he was gone, and the world didn't change at all with his absence. The stock market wasn't affected. The buses didn't slow. My father meant nothing to the world.

But he meant the world to me.

How cruel a gift for my mother to make me live through this again.

Dagney wrapped her arm around my back. Standing steady. Strong.

We should get out of the water, but we didn't move.

Isabel's boat had been covered in flowers, and the pale yellow blossoms floated in the glittering water marking the last place we saw them.

We stood vigil longer than we should have.

The sky was broken, and Grig was out there alone, and we had a game to win. But we knew as soon as we left, the scene here would end. As soon as we left, no one here would mourn Isabel or Marcus. The

Kneult would go back to hibernation, and the bodies would stay in the water until the diseased sky swallowed the last of their bones.

Dagney moved first. She wiped her eyes on my shirt. "We need to find Grigfen. I can't let this happen to him."

"Where is he?"

She closed her eyes. Then she pointed across the harbor toward the Island of the Savak.

I swallowed.

The wailing song finished; the mourners traded for Marcus and Isabel's belongings, trading with memories, not money. A pair of boots traded to a boy about my age for a brief tale about a hunt, a shaving kit to a little girl for a story about how Marcus had taught her how to read. But did that mean the real Marcus liked to go hunting, or taught his little sister how to read? They traded Isabel's paintbrushes for a story about a kindness to a friend, and they gave her small dog to a woman who looked like her mother who stood and couldn't say anything at all.

When they brought out Isabel's armor, they brought it to Dagney. "For your help carrying the bodies, we'd like to give you this armor."

Dagney inhaled, her eyes tabulating the stats of the armor, and then for a moment, she dropped her eyes. "Thank you."

They turned to me. "And you, Prince Ryo. Yes, we know who you are. We honor your father's service, and the duty you've performed today. We offer you the armor of Marcus, and your father's sword."

"What about my mother?" I said, frustrated the queen wasn't honored. "I lost her too."

The truth of my statement tore my throat ragged. I missed my dad every second of my life, but I knew he didn't choose to leave.

I lost my mom the day my dad died. And every night she didn't come home, every time she heard me cry and didn't check on me, every time I grieved my dad on my own, was her choice.

They couldn't just forget that loss.

We could have grieved him together. Instead she made this worthless game that was trying to kill me, and then forced me to relive my grief as realistically as possible.

What was wrong with her?

Dagney cleared her throat. "Thank you for your trade." Attention turned to Dagney, like a weight pulled off my shoulders. "We'll be leaving now."

The game paused like it was waiting for me to say more, but I just stared into their computerized faces and waited for them to move on. I wasn't going to take my words back. I'd just found them.

They handed me the king's sword, and I leveled up. Light shone from the sword in my hand, brighter than this harsh sun, highlighting the shimmering silver and the bronze handle.

I wasn't just a hunter now. I was my father's son.

And we were going to win this game for him.

Dagney had leveled up too, her health full, her cheeks glowing.

I held up the breastplate. Marcus had worn this, earned it over his time in the game. His thickly plated armor had maxed-out protection and speed. The thick silver armor didn't match the outfit I wore underneath, but he'd worked so hard for this. It was an honor to wear this before the final battle. I'd carry him on my shoulders as a thank-you.

Isabel's armor fit small on Dagney, leaving vulnerabilities at her side. The Axes of Creation and Destruction formed an X behind her back. She put on a helmet, the helm shadowing her eyes. I crossed to her and pulled off her helmet.

I wasn't ready to not see her eyes.

I gave her a kiss, soft and brief.

"For luck?" she asked. Her bottom lip tucked behind her teeth.

"Because I wanted to kiss you. You're not a rabbit's foot."

She grabbed my collar and pulled me down for another kiss.

And when she moved back, she smiled. "And don't you forget it."

I rested my forehead against hers.

"You were really brave," she said. "You okay?"

"We don't have time for okay." I put on a smile. "We have a queen to see."

We could do this.

Dagney was only at level twenty-one. I was nineteen. I'd have preferred to be at least above level fifty before we went against the queen of the Savak. I'd have preferred to have an army at my side, mechanicals at my flank, weapons buffed.

All I had was Dagney. She grinned at me and my muscles relaxed. They didn't stand a chance.

"The Island of the Savak is mostly mountain, and if I mistime it, we might end up encased in rock, so I'm going to take small steps. I'm aiming for that ship." She pointed to the horizon, where a fishing vessel sailed toward the Island of the Savak. "They might not take kindly to stowaways, so whatever happens I'm not going to stop walking. Hopefully there will be another ship beyond it, but if we land in the water, hold your breath, and hold on tight to me."

I tucked my fingers into the straps of her armor. Electricity drew us closer as she stepped toward a rocking boat. Sailors shouted at our arrival, but she stepped again, to a wrecked boat, covered in ashes. The wreckage dipped under our weight, seawater soaking up to my knees. There was nowhere else to step except the sea. The Savak were beyond the horizon, but I couldn't see their island. All I could see were waves.

Our eyes met and we took deep breaths. She studied my expression and gave a small nod.

Then she stepped right into the deep water.

The ocean tore at us. There was nowhere to step in the deep swirling sea. Dagney's eyes widened, her nostrils flaring under water. I threw myself forward and dragged her by her waist, pushing her legs forward. Light shifted around us as the next step landed, still underwater, ankles deep in demanding sand. The dirt swirled around us, sucking me down. Dagney held my armor tight and stepped off my knee. We shot forward again, deeper under the surface, the light of the sky so distant I couldn't see anything other than swirling black shadows and sharp circling fins.

Bubbles escaped her mouth, and my lungs ached. Her eyes widened in fear and I didn't pause to look at whatever creature she saw. I pushed her forward again. The drag tore at my grip, the ocean prying her nearly out of my hands. But she didn't quit. Not until we stood on the pebbled shore, ocean water to our shoulders, the water jostling us forward.

I coughed seawater until I could breathe without the rattle of salt in my lungs.

Dagney exhaled sharply, her soaked hair plastered to her face. "Disengage boots!" she shouted.

Both of us breathed out labored breaths.

We'd made it to the Island of the Savak.

27
GRIGFEN

When the world went back into focus, I kicked my bare feet against the ground and brought my legs into my chest. The agony in my ribs, sharp and stinging, blurred my vision. I could only take shallow breaths.

But I was alive, I hadn't broken my promise to Bluebird. Not yet.

A shadow loomed over me. I skidded backward, something metal and hard digging into my shoulder blades. A firm hand steadied me and something cold brushed my lips. Bitter drink quenched my dry tongue and slid down my clenched throat. Light followed that tea, awakening nerve endings. My broken ribs were still tender, but crusted over like the tea had grown armor inside me. Hibisi. Someone had brewed those blossoms. My eyes cracked open.

"Needs honey," I croaked.

A bloke in a horned golden mask knelt in front of me, holding a glass jar. His body was painted in Devani symbols, his bare chest was wrapped in a metal harness, and behind him were skeletal wings—gold and spindly, creaking under a pair of gears. An orange player indicator floated over his head.

At least it wasn't McKenna. "Thanks for the healing. I'm Grigfen314."

"ShadowscapeXI," his voice low rumbled, "but I go by Andrew here." I dropped my chin to my chest. I'd played *Ashcraft* with him before. He was quick and sometimes impatient, or short tempered with a loss, but he was alive and I was alive, and I was not picky on mates.

Darkness still coated my vision. It seemed even the sky had turned into shadow. "Where's McKenna?"

The cold marbled floor, covered in a mosaic tile, led to a filigree railing. We were on a rooftop, the open sky the only ceiling on the tallest tower of the castle. The twin moons left a highlight on the water.

"*Shhh!*" He shot a look behind us. The haze of loyalty around his shoulders was a mix of orange and red. "She's crafting. It's best to let her work."

He didn't have to tell me twice.

I stumbled to my feet, my balance top heavy. Golden bars strapped to my bare chest, a glistening clear stone right over my heart. Spindly golden wings grew from my back, heavy and sharp. These wings were not made for flapping.

My shirtless body had been painted in kohl. I looked like a drawn skeleton. Shaky lines traced over my bones and across my ribs. From the itch on my cheek and under my eyes, my face had been painted as well. I touched my nose and black kohl smeared onto my fingers.

It was, in a word, chilly.

I was grateful I was still wearing my trousers.

The cut in my side had been healed but my ribs ached. How long had I been unconscious?

The crown slid down my forehead. In the skill section of my stats, the words *Equip Crown of Visions?* highlighted.

I glanced around. A swarm of Wingships darkened the broken red sky above me, each one armed and watching the harbor, while a trio of zomoks flew around a hovering Wingship at the center that tossed oranges and whistled out commands. The jagged mountain peaks seemed low compared to this tower.

If not now, when?

Equip crown.

Electric shock rocked down my spine. The crown straightened itself on top of my head, as if by magic. A flicker. A flash, like a spurting video, and then the vision showed me Queen McKenna pressing a jewel bracelet like she'd clicked a button. I heard gears tick behind me, and then the sharp wings bolted to my back swung upward, through my ribs, and the bloodstained tips crisscrossed through my chest. McKenna let go of the button and smiled at me as my vision shadowed to black.

Regular game play shuddered through that black. I'd fallen to my knees, my heart racing as I touched the place on my chest where the blades would strike.

Deactivate crown.

That wasn't a future I wanted to see.

At the left, a large group of Devout knelt on all fours, manacles slung around their ankles. I stepped toward them, and their gaze turned to me. I knew a few of them—Rogi, Boll, and Vaika. Their loyalties flickered green for an instant as we met eyes, before shifting back to red as their shoulders caved in defeat when I joined them.

They sang a low hymn, forming ghostlight into a low hanging green mist, which siphoned into a trailing snakelike shape toward a pile of black lumps at the center of the ballroom floor.

I raised my voice with theirs, ghostlight pulsing forward toward robes covered with raven feathers, lying like lumps on the polished floor.

Historians. She was making Historians?

McKenna knelt in the middle of the lumpy piles of robes and gears, a screwdriver held between lips painted the color of blood as she fiddled with a mechanical. She was dressed in breeches, a pale billowing tunic, and a sheer red coat, which tapered sharply at her waist and fell to her mid-thigh. And the bracelet from the crown's vision that would trigger my death was tucked into the work belt slung over her hips, like just another tool.

She motioned with her fingers and Andrew joined her side. He twisted a stream of the snakelike mist around his fingers then blew it into the gears.

The mechanical engine coughed a green exhaust before the gears purred to life, making those raven feather–covered lumps rise. They stood at attention, and then they began to spin, an army of Historians, dancing to silence. Each one touched spindly hands and spun again, their robes spreading in the movement, revealing flashing blades at the ready. Their carved silver masks sparkled like empty starlight. The Historians were not supposed to dance. They were made to record history, not to be music box spinners, and certainly not to carry weapons.

"What do you think?" McKenna asked, watching me.

Um . . . luckily she didn't wait for my answer, because at the moment I was still struggling to find words.

"They're not too much, are they? I was going to try and train my army to dance. Imagine a cast of thousands in an epic ballroom scene. But they were not as coordinated as I'd hoped for people who know how to fight. Five, six, seven, eight, slash, turn, stab. You'd think it was the same thing and that they could at least pick up a box step, but nope."

She pressed a button and the Historians took another turn about the ballroom, robes spinning, blades flashing.

"Now, that's charming. And a bit unnerving. It's right in that uncanny valley between human and not human, and it just puts my teeth on edge in the most gorgeous way, don't you think?"

"It is impressive," I said carefully.

"It's partially your doing. As soon as I earned your loyalty a whole bunch of crafting unlocked. With Andrew I have access to Devani magic, and now with you I have Devout magic, but the really cool thing is when I braid the two magics together. Not that I can use magic, but I can craft it a bit. Speaking of which, can you come here for a minute?"

A chill ran up my neck.

I turned back, but Andrew was gone. He'd crossed past the Historians to prisoners marked with Devani symbols who huddled at the edge of the sharp precipice. Their drawn symbols shone with specks of color hiding behind kohl, cobalt for ice, red for fire, silver and black and a thousand different shades all meaning something powerful, something I could not understand.

"Me?"

"Andrew already did his part, but I need you to seal this magic closed with a concentration of ghostlight. Once I earned your loyalty I could use the NPCs' ghostlight, but only to a point. There are spells only players can do."

The Historians were too deadly already. I didn't want to think about what they'd do to Dagney and Ryo if I helped her. What else could I do? Maybe I could grab the bracelet from her belt.

An itch nestled between my shoulder blades. I startled back. The gears on my chest clicked and then spluttered.

McKenna twisted a strand of her pale hair around one finger as she watched me through sharp eyes and touched the jeweled bracelet.

My loyalty must have shifted colors. She studied me like she could smash me underfoot, and then she locked the bracelet around her wrist. "Do you need a demonstration?" she asked, her voice lowered. "Andrew, come here," she said. "Your part in my finale is done. I'd love to show Grigfen how your wings work."

I swallowed hard. "No, you don't need to. The Crown of Visions showed me enough."

She blinked. "Ah, good." She seemed almost disappointed.

As was her right. All hail, McKenna. Mighty and wise. May she win quickly with no obstacles.

I lifted my hand and surged a ray of ghostlight into the Devani gear box. Sorry, Ryo. Sorry, Dags.

McKenna clapped twice and then shut a flap and twisted a bolt to keep the metal shut.

She must not know what she was doing. Maybe now that she had my loyalty, she would listen to me.

I approached her like I would a rabid animal. "McKenna."

"Don't try anything."

I softened my voice. "I have to tell you something."

She let out a sigh and then gestured with a palm before she focused on her work. "Go ahead."

"It's not your fault, but something in the game has gone wrong. That's why you feel pain. You have to know the rest of us feel pain too. And when we die in the game, we die in real life."

She lowered her wrench. "I don't feel pain."

"What?"

She plucked a blade from her bench then sliced her palm, a line of red pulsing. She sipped a glass jar, and the red pinked over, turning scar to solid perfect flesh. "So you can put your lies and tricks away."

She grinned and went back to her mechanicals.

My throat tightened. Why couldn't she feel pain? We all could; that was the problem. Why was she the only player not attached to the pain receptors? Did that mean she couldn't die here?

Then how could I convince her that the rest of us could?

I had to try. "McKenna. You don't—"

She gestured with one hand. "You're blocking my light."

I hunkered down until I was eye level. "How many players have you killed?"

"I don't know, read my stats. Like six or something."

My blood pulsed. She had to know. Even if she wouldn't believe me. "They really died."

She let out a small laugh. "Whatever."

"I'm not lying. They really died. The pulses from the pain centers of their brain killed their bodies back at Stonebright." How was I going to get her to understand? "Have you ever watched *Sword Art Online*?"

She stood. "You think just because I'm a newbie I don't know how video games work."

It's pronounced noob . . . That doesn't matter. "There was a glitch—"

"You're getting annoying. My lower ranking doesn't mean I'll fall for your tricks. I'll concede that it's an original way to go about it, trying to make me feel guilty about this role I'm playing, but I'm not an idiot. I know how video games work. I won't fall for this tactic, or this distraction, and you know what, all this talking is boring so they won't use these shots anyway, so go back over there with the Devout and get them to sing louder. I need more ghostlight storage."

But she had to understand. This wasn't only my own life I was trying to save here. If I couldn't convince her, then she'd take out the rest of us too.

"I swear it. If it's not true, I'll never play video games again. I would pay you every pound I earn, I would dance naked in front of millions of people, just believe me. McKenna. Don't kill anyone else. I will do everything in my power so you can win. I swear it, I will. Just don't kill anyone else."

She raised a button on her bracelet in response. Not a blade, not a weapon. But she held it like it would destroy me, and I believed her though she would not believe me.

"You're alive because you are useful to me. Stay that way, or else I'll send you back to Stonebright with the rest of the players I've already tagged out."

Tears burned my eyes. "Please. Don't kill anyone else." Her thumb lingered over the button and ghostlight started to fill the jewel over my chest. The jagged wings behind me clicked.

I held up both hands and backed away slowly until I knelt with the captured Devout and joined in their singing.

McKenna turned back to her machine. She didn't look up to see my tears.

She'd think I was acting if she did, that my tears were a trick, or a strategy to beat her, and I couldn't blame her. If Bluebird hadn't been the one to tell us that players had actually died from this, I couldn't know if I'd have believed me either. And if I had accidentally killed people, I'd fight tooth and nail to make it not be true.

McKenna strutted away from her gears and shouted out orders to her servants to clear the ballroom for incoming guests, her hips waving and shoulders spread wide. She relished this role she played.

But she wasn't the villain. She was the first victim, and she didn't even know it yet.

Ghostlight poured like mist around us. I pulled against the gold bars that strapped those sharp wings to my chest. The metal was forged closed, and no matter how I pulled against the seams, they would not bend. The gear placed between my shoulder blades clicked, and the wings attached to that spring had been filed into blades I could remember sliding through my ribs.

Don't come here, Dags. Don't bring Ryo.

At least Bluebird wasn't here for this.

This was a battle we could not win. How could we defeat a villain we could not kill?

She could destroy us without a problem. Like she was smashing a goomba.

Or pushing a button.

28

BLUEBIRD_OFDEATH

What does she mean she can't feel pain?" Ms. Takagi said as she opened the door to the players' bay.

I lifted my head from the side of Grig's bed, his cold hand limp in mine. After the source code failed around me, I'd moved down here. I couldn't help him, but I could sit by his side. His cheek slumped against his shoulder. His palms were up, one finger twitching every few seconds.

Mr. Carrington rose from his post next to his daughter's side. "Now, before you get mad—"

Oh no, my dude, you never start a sentence like that.

"What did you do?" Ms. Takagi asked.

"I didn't want you sending shock waves into my daughter's brain."

"You were the one who insisted she play."

"For the PR! But that doesn't mean I'd allow you to hurt her."

I didn't follow. "What does that mean?"

He huffed and held his fists to his hips. "I tried to protect my daughter. Not that it worked. She's still connected to the world, to some of the sensations, but I didn't want her to feel pain. And can you blame me? You did the same thing when you gave Ryo extra lives. Rules are rules, but not when they apply to our children's safety."

I could blame him. "You were the one who damaged the code?"

Ms. Takagi shook her head. "He doesn't have the skill for that. Who'd you use?"

He adjusted his glasses. "Abrams."

Ms. Takagi paled. "I fired Abrams for incompetence. And you let him play with my source code?"

"I had to. You never told the players you were sending shock waves into their brains. You inadequately warned them of the dangers involved."

"It wasn't dangerous until you broke it. Seven children are dead."

"My daughter could be next, and whose fault is that?"

"Yours! You messed up my code, and your daughter—"

"She doesn't know what she's done. She'd never hurt anyone in real life. She doesn't realize it's more than a game now."

"Someone needs to tell her," I said.

Ms. Takagi let out a sharp breath. "Grigfen314 already has. She didn't believe him. I hope Ryo can convince her, but . . ."

Mr. Carrington pressed his hand against his forehead. "This was not what I intended. No one said anything about anyone being killed."

My arms shook. Doing nothing was torture. I had to do something. I couldn't just sit here and watch Grig die. He was too dang adorable to die without me telling him so.

And I was the only one who could get into the game. I was the only one who could reach McKenna.

They had to let me try.

I let go of Grig's hand. "Let me go back in."

They faced me.

"No," Ms. Takagi said.

"I can make her listen. I'll give her a message from her dad like I did with that sultan of three moons thing for Ryo. You can think of something she will believe is from you and I'll tell her to put her weapons down."

Ms. Takagi bit her thumb then shook her head. "The code is too corrupted. If you go back in there, we won't be able to pull you out again."

"Then leave me in."

Mr. Carrington lowered his hands. "It could work, Nao."

"You don't talk to me." Then Ms. Takagi stilled, considering. "No. I won't risk another life. I can't. It would damage the code and accelerate the corruption."

I could do this. But if she was right, then it meant risking my life, everyone's lives, to do it.

I knew better. My life mattered and I always would fight to save my own life.

But I was the one who people always helped. I was the one with the need. And now there was something I could do. Something only I could do.

I wanted to save Grig. I wanted to be the one to save all of them.

"I can do this. I can convince her to stop. They'll get the armor and win the game and I'll be freed with the rest of them."

Ms. Takagi clenched her eyes closed. "I promised your mother you'd be safe."

Oh, my mom would be so pissed if I did this. But I'd deal with that argument with Grig at my side. "Even if it means I could save your son?"

Ms. Takagi's jaw pulsed. She studied her son from a distance. "Even then." She swallowed. "I can't allow you into the game. That's final. They are on their own."

I dropped my hands.

"Excuse me." She fled out of the players' hall, her hand covering her mouth.

Mr. Carrington sniffed and studied me.

I couldn't give up. Maybe he would help me break in. He'd already changed the whole game.

"I'm sorry for your friend," he said in a quiet voice. "I'm sorry for what I put in motion."

I rolled my chair closer. "Then you need to help me fix it."

Purple and pink columns skimmed over the ocean like a skipping rock. "Wow," I said under my breath, "they sure travel quickly."

My nervous stomach churned with stage fright. Dagney Tomlinson and Ryo Takagi-Vinton. Ryo was a main character of the whole game, so surely his skills were maxed out, and Dagney's ranking was in the top three. Plus they'd been working together, so they'd have the advantage of having a teammate.

I'd use Grigfen's death as a distraction and take them out.

It was a solid plan. Otherwise they'd team up against me, and the one thing I would not accept was to die a pathetic death. No tripping over the edge, no being crushed by a statue. No. If I was going to die it would be with blood on my hands.

There was so much to do before the next scene really started. I needed to get my costume on, my makeup, make sure everyone knew what to do.

"Places," I shouted. The Devani turned to their poses, some kneeling to create levels of interest, some holding magic between their fingers, some in poses inspired by Bob Fosse. I rushed to Grigfen's side. The three had spent time with one another, so he needed to be down center in the heart of the action.

I pressed his shoulders parallel to the edge. "Chest out so you don't show your back to the cameras, and when in doubt say nothing. I'll help keep the scene moving forward, so don't worry about that. Just try to act afraid, and don't move. Your death will be quick and painless, and I promise it will be at the most dramatic time possible. Okay? You're sure to get plenty of screen time."

I glanced at Andrew. He knelt on the ground, his blade wings arched. I really should kill him now. It was just so many elements to try to balance at once.

And if they turned his loyalty to their side, which they probably would since he was a spineless traitor (in the game, in real life he was kind of charming) . . .

I should probably kill him.

But waiting, in a way, amped the drama. We had to keep the audience guessing. Besides, I liked him too much to give him a boring death. We'd spent a few hours together tasting Savak delicacies. I could eat anything here and not think of calories even once. It was glorious.

I paused and took in the set. The Historians spinning at the center of the ballroom, Whirligig lights floating above the Devani and Devout, making a perfect tableau. Servants in the graceful livery I'd designed, the mosaic tile floors glistening in the moons-light. Only the tears in the sky marred the perfection of the scene. I scowled at it. If there was time, perhaps I could have made a screen to block the flaw in an otherwise perfect stage. But my armies would fly in from above when the time came, so it was best just to ignore it.

The show must go on.

Costume, weapons, and crafted tricks for up my sleeves. That's what I needed to focus on.

"No one move," I said. "I need a quick change but I will be right back."

It was finally time to wear my favorite costume. My army at the beach would keep Dagney and Ryo busy for a while, but as quickly as they moved, I'd have to cut the makeup I had planned, which was an absolute shame.

Stealth mode.

I flew down the stairs toward my rooms and most especially my costume closet. My heartbeat raced, but it was just preshow jitters. Warm-ups should calm it down. "Unique New York, unique New York. You know you need unique New York." I blew raspberries like a horse to loosen my jaw and shook out my arms so I could get blood flowing. I needed every inch of me to be awake and active. Dynamic fingers. Fill that stage with your presence.

In my rooms, I glanced in my triple lighted mirror and opened my closet door.

More than any other scene I'd done so far, this moment was what would make me a star. I would either kill them all to claim my victory, or else they'd team up and I'd have the most epic death scene since Romeo and Juliet. Either way, I needed to channel Meryl and earn it.

My costume was steamed, loaded, and hung on a hook on the back of the door. I dressed in stealth mode. The cameras may have caught glimpses of the costume as I constructed it, but I was not going to give away the full effect until the right moment. In stealth mode, the cameras couldn't see the gilded crown rising like horns above my head, or my smallest helmet, designed more to hide my hibisi drip than to offer protection, highlighting my cheekbones. I wore a stark bloodred dress, expertly cut with long bell sleeves to hide the poison blade shooter, a high neckline and a low back, perfect to display my stained glass Wingship.

I folded my mechanical wings tight against my back, and then wrapped myself in an ordinary Historian's cloak. I lowered a plain mask, and the only thing that marked me different from another Historian was the tips of my horned crown, which stuck out an inch.

Stealth mode ended. All the cameras would see was a common Historian, not unlike the ones spinning in the ballroom directly over my head.

The remaining players would not see me coming.

This reveal would send chills up the audience's neck.

Stealth on.

30
DAGNEY

A seagull squawked and the ocean rumbled as waves crashed against the shore.

I measured the distance to the castle and did a little estimating while my new armor chafed against the ocean-drenched clothes I wore underneath. My head ached with exhaustion and all I wanted to do was find a cozy bit of blankets, something yummy, and maybe a book, but I had a brother to save first.

20 percent, I estimated. I timed the step and we took off from the shore, zooming until we reached a large expanse of grounds right at the base of the Savak castle.

The castle looked like a knife, towers filed sharp, cutting the sky with flags.

All around us, from the ground and flying higher, a wall of Savak Wingships loomed like buzzing flies. Boxes of treasures hid on the ground, and I could count the levels we'd amp if we had time to just fight the Savak army that watched our approach.

A couple of soldiers brandished weapons and rushed us.

Ryo let go of my hand and drew his sword. Now would have been a good time to use that army Ryo had started to assemble but we'd had to leave behind. My fingers itched to grab my axes and crush a few NPCs. Let out this tension and pressure that had built between my shoulder blades.

But we were doing a speed run here. We needed to grab Grig, find any of the remaining armor, and get out of this creepy place.

The arrow pointing to Grigfen turned upward. Ryo's sword crashed as he fought the Wingship.

I cleared my throat and did a little math. The castle was massive. Maybe 10 percent?

I lunged for Ryo's arm and with one magic step we zoomed to the top balcony of the castle.

The platform at the top of the tallest tower looked more like a ballroom than a battlefield. Historians danced at the center, each spin mechanical and whirling. An orchestra of Whirligigs played in a dark and empty corner, gears shifting as bows ripped across strings and sticks attached to a slowly spinning wheel banged on drums. Loyalties and magic lit the sky, so much red fog; it felt like blood had filled my eyes. The shattered sky had swallowed the sunrise, and every minute more of the sky dissolved.

We were running out of time.

The arrow in my mind disappeared. Grig had to be up here somewhere.

Disengage boots.

I let go of Ryo and armed myself with a battle-axe in each hand. I hadn't really had time to test out these axes, and there wasn't time for a tutorial. I scanned the prisoners lining the edges.

Devani on one side. Devout on the other. Each chained and working, their magic or ghostlight seeping out of them, pulling into the center of the room where a sitting mechanical hummed. The queen of the Savak had turned these people into fuel.

And then made them stand pretty while she drained them.

A green player indicator hung above a winged man covered in paint.

Grig.

We rushed to his side. Grigfen's skin glowed pale as a bone, his shaved head painted to look like a skull with pointed teeth, a black crack lining his forehead where the Crown of Visions perched crookedly. While I was worried about him, he'd earned another piece of the armor.

Badass.

He didn't move or celebrate or even grin. He stayed on his knees. His loyalty only flickered from red to purple for a second before shifting back to red, even as Ryo knelt at his side.

"Hey, gang," he whispered. "Can't move. Sorry about that."

Why wasn't he moving? Ryo pulled a jar of hibisi tea.

Grig stared at the dance floor, his pale eyes devoid of hope. He nodded. "I'd love a nip, thank you." He drank and his cheeks warmed with color as his stats improved.

"What happened?"

"So much. I'd love to tell you the long version, because it makes me look quite impressive, but the short version is I betrayed you all in order to keep breathing, but McKenna doesn't trust me, so she's strapped me with wing swords posted above my back and if I sneeze wrong she'll push the button on her bracelet and I'll die."

He was right. The wings were filed sharp, the tips stained with either blood or red paint, I wasn't sure. They were attached to gears between his shoulder blades and a sliding spring that would shove them into his lower back.

"How far a distance do you think the button will work?" I asked. "If we grab him and—"

"I'll check." Grig's eyes flashed white and his spine arched upward. The Crown of Visions must be showing him a future. Ryo tugged at the bar around Grig's chest, looking for a clasp.

Grig's eyes flashed back.

"It won't work," Grig said. "You have to get the bracelet off McKenna."

Ryo stepped back. "Or convince her not to push it."

"I tried. She doesn't believe that this is real."

"Perhaps I could be more persuasive?" Ryo asked. He pulled back one more time, and the gears clinked forward.

Sweat fell down the side of Grig's face, leaving a trail of skin down his painted cheek. "Stop. She won't believe us. She can't. Her win condition is killing other players, so . . ." He winced and his loyalty colors flashed back to red.

Ryo met my eyes. "How many did she kill?"

"Loads. But she doesn't know it's real. I told her, but . . ."

How could she believe it?

"Hey, you're alive," I told him. "You've done well. And we're here, okay. We won't let her kill you." But how could we stop her without killing her?

"She's not attached to the pain receptors, so—"

The soundtrack suddenly went very *very* quiet. Grig paled. "I can't talk longer."

With a shudder he fell to his knees, ghostlight pouring from his hands. He began singing a Devout hymn.

A red diamond floated over the dance floor.

McKenna was here.

The Savak I saw did not match my father's stories. McKenna must have taken some creative liberties.

I had no idea how to defend against them, and neither did my game vision.

"What do we do?" I searched the ballroom for whatever had made Grigfen and Dagney go so still. "We can't kill her and we can't leave Grig with her."

"What resources do we have?" Dagney whispered. She raised her axe. "I could try to cut Grig's wings off with this. It's the Axe of Destruction."

Brilliant. "Test it out on something else first."

Dagney swung the axe into a large self-playing cello. The thing collapsed into itself, its center a black boiling acidic liquid that kept spreading.

"Don't try that on me!" Grig whispered sharply.

The black ooze seeped down from the ruined cello, eating a violin, silencing the string instruments, and tearing off a section of the balcony.

"What did you do to my set?" A female voice rang out from behind us.

I lifted my sword. A feather cape ruffled before it disappeared back in the dancing Whirligigs. She was hiding . . . Why wasn't she just attacking? Why wasn't she pushing the button?

"Maybe I should try the Axe of Creation," Dagney said, one eyebrow raised.

What could I do? "I'll try to turn her prisoners to our side. The Devout seem pissed. I can use that."

"Be careful."

I nodded, and for the briefest of seconds we shared a look shaded by hints of goodbye.

Then she turned away and slammed the other axe into the railing lining the edge of the balcony. At the impact the material in the railing doubled, growing taller, like a hedge, the iron bars twisting up and crisscrossing over our heads.

The red player indicator reappeared, and for a moment I saw McKenna, her eyes entranced in the axe's creating. Her fingers lifted to the mask on her face, and a golden bangle with a jewel slid down her wrist.

Her focus was on Dagney's axe. Not me. Every speck of gamer in me disappeared, and suddenly it was Friday night, and I stood on the line of scrimmage staring at a quarterback with his eyes on the other side of the field and a direct open line down the middle.

Hut, hut, hut, hike.

I rushed forward, my head low into a tackle. At the last second, she turned toward me, the whites of her eyes flashing. She disappeared. When I reached the place she'd just been, there was nothing to tackle but air.

Something I could not see sliced at my arms.

Dagney

What part of "Go turn the Devout to our side!" meant tackling the person who was trying to kill us?

McKenna had sliced at the wrong girl's teammate and occasional make-out person. I swung my axe and growled.

But she'd gone back into hiding like the spider she was.

"Ryo," I shouted. I tossed the hibisi to him. He caught the jar and sipped some of the tea.

He seemed properly embarrassed as his arms healed. "I know. I know."

He tossed the jar back to me.

The army from the beach was flying up the side of the castle. The wall I'd formed blocked the sky a little. That would help, but I needed Ryo to use his Charisma to turn the NPCs to our side. "There's your army," I said, pointing to the Devout and Devani. He nodded.

Then I went searching for a spider.

Ryo turned to the Devout and called them heathens or something. I only half listened. McKenna had the ability to go invisible.

Which was really the worst idea Ryo's mom ever had.

I knocked a spinning Historian off the track. The Historian swung at me, blades slashing at my arms.

OW. I slammed my axe into it. Twice for good measure.

The Axe of Destruction left a black acid-like substance behind, which burned the marble floor.

"Stop!" McKenna said from the empty air. "Do you have any idea how long it took to make those?"

I slammed my axe into another Historian. "Give me your bracelet and I'll stop."

Whatever Ryo said to the Devout seemed to work. Grigfen kept singing, but the rest of the Devout succumbed to Ryo's Charisma and stopped powering the dancing Whirligigs.

The Historians stopped spinning. I smashed another anyway, swinging my axe like a baseball bat.

"Ghostlight!" Ryo said, his eyes lighting.

The Devout with purple loyalties sent a wave of ghostlight into the ballroom, a bright green fog that seeped over the floor and outlined a large shape that might have been a human in a cloak.

Clever. "Found you," I said.

McKenna flashed visible, sliding the Historian cloak off her shoulders and removing her mask.

She was every inch an evil queen. Her dark wings spread wide, reflecting light through the jewel-tone glass. Her bloodred dress was stunningly cut, showcasing her collarbones and the sharp angle at which she held her head. She captured the ballroom, just glowing with the Charisma Ryo was programmed to have.

She raised her wrist, flashing a bracelet twisted with two jewels, and pressed a button.

Blades whirred as swords struck through flesh.

McKenna

It was gratifying, really, to watch their jaws drop when they saw me. Even more so when they turned at the sound of the death wings striking through flesh.

Oh, this was especially dramatic.

I flicked my wrists and palmed a dagger in each hand, waiting for them to come for me. I wanted them to die with their eyes on mine.

But they didn't come for me.

It was like they dropped character completely, and they rushed to the player with the blood pooling around him.

Which button had I pushed anyway? Both bracelets were strung together, but I'd only struck one.

I turned, following Ryo and Dagney with my eyes as they knelt in front of the Devani.

Andrew.

All the Devani-enhanced crafting had disappeared from my stats. Shame.

I lifted my palm and focused down the length of my arm to aim. Dagney kept pouring hibisi down Andrew's throat, and Ryo tried to stop the blood with his own cape. The endeavor was pointless; I'd already killed him.

I aimed my dagger for Ryo's throat.

Now, while they were distracted.

I fired.

BLUEBIRD_OFDEATH

The elevator lifted slowly, the Muzak sickly sweet, doing nothing to calm my racing heart.

Any second now, Ms. Takagi would see we weren't in the players' hall. Any second now, McKenna would kill Grig and then he wouldn't wake. I had to get in there. I wanted my raven cloak and I wanted Grig's hand in mine.

"What do you want me to say to McKenna so she'll trust me?" I asked Mr. Carrington. His shirt had wrinkled, and he wouldn't look at me.

He lowered his hand. "Perhaps 'the world was wide enough' to let them live."

"Is that a *Hamilton* reference?"

"If that doesn't work, say, 'One singular sensation.' That was her last recital song, and it will at least distract her so you can disarm her." The elevator dinged and the doors opened.

Neither of us left.

"It's really brave what you are doing." He met my eyes. "Foolish maybe. But I'm grateful. McKenna is my princess and I—"

"Don't worry about it, Mr. C. I've been rescuing princesses from castles since I was three years old. I got this."

He followed me to the chair I'd used earlier and strapped me in. He started to lower the harness but stopped. "I'm not sure this is the right thing to do. If you go in as a full player you'll be connected to the pain receptors. You could die."

I closed my eyes. "We all could die, Mr. C. We all only have one life over our head."

I was born with the words *return to sender* stamped on my forehead. I was never going to get better. I'd never regain the muscle strength I'd lost, and one day the disease I fought was going to kill me.

But until that day, I'd live. Living was a form of fighting back.

And I wanted my life to have Grigfen in it.

He gave me something to fight for.

I dipped my head. "I can help. I'll give her your message and no one else will have to die."

He lowered the harness and strapped on the diodes.

"Last chance."

It was my choice, and I knew the risk. "Time to summon Exodia."

"Excuse me?"

I shrugged my shoulder and smiled. "That means yes."

——— ——— ———

I woke in the middle of a ballroom. In front of me, the queen of the Savak fired a dagger. A whiff of smoke expelled from her wrist. My whirligig-assisted leg braces slid into attack mode as I reached into a Historian's cloak and drew a blade with each hand. I spun and cut that dagger down.

The queen stared at me, and then flashed invisible.

I breathed heavy. Searched around. She was hiding somewhere. I knew it.

I had no idea what was happening, but I knew a battlefield when I saw one. I sniffed deep. No sign. Last thing I remembered I'd been given an assignment with my fellow Everstriders. The general had gone missing, rumors whispering that she'd signed her name on a contract giving our kingdom to the Savak. Last thing I remembered, it was morning.

The green fog cleared and a girl kneeling by Prince Ryo turned, gorgeous axes held in each hand.

Her expression seemed surprised to see me for a brief second, and then she gestured to the side. "Take off Grig's wings now."

She pointed to a painted boy on his knees. Sharp metal wings sprouted from his back.

I had no idea what was happening, but I recognized the order in her tone. I pulled off the Historian's cloak, revealing my Everstrider uniform and the Mechani armor I called Voyage, which helped me walk. I marched to his side.

His hopeless eyes met mine, and the loss in them dimmed as if snuffed.

"Bluebird?" he whispered.

How did he know my name? He didn't seem familiar, but nothing seemed familiar. "What is happening?" I said. My voice seemed too loud. Why was everything so loud? My Everstrider uniform seemed so bright, gold medals gleaming, leather boots tucked into my armor, and coat pulled tight at the waist and trimmed at my knees with bells that only rang when ghosts were nearby.

They were ringing now. "It's okay. It's okay," he said. "You haven't drunk seer water yet, so you don't have game vision." He wiped his eyes and sat up.

I looked at the metal harness fused around his chest. I slipped my fingers between the metal and his chest and bent, but even my elevated strength wouldn't budge the metal.

"Don't bother with the wings. Their likely to snap shut if we do too much fiddling."

"Then what do I do?"

His eyes softened and glistened with tears. "You're not supposed to be here."

I snorted. "Tell me something I don't know." Something clashed, like metal against metal. I turned, but that wild girl just hunted the empty air. "I should be at my barracks. I don't know what's going on."

The girl roared out a growl and lunged for the Savak queen. Her black hair was chaos and her green eyes were made of fire. She swung her axe above her head.

"What is my mission?" I asked. "If I can't help with the wings, there has to be something I can do." There was something else. Something important. But I couldn't remember.

"We're your allies," he said. "And it's our job to fight the Savak queen. Do you understand?"

That wasn't it. I knew there was something else. But I nodded and held up my sword. I was a weapon, and all they had to do was aim me. I didn't need to think. "Hulk smash?" I asked. I blinked. That wasn't right. What was a Hulk?

He smiled as if my words made sense. "You . . . You are a pre-seer water player with a fresh download of memories from another life, dropped into a final battle with no recollection of why, or who you are, and you can still deliver a perfectly timed reference to a Marvel movie?"

I didn't understand anything he said but I shrugged.

"Your nerdiness truly knows no bounds. I love you so . . . um . . ." He flushed red. "Sorry."

I leaned back. "Wait, what did you just say?" It wasn't even the first bit, it was that last sentence. I looked at him again, really soaking in the curves of his cheekbones, the color of his eyes.

I knew him. Somehow I knew him. Why wasn't my brain working right?

He stood and raised his hands. He let out a breath. "We'll talk about that later. Now let's keep that queen so busy she can't push the button on her wrist."

I stood at his side like we'd fought as allies before.

Then I ran forward toward the only thing that made sense.

That annoying queen would not stop disappearing.

Hunt the queen. The arrow in my mind followed her, even when she flashed invisible. It was a limited-use skill, so it only worked for a short time. I counted the space between disappearances.

Nine. Ten.

Ten seconds of invisibility.

I wiped Andrew's blood off my hands and onto a Historian's cloak. Then I gripped the handle and slammed the Axe of Destruction into a swirling Historian. The thing broke off its spinning axis and was finally still.

McKenna grunted. It was the only thing I knew she cared enough about to try to threaten her with.

Ryo joined my side. "The Devani are fighting off the Savak Wingships, and the Devout are helping them. It's just us and the queen."

"Good work."

Bluebird returned. With her armor, her strength and endurance were incredibly high. She'd be the perfect tank. And best of all, she'd brought Grig back to his feet.

"You sure?" I asked when he joined us.

"If I'm going to die," he said, "I'm going to die playing."

McKenna reappeared. She crept to the center of the room, her fingers brushing the button on her wrist, which she didn't push.

My heart thundered in my chest. "We don't want to hurt you," I shouted. "But we will. Take off the bracelet and we'll leave."

"Why would I do that," she said, "when I'm seconds away from victory?"

"She doesn't feel pain?" I asked.

"Nope," Grigfen said.

She lifted her wrist so her hand framed her face.

Activate boots.

Her other hand reached for the button.

1 percent

Before my boots hit the ballroom floor, I swung my axe and cut off her left hand.

Her eyes met mine. A wave of invisibility crested over her head.

The bracelet fell with her polished fingers. The severed hand crackled as the ooze burned the blood. The metal bracelet caught in the destruction, sparking once. Twice. The jewel cracked right down the center.

The sparkling black spread from the bracelet to the jewel at the center of the harness at Grig's chest. The metal bar cracked open. He threw it off him just before the destructive ooze hit the gears and the blades snapped closed.

"Oh Jesus, Mary, and Joseph," Grig said as he pressed his hands to his chest.

I grinned.

Then a blade, shaped like a feather and coated in a dark orange smoke, slid into the space at my side where the armor didn't cover. The knife stabbed between my ribs.

I didn't even have time to be mad.

Ryo

Blood trailed from McKenna's severed arm as she held her handless wrist to her chest and fired a blade at Dagney. Bluebird lunged for her, her sword lifting as she pushed their fight to the blurs at my peripheral.

But all I saw was the moment Dagney fell.

I rushed toward the center of a ruined ballroom.

She gasped, her face crumpling. Her sharp green eyes found mine, and time stopped.

Dagney pressed her hand against the blade stabbed into her heart. She'd be okay. She would heal from this. She had to. I'd seen hibisi heal plenty of injuries. And if not, my mother would make this right.

But my mother hadn't healed Isabel, or Marcus, or any of the others. She couldn't break the game to save Dagney. She didn't know how special she was, how much she meant.

How could she, when I was just figuring it out?

The world sped back up. I ran to her side. My throat burned.

Dagney covered her side, her hands stained with her blood. She growled half a swear word, half a moan of pain.

A Savak Wingship broke through the Devani line, blocking my way. *Activate gloves.* I reached forward and pulled the Savak aside, my gloves shoving him over like an open door.

Another came for me. We'd lost control of the battle. I shoved past the guard. He slammed his fist into the side of my face, the impact tearing the skin on my eyebrows.

I wouldn't reach her in time.

"GRIG!" I commanded. "Dags has the hibisi!"

Grig threw his hands back and flew forward with a wave of ghostlight.

No matter how I brawled against the Savak, I barely slowed them. "Help me," I commanded to the Devout and the Devani beside me. My Charisma strengthened their resolve, and they held back the Savak, their magic levels doubled. They were a wall now, a wall of death no Savak could break through.

I ran forward without looking back. "Please," I whispered. "Dagney, fight this."

Grigfen had reached her. He poured her hibisi in her mouth.

Please heal.

Between stinging punches, Dagney stole jagged breaths, her eyes blinking, her jaw arched as she held her insides in. Light cascaded from the moons above, touched her cheek, and brightened her hair. She was so beautiful.

And then she was so still.

Dagney

My lips were wet with my own blood, and my lungs sloshed with each rapid breath. It hurt too much to cry.

But I still did.

Eventually the pain receded. Eventually my vision faded to black. And for a second, I wasn't in the game; I was trapped inside my body. My spine arched and there was a beep, and stabbing pain through my eyes and into my nerve endings.

Wake up. Wake up.

"Come on, Dagney," someone said. It sounded like Ms. Takagi. "Fight it."

I tasted something citric and warm. Light flashed bright white behind my closed eyelids. Heat spread from my mouth to my toes as fire twisted through my veins and nerve endings.

"You can do this, love. Breathe. Please. Breathe for me."

I reached out. "Ryo?"

"No, Dags. It's me, Grig."

I tried to sit up, but couldn't.

"Whoa. Slow your horses. You're still stabbed here." He placed something cold against my lips. "Drink more. The hibisi is not working. I'm gonna pull the dagger out. It's going to hurt."

I opened my eyes to see my brother kneeling over me, his hands shaking as he poured hibisi into my mouth. I touched his hand. It's okay. It'll be okay.

The words wouldn't come out of my ragged throat.

He held the blade where it stuck between the ribs on my left side. He pulled it out—no ripped it out, the blade slicing my insides. It was so intense I couldn't tell the moment it was out, there was no relief, just a raw open place that stung in the icy air and swelled with hot blood. He pressed the wound closed, the pressure agony against my ribs, and then he poured the hibisi into my mouth. The sweet tea still tasted like kale, but as I swallowed the pain seeped back, dimming like a light switch. Praise Kale. Kale for everyone.

Ryo crashed to my side. When I looked at him I saw terror—naked and unmasked. A split marred his lip, his battered eyes bruised and hurt. "Dagney," he spluttered.

I reached for him. "What did you do to yourself? Check your healing."

Blood filled my throat and I could not breathe, but he crushed me to him, his sweaty cheek salty against my lips. His laughter seemed bitter and grateful at the same time.

A stinging sharp sickness spread through my body. I dropped my head back.

The painted skull on Grig's face smeared with his excess sweat. "The hibisi isn't holding, mate. There was poison on the knife, so it keeps wounding her. She needs more than this."

He held the hibisi to my mouth again and the pain slowed for a moment, but it came back as sharp as a barbed wire. The relief sharpened the return. It'd be better if they let me get lost in it. If the pain swallowed me completely I could forget how sweet it was to be without it.

The world darkened, but the pain would not dim.

"I'm not going to let her die. What do we have that's stronger than hibisi?" Ryo muttered. "The last item. The Breastplate of Healing. Of course. I'll go get it."

The arrow in my game vision spun but wouldn't settle.

Grigfen darted a glance toward the collapsing sky. "I'll stay with her."

"Keep her breathing." Ryo knelt by my feet. "Dags, can I borrow your boots?"

I shook my head. "Trade." It won't work if we didn't follow the rules of this world.

His eyes lit and he reached into a pocket and pulled out something small and dark. A coin?

It was my mother's ring.

I held it and tears blurred my vision. I never used to cry. I hadn't cried when I saw Sir Tomlinson's body, or as we stood vigil for the fallen players. I didn't cry when my mom asked if it was my fault that I got pushed down a flight of stairs, or when I ate lunch alone and the table full of my former friends started to moo. I didn't cry when their names hurt me. When I was lonely.

I never allowed myself to feel safe enough to cry.

But I cried now, holding this ring, knowing my mom was missing me. I couldn't die. I couldn't let this be my end. I had to keep fighting, because I wanted to go home.

The boots fell off my feet, like I'd released them.

Ryo put on my boots and then crawled to my side. He traced my cheek with his metal fingers, bent closer, and kissed me. Brief as a goodbye. "I expect confetti when I return. Perhaps a parade."

He would never let me forget I let him save me. "You're the worst. Drink some hibisi."

As he stood, his cheek creased in a grin that felt like a dare. "Make me." Then he raised his gaze and jumped.

And the boots transported him away.

The boots clicked on.

Run tutorial?

Nah, I got this.

I didn't need a tutorial or Dagney's directions to know where the Breastplate of Healing was hidden. I had a story.

I glanced up. Hope the moon was only one step away.

100 percent. I leapt straight up.

My father had told me the story of the sultan of the three moons.

Once there was a little boy, loved beyond measure, but born without a soul. He'd been formed with clay and wax, tears and prayers. His mother molded his cheek with porcelain, his father made his legs with a soft pine. They pulled all the ghostlight they could to make his gears turn, but the ghostlight always used up and he would turn back to a lifeless thing.

If he were a real boy, he wouldn't have needed ghostlight. His own soul would turn those gears. But he needed a little extra help.

So his parents used their magic to form armor to keep that soul in. His father was a healing witch, and the spell he used to form that Devani breastplate cost his life. The boy and his mother mourned the loss, but eventually lived happily together as mother and son, until old age hunched her shoulders and sent her into the Undergod's embrace. The mechanical boy lived on.

He collected gold. He collected titles. He even tried to collect the moons. But his gold and his titles and his moons collected dust. And all those who served him fell away to old age while his gears kept spinning.

After he lived a thousand years, he took a trip to the favorite of his three moons. He watched the sunset behind the world that loved him, and then he removed the breastplate. His pine legs petrified, his porcelain face cracked, and the ghostlight that had spun his gears for so long it had turned to a soul seeped from his wax heart. His ghostlight soul found his mother's and father's ghostlight. They mixed together until it was one. One heart. One soul.

Loved beyond measure forever after.

I missed my father's stories.

The Breastplate of Healing was hidden on one of the moons. And the only way to get there was to use the Traveling Boots.

Or invent NASA. Whichever one was quicker.

I glanced down through the rippled upward step. I was high enough to see my castle, see the ruins of my city. I saw the long line of glitched sky, wrapped around the curve of the world. I had to hurry.

I looked up at the quickly approaching moon. Growing larger. Closer.

The rush of traveling tickled against my skin and sent a surge of adrenaline. I fought against gravity as the air became colder. Thinner.

Still. I had to admit my mom's game wasn't boring.

I more crashed than landed on the surface of the moon.

I stood. The desolate silence wrapped my neck, the ground crunched like hard gravel, but the view . . . the view was incredible.

The world was a moon too large for the sky. White clouds spiraled around the globe and torchlight sparkled like stars from the cities. I could see every playable country from here, cut through with rivers and oceans. Beyond the lands I knew were small peninsulas and continents I'd never heard of.

I only knew my own side of the world. If I'd seen the planet laid out like this I'd have notice that the continents spelled out my name.

My mother had formed the world as an Easter egg for me.

I didn't know I was her whole world. I'd never been a whole world before.

My eyes prickled with tears.

Then I turned away. No time to explore or get sentimental. Dagney was dying. I scanned the moon's surface, but it was simply too basic for my mother to have hidden the breastplate here.

The Little Mother was barren.

I needed to reach the other moon, the one called Father.

I took a running start, each step throwing me across the moon's surface, and I wasn't even using the boots' magic. Gravity worked differently here; each jump threw me faster. How was I supposed to estimate the distance between the moons, and . . . how would gravity affect that? I couldn't just go 100 percent, because they weren't that far from each other.

I knew enough about math to know I was way out of my depth here.

My mother would make it possible. She'd make it difficult, but it had to be possible.

I just had to take a wild guess. I threw my hands backward and exploded into a running leap. *40 percent?*

The moon loomed larger, larger; oh crap, I aimed too far. I reached the larger moon with an impact that jammed my joints as it shoved me through the surface and deeper, down below the surface, lodged between the moon rocks. The tight and heavy rocks formed a Ryo shaped hole deep into the surface.

But at least I'd stopped.

I climbed upward, ignoring the aches in my ribs and the way the impact into the moon's side had made my joints crack and left a splatter of blood on the moon's surface.

I searched the moonscape until I saw the ruins of a boy made of rusted gears, pine legs, and a porcelain smile. I stepped to it and bent down, undressing the ruins of my favorite story. The solid gold breastplate was covered with copper moons. I exhaled and looked up.

A third moon hid in the distance. Just for me.

With my name a world, and a secret moon hiding beyond, I knew my mother was watching me. No matter what we'd been through, or the times she wasn't there when I needed her, I knew she waited on a different world, cheering me on, hoping and praying and waiting impatiently for the moment we'd be back together.

I knew it like I knew my father was doing the exact same thing.

"Hi, Mom," I said to the empty surface of the moon. "I'll be home soon."

Now, how to get back?

100 percent again? Dagney would have had a map of the stars and been able to estimate perfectly by their position. I had to get back to her so she would do the math for me.

I timed my step and leapt. The light from reentry curved in an arch of sparks and lens flares. I hurdled through the dark and into the atmosphere.

Ahead of me, a cubed line of glitch floated like a cloud in the sky. I barely recognized it before I realized I should try to avoid it, and then before I could even think of how, I went through it.

The boots unequipped and my game vision sparked, and then went out.

The hair on my arms stood on end as I fell through the sparks. Stripped of powers, magic, or even my stats, I had nothing but the ever-approaching surface and the healing breastplate that Dagney needed. Gravity snatched me and the leap became a fall.

The wind ripped at my clothes, but I didn't stop, not as I fell through thick and bristling clouds. The breastplate shook in my hand, the copper circles ringing like wind chimes. I was too high, my descent too fast. I'd made myself a meteor. The g-force pressed my neck backward.

I could see the castle, but it was nothing but a speck in the distance. I wasn't going to make it. Not unless the boots restarted.

I opened the Breastplate of Healing. My only hope to survive was to put this on. Unless my extra lives would save me? How many did I have?

My stomach rolled. My time to make this choice grew shorter with every inch I fell. Come on boots, come on.

The extra lives might save my body here, but the impact would kill me for real.

My game vision flickered. I saw a flash of my stats, my health bar fading. And a warning. Bold and loud. *This item can only be used by one player.*

The breastplate would only work for one person.

I could save Dagney, or I could save myself.

There was no option three.

expected Dagney's death to feel triumphant. I expected the light of leveling up to brighten my tired eyes, and to feel the relief of having one less person trying to kill me.

And I wanted some kind of justice for the hand she cut off.

I drank my hibisi and turned on stealth, moving away from where my hand dripped blood, moving where no one could see me. The skin at the end of my arm turned solid. A clip appeared at the end of the stub. I could attach a mechanical hand if I wanted. I glanced at the Historians I could recycle for parts.

But then I paused and glanced over.

I didn't expect the look on Ryo's face. I didn't expect Grigfen to abandon his work, to walk away from the discarded death harness, and rush to Dagney's side.

But they moved like they'd stopped playing the game.

They'd broken character when Andrew had died, but this was different. They worked to heal her as though the game didn't matter without her.

The new Everstrider lunged through the Historians, hunting me with a sniff, as if she could track my smell.

Grigfen looked over his shoulder. "Don't kill McKenna, Bluebird. If she dies in the game, she dies for real."

"Disarm and imprison. Got it," Bluebird shouted.

Bluebird . . . As in *bluebird_ofdeath*?

Why would Grigfen lie to his partner?

Stealth ended.

I didn't have a place to hide. Bluebird lunged for me, her sword swinging. I fought back with my wings, but doubt had undercut my performance. She slammed her sword down and I blocked her again, spinning once. She hit the butt of her sword into my helmet, knocking me over.

I slammed into a Historian, the glass at my back shattering. I thought that might happen. I snapped a switch and my wings covered with a fan of gold.

Why would they add another player right now? They already had a team, and now someone came in out of nowhere? Why would they mess up the rising tension like that?

I spun and shot a blade. It missed her heart, the blade spinning wildly, cutting a line through her uniform sleeve. She gasped and grabbed her arm where the blade had marked a line of blood. I should have used a poisoned blade.

Next time.

"Does it hurt?" I asked with my queen's smile.

She came from outside the game so there hadn't been enough time for them to tell her the rules of this trick. I was going to catch them in their lie.

Her eyes lifted to meet mine. "Like you wouldn't believe."

I froze.

How did she know to lie?

She showed me her palm, painted red.

I aimed my remaining blade launcher at her. She grinned, and quicker than I thought possible, she rushed for me, twisting in the air in some high-flying trick before she slammed her feet into my chest.

She stood over me with a sword in each hand held to my throat, her armored heels holding my arms down to the ground.

I tried to fight, but I couldn't. This was not my glorious death scene ending. It was pathetic and confusing. Could the cameras just turn off for a second? I couldn't remember the lines I'd written for this moment. I couldn't imagine what my character would be feeling right now.

They felt pain?

She studied my expression. "I have a message for you. I know I do."

Her grip stayed at her hilt, but she didn't swing. She didn't hurt me. Why didn't they hurt me? Ryo had left, but Grigfen huddled over Dagney's body, his back to me.

I aimed toward his back. My blade launcher had armed, but I couldn't press the trigger.

This had to be a trick.

But why wouldn't they use this trick to hurt me? Why didn't they just finish me off?

"It was a message from your father. Something about a princess. Something."

My dad? He always called me princess. "You need seer water." My voice was ragged.

If she really had a message from my dad, I'd do anything to hear it.

"Does it really hurt?" I said in a soft voice. "Break character for a second. No tricks. No lies. Does it really hurt?"

She nodded and I closed my eyes. But there was no hiding from this.

So they felt pain. That didn't mean anything.

Andrew.

I didn't see it happen, but I knew from when I demonstrated the wings on the Devani princess what it had looked like. His mouth would have widened as the death wings he'd been wearing unfurled, the Whirligig engine humming. He'd look for me, but I wouldn't even meet his eyes as the sharp golden wing folded out and stabbed through his back, coming out below his collar—the tips red with blood.

He would glance down at his chest, more surprised than in pain.

But he'd felt it.

I gave him a dramatic death scene, but I hadn't bothered to watch.

Clouds gathered above Bluebird, blocking the moons I'd flown past to kill Sylvania. She'd nicked my dress with her blade, and I'd been so upset about my outfit that I'd shot her thirteen times. I remembered the way her blood gathered. The moment the light in her eyes dimmed.

They were hurt, but they'd gone home. They woke up. I knew they'd woken up.

But why would Grigfen have told the truth about the pain, but not about the players who'd died? I didn't understand.

Her heels cut into my wrists, but I didn't feel it. The shattered glass in my wings cut into my bare back, slowing dimming my health. But I didn't feel any pain.

There was something different about me.

The sky shattered with a fresh glitch. There was something wrong with the game.

My breaths rasped. It was true.

Marcus.

Sylvania. I rocked my head back and forth. *Catherine. Isabel. Sam.*

I didn't know.

I didn't know.

I screamed but nothing was louder than my thoughts. There was something wrong with the game. I killed them. I really killed them.

Bluebird held her blades to my neck.

"Stop," I croaked with a throat too raw for me not to feel it. "Please stop. I won't hurt anyone anymore."

"I don't believe you."

I squeezed my eyes shut. I didn't know. I didn't know. I . . . "The world was wide enough," I whispered.

The pressure on my wrists lightened.

"What did you say?" Bluebird asked.

My hands were free. "I didn't know."

Behind Bluebird's shoulders, a column of purple fell from the sky. Ryo.

I shot backward and my mangled wings lifted me to my feet. *Stealth on.* I flew past the players I'd killed, past the ruins of the stage I'd worked so hard to build.

I didn't know.

I flit through the battle in the background. "Commander. Retreat!" I ordered to the Savak. My army exited the sky, and then it was just me and Ryo plummeting to the ground.

I pulled the anchor line with my surviving hand and spun it around him. He held a golden something to his chest and flinched backward as I approached.

I caught him around his ankles and dragged him up. He reached toward his hilt.

"I'm not going to hurt you," I said. "I didn't know it was real. I didn't know."

For a second he stared at me. Then he bowed his head and released a shaky laugh.

And for the briefest of seconds his loyalty shifted the brightest red.

T he world was wide enough.

That was the message. That was it. A weight lifted from my back, and a light brightened on my arms. I'd accomplished my mission, even though I wasn't the one to give the message. McKenna gave it to me.

Why wasn't my brain working like it was supposed to?

I searched the battlefront. Devani and Devout scanned the skies for an attack that had stopped as the queen had flown through it. Grigfen still knelt by the injured girl's side, feeding her hibisi while her wound festered at her stomach.

That was poison if I ever saw it.

"I'm out," Grigfen said. "No, no, no. I need more hibisi."

I stepped forward.

Everstriders always carried a pouch of hibisi blossoms at their belt. I handed him the whole pouch off my belt and then I stood over him, my blades in hand, searching for the Savak queen to go visible.

"Thanks, love," he said. "Dagney, you're going to have to chew. Hang on for me. Ryo's almost back."

The ballroom was an empty war zone, the ground scorched and folded like Kne巴k paper cranes. Empty Historians paused mid-step, while their partners lay destroyed, their raven cloaks charred, the cloying smell of burnt feathers mixed with the copper scent of blood. A Whirligig orchestra still played on, those instruments untouched by the violence.

There was a hole in the sound where the orchestra was missing important instruments.

There. In the sky. She flew toward us carrying something. I squinted, and it was as if my senses sharpened and I could see the distance much closer. No, it wasn't something. Someone.

"Prince Ryo," I said, judging from his purple cloak.

Grigfen looked up. "Oh thank God." She was zooming toward us at breakneck speed.

I gripped my sword tight. "She's using him as a hostage. We should gather the Devout and Devani—"

Grigfen touched my leg. I froze, the skin where he'd touched tingling. "No, her loyalty is purple. She's on our side now." He placed a blossom on Dagney's dry tongue.

"That's impossible. The Savak queen—"

He met my eyes, and I swear I heard bells. "You've got to trust me, Zoe."

Footsteps thudded behind us as McKenna dropped Ryo on the marble floor.

But Ryo didn't spare us a glance. He rushed to Dagney's side, copper armor chiming as he ran. McKenna flapped her wings higher, abandoning us and this battle like we'd try to kill her if she stayed.

She wasn't exactly wrong. She hovered over us. I think I could aim a spear and still hit her, but Grigfen asked me not to.

I trusted him. I didn't know him at all, but I trusted him like I didn't anyone else.

But why?

Ryo bent next to Dagney, pulling off her blood-damaged armor, pressing the copper plate to her chest. He wrapped the breastplate around her, tying the ribbons with gentle fingers.

Grigfen stood at my side, his face softened. "It's working," he said for my benefit. "She's healing."

Dagney gasped, and her gray cheeks brightened to a glowing pink. She opened her eyes and then Ryo bent and kissed her lips, his blood-painted fingers leaving a streak of red on her cheek.

I turned away, their moment too personal to observe, even for a former Historian.

"I'm sorry," McKenna said from above, "I didn't know."

Years of Everstrider training had taught me the priority of battle. First, you save. Second, you heal. Third, you run in smacking.

We saved who we could, we healed who we could, and now it was time to fight.

I pulled Grigfen away from the rest of them. "We need to make a strategy," I said. "I know you believe she's on your side, but this is the Savak queen we're talking about; she's not the kind of person we should turn our backs on, or enlist on our side."

"Our side?" he asked softly. How did I know his face well enough to see it soften? He saw me. It wasn't through a crowded room. It wasn't through a magic glass or a few thousand miles.

It was close enough to touch.

My eyebrow twitched. "You're my ally. Right?"

That was what he said.

His skull grin cracked into the widest smile. "Is that what I am?"

I glanced around. The Savak were gone, the Devani and Devout tending to their wounded, or sleeping, weak with overuse of magic.

"She's not going to hurt us, love."

I let go of the hilt. My chest lightened as Voyager shifted into rest mode. "So we're not . . ." I cleared my throat. "Fighting?"

"At the moment, no one is trying to kill us." He moved closer like

I was his victory, wrapped me in his arms, and lifted me off my feet. "I'm so glad you're here."

He lowered me to the ground. He gave a quivering smile but didn't look away from me, not for a second. I should not feel this comfortable with a stranger. I'd never been good at talking with . . . well, anyone. I babbled when I was nervous, I said things wrong to nearly everyone I met, and then I would lie in bed for days afterward going over my foolish words again and again in endless blithering circles. But with this oddly painted, strangely sad, handsome no one, my muscles loosened, my heartbeat steadied.

It seemed the most natural thing in the world to step inside his shadow, to breathe in his smell—incense and tea, something herbal and softly sweet.

He pulled off his crown as though he was going to give it to me. It sloshed in his hand so he peeled back the leather that capped the metal, and inside clear crisp water glowed in the moons-light.

"Fancy a drink?" he asked.

"I've never drunken from a crown before."

"If you'd prefer, I could fetch you a skull for a cup."

"Oh no, I've done that thousands of times." He grinned and I lowered my voice. "Seer water?"

"Yeah. I'll watch your back."

I drank.

— — —

After those last three notes played, my mind was finally my own. HOLY BATMAN I'm really here. Look at those stats! What skills do I have? Tracking. *Yes.* I knew my senses were stronger than I remembered. And my stamina and endurance were buffed like whoa. And . . .

Grig touched my arm and I squealed my loudest nerd squeal.

"THIS IS THE GREATEST THING TO EVER HAPPEN! Lookit those graphics, it's like we're really here inside a video game!"

He held my face in his hands. "Only you would sneak into a death-trap and squeal about the graphics."

I leaned against his palm. "Oh, you'd do it too."

His copper eyes specked in the light. "For you I would."

I touched his cheek. I was so glad to have my brain back. So glad to know why I knew him.

I knew the way his lips curled when he smiled, I knew the silly faces he made when he thought he was funny, and the way his mouth dipped at the corner when he was sad, but there was no warning for the way his kiss stole my breath. There was no preparing for the way his lips pressed against mine.

It was like going home.

When I dared peek after, he grinned with his painted eyes closed. His fingers grazed my cheek. "Ten out of ten, would play again."

He kissed my cheek and then my lips again. This time my lips parted with his, and I wrapped my arms around his shoulders, and he held me tight against his chest. My insides bubbled like champagne and I felt like laughing, so I did, even though it broke through the kiss too soon.

His eyes shone, and when he closed them and rested his smudged nose against mine, a tear slid down his cheek leaving a line in the black. "I'm both devastated that you are here, and simultaneously embarrassingly grateful to see you."

His grin changed to a straight line, his eyes steely as his focus shifted to behind me. I knew this look too. I reached for my sword before I turned to face an enemy.

A pulsing white line ripped open the sky.

Ryo helped me up. The breastplate felt tight against my chest. He pulled me to him and kissed me again in victory. Kissing Ryo was like the moment the armor closed around my chest, as if his lips on mine had shut out the pain. I didn't care about the people watching. I didn't care that he saved my life and was probably going to rub it in my face like the jerk he was. I kissed him and my brain shut off every other thought I'd ever had except happiness. It felt like eating my favorite food, or snuggling under a blanket with a good book while it rained outside my window, or like the feeling when my highlighter markers were arranged in the colors of the rainbow. Like things were right and good and I didn't have to die. I slid my hand around his jaw and held him closer. I didn't die! That was worth celebrating.

I pulled back and beamed at him. "Let's go win this thing."

The sky cracked open.

That obnoxious sky. "And quickly."

"Yes, now is not the time for snoggin'," Grigfen said, his grin back where it belonged, although some of the makeup from his face had somehow marked up Bluebird's cheek. I decided to be saintly and not mention it.

Ryo, however, pointed and laughed.

I would have smacked him, except for the swell of pain on my left side. I clutched my side and glanced down. The poison was still in me, trapped under the breastplate, tearing through my flesh, the ache sharp and wheezing. My bones felt weak.

Activate breastplate. The metal warmed, and the pain slowed. I'd thought the breastplate would have just healed me once and for all.

But that had never been my luck.

"Let's go," I said.

McKenna hovered above us, her shattered wings barely keeping her afloat, a single tear glistening on her cheek.

"No one blames you, you know," I said. "It's not your fault the game got screwed up."

Ryo inhaled sharply. "No, it's not."

But I didn't blame his mother for this either. Sometimes things just go wrong. Life wasn't like a video game; there wasn't always one villain you could kill and things would be better.

"I don't think I should go with you," McKenna said. "I'm not supposed to be in the next scene."

"Screw that. We need all the help we can get," I said. She was a Rogue with crafting expertise, great aim stats, plenty of charm, and ranged attacks. She'd be useful.

OW. The pain in my ribs flared again.

"There's plenty of blame to go around," Ryo said, "but you didn't hurt anyone on purpose. It's just good Dagney didn't get your part."

I pressed my stomach. "Yeah, you'd all be dead." I meant it as a joke, but it was true. If I didn't know, I'd have played much dirtier than McKenna did. I really would have. "This isn't your fault. And you're great so long as you don't shoot anyone with your poisoned daggers."

Activate breastplate. The pain softened.

McKenna landed and disarmed the blades. They fell to the ground and then kept falling.

"How many bloody blades do you have?" Grig said.

"Oh, one more." She tugged a massive dagger from her boot. Then she reached beneath the helmet covering the side of her face and pulled down a thin tube. She jammed it into the blade launcher on her handless wrist and test fired. A splash of water hit the ground. "Maybe I could act as a healer?"

"Mother of Mercy, is that a hibisi Super Soaker?" Grig asked.

She sprayed him in the mouth, and his stats shot up.

"I've got about five gallons," she said.

"Where did you keep it?" I asked. Her finely cut dress lay flat against her body.

Bluebird's eyes were shaded in worry. "We've got to hurry."

Right. I turned to Ryo. He had the boots. He sighed. "Please. Please don't make me do math."

"I'll trade you for them . . ." The pain started pulsing again. Oh, this was going to be annoying, I could just tell. I let out a growl. "What do I have to trade?"

His eyes seemed concerned. "Here, let me carry your bag."

I gave it to him gladly. The thing was starting to get heavy, or else, my legs seemed weaker. "So you're saying you want everything?"

"They are very useful boots."

Activate breastplate. The pain stepped back into hiding, and I managed a weak smile. I put on the boots while Bluebird and Grigfen raided the ballroom for loot.

When they were done and before the pain came back, I stood. "Everybody hold on to me."

Grig rested his arm on my shoulder, and Bluebird tucked in, touching my lower arm. I stood between McKenna and Ryo, holding both of their hands.

On the way from the Kneult harbor to the Island of the Savak, I'd added up the percentages it had used to make it across the ocean, but the Kneult shore was about ten miles closer to the Island of the Savak than our kingdom. 35 percent.

Activate boots.

We transported back to the docks in one step. Nailed it. Yes. It just took the whole game to finally master the boots, but finally I did that.

"Whoa," Bluebird said. "That's like—"

"Incredible!" Grig finished her sentence. "But . . ." He pressed a fist to his mouth. "I think I'm gonna be sick."

McKenna splashed his face with hibisi.

Ryo burst out laughing.

I scowled. The wound in my chest was acting up again. "Don't waste it."

From the slight smile on McKenna's face, I think splashing Grig in the face was worth whatever hibisi it took.

The city seemed empty, frozen, like the Kneult city. Of course. There was no one here to play.

"Those boots would have been very useful," McKenna said as she shook out her wings and we turned toward the castle. "Those flights back and forth were . . ." Her face darkened. "It's probably for the best I couldn't use them."

I squeezed her hand, and then squeezed too tight because overwhelming pain had come back with a vengeance. *Activate breastplate!*

The city skyline flickered with static, like it had caught up to us being here. Flames erupted, buildings fell, and a dark green haze settled over the city. The drumming of battle music started.

I growled.

"Don't look at me," McKenna said. "This wasn't the Savak."

Bodies broke through the ground, skeleton arms reaching through the city, Lurchers floating above, swallowing Whirligigs with heads that spun.

"HORDES OF UNDEAD!" Grigfen shouted, both his hands held above his head.

"I'll take point," Bluebird said, grinning. "McKenna, you keep Grig's healing up."

He flexed his fingers. "It's magic time."

I growled under my breath and then grabbed my brother by his collar. "We don't have time for this."

"Wut?" he protested.

"Grab hold," I said to everyone. "Let's just get to the throne room and win this thing already."

I measured the distance to the castle and fast traveled us to the steps.

"Fifth floor, center of the building," Ryo said, his eyes measuring my expression.

A Lurcher swarmed at us, and Grigfen shot a wave of ghostlight to knock it over. Wasteful.

I stepped up and fast traveled toward the throne.

The throne room seemed larger than I remembered; the arched ceiling lifted nearly a story higher. The glistening room was cleared of every other piece of furniture. Mosaics glinted on the polished walls, while large arched windows opened to the damaged sky. In the back of the room, on a raised dais, light struck a large golden throne. We stepped inside, the hall doors slammed shut behind us, and the battle music played.

I flexed my fingers and muttered under my breath. This could never just be simple.

The throne was suddenly occupied.

"Hello, Nephew." King Edvarg sat on the throne, his legs long and spindly, his eyes sunken, and the whole room buzzed with a pale green light.

"A lich king on the throne! A lich king on the throne!" Bluebird squealed.

Grigfen looked at me with big kohl-streaked eyes. "Can we, Mum?"

I made a face and then palmed my axes in each hand. "Oh, go play."

McKenna leapt up, her gold wings spreading before she flashed invisible. Grig and Bluebird rushed forward, Grig's hands waving in giddy ridiculousness and Bluebird's head down, her focus deadly.

I almost felt sorry for Lich King Edvarg.

"Left!" Grig shouted. Bluebird ducked and rolled while Grig sent a wave of ghosts over her left shoulder. The bones converged into a skull-and-bones monster, nearly half the size of the king.

McKenna sprayed Grigfen, lifting his health back to full strength. His magic creature roared.

Meanwhile Bluebird sneaked behind Edvarg's back and started doing some major damage, flipping one way, twisting another, stabbing his ghostly flesh.

I worried for a second when King Edvarg clawed at her, but her armor's endurance was so high that her health barely budged. He knocked out Grig's skeleton monster and then flashed green.

"To cover!" I shouted. Shouting sent a wave of pain into me again, sharp and oozing.

OW.

Breastplate.

King Edvarg roared and shot out a wave of bones. Bluebird blocked the ones from hitting Grig and then rushed forward again before the last bone fell.

I gripped the axes but didn't move.

"Why aren't you playing?" Ryo asked, watching me carefully.

I grimaced. "I am. I'll step in if I need to, but my job right now is to protect you. We can't win until we put the rightful heir on the throne."

A glowing skull rushed toward us. I swung the Axe of Destruction and the skull flew back, striking the right side of Edvarg's head. The black ooze struck and started melting his flesh.

I loved these axes.

"Why aren't you?" I asked.

He didn't answer right away. His health was fine, but his eyes were dim. "I'm just ready to go home."

I swallowed. Home. What was that going to be like? What were we going to be like?

"Okay, let's end this." *Activate breastplate.* "McKenna, watch Ryo!" I ran forward while Grigfen and Bluebird kept Edvarg's attention on them. I glanced up. *1%.* I flew to the ceiling, kicked off the wall, and chucked the Axe of Destruction. I fell. *1%.*

I landed by Ryo's side and then almost collapsed with the sudden crushing pain.

BREASTPLATE.

My axe continued to spin from where I threw it, blade over handle, blade over handle, and then lodged into the side of Edvarg's bony neck. The black ooze bit through him.

He fell with a heavy boom.

We froze.

McKenna landed. "We did it!"

"Wait." Grigfen threw his hands out.

"No, it's okay," Ryo said. "This was his third form. He's dead."

As if to prove it, the throne lit up. It matched Ryo's uniform, gilded gold with bronze and silver foxes, covered with purple jewels.

Ryo let out a breath and then jogged up the dais.

I offered a small smile. We had every item, and he had all our loyalty. This should work.

Ryo sat on the throne and nothing happened.

I *HATE THIS GAME SO MUCH.*

"What else do we need to do?" I kicked Edvarg's fallen body. A bit of poisonous gas expelled, so I stopped.

"Maybe you need to be in costume?" McKenna said. "Should you be wearing the armor?"

"We're a team, though," I said.

"That makes sense to me," Bluebird said.

"Yeah, it's worth trying." Grig pulled the crown off his head and offered it to Ryo. A jewel on the throne lit. He didn't have to trade for it. The rules must be different for me because I was Trader class.

"Yes," Bluebird said. "It's working."

"Well, I have three pieces." I crossed up to the dais to hand him my axes. Ryo stopped me.

"The Breastplate of Healing," Ryo said, his voice low. "You can't. You can't take it off."

I touched the metal covering my stomach.

"That means you have to be the one to win," he said, like that didn't cost him anything.

It was his mom's game.

And I got to win it. I GET TO WIN IT.

The ceiling cracked through with a glitch.

QUICKLY. "Okay, fine. Let's do this."

"How do you win?" Bluebird asked.

I raised my hands in defeat. "I don't know. Ms. Takagi took over my seer vision so I didn't get to hear my win condition."

What do I do? I thought I was an assist character, so I could win as a member of Ryo's team, but win by myself? How—ow. *Activate breastplate.*

I couldn't even think solid sentences right now. How was I going to figure this out?

"Here." Ryo handed me all the armor he had. The jewels dimmed like someone had snuffed them out.

So he couldn't just give me the armor.

"Well, then what about this?" Bluebird asked. "You're Trader class, Dagney. So maybe you have to trade for the victory? Or maybe you should marry Ryo and win by marriage."

Ryo and I shared a quick look. I knew getting married in video games was a thing people did sometimes, and it didn't actually mean anything. But Ryo meant something to me. We'd had enough blurred realities. I didn't want to cheapen it. And besides, if I was going to win, I wanted to win on my own.

"Let's try trading," I said.

But what could I trade? Ryo already had my bag, the gloves, Grig's crown, and the throne. Every gilded inch of that throne was made for him. He was the main character. He was the one who was supposed to win.

I had nothing worth a kingdom.

Nothing. Except my heart.

Nope. Not going to say anything that cheesy.

My hands turned clammy. *Activate breastplate.*

But the breastplate didn't slow my panicking heartbeat. There had to be another way, and I swear if I had full access to my brain I would have figured one out, but this would work. It had to be something Ryo would value, something that came at great cost to me.

MY PRIDE WAS A COST TOO HIGH. Not going to do that. I stared at the pixilated ceiling that was ready to swallow us all. The light so bright it burned my eyes. Light bright enough to dim the pain that was starting again.

I didn't have time to argue with myself about this.

But, oh gosh, I'd look so stupid. And what if Ryo didn't say it back? What if . . . I couldn't. Nope. I needed to make a list of pros and cons, and not be dying, or in the middle of a story that wasn't my own to know for sure. I couldn't untwist my barbed wire heart enough to give it to him, not until I knew how he would treat me when he saw me in real life.

I couldn't just say it, not until the game was finished.

I let out a breath and shook my head.

I hated this.

"Ryo . . ." Oh gosh. Don't do it. "I love you, you ridiculous boy." Oh my gosh. "Will you trade my heart for your kingdom?"

I covered my eyes with my hands.

My heartbeat thrashed. *Activate breastplate.*

This was so embarrassing. I was going to die and it wasn't even the game that was killing me.

Ryo pulled my hands away from my face. His glistening eyes were soft. Happy. "Dagney. It's okay. It's okay."

"It's so embarrassing."

He cupped my cheek and shook his head. "It's not. I love you too."

"Really?" I whispered.

He cocked a lopsided grin. "And that means I get to keep all your stuff."

I hit his chest.

He kissed my nose.

"I happily accept your trade." He led me to the throne and helped me sit.

The jeweled throne lit. Ryo slid my axes into their sheath on my back and held the gloves open for me to slip my hands into. The items, one by one, added to my inventory, and the jewels lit a soft pink.

He placed the crown on my head and then grinned at me like he had a joke hiding behind those eyes. I smiled back. I felt like some kind of warrior princess and barely noticed the pain, still swelling. Light ripped through my eyes, streaks of white shooting from my arms, from my skin. The victory music rose to a crescendo, and the muscles at the back of my neck relaxed, as though the game had released its grip on my brain.

Ryo and Grig wrapped their arms around each other's shoulders, both of them grinning as wide as the skies above us. Bluebird watched the sky as it tore through the upper floors. And McKenna dabbed her cheeks with her blood-soaked sleeve, and turned away so her back was to whatever cameras were watching.

Every one of the other player's loyalty had shifted pink.

But not one of them brighter than my own.

39
MCKENNA

I never wanted to face this music.

But when the light touched me, I felt a release in my brain and then a shift in my senses. The soundtrack changed to the murmur of voices and a sharp beeping that drummed in time with my heart. My beautiful clothes transformed into wires and needles and tubes. Someone grabbed my hand as I tried to yank out the tube in my throat.

Black spots dotted my vision.

Someone called out my name. I fought emerging from this dark pit. I fought that voice.

But it was my dad's voice calling me "princess," so I had to answer.

The world seemed so dim when I opened my eyes.

There weren't enough people here.

And it was my fault. No matter what they said. No matter the part I was playing. I was the one who killed them.

My dad's clothes were covered in wrinkles, his hair matted to a greasy forehead. He lifted his thumb and gave me a smile from where he sat at the base of my hospital bed.

I turned away.

He didn't need to see my tears.

I was alive.

And maybe one day that fact wouldn't fill me with guilt.

Ryo

When I woke in a different world, my mother was there waiting for me. I lifted my weakened arms, tugging at tubes and wires and everything she'd used to keep me living.

I wrapped her in a hug. We made it. We made it out.

Her shoulders shook. "I'm sorry, I'm so sorry."

"It's okay, Mom. I'm okay."

She pulled back. "I wanted you to live in a world where he still did. I painted that world with my grief and it almost killed you."

I wiped her tears from her cheeks. "Dad would have loved it."

She held my face in both hands. And I knew she was holding her whole world.

Grigfen

When the white pixels in the sky found me at last, they sent me home.

Her bed was across from mine. I pulled the wires off me and then stood on wobbly legs. I crossed through protesting doctors and nurses until I reached her bed. I fell next to her. The nurses and doctors tried to stop me, but I ignored them and took her hand in mine. Her skin was cold, so I rubbed her fingers to warm them up and pulled the blanket over her shoulders.

"It's all right, love. It's over. You can wake now."

Her eyelid twitched. I pulled her hand to my lips. Then I lay back on her pillow. The wires across her forehead were cold against my neck as I wrapped my arms around her shoulders, my legs pressing against hers.

Her breaths were soft against my chest.

"Wake for me, love. Come on."

Bluebird

I watched my friends disappear one by one.

A victory song played until the castle's ceiling above us faded and the twin moons glowed. A pulse wave of light exploded from the Seer Spring across the ocean and lit the night sky until it was as bright as midday. The light brightened until it seared my vision.

The walls flattened and the ground rushed up. The castle deleted into a plain white sphere with an ornate throne at the center. The sphere of white spread, sucking up King Edvarg's body, spreading out past the Savak and strangers, and everywhere the light touched more NPCs disappeared.

Until it was only me.

The victory song played the notes faster and faster, the melody sharpened and distorted. The world slipped away no matter how hard I held on to it. I glanced down at my armor, my Voyager, and wished I could bring it with me as I left. For a moment I took in the design, the gears, and the hardware, and my thoughts began to whirl. Could this design be replicated in a real world setting? Hmm . . .

A Whirligig flew around me once, and then it too disappeared, into a spark of pixels.

The music played on in my mind. I clenched my eyes closed and lived there alone in the retreating world we'd created. I didn't stay forever.

Just until the last note played.

Every inch of me hurt when I woke. Tubes cut through my skin, and my thin arms hung at my side. I couldn't lift them. When the song finished, I opened my eyes and faced my real life. My vision blurred as

I counted my fingers and tried to bend my knees, and I was grateful, so embarrassingly grateful, for this battered body I called home.

Grig released soft even breaths, his air swirling sweetly against my cheek. His body curved perfectly around mine.

I loved him. That much I knew, like I knew *Frostborn* one and three were my favorite games, but two was never to be spoken of, like I knew my mom would kill me for what I'd done to break into the game, and for having a boy in my bed.

The fact that I loved him was a measurable evidence-based fact. Surprisingly, another evidence-based fact was that he loved me too.

Loving was a form of fighting back.

And I was nothing if not a warrior.

"Hi," I said.

He grinned. "Nice to meet you, love."

40
DAGNEY

THREE MONTHS LATER

The rules of the game were simple.

There was a ball, and two teams in tight pants who wore thick pads over their shoulders. And also nachos.

So if I tried, really tried, I could separate the idea of football from what I used to believe it was to whatever this thing was that Ryo loved so much. Truth was, I never went to a game at my old school, and would not even if you paid me. So how was I to know if it was actually as bad as I imagined? Since I'd been back, I'd been surprised by the number of people who didn't hate me.

And surprised by how little I cared about those who still did.

Still, as I sat on the cold metal bench on the front row, I couldn't help but notice the way the boys got to play while the girls got to wear skimpy outfits and cheer for them.

I growled under my breath.

I held my phone in one hand and waited for the band to start playing Ryo's school song. It was the last game of the season, and the first one Ryo had been cleared to play.

Luckily it was the night before our internship started, so we'd all flown in early so we could watch him play.

They offered each of the surviving players the internship prize, and all of us, except McKenna, had accepted it. They also gave each one of us the full prize money. A drop in the bucket compared to the money they gave to the families of the players who died.

And it wasn't enough. Not to replace the eight missing lives.

After Mr. Carrington was fired and the lawsuit settled, Ms. Takagi had closed Stonebright and opened a new studio. It wasn't as big, but I was excited to work with her there.

And to be able to see Ryo again. Our daily phone calls didn't have nearly enough kissing in them.

My phone buzzed with a text.

It was from Ryo.

You coming?

I spun my ring around my little finger and then texted him back.

Already here.

After a few minutes, I switched to McKenna's number and texted her.

It's not too late. You can still come to the game.

It took a second, those three dots appearing, and then disappearing. Then her reply.

Can't. PSATs.
Is that what they are calling Netflix these days?

I snorted when her reply beeped almost immediately.

Shut up. It's part of my healing process. My therapist says self care is super important.

I typed,

Well, for my self care, I'm going to go change into a hoodie.

DON'T YOU DARE! I picked those clothes special.

You looked gorgeous in your selfie.

I snorted.

I'm changing! Ooh what do you think about snuggies?

I WILL KILL YOU.

Three dots appeared. Then disappeared.

Sorry.

She didn't reply for a good minute.

You're still wearing the clothes I picked out?

I was about to type *Come to the game and see*, but I'd already pushed her too much today.

Her clothes were here. That was enough.

For today.

I made a face and sent her another selfie.

In the background, dark clouds rumbled. Maybe there'd be a rain delay, and the game would be canceled, and we could all go out to dinner or go see a movie.

No such luck.

Zoe and Griffin arrived at the stadium right before kickoff. The clouds were thick, but no rain fell as they sat next to me in the front row in the handicap accessible area. Zoe rolled right next to me. "Dags!"

She wore her usual leather boots, jeans, and a tee shirt that said *SINGLE PLAYER AND SINGLE PAYER* in bright pink print. Her hair was dyed a fresh purple since last time I saw her, cut short at the sides, her natural hair tight compared to the polished curls she wore in the game. Her smudged blue-framed glasses slid down her nose. Griffin wore all orange and green, Ryo's school colors. Even his face was painted, though he didn't go here.

I was officially overdressed in my cardigan and flowered skirt. "I hate you both."

"You look nice," Zoe said.

Griffin dropped their bags. "Did you hear? It's official. I'm starting a band. I just got to get a load of trumpeters interested." He handed me one of his goodie bags full of snacks. A pom-pom fell out.

I grinned. "I like your school spirit."

He raised his eyebrows. "I *am* nine-tenths ghost. Might as well play the part."

"Why are your jokes so bad?"

"Years of practice." Griffin tapped Zoe's knee and rustled inside his bag. "Bean dip?" He pulled out a glass Pyrex dish and a bag of tortilla chips. "You'll never guess what the secret is to making a perfect bean dip, so I'll tell you."

"It's not really a secret if you tell everyone," I said.

"Right, but you're not everyone, now, are you?"

The band blasted my eardrums and the crowd erupted in cheers. The players streamed out, and everything grew even louder. Last game of the season. Everybody was here, their focus on Ryo.

And I wanted to cover my head and disappear.

Zoe smiled encouragingly at me. "You are making a bigger deal than it is. I promise."

"What's going on now?" Griffin said, looking around.

"Don't worry about it, Grig," Zoe said. "This is a girl thing."

I bit my lip and sucked in. Zoe's words helped a little, and I knew better. My worth was not based in my appearance, and Ryo didn't want a trophy, he wanted me.

But he had to notice the way the cheerleaders looked at him, or the way the girls along the fence were all adoring fans in such tiny packages.

But even with a thousand people cheering his name, Ryo looked for me.

When our eyes met, his shoulders dropped and he grinned like he was relieved. He wouldn't ever admit it, but he needed me here to support him.

Dark clouds rumbled above us.

Ryo crossed the field to greet us, his arms wide like he was hugging the whole world. "Sun's greeting, fair travelers!"

He and Griffin bumped shoulders first, but then he held me close. I leaned against the cement barrier as he kissed me hard, right there where everyone could see. In that second, everybody else disappeared, until it was just him and me and a kiss that I wished went on longer.

Brownie Blizzard sundae.

Ryo rested his forehead against mine. "I'm so glad you made it."

My whole insides warmed. He didn't look at me any differently than the way he looked at me in the game. "Of course. I love you, you know?" I expected my stomach to twist, but I didn't feel nervous. It seemed like the most natural, honest thing I could say.

"Dagney," he said, his expression the kind of happy that I knew couldn't be faked.

"And that means I get all your stuff." I pushed his shoulder. "Go get me a victory."

His eyes twinkled. "Yes, my queen." He tapped Zoe's nose and then he ran back on the field, those tight pants of his increasing my appreciation for this game tenfold.

A whistle blew as he lined up with the rest of his team. He put his helmet at the top of his head, but for a quick instant before he lowered it, his focus shifted up to the top of the stands.

Where his mother cheered with both arms raised.

ACKNOWLEDGMENTS

Dear friends,

I owe this book to the following:

- Holly West, my brilliant editor, took a messy draft of this book and found a path to a story I love. I owe her Dagney's Pathfinding. Holly brought with her a team of extraordinary people including Ilana Worrell, Raymond Ernesto Colón, Kerianne Steinberg, Katie Klimowicz, and so many others who had a hand in making *Glitch Kingdom*. A special thanks to the sensitivity readers. Thank you to the whole team at Feiwel and Friends and Macmillan—I've been in such good hands.

- To my agent, the mighty Jessica Sinsheimer, I owe Ryo's Charisma. Thank you for changing a group of uninterested people into a book deal, and for always knowing the answers to my questions. Go team!

- I owe Bluebird to three incredible women. Isabel Ibañez gave me Bluebird's Stamina, her drive, and her armor. Isabel, you are my general of light-and-also-making-me-write-things. Thank you for dragging this book out of me. My best friend April Clausen gave me Bluebird's Heart. You take such good care of me, friend. Thank you for the milk shakes, the french fries, and the everything. Megan Grimit gave me Bluebird's Intelligence. You've taught me so much, my friend, my mentor, and my twisted sister. I am not worthy.

- To all the writing friends who saw ghosts of this book's past, (and all the stories that came before it) I owe you Grigfen's Magic. Thank you to Kendra Lusty and Gina Francesconi for being my first friends, my first readers, and my first supporters. Thank you to my Hale-ians, because you gave me my teenage years (especially you, Emily McDougal), and thank you to Barbara Fields for helping me survive them. Thanks to Andrew Beck for being my brother who is not my brother (I salute you). Thanks to Sabrina West and Melanie Crouse for sharing my brain and for being so kind when I asked for it back.

- To *Glitch Kingdom*'s beta readers: Rachel Larsen, Cassandra Newbold, Stacey Goldstein, Heather Dean Brewer, Laura Valín-Peñalba, Jana Nelson, Isabel Ibañez, April Clausen, Sabrina West, and Kate Meadows, thank you for shaping this story with me. Thank you to Dr. Anne Lipton for explaining to me how brains work, (who knew?) and to Dustin Hansen and Dillon James West for your insight into video game history and into those who develop them.

- A special thank-you to Brenda Drake and the Pitch Wars class of 15, my community of weirdos, for being there every step of this book's life. Thank you to the Prosers (especially MaryAnn Pope!), Hatrackians, Storymakers, Pitch Crit Crew (PCC!), and my Twitter friends for everything you've taught me. To my Young Women, thank you for your love and for reminding me how teenagers actually talk. And of course to the thousands of writers whose work gave me the tools to make my own.

A special hand-to-the-heart thank-you to all the bloggers, librarians, booksellers, booktubers, and readers who put the right books into the right hands. Just like Grigfen's seven-layer dip, I believe any good thing is always two layers deeper than gets credit. Thank you to everyone who does the invisible work.

• To my family—My mom, for teaching me to read, for taking me to the library, and for letting me climb up in the branches of the giant tree in my backyard with a book. My dad, whose books I so often stole and sometimes dropped in bathwater. My sister Jana whose bookshelves I envy. My sister Tyana for teaching me how to swear. My brother Ben who let me be Luigi and who talked through this idea when it was a baby. My children, who I love to the moon and back, and whose names shape my world, and to my sweet love Darren, for every single day of forever. Thank you for giving me McKenna's ability to turn invisible. I love you, you awesome nerds.

And now, dear readers, THANK YOU for reading! This book is yours. No matter your size, no matter your health, you are enough!

Thank you for reading this Feiwel & Friends book.
The Friends who made GLITCH KINGDOM possible are:

Jean Feiwel, Publisher

Liz Szabla, Associate Publisher

Rich Deas, Senior Creative Director

Holly West, Senior Editor

Anna Roberto, Senior Editor

Kat Brzozowski, Senior Editor

Alexei Esikoff, Senior Managing Editor

Raymond Ernesto Colón, Director of Production

Emily Settle, Associate Editor

Erin Siu, Assistant Editor

Rachel Diebel, Assistant Editor

Foyinsi Adegbonmire, Editorial Assistant

Katie Klimowicz, Senior Designer

Ilana Worrell, Production Editor

Follow us on Facebook or visit us online at fiercereads.com
OUR BOOKS ARE FRIENDS FOR LIFE